Alchemical Assistance

A Matt Hunt Mystery

Rev. Stephen Rodgers

Alchemical Assistance

Printed through Creative Space

Publisher of Record: Sage Center Publications

ISBN-13: 978-0615854953 (Sage Center Publications)

ISBN-10: 0615854958

Front and back cover design by Luke Rodgers

Acknowledgements And Dedication

First I want to acknowledge the reality of God in my life and of all life whether we choose to see it or not. There are many tools we can use to deepen our relationship with the Creator and yes, personally I believe that people must go through Christ to have perfect union with God—in this life or the next.

Alchemy has been one of those tools that Christians have used for well over a millennia.

Bringing together the fun of a murder thriller, the metaphors of alchemy, and the passion of God into one book has been quite remarkable, I can only hope the reader enjoys the ride and may learn something as well. I have no alchemical teacher other than reading. Carl Jung gets credit for brining alchemy into modern times through the eyes of psychology. There are many websites surrounding alchemy. As is true with theology, one must be careful who you give authority to speak the truth. In the end, you are the authority for what works for you. Discern well!!

Many thanks to the Freak Mountain Ramblers for their music and willingness to be part of this book. You can find their musical schedule (they play just about every Sunday as mentioned in the book) at freakmountain.com.

The other "real" person is Dave Marshall, oldest and dearest friend. He is a real and fabulous stock broker and financial consultant with Baird Investments in Portland. I'm sure he continues to manage the money he was given in this book very well. LOL.

All other names in this book are fictional; if you think they are you, enjoy the fantasy. I am the editor of this book—sorry about that.

If you aren't sure what alchemy is I suggest you take a minute and look it up on the net before you start, or go to page 170 for a brief lesson.

For Glyn, my son, in whose memory I dedicate this book. In his death I have no doubt he has found and is with the Stone of Stones

1 MATT'S FIND

The large ancient wood door was unlocked. I recognized the carvings on it from my studies of alchemy—the sun and moon, king and queen, metaphors of the unconscious abounding. As is usually the case, I let myself in. The person whose home was being invaded was either in or past trouble. From the outside, the humble abode was unkempt, weeds overwhelming the struggling grass. The summer had been long, hot and obviously they saw no need to water or perhaps they just couldn't be bothered. Curtains were all closed and any sense of joy had long since vacated the premises. Fall was now upon us, a slight change in the temperature, leaves starting to change.

I knew the second the aroma hit my nostrils that death was near, and not a pleasant death or my body wouldn't be here. Perhaps we should back up before we get too far astray.

Born with the name Matthew Hunt, most just call me Matt. I am a priest, once married, two adorable grown children, the head of a large church, and I have a gift. For lack of a better term, let's call it the gift of sensing. No, it's not like being a psychic or clairvoyant, my senses just pick things up and I trust them. I smell things others can't and see things that can't be seen. These are gifts from God, given in order to seek justice. Now, before you get all excited under the collar, let's understand this is not a book about conversion. There won't be a lot of Jesus talk, although without him my gift wouldn't exist and you can't understand what I do without some. Somehow the Spirit opens my senses to become aware of injustices. I simply try my best to allow the Spirit to use my senses and I heed them and follow their lead. Wondering why God leads me to

certain cases has never been part of the package. That question is on my lengthy
list that will be presented upon my hopeful arrival into the Kingdom.

I didn't want to disturb what was a crime scene, but rarely being able to resist, I entered. Whatever had taken place in this home was done several days previously. The stench almost made me gag. Were it not for the numerous autopsies and gory situations I'd been to before, gagging would have been the least of my problems. There are parishioners who ask to come with me when one of these senses comes upon me. I laugh. Does it say more about them or more about me?

There was nothing abnormal about the house, other than the trail of blood heading along the right side of the hallway, that was odd. Down the stairs, around the corner and to the back of the house the red stripe moved—quite deliberately. I was amazed how much light entered, even with the curtains drawn. Careful not to touch anything or put my feet in the blood, I moved down the hall. Pictures on the wall led me to believe that someone was an artist, stunning abstract paintings in bright colors, reminiscent of Kandinsky. There was more artistic work based on a deep understanding of the alchemical world. Interspersed were photographs of what I could only assume were family members. But then we all know what happens when we assume.

Somehow I knew the room I was about to enter would be different. Having been drawn to over a dozen major crime situations since acquiring my gift from God, my heart still started to beat faster. Odd that I would call it a gift when it always seems to lead me to murder and despair. People don't kill out of joy but out of fear and hopelessness, a sad chasing after control, even in war. You'll have to forgive my preaching from time to time, after all, I am a priest.

I felt the room before entering. Literally felt its presence. There was texture to the air, a life being breathed within the walls and a life being taken away that drove the room into mourning. The space wasn't an ordinary room, but rather a laboratory. The tables were filled with books, notebooks, beakers, test tubes, Bunsen burners, and other equipment I didn't have a clue about. All was in order, well at least in a way that led me to believe the perpetrator of the crime hadn't torn the place to shreds. This was not a modern laboratory like you'd see in a movie; this reminded me of more ancient times.

Death, no matter in what situation, is not a pleasant aroma after a few days. She'd been dead at least that long, my guess was longer, but something kept her from decomposing more rapidly. Her beauty was undeniable, even in death she held grace in how she lay. The knife wound must have been quite painful, not to mention being dragged down the stairs. The second stab wound in her heart caused her to die quickly. How was it she died with a smile on her face? She was aware of something I longed to find out about.

I noticed that I was taken aback when first seeing her. There was a familiarity to her face I couldn't place but intuitively felt I'd met her. I let it go.

Admittedly, finding a woman inside a laboratory, in her house, stabbed to death is pretty rare. Because of the length of time she'd been dead I was already thinking she didn't have many friends---where were they? Why did God feel it so important to bring me here? A chuckle came out of my mouth as I thought about all the CSI type shows. Of course they'd have it figured out in an hour, all their tests happening within the blink of an eye---reality is a bit different. I did know however that the first 24 hours after a person's death is critical and that option had long since passed. The blood, even pooled, was dry.

The attack had come in the middle of the night, her pajamas on. There were no ripped clothes, no signs of a struggle—I wondered about the front door being open, she probably never locked it. I didn't need to spend a lot of time with the body, the CSI people would do that. I was more interested in the why behind the whom. Motive, motive, motive.

There was nothing in the lab to indicate who this person was, although I knew exactly what she'd been up to and wondered how close she'd come, perhaps too close.

I went through each room in the house allowing my senses to be bombarded. There was little to be felt. I did notice a few interesting things, at least interesting to me. No telephones existed in the home. She was a loner. There were no indications of visitors, no calendar, no date book, and no evidence of mail. Her life existed within the lab. Her bedroom was for sleeping, the kitchen for eating. She was extremely neat, albeit probably because she didn't really live in most of the house. The bed was made, an antique quilt resting on the mattress. Cupboards were lined with plates and glassware in an orderly fashion. No dishes in the sink or drying rack. Then it hit me.

I ran back to the lab, grabbing two pictures off the wall, to hell with the police. I stared at her. She was no more than 40, a grace to her beauty, even in death. Somewhere in the lab had to be evidence of her existence, her name. The writer of Ecclesiastes said that to everything there was a time and place. She believed in those words.

The Holy Spirit and I have a good relationship; you might say we are on speaking terms. The difference with me is that when I say the Spirit has told me something, something always happens, always. It's not like people on TV or books that make claims that not only don't come true, but are flat out lies leading people away from God. I asked the Spirit for her name. I don't always hear what I want to hear, but things happen.

I don't hear voices, I sense things, past, present, and yes, future. This woman lived a life of patterns, it was part of the process that had brought her to where she was. There was a corner of the laboratory where a desk sat. It stood on carved legs and had a front that folded down. I pulled it open, revealing a series of cubbies, drawers and doors. Nothing was on the desk, unlike virtually every other surface in the room. When I sat down at the desk I opened each drawer, some large some small. Nothing to be found other than paper, pens, and some writing. They were all hand written and in multiple languages. I recognized French, German, Latin, Chinese, and Spanish. As to her identity, it was a void, but I knew something was here. I was more methodical the second time. Behind a door in the middle of the desk were two shelves. The second shelf looked worn. I pulled it out, another door behind it. I own a desk left to me by my father that has a secret compartment in it.

Within that door lay what I'd been looking for, a checkbook. Mary Elizabeth Weathers. The ledger showed that bills had been paid; I suspected she threw them away or burned them in the furnace that sat in the middle of the lab. Now the police could be called. As always, they'd have lots of questions and I would not have many answers—yet. Over the years we had come to an understanding—they tolerated me solely because I produced. An odd profession, turning up dead bodies or finding stolen goods. And just in case you were wondering, I do not accept money. Because this comes from God, it's hard to justify an honorarium. Being hopeful that everlasting life is my pay for using what God has given me to help others and bring justice is more than a just reward. Besides that theological point, I can't lie, I enjoy the thrill. There was also a small booklet. I opened it quickly, saw that it was some kind of diary and stuffed it in my pocket.

Just as I was about to call the police my cell phone rang.

"Matt?" I had good voice recognition and I knew this one well, very deep and rich.

"Hello bishop."

"What are you doing?"

I hesitated in telling him. The bishop didn't like what I did, feeling all my time and energy should be put into my parish---which by the way was one of the largest in the diocese. He was kind of stuck. He couldn't really boss me around because a not insignificant part of his salary came from our church. Our theologies collided as well and I wasn't the meek quiet type. In the end, I don't like lying.

"I'm sitting in a house with a dead woman on the floor, just found her." I knew it would get a rise out of him.

" Oh my God Matt, have you called the police?"

"Not yet, it's next on my to do list."

"Well, perhaps you could call me later, now is probably not a good time."

"It's fine bishop, she isn't going anywhere and the bad guys are long gone."

"You can be so morbid sometimes."

"I think it's genetic, my mother was like that."

A long silence ensued, he was trying to figure out whether to proceed or not.

"We need to have lunch."

"Whatever for Jim?" He hated it when I called him anything but bishop. I suspect it was rude of me to not call him bishop, but he needed to be humbled from time to time. "I'd rather not talk about it on the phone, how does a week from Friday work?"

I pretended to hum and hah. The bottom line is that he is my bishop, I didn't have much choice and his voice had a tone of urgency and concern in it.

"I'll see you at Chili's at noon," I replied. "Why in a week if it's so important?

"I have to leave this afternoon for a series of meetings, you will be my first appointment when I get back."

"See you then." My mind started imagining what could possibly be on his mind. He is a very political man, many bishops are, I take that back, all bishops are. Hard to be successful in that job if you aren't a good politician and I hold many politicians in high regard. Then I let it go and dialed Officer Tom.

"Tom?"

"Yes, is this Matt?"

"Fraid so."

"This can only mean one thing, a body, and I thought the crime rate was going down because I hadn't heard from you in a while."

"I guess I was too busy with the church to hear the wonderful voice of God."

"Give me a break, just tell me where you are."

"2221 NW Garfield, but there is no hurry, she's been here awhile. I'd be prepared for a strange case Tom."

"Why do you say that?"

"You'll see when you get here, how long will I have to wait?" I knew he had the potential to make me wait hours. "I'd hate to dig through too much evidence." That put the pressure on.

"Alright, we'll be there in 10 minutes, can you keep your hands off things till then?"

"I'll do my best."

As soon as I hung up I called my friend Sue. She was an information specialist, well that's what I called her. A computer genius who loved finding information—and getting paid for it. I gave her Mary's name and address and asked her to find what she could. I told her she was about 40 and gave her the bank account number.

Tom was an officer who had been dealing with me for 6 years. He was 5 years from retirement and his body showed it. Let's just say he wouldn't be chasing 70 year old people down the street. The first time we'd met I was a suspect in the case. I'd walked into the police department, my head high in the air, my nose sniffing the heavens with ego, and told them about a murder. I'd been right of course, but telling them I got my information from God didn't go over very big. I'd mentioned they'd often used psychic detectives, at least that is what I saw on TV. Tom was quick to point out there was a reason those things were seen on TV and on the front page of the National Inquirer. He did pull back a bit and admit there had been a few circumstances where they had been accurate, very few, and the time they spent chasing down bad leads wasn't helpful. With that in mind he said thank you and sent me on my way, quite dejected I might add.

In sports they tell you when the going gets tough, the tough get going. In my faith we talk about the ability of deep faith overcoming all doubt and faith which was not something of which I was in short supply. I literally ran back to the church and prayed. I remembered in the Bible how God had hardened and opened hearts, I wanted Tom's to be bleeding, not literally mind you. After praying I went back to my office and met with a couple who had come in for pre-marital counseling. At the end of the session we came out of the office and two officers were standing there, Tom and another—in uniform. The couple left quickly, never to return. I didn't know if it was me or the police that scared them off.

Tom asked if we could talk. I was excited to see them, Julie, my administrative assistant was speechless.

"Has there been a theft pastor?" she asked.

"No Julie, a murder," I replied, turning my back and heading back into my office, knowing that the phones would soon be ringing off the hook in the parish.

To make a long story short, you can read about it in another book if you'd like, Tom told me they found the body, just where I'd said it would be. This led to days of interrogation. Fortunately I had an airtight alibi and they found the murderer fairly quickly or I'd still be a suspect. Tom still hasn't accepted how I know what I know. Maybe he believes people come in and confess things to me (which I can't tell anyone because of confidentiality) and then I tell the police.

"Tom, I normally don't hear confessions of people I don't know. If I do, I start by telling them that confidentiality does not apply if they tell me they have done harm to someone else or are going to do it to themselves. By knowing that going in, if they say something, I can get them help without breaking their confidence."

He believed me, at least in part. Over the years he'd come to trust me, he even sought me ought from time to time. But with me, that isn't how God works, he chooses when and where. I wish God would give a million people the gift I have, we could solve lots of crimes.

Tom called back and was on his way.

"Ok, so what can you tell me from what you've seen so far?"

"There was no fight, she was stabbed upstairs and then taken to the lab where she was stabbed again and killed," I said with a smile, proud of my reasoning.

"You've been through the house?"

"Of course, what did you expect?"

"You'll never learn will you?" he said a bit exasperated.

The lesson that had been learned was as soon as he arrived I'd be out and any chance for looking around would be gone for at least a day and in murder, every day counts. I didn't respond to his question—he didn't really expect me to.

As we were talking he and his partner drove up. As a detective he didn't wear a uniform and his car was a boring unmarked Chevy. I keep trying to convince him to move up in the world, at least get a Jag. He would laugh, but admitted being jealous of my Ferrari. I inherited it from my grandfather, a rather wealthy man. The nice thing about being independently of means is you don't have to play politics with parishioners or bishops, I can always leave. I'd told myself I could have a nice car for a year, and then it was back to my used vehicles which drove my wealthier parishioners crazy. For me a car is simply transportation. In my line of work if people are concerned about my show of status, we have larger issues.

Tom stepped out of the car. He was a huge man, having played tackle for the USC Trojans. Let's just say he hadn't stopped eating when he left college. Probably 6'5" and 280 pounds, he was in much better shape than he let on. He had that football player look to him; lack of a real neck, short hair, and broad shoulders. His face however gave him some deniability. His features were soft. Were it not for his size he'd be a great chaplain.

"Hi Tom, where is the rest of the gang?"

"On their way."

"Matt this is my new partner, at least for this case, Steve."

"Glad to meet you Steve," I said reaching out my hand to shake his.

"My pleasure---what was your last name?"

"I didn't give it. So Tom you ready for this?"

"I'm never ready. I hate death."

"I knew there was a reason you wouldn't be a good chaplain."

We walked in front of Steve, a new recruit, probably a friend of the chief's.

"Go easy on the kid."

The door was open as we walked in.

"How did you get in?" Steve asked.

"The door was open."

"Did you know her?"

"No."

"You usually walk into homes of people you don't know?" he asked becoming impatient.

"Only when someone dead is inside."

"How did you know that?"

"Do you have a nose?"

At that moment he gagged. He'd been so caught up with trapping me he'd forgotten to smell. We all do it, turn our senses off and on as we need them. It is often said people who lose one sense have the others strengthened. I believe them.

Tom chuckled under his breath as we entered.

"Ok, so what have you touched?"

He knew me well. "Just her desk trying to find out who she was."

"And?"

"Mary Weathers."

"And where is Mary, or need I ask," he said, his eyes following the trail of blood. "She's very neat, doesn't seem to have a lot of company."

Tom walked around the lab, gloves on, looking taking notes. He actually paid little attention to the body, but then what could he do?

"How am I supposed to figure out what was taken, if anything?" he asked.

"I've been thinking about that and have some ideas but I'm not quite ready to spill the beans."

"Come on Matt, can't you and God give me a clue?" he replied with some humor.

"We don't want to send you on a wild goose chase."

Steve had come in, having gotten a grip on his revolving stomach. "Maybe it was a robbery?"

"Tell you what Steve, roam around the house and see if you find anything of value in the place, or something that would give you an indication of what they might have taken." Tom knew full well, there was nothing here worth a robbery, whatever it was, was in the lab. "Matt, how many people do you know have a laboratory in their home? I looked in the living room as we walked, hasn't been used in years."

"I noticed that as well. The same is true with the rest of the home. She spent virtually every waking moment in this room.

"Do you know what she was working on?"

There are times in life you have to tell less than the truth. "Haven't a clue."

"Maybe our people can figure this out."

"Tom, what do you notice about the notes?"

"They are in a bunch of different languages I don't read."

"What else?"

It took him a minute, and then the reality hit him in the face. "Oh my God, sorry, they are hand written—by the same person I'd predict."

"By her."

"Wow, one bright lady."

"Very bright. To be able to read and write in 6 or 7 languages, how many people do you know that can do that?"

"None."

"Exactly."

"So did you find anything interesting in your time alone with Mary?"

"Just her checkbook," I said, knowing that the diary was all I had and that I wouldn't see the rest of the documents for at least a few days. I handed it to him. The hope was Tom wouldn't ask for anything else since I freely gave him the checkbook—although he should have known better, or perhaps it was a choice he made because when I took things I always came back with information he probably wouldn't have found for a long time.

Steve re-entered the lab. "Pretty sparse around the house, probably not a theft."

"Good assumption, you catch on quick," I told him. Normally I like humbling people with quick wit, sometimes I just use a bit of sarcasm and hope they catch on.

"Thanks." He didn't catch on.

"How old do you two think she is?" I asked.

Steve, bending over the body, "45 tops."

Tom leaned around the counter, "Agreed."

Standing up, Steve looked around the room and picked up some of the papers. "She was into some strange stuff."

"How do you know that," Tom asked.

"I read French and German."

"So tell us what it is about," I coached

"Well, here she is talking about the sun and the moon, this one talks of bifurcation and mercury. I don't get any of it.

My phone rang.

"Hello? Hi Mary, what do you have? "There was a long pause. "Have you double checked? You are certain? Can you find a picture? If you do send it to me on my phone, thanks for your help, I'll be in touch."

My face must have gone white.

”What’s wrong Matt,”? Tom inquired.

“Hold on.”

I ran to the hallway and looked at the group of pictures. They appeared in chronological order. I could pick her out near the end and tracing backwards believed I could find her in each picture getting younger and younger. Finally we got back to childhood and a baby picture. I took it off the wall and on the back was the year it was taken, 1926. I gasped. I looked at the last picture which could have been taken the week before, she looked exactly the same. I was nervous but took it off the wall. On the back was the date, 1966. In the picture she was 40. On the floor, murdered, she was 80. I think I had a motive.

2 BOB'S DELICATE TOUCH

Hello, my name is Bob, perhaps not my real name, but if you want to do the research you can figure it out. Matt told me he was writing his side of the story and offered me the chance to write mine. Nothing else to do, so why not? Besides, Matt seems to think the story is over, far from it.

The world of alchemy is a mysterious one. Most alchemists do their work in secret, fear of secrets being spread, treachery or greed running rampant within their community. Most of us would call it paranoia, but the history of alchemy bears out their fears.

I've been studying alchemy for about 30 years—a beginner in comparison to some. I've had affiliations with 15 or more people who have been wrestling with it for over 60. Most people think of us as crazy. After all, isn't alchemy about those people that try to find a way to turn everything into gold? Like the Midas touch? Yes, the more public persona of alchemy has to do with changing things into gold, but behind that was and continues to be the true nature of the work----turning oneself into a work of perfection—of gold. Infinite wisdom, power, immortality, these were what I and others seek. You see, I am an alchemist.

The work is mostly symbolic, just like the work of Christian mystics. What many religious people don't understand is that in order to comprehend and understand the infinite—God—you must get beyond the rational and enter the mystical and symbolic. It's interesting to watch Christians. They all get to a certain point and stop their maturing process. Why? They don't crossover to another way of seeing the world about them. The Bible tells us not to stop maturing till we reach the full stature of Christ. But what do you see when you read about Jesus? A world of symbolic and metaphoric language because Christ knew you couldn't ultimately come to know God without it. There are no words in human language for whom and what God is.

I was after the Philosopher's Stone, the essence of what the spirit is, and the key to the power of the universe. If you are a Star Wars junkie, it would be the Force. Perhaps the Holy Grail to some or a couple of levels above enlightenment. Many have found it throughout history. Why do you ask, if they are immortal, are they not with us? One of two reasons. They either chose to not live anymore and to die to be with God, or they are still here, moving about so no one can see them fail to age.

My work had taken me around the world. I'd found and worked with many alchemists who introduced me to new ways of working on myself. They showed me the power of free will and that the essential powers of the universe were neutral, neither good nor evil. God struggles to have us use them for good and Satan for evil.

Over the past few years I'd made some contacts in the States. Alchemists are everywhere, quietly doing their work, they always have been.

Alchemists are the founders of modern chemistry and medicine. As they healed others through science, they were healing themselves through symbolic internal work. I knew I could become one of the great ones, I was possessed by the need to reach the end game, no matter what. Some times in history great prices needed to be paid. I was willing to pay any price to merge the Yin and Yang, the Light and the Dark, an essential part of the work. While most of the work is more mental, there are specific things one can do as an alchemist that are more practical. Going beyond the limits of science is amazing, if not secretive. You can't mass produce the elixirs alchemist's make, so there is no profit side to being an alchemist. But I have not been sick a day in over a decade and I think I have slowed or stopped the aging process in my body. Aren't those worthy pursuits in and of themselves? I'm not satisfied.

I moved to Portland to be closer to a person I knew could help me if she wanted, Mary Elizabeth Weathers. Her grandfather had been an alchemist, although not one obsessed by the work. Mary became intrigued in college. She studied chemistry, then medicine, along with her ability to learn languages. But all of her studies were focused on the work of alchemy. She never worked, she didn't need to although I never quite figured out how. Her father was not a wealthy man. I always wondered if indeed she'd learned how to change things into gold, but I never saw or heard of any evidence of it. Mary was a humble alchemist, keeping to herself, although I had a notion of who her teacher might be.

We met on the internet months ago when I was living in California, seems to be the way of many nowadays. At first it was casual, just a curiosity. There are chat rooms for everything, including alchemy. You learn quickly who the serious people are and who the freaks are. When I was young I'd gotten interested in computers. I was quite facile and had a home packed with technology. You can't cheat and find out for certain what a stock will do over a given period, but you can break into a stock company and purchase stock at the initial offering and get into emails for insider information. I invested in Apple, Microsoft, and Starbucks. I don't need to work.

I tell you this simply because you need to know how I found Mary. I hacked her IP address and tracked her down through her host. For those who may not be up on the lingo, I traced her chat back to her home. Yes, it can be done.

Mary never met anyone she'd chatted with on line. I found it quite frustrating. She, like the rest of us was paranoid and with good reason, she was close to finding the answer. The problem was I needed the answer and was aware if I didn't get it from her soon, she'd disappear never to be heard from again, save in strange tales.

One of the most famous alchemists was a man by the name of Philips Aureolus Theophrasus Bombastus von Hohenheim. Quite a name isn't it. He took on the name Paracelsus. He fundamentally changed alchemy from being a search from changing matter into gold to finding the spiritual center of our being and healing others. He died for the cause and many consider him to be one of the founders of modern medicine. A significant part of his work was to find the Archaeus and to seek ways of strengthening it.

"The Archaeus is an essence that is equally distributed in all parts of the human body. The Spiritus Vitae (Spirit of Life) takes its origin from the Spiritus Mundi (Spirit of the Universe). Being an emanation of the latter, the Archeus contains the elements of all cosmic influences and is therefore the cause by which the action of the cosmic forces act upon the body." (alchemylab.com/alchemical_theory.htm)

Jesus knew this, he was in complete touch with the Archaeus. Christ was the ultimate alchemist. He just wasn't stable enough to own a laboratory. His lab was the people he lived and worked with and the world about him.

Paracelsus started the introduction of metals and minerals as part of medicine along with herbs. Perhaps he was the first pharmacist. Does anyone take vitamins that don't contain minerals? Thank you Paracelsus and alchemy. He also introduced the foundation of homeopathy—the idea that taking small doses of what makes us sick can make us stronger against those very illnesses.

Above all, he believed the answers to humanities problems existed in the realm of the spirit, not in the realm of the intellect. He was committed to truth and called out falsehood wherever he saw it. Eventually the church turned against him.

Mary had the answer, or was at least close to it. I could tell from her writing she had something the rest of us didn't have, but she wouldn't share it and I could not let her get away with that. She held onto what Sir Isaac Newton once said, Newton being perhaps the best known of all alchemists:

"It may possibly be an inlet to something more noble, not to be communicated without immense damage to the world if there should be any verity in the Hermetic writers, therefore, I question not but that the great wisdom of the noble Author will sway him to high silence till he shall be resolved of what consequence the thing may be either by his own experience, or the judgment of some other—that is of a true Hermetic Philosopher—there being other things besides the transmutation of metals, if those great pretenders brag not which none but they understand." (in a letter from Newton to Robert Boyle)

He was well aware of the dangers of letting secrets out, for the pretenders would abuse the knowledge and once again blacken the name of alchemists.

But I am no pretender. I seek the highest aim of alchemy, and Mary wouldn't let me in. I'd come to realize she was a pretender, and I couldn't let that be.

Mary was not stupid. She'd done her homework and done a good job of keeping me from discovering who she was. Firewalls and back-dooring other sites to further block her identity all made it tough for me. She made one mistake, she underestimated me as have others. I never let on I was tracking her. She didn't think computer geniuses would chat in an alchemy room—let alone believe what they were talking about. For the most part she was right. All others I met in that room were computer imbeciles. I could have helped many with their techie questions, but that would have given away my abilities, something I couldn't have.

I remember sitting at my computer, watching people come and go from the chat room, sharing little pieces of information, entering the host's main site via a back door, then tagging her address. It bounced around quite a bit, to Europe, New York, Mexico City, and then Portland, Oregon.

I'd done the same thing with Philip. He'd come upon a process for discovering a miraculous compound for rapidly healing cuts. I wanted it and he wouldn't give it up. I tracked him down to Salisbury, a small town in northwest Connecticut. He lived on a farm, his lab in the barn, and a beautiful lab it was. But no one holds back on me. I tried to be nice several times, he grew meaner and meaner. I changed tactics and became nice and didn't ask for anything. He relaxed and before long we were "friends." He told me he was going away on vacation and would be in touch when he got back.

I flew to Boston, rented a car and drove to his house. I spent two days going through the barn. I put his computer in the trunk of my car. I found his lab book which kept his best notes, well hidden under a floor board. But he'd been using the same board forever and it didn't take a rocket scientist to find it. As smart as these alchemists are, they can be very naïve.

Philip, like most serious alchemists was single. Being married or having a family didn't fit with spending countless hours, day after day, month after month, year after year involved with secret work that few understood.

I couldn't really have Philip knowing I'd done this and he was smart enough to put two and two together, although he thought I lived in Texas. He'd told me what kind of computer he had, so I replaced it with a used one. I knew the fire would destroy it, but at least he wouldn't think it had been stolen. I started the fire near his electric board; I didn't want arson investigators getting into this.

Every lab has a furnace in the middle. A furnace that takes enormous amounts of energy for certain practices. With lots of energy comes lots of opportunity for fire. I felt a bit sorry for him, all that work, but he had become greedy and was now paying for it.

I stayed long enough to watch it start, to ensure it would go. Living out in the middle of nowhere didn't help. I don't think the volunteer fire department got the word for at least 30 minutes. Then they had to get out of bed, get the truck and come to the house. There would be nothing left by the time they put it out. What would Philip say, "that was my entire life's work, I was close to finding the Philosopher's Stone and some medicines that could change people's lives?" They would laugh at him. The fact was no one even knew how to contact him. There was an article in the Lakeville Journal the following week that talked about the fire and had an interview with him.

"It was just a barn, a workshop where I built things and kept my tractor." That was that. I'd gotten what I wanted and taught him a lesson. It would be the first of many lessons taught to those who stood in my way. He was lucky, no physical harm done to him.

The better part of two months was spent finding Mary. Then I needed to figure out what to do with the information. I could knock on her door and say hi, maybe she'd take me on as a disciple. I doubted it. Had she wanted a disciple, she'd find one on her own. Besides, if someone came to your door and said they'd found you by hacking your chat room account, you might be a bit reluctant to trust them. She would be. So would I, although I was different than others.

I rented an apartment a few blocks from her house. The landlord thought my mother was very sick in the hospital and probably wouldn't be coming out alive. I would pay cash for three months' rent, but couldn't sign a long-term lease. She was very understanding. Tears came to her eyes and she asked if there were anything she could do. I feigned a tear and told her no.

I was stunned when Mary came out of her house the first time my eyes laid eyes on here. I knew Mary had to be over 70, yet here stood a beautiful 40 year old woman, if that. It was then I was sure she'd made a step few others had made and I needed to know how to acquire the same state of being. Being sick was not long an issue for me, but stopping the aging process was something well down the road.

For the first few days I just followed her, which meant once I went to the store and another time I followed her to a church. Many alchemists were Christians, but I never quite understood why, other than the symbolic language was certainly Christic.

While Mary's home was in a residential neighborhood she didn't have far to walk to stores or the university. I got bored sitting all day staring at a house. It took some doing, but I set up a camera to watch her house. Motion detector software was put on it so when something entered the field of vision it beeped on my computer and I could see what was going on. Meanwhile I could do research at the library and think about what I would do next. One nosy neighbor did ask what I was doing on the telephone pole and where my special truck was. My reply was to let him know I was called in for special issues, worked by myself and didn't need all the equipment in the trucks. That seemed to satisfy his curiosity.

After two weeks I decided I needed to know more about her. In the end, I might have to take her life, I should at least get to know her and give her a chance for redemption. She attended a weekly bible study at a nearby Episcopal church. I joined them.

There were about 20 of us, and as far as I could tell, 4 were like me, new. The minister had us make introductions. I was Bob, just moved to town, an ambulance driver. Mary introduced herself as Mary, a retired woman seeking God. She watched me from the moment I entered the room. Paranoia crept in. Her eyes felt like lasers.

We were talking about Matthew, chapter 6. The pastor talked for a bit about the passage from a historical perspective and then asked people to share what it said to them. Several offered ideas. Then Mary looked straight at me and said, “Bob, has the salt found its way into your life yet?”

Salt was the end element of the process. It has been a preservative throughout history, a mineral of great value in ancient times, one that adds flavor, tenderizes, and preserves. Jesus used it as a symbol for his disciples, but I knew her intuition put her onto me. I’d made a mistake in coming. Now the end was known, I just had to figure out when.

“Mary, that is a good question,” I said cautiously. “I think I'm close to finding the salt to bring it all together. But I know it can't be done alone, I’ll need some help, some spiritual direction.”

“Of course Bob, we all do, but in the end, you have to make the choice, you have to choose to follow the right path, no one can make that decision for you."

"I've made that choice, I'm on the right path."

"Are you sure?"

I wondered how she could possible know, then I remembered one of the things that changed as you got close to the end was your intuition. I remembered how Jesus was able to know about the woman at the well and her 4 husbands, read the minds of the Pharisees that were trying to trap him, and constantly knew what his disciples were thinking. She was very close. I decided to play into her hand.

"That's why I'm here Mary, to learn with and from others, to find God. To see how God reveals himself in his Word."

"I'm glad you are here Bob," said the pastor, trying to bring Mary and me back into the fold. There was an odd tension that was palpable. I'm sure I looked strained; she looked like she was sitting in an oasis of peace.

That was the end of the study and we all left. When we reached the door Mary turned, looked into my eyes, touched my shoulder and said, "I know."

Shivers ran down my spine and electricity coursed through my body. I couldn't believe it, yet I had no response, I was frozen. I thought of Jesus being in control, even to his death. Well, she might be in control, but it was still going to cost her.

I went back to my apartment and knew I had to do it today, the more time I let go by, the more chance she would have to tell others and protect herself. It did occur to me that if she already knew, why even then wasn't she protecting herself. She could have fled, disappeared and moved her laboratory. Was she setting a trap for me?

I packed my bags and put them by the door. When I was finished with Mary I would be going home. I walked to her house. The light in the lab was out, but her bedroom light was on. The door was open and I let myself in.

The house was very solid and no creaks sounded as I went up the stairs.

"It's alright Bob, I know you are there."

I no longer pretended to be sneaking about. I walked down the hall and into her room. She sat on the bed reading a book.

"Hello Mary."

"Hello, what is your real name?"

"Thomas."

"I should have guessed, how appropriate."

"What do you mean? " I asked.

"Surely you know of doubting Thomas, thought he had the answers, needing proof when the answer lay within him."

"I don't have time for games Mary, just give me what I want and I'll leave you alone."

"You can't leave me alone and even if I gave you what you want, it is not what you need and that is more important."

"What are you talking about?" I was getting angry.

"Do you remember the story in the Gospel of Mark about the man who was paralyzed? His friends dragged him to Jesus, but there was no room, so they dug a hole in the roof and lowered him down. They expected Jesus to heal him. At first, he didn't, he said, "your sins are forgiven." Jesus knew what he needed. Even if I give you what you seek it won't work, you aren't ready."

"I'll take my chances."

"Tell me, have you had success with what you stole from Philip?"

I was astonished. "How did you know?"

"A good guess that turns out to be true."

"I'm very close to having an understanding not only of his work, but of discovering the Stone, I just need your input."

"Death is meaningless to me, you must know that, and you aren't even close to the Stone."

"Don't you seek immortality?"

"I feel so sorry for you, you've missed the point of the work. The point is not to live forever on this plane, but to be at one with the One who created the work. That is when the universe opens its arms. Whether I find that now or in heaven doesn't matter. You only make your journey more difficult by going the path you have chosen."

Fury enraged me, I'd had enough. I pulled the knife out and stabbed her in the thigh. She screamed and grabbed her leg as blood poured out.

"Now show me," I yelled.

I dragged her down the stairs. She didn't cry, she smiled at me.

"You have just destroyed what little hope you have."

"Soon I will have all the answers," I replied. How could this woman not be screaming and crying?

"The truth is you have no answers, you don't even know the question."

"Where is it?"

"Thomas, tell me exactly what it is you seek?"

"Your notes on the merging of the sun and the moon."

"That is all?"

"I think it is more than enough."

She hobbled over to her table and handed me a notebook. "Here, it's all yours."

I stabbed her in the chest and watched as she slid to the floor, dead, a smile on her face. Killing someone was far easier than I thought. My anger subsided now that I had what I deserved. On one level, she was competition and the competition was now gone. Her help in the process would have made my life easier, but I didn't need her or anyone.

I couldn’t make it look like a robbery, there was nothing in the house to rob. Burning the house down wouldn’t help, not with a stabbed woman on the floor. I knew I hadn’t left any clues so I didn’t worry. I briefly looked around for other things to take. I grabbed her computer.

Mary had given me the keys to the kingdom. She thought I wouldn’t understand or be able to use what I now had in my possession. She was wrong, she’d underestimated the neutrality of the spirit.

3 THE PENDANT--MATT

"You're crazy, there is no way she is 80," exclaimed Tom.

"Well believe what you want, she's 80. I have proof, but for now come here and look."

I showed him the pictures on the wall, taking it step by step, showing him my logic.

"I'll be damned."

"It must be her daughter," said Steve.

"Trust me, it's her. You can believe what you want but you are wasting time, we are already a couple of days behind the killer, maybe more, " I said.

"What makes you say that,?" asked Tom.

"We both agree she doesn't look close to 80. I don't know what process helped her stop aging at 40, but whatever it is may also slow rigor. You'll have a hard time pinning the date down, this is no normal human being and this is not going to be a normal investigation."

"On that we agree. By the way, what was said to you on the phone?"

"A friend of mine did some background work."

"That fast?"

"This person is good," I said proudly.

"I might need their name."

"Not a chance. Through the bank, she got a social security number which led to a college picture and a clipping of some work she was doing at the university in the 60's, probably just before that picture was taken. My guess is you will not find any more recent pictures. Once she stopped aging she disappeared."

"Come on, she didn't stop aging, she had good facelifts."

"Tom, ask your coroner to do whatever scans you want, she will test as a 40 year old."

"I still don't get why they murdered her?" asked Steve.

"If you had figured out a way to stop aging, what do you think that would be worth?"

"I get your point."

"The field of possibilities is fairly large," Tom said.

"She was a very quiet person, clearly not interested in money. I doubt anyone knew."

"Someone knew."

"Well, I don't think they killed her for the money. Look around, do you see any pills, juices, or concoctions that would do this? There is something much deeper going on here."

"How the hell am I going to get all this translated?" he said looking at all the papers.

"If I were you I'd call in advanced students at the university in each language. Give them some tips on what to look for and let them loose. There is no need to translate everything"

"Just one problem……"

"We don't know what to tell them to look for."

"Bingo."

Steve entered the conversation. "It's easy, look for things about extending life, or immortality or eternal life." I had to appreciate his desire for the obvious, but it was also annoying.

"Look Steve, she found whatever that was in the mid-60's. She was well beyond that now. I can't conceive of what it was, but stopping the aging process was small potatoes, a way stop on the way to her goal. Unfortunately, she never reached it and I'm a bit nervous about the person who will kill to get their hands on her secrets. I'm going to leave, I'm sure you can handle it from here."

"So glad to hear of your confidence. What do you think he stole?" said Tom with sarcasm.

"Well, her computer is gone, although I doubt there was much of value on that. My best guess would be he got a notebook of some kind, or he left empty. Will you let me know if you find anything?"

"Of course, and is the feeling mutual?"

"I called you didn't I?" I winked and headed out the door. "Oh, glad to meet you Steve, best of luck!"

"Thanks."

Steve wasn't going anywhere fast, but at least he wasn't dangerous or a complete idiot. As I left the house I had that feeling of sadness again, like the house itself was mourning Mary. Something told me the house wasn't going to live very long.

Along with the diary, I also took a piece of Mary's clothing, a small picture, and a candle I found in the lab. I wanted the Ansel Adams print but felt that was going a bit overboard. It was an original with a note to Mary on the back. The thought of the state getting their hands on it made me quiver and I suspected she had no relatives, so I grabbed it on my way out—a justifiable sin? I put it back.

I returned to my office, enjoying the ride through streets. Our parish was downtown so I get to know the regulars in the neighborhood and in the summer have my windows down and say hi. Portland is such a vibrant city, a remarkable amount of creative juices flowing and greenery everywhere you look. Beautiful gardens in people's yards, trees lining the streets creating shade and amazing textures of green.

The church had remarkable people that took care of the grounds, mostly retired people who had great pride in the church grounds. We had two acres, so there was quite a bit to take care of. The church itself was quite modern and open, although it had 15 large stained glass windows, each representing a different era or style of glasswork. On a sunny day the inside glowed and at night we put the lights on inside so passers-by would enjoy—our little piece of evangelism. When the church was built they wanted it to be both sacred and well used. Having a large structure sit there empty 95% of the week drives me nuts. Many groups use the space during the week and I think God appreciates the stewardship. The original church sits on a corner of the property, a reminder of our humble beginnings and a charming wedding chapel.

As I walked in, Julie handed me a long list of messages. Fitting criminal work into the schedule was often difficult, but most of the time I made it work. I was often surprised by how God would use something I had to do for the church to guide me in the other efforts. I looked down the list and nothing leapt out at me as a sign from God. A question about the pot-luck, a comment on my sermon, two more outreach ideas, a need for a visit, two I didn't have a clue about, and one from another clergy person about the upcoming convention. I knew she wanted me to make waves—I wasn't sure this was the year.

"Julie, when is my next appointment?"

"20 minutes."

"And what is it?"

"Linda Dumar and Brad Johnson, premarital counseling."

"Ah yes, great young couple. I think they have been helping out with the youth program haven't they?"

"Yes."

Usually when Julie was mad at me about something she was very curt. "Is something the matter?"

"No, it has nothing to do with work."

"Well, I'd be happy to help even if it isn't work."

"Later maybe."

I knew to let well enough alone. I walked into my office and sat at my desk, plugging the camera in and downloaded the pictures. Did I forget to mention I'd taken about 50 pictures at the scene of the murder? Knowing I would never see most of the crime scene again, I always took pictures and never told Tom. Whenever I would bring something up about the crime scene I'd just tell him I had a photographic memory. Not a complete lie, and although I remember things well, having a camera with me 24/7 seemed to come in handy more often than not.

While they downloaded I sat back and relaxed, opening my heart and mind to the Spirit. It came at me like replaying a movie. "Julie, can you check a name on the register for me? Mary Weathers." I had a vision of Mary coming to our church a couple of months ago, but couldn't place why she didn't return or what she'd said.

I looked at the pictures one by one hoping something would leap out at me, but nothing did other than a small pendant on a lab table with the following on it:

I had no clue what it was or meant, although I would find out. I printed out several sheets of photographs and planned on having them translated or interpreted when I went to the university later on in the day. I always try to stay one step ahead of the police. They more often than not got there before me, but I enjoy the challenge. Besides, I have God on my side.

The diary was sitting on my table. It was well weathered, a leather cover and had only been used for about a year. This was not a lab book, but notes that pertained to other aspects of her life. I knew its age by looking at the first and last pages. About 90% seemed to be in English so I was in luck. Having forgotten the world I sat back for a good read. Normally I would never think of reading someone's diary, but in this case she wouldn't be able to complain.

Just then there was a knock at the door. How quickly we forget!!!!

I opened the door to the smiling faces of Linda and Brad. We reintroduced ourselves and sat down. This was our second meeting. They were a delightful couple, very committed to our Lord and anxious to deepen their own relationship. Our first session had taken place a month before. Pre-marital counseling was fairly routine. There was a system most pastors ran the couple through. Some don't even do it themselves, they farm it out, claiming to be too busy. To be too busy to meet with two people who want to commit themselves to each other in the presence of God and be blessed by a priest is rather strange. Other clergy have official counselors doing the work, feeling they will do a better job—ie. cop-out. On the other hand, priests are not trained to do everything, to be all things to all people, albeit convincing some parishioners of that is difficult. I guess I should be thankful clergy own up to what they may not do well and delegate that job to someone who has the gift. I have never heard of pre-marital counseling making a life changing decision in a couple's life—OK a few times, but quite rare.

I tell the couple these sessions are primarily for me to get to know them and visa versa, to ask a few questions to try to make sure they communicate well and have covered the bases and to hear my lecture.

I had one couple come in who had been living together for 3 years. They wanted to get married. I started going through my list of questions. When I got to the one about kids, I asked, "And what about children? At the same time the man said, "Can't wait," and the woman said, "Don't want them." They stared at each other. Somewhere inside they knew what the other would say and didn't want to face it because they truly loved one another. After another half hour of discussion it became apparent both were adamant about their feelings. They left and called a few days later thanking me for my help and telling me the relationship had ended. I was sad it had ended but thankful they'd figured it out before getting married.

Today was lecture day. Not really a lecture, rather sage advice from someone who'd seen more than a few relationships. I include it for two reasons, the first is that the reader will find it useful in their own relationships---of any kind. Secondly, well you will soon see, it impacts the story.

I love meeting with couples before marriage, their eyes radiate with passion, their faces glow and their lips are always moist. Hands are often held and bodies are close. I'd given them some literature to read and a book, WE, by Robert Johnson, a fabulous work on romantic love.

I should probably tape this little talk of mine and just hand them the CD, it's pretty much the same every time. But I like seeing their responses and hearing their questions. “So today, we talk about C.I.A. Normally at this point I see that quizzical look in their eyes. Most people who come in know of my “other” work and when I mention the CIA flags go up.

“Don’t worry,” I say, “it’s just an acronym for what a marriage counselor once taught me were the only three core issues in a marriage. Usually couple’s come in and tell me they have a sex or money problems. Upon further digging I have yet to find a case that doesn’t end up being one of these three issues. Any guesses as to what the “C” is for?”

I wait.

“Control,” Linda says.

“Excellent,” I exclaim, proud of her insight. “Control issues are probably the number one issue of the day.”

“I thought it was communication,” said Brad.

“But communication is something we control. If you stop talking with Linda, it’s a choice you are making, you are choosing to determine what conversations are about, to not make yourself known or vulnerable. It's merely a different form of communicating. Not communicating is not possible. Sometimes we aren’t even aware we are controlling, it’s unconscious. That’s why it is so important to take care of the marriage and to seek help as soon as things go wrong. Counselors, good ones, see things you won’t. Some of the best marriages I know go for counseling a couple of times a year just like you take your car for a tune-up.

“That makes sense,” responded Brad.

“Is it always an issue? Can't being in control or letting go of the need for control be a good thing?” asked Linda.

“Of course. The idea is to be aware of our own control needs and to share them. Problems arise when there is conflict around control. Relationships all have dynamics of control, the question is what we do with them. Anyway, let's move on. "I" is for inclusion and conversely, exclusion. This is when one person feels excluded from the other's arena. I had a couple where the man had a group of friends he went out with every week, and she was specifically not invited—ever. It made her angrier and angrier. Finally, he invited his friends over, she met them and all was well. It was the idea she was being kept out of his life that bothered her, not that she cared if he went out with friends or not.

"I think we are pretty good on that one right now," said Linda.

"Does that mean we aren't good on control?"

"No, that one is ok too." They laughed.

"Don't worry, it's a very long process, nothing is perfect and forgiveness is a big part of marriage. "The "A" is for affection. This is when one partner or the other is feeling like they aren't getting enough affection; physical and emotional. It usually lags behind the other two. Everyone has different physical and emotional needs. You have to make sure you make your needs known and do your best to fill the other's needs that you are able. But know that you can't possibly fill them all and don't assume your partner knows what you need, tell them."

Multi-tasking has always been one of my strong suits. I can be completely attentive to one thing while a different part of my brain is working on something else. Now and then the two collided.

"Oh my God, that's it!" I said with great joy.

Brad and Linda looked at me. "What are you talking about?" as if they had said something miraculous.

"I'm sorry, but you've just helped me figure out a key to the puzzle."

"What puzzle?"

"The why for the murder I just discovered." I tended to be fairly open with my work, other than details.

"You are working on a murder while doing pre-marital counseling?" Linda quipped a bit annoyed.

"I'm almost always working on a murder or some crime, whether I'm counseling, preaching, or sleeping. Perhaps I should say the Holy Spirit is working within me while I do other things."

Linda, the more curious of the two asked, "So what did you figure out?"

"I think most murders are like other relationships, something goes astray along the lines of control, inclusion or affection. In this case, mostly inclusion and control. The murderer thought he could control the one he murdered. When she excluded him, she took the power and he couldn't stand it, so he killed her. I doubt he got what he wanted from her."

"And what was that?" Brad asked nervously.

"That I don't know Brad, I plan on finding out though. It's interesting, Jesus was well aware that control was a pivotal issue in humanity. Remember all his tangles with the Jewish leadership? They perceived him as a threat to their power and control, not to mention to their authority over scripture and theology----all very understandable. But remember what he said, "You will not find yourself until you die to yourself." Your ego must die and be replaced by the mind of God if you are to truly discover what it is to be fully human. That is the story of Adam and Eve, they gave up full humanity when they denied the mind and will of God. We do it all the time, it's called sin."

"Brad, I think Pastor Matt is busy, so maybe we should let him go," Linda said.

"Oh, sorry pastor, it's just so fascinating."

"I agree Brad, never a dull moment." I suddenly got this nudging in my brain. I sat quietly, listening, closing my eyes. They must have thought I was off my rocker.

"Are you OK?" asked Linda.

By that time I was gone, mentally in a totally different world trying to feel what the Spirit wanted me to do. Somewhere in my mind I heard the door close and knew they'd left. Then I felt something inside of me like a kick in the ribs.

I jumped and ran to the door. "Wait," I screamed.

There were probably 8 people in the outer office, including Brad and Linda who were setting up the next appointment.

"Someone in here reads a foreign language, who is it?

All eight raised their hands and looked at each other.

"Wow!!!!" I smiled.

"What language are you looking for?" asked.

Normally, when the Holy Spirit leads me like this I didn't hesitate. But dragging these people into the crime may not be the smartest idea.

"Well, let's see, Latin, German, French, Chinese, and Arabic, I think."

I was stunned, each went around and every language was covered to some degree. I told them to meet me in the classroom in 10 minutes. They were all very excited. I don't know why I am always amazed at the work of the Spirit, the web is vast. Well, more on the web later on, and this isn't the internet web I'm talking about, but the spiritual one.

I went into my office and printed off all the pictures that had writing. I did my best to separate them into languages. Then I took them to the collective consciousness that had gathered in the classroom and set the passages before them. I'd also photo-copied the foreign language passages of the diary and gave them those.

"These all have to do with a case I'm working on, you probably figured that out." They laughed. "Just translate what you can. If there is anything that you would think would be significant to me and the police, let me know."

Fortunately, Tom didn't go to church at the moment. I am sure that discussion of this meeting would be the talk of the church on Sunday and he'd want to know how I got my hands on the writings. Were he really thinking, he'd wonder where the extra words came from—the diary. It was a crime to take it and I would certainly pass on any pertinent information, but I was not about to admit to taking it. Not at least until after the case was solved and we had a few beers, ok, several beers, in us.

They looked like a group of scholars who'd just found the Dead Sea scrolls. Some worked by themselves and others worked together, talking back and forth, sharing ideas. Now and then one would go to the computer and track down a word on a website—thank God for the internet. I was most puzzled by Mildred. A woman in her 60's who helped regularly at the church but was very quiet. Even though I'd talked with her on numerous occasions, I knew little. She'd been raised in China, which I knew but had forgotten. She had several pen pals still there, went to Chinatown once a week for a meal and read the Chinese newspaper. She moved up my list of great contacts to have.

Whenever the phone rang, Julie left her work on the Latin text, another surprise for me. I had no idea she read Latin. But then I hadn't known she was a talented cello player either, until she played a solo Christmas Eve one year that made us all cry. The music director found out, but I didn't know. Sometimes I wonder if I'm in the right job.

Mary Weathers was not a scholar in one sense of the word, she never included her sources. Lots of formulas, quotes, and ideas, but no reference as to where they came from. My guess was were she alive she could tell you everyone from memory.

The "scholars" gave me bits and pieces as they translated them. Most were not surprises. I knew enough about alchemy to know some of the language and this was all alchemy. Mercury, sun, moon, coagulation, purification, salt and other chemicals abounded. My guess was the formulas were symbolic formulas but would take a great deal more knowledge than I had at present to figure out.

They'd been at it for two hours and had more to go. "If you want to take these home you can, I have to leave for a while."

"Pastor," Julie stated. She called me Pastor when others were around and Matt when they weren't. I preferred being called by my first name. "Here are the notes on Mary Weathers."

I took the notes and thanked her.

None of them even raised their head to say goodbye, they just kept on. I told Julie where I was going and to have people leave their findings on my desk.

The notes were brief—as always. When someone visited the church and I talked with them I always made notes about that meeting for future reference. Mary had stated she was interested in a Bible study and in the more mystical side of life. I'd asked her where she lived and she told me. I told her I'd enjoy having her in our parish but the priest she wanted to work with lived in her neighborhood. I gave her the name and address. She also told me she admired my work, I even wrote down a quote because at the time it seemed so odd. "Matt, soon you will need all your gifts and more, trust." Now that made more sense. She also said something else I wrote down that I'd totally forgotten. "Do you like the work of Ansel Adams?" I'd stated he was one of my favorites.

"Good I may leave something for you." That was it. I was stunned.

The ride to Portland State University took about 20 minutes, traffic got worse and worse all the time in Portland. I didn't really want to go downtown, but they did have the best library and besides I enjoyed being around all those young people, trying to figure out what they wanted to be. Years ago I'd convinced the President of the university to give me a permanent library card to help me with my work. A sizeable check didn't hurt. Then I decided to get my M.B.A. Running a church with a $4,000,000 budget and a $35 million endowment can be a bit tricky. I tried to keep administration to a minimum. The vast majority of money was given away to causes with which we had direct involvement, including the orphanage in Peru where we sent doctors and helpers every year. It wasn't that I didn't trust our treasurer, Edward was a saint. I just felt understanding what we had and what we could do with it made sense. A few strong suggestions from my friend Dave, a broker, were made and had turned a $17 million dollar fund into what it was today in 3 years.

I sat down at one of the library desks took out my laptop and waited for it to connect to the wireless network. How could you not love technology? Shortly I was up, running and searching their vast data base. I started with books that were in the library. While there weren't many, I found 8 that would be useful. It turns out one of the main sources for research is at the British Museum. I thought about a field trip, but knew at this time of year I'd never get away with it and I didn't really know yet what I was looking for, mostly a giant fishing game.

Looking at articles for about an hour I realized one of several possibilities existed. 1. Alchemists were whackos. 2. They had created a language only they understood, a language so symbolic you would have to study it for years to really know what was going on. 3. They were horrible writers. 4. It was all a huge 50 century scam. Those who figured out the scam had given so much time, they couldn't admit their waste, so they became part of perpetuating the scam. I'd read C.J. Jung's works once, two or three of them were on alchemy. I wasn't sure he understood it either.

I knew that 1 and 3 were probably wrong, at least for some. There are whacko priests and bishops (I might be one) but certainly not all alchemists were crazy and it was evident some were brilliant writers. I just didn't get it. That left 2 and 4. I chose for the moment to go with 2 because I couldn't figure out how an 80 year old woman had stopped aging. That was fact, not a scam.

My phone rang. I saw the number and smile.

"Which part did I get right Tom?"

"How did you know?"

"You never call me this early in the investigation unless I said something that was right."

"She's 80."

I tried hard to suppress a smile and a laugh. "How did you find out?"

"First was the same way you did, we just checked the bank and past history. Then there were the neighbors—we do that sort of thing you know. While they rarely saw her, they'd known her for 25 years. They said they'd noticed that she didn't age much; they thought she ate right and exercised. These people were 80 and looked it. Then there was the coroner. He is currently trying to prove himself wrong. There are a variety of tests they do, but he says some come back as 40, some 60 and some 80. But a 40 year old cannot fake it as an 80 year old. He's not sure how an 80 year old fakes it as a 40 year old."

"So what is next?"

“The lab boys are still at the house, that could take a couple of days, there are a lot of papers in there. Get those translated and go from there. We are analyzing all the bottles of stuff we found in there, that could take a while in and of itself. “

“Well, good luck.”

“And you, what are you doing?”

“I’m at the library learning about alchemy.”

“A thrill I’m sure,” Tom retorted.

“I think I might have to learn more about it, from the inside.”

“Oh please don’t do this again, you almost got killed the last time. Don’t forget you are not a cop, you are a priest.”

“I haven’t forgotten and I learned my lesson, trust me, but I think I can get in without getting that far in.”

“Don’t go anywhere physically without telling me.”

“I won’t Tom.”

“Promise—on the bible.”

I laughed. I don’t make promises, my yes is yes, but the Bible thing doesn’t really do much good, God usually doesn’t strike people down for lying. He’s not happy about it, but no lightning bolts.

The hour was getting late and I needed to get back to the church, pick up the work parishioners had done and call Sue. It was doing to be busy tonight, talking with alchemists, trying to single out the murderer, assuming that is I could find them and him or her.

4 BOB SETTLES IN

Driving around Portland on a nice fall day was just what I needed. I'd crossed a level I'd never done before, killing, and I was shocked by the thrill it gave me. But the larger excitement came from what I held in my hands, her notebook. I was a bit perplexed as to why she gave it to me so easily. Perhaps she knew her time was up and I would trash the house to find it. Alchemists have a relationship with their labs and they will protect them as a good parent would their child. In hindsight I probably should have rummaged through the lab for a while longer. Who knows what I might have found. I was nervous about leaving a trail and a bit paranoid about getting caught.

A brief look in the notebook let me know I would need some dictionaries; Latin, French, and Arabic. My Latin and French were pretty good, but Arabic is not my forte. It didn't seem to be Mary's either. I went to Powell's bookstore, a large and busy store where no one would remember me. I loved books and spent an hour browsing their shelves. Not surprisingly, the section on alchemy was weak, but the city had other more esoteric stores for that and I didn't really need those anyway. I purchased the books and then headed to the waterfront.

The sun was out, lots of people strolling along the walkway by the Willamette River, and I found a bench on which to do my work. My own home is in the country, but I was enjoying this respite in the city. Lovers strolling down the quay, street people sleeping under trees, bikers and joggers out for their exercise innocent of what was happening around them. I remembered reading about the year of the floods in the late 90's in Portland. The river came up to the edge of the wall and almost poured into the city. Hard to believe since the river was currently a good 20 feet down the wall. I opened her notebook and started to read. The first several pages were in English.

"Mercury conversion to salt has transmigrated the optimum levels of energy through the animus."

My God, I thought, she's done it. She's found the ultimate source of power and she's used it.

I kept reading, transfixed by the work she had done and on another level by the power I had in ending it all. I was a bit perplexed that I felt no guilt, but I didn't. I had asked nicely and she'd refused, so what was I to do? I have never been one for reinventing the wheel. If someone has already created a good drug to get rid of diabetes, why should I invent another, just use theirs. Alchemists are not known for sharing their work with just anyone, but most of us have someone we mentor. I was wondering if Mary was teaching someone, I'd have to find out.

I won't bore you with many more details about Mary's work, you wouldn't get it anyway, at least not without years of work. The linguistic system has to be embedded in your heart to fully grasp what is going on. Leafing through the pages I noted two amazing formulas I would have to test soon. I wasn't about to risk my life trying things in this book, better to use other people to test her integrity, and that is what was on the line, whether she was being truthful with me or not. As the sun baked my face I wondered what I would do if this was a fake. What if Mary knew I was coming and put together a fake book to throw me off course? Perhaps I should have kept her alive just in case. Two more maxims that keep me moving forward---no regrets and no looking back.

After underlining some things, I closed the notebook and looked to the future. What were the next steps? I needed to ensure there were no tracks that would lead back to me. Obviously I couldn't go back to the house. I had paid for everything in cash, not shopped at the same store twice or eaten out at any regular place. Even if they were able to find a fingerprint somewhere, I had never had mine taken, so there is no record of me anywhere that would give them a clue. I felt secure and decided to head home.

The world is filled with centers of power. Carlos Castenados talked about them in his Don Juan series, shamans and priests of every religious tradition know of them, and most alchemists with any brains do their work near one. I'm sure you aren't surprised that Jerusalem is a powerful center. Part of the tension between religions in that region is because they are fighting over a spiritual center of power. The problem is none of the people fighting are spiritual. If they were, fighting would cease, children would not die at the hands of those who blasphemy their religion, and the spiritual forces at work in that area would be able to do amazing things. The actual focal point was where Jesus was crucified. He made it that way, knowing what was possible. He had the power to stop his death, yet chose not to, I've never understood that. I would have wiped them all out.

Some power centers are easily found, like Jerusalem. Others need to be felt. Mary knew Portland was another intense spot. Native Americans long knew of the forces at work in this locale. I can feel it breathe. Part of me would love to stay here in this beautiful city, the culture rich, the geography amazing, and the people pursuing the spiritual realms probably higher than anywhere in the states. They are also a well-read populace. In Multnomah County, their 17 libraries check out more materials than any other county in the country, that includes New York and LA. You might ask why that is important. While alchemical work is done primarily in solitude, the energy of others has a great impact. You could never get anything done in an area of violence. Mary knew how to find the right spot and she'd done well, but not well enough. I would retreat to my lab, I missed it.

There were two other reasons I needed to leave Portland. The first was I didn't know what impact some of my actions would have on the energy fields I needed. I preferred to be in my own lab where all the vibes were good. The second was I had a feeling someone was after me. This was not the ordinary feeling of paranoia I get. This was physical, I didn't think, I knew. I can't not fathom how this person is tracking me down, but they are and I needed to leave town. The trail would go cold when I left. This other person was using means to trace me far beyond what police could use. I wondered if there was an alchemist like me, doing what I did, coming after me as I went after Mary. I would have to be careful.

Two weeks had passed since Mary gave her life to me. I'd watched the papers and news and walked by the house a few times. All was quiet. My guess is her file would be put away shortly. She had no relatives, no real friends, and no pressure from the public to find the reason for her death. Police tend to put their focus on the cases that get attention. Police around the country were far too isolated from one another to put together the string of events of which I'd been a part.

I loaded my car with the few things I had with me and headed south. I told the landlady my mom had died and I was heading back to Ohio. I'd never parked by the apartment, so she didn't know the license was from California. I'd been to Ohio several years before to take care of another situation and while I was there I picked up an Ohio license. It's what I used whenever I was out of California.

Interestingly enough, most of the "potions" alchemists make are not that difficult. Think about it, they were making these things over a thousand years ago, they didn't have fancy labs with all the toys we do. The problem is science is missing out because they have tunnel vision, they fail to accept the reality of spirit. Their loss is my gain.

One of the first things I was going to have to do when I got home was to head to Santa Barbara and visit the hospital---after I created a batch of Mary's formula. It would be the first test.

While I was excited to try this out, I was in no hurry, patience was one of the biggest lessons we all have to learn and part of patience is delayed gratification. I'd rushed into a few things before and they rarely turned out well. My mind and spirit needed to be in tune and taking the long way home, slowly moving down the coast was just what I needed.

I was just south of the city when it hit me. I pulled off at a rest area and sat there. I was thinking about the bible study, what had been said and left unsaid. Truth was, I didn't want the study to end, I was enjoying myself and frustrated the pastor wasn't really taking part, after all, he was the expert. I don't know why, but I needed to know what he thought. The hour was early, so I turned around and headed back to town to have a chat with him.

When I first entered the church I hadn't taken notice of what type of church it was, I didn't care because it was where Mary was going. Had she been going to Mormon Church I would have followed her. Now I was more curious. There must have been a reason she went here.

The church was not large, probably built in the 60's, that famous A-frame shape of so many. The structure showed its age. My guess was they had about a hundred people attending on a Sunday morning. I wasn't surprised to find it was an Episcopal Church. Mary would feel at home here, a church rich with liturgical tradition and yet open to a wide variety of beliefs. As of late they seemed to be floundering in what they really did believe. Jesus was at the core, but what that meant and who he was caused no end of grief, especially since they didn't really like to talk about it. Their church was more focused on politics than the spiritual message-one of the main reasons of their slow demise.

The grounds were well kept and they had a lovely view of downtown from their perch on the south hills. On a clear day several snow-capped mountains could be seen. I couldn't quite figure out why the church had no clear windows. Maybe they felt by blocking out God's creation, they could concentrate on God more fully. My laboratory had no windows. I didn't want people looking in, I didn't want to know if it was day or night, and I didn't need the distraction of nature. This was clearly a neighborhood church, no parking lot and surrounded by beautiful homes. I'm sure several thousand people could walk to this church on Sundays. My guess was that less than 100 attended. While Portland was certainly a spiritual city, church going was not high on the list.

I entered the door. It was a Thursday and no one seemed to be around.

"Hello?" I said. "Anyone here?"

I walked around the building. The sanctuary was simple, yet sacred. A sense of peace resided here, as in most churches. I sat in one of the pews enjoying the quiet and stillness. The stained glass windows were from the 19th century and depicted central stories in the bible. Adam and Eve, Moses, David and Goliath, Jeremiah, Jesus feeding the 5000, turning water into wine, and of course, the crucifixion. I'm sure there was a story behind why these images were chosen. From the looks of things, I'd say this was a pretty traditional parish. The organ was the only musical instrument and only a hymnal in the pew racks. It was a bit chilly in the church, but not unpleasant. It had that old church aroma. A door squeaked somewhere behind the altar. A few moments later the priest came out, carrying things he put on the altar. He was unaware I was there.

'Hello father," I said.

My voice startled him. "Oh, hi, I'm sorry."

"My apologies for startling you."

"Don't worry, is there anything I can do for you?" He looked at me and I waited. "You are the young man that joined our bible study a while ago."

"Yes I am."

"What can I do for you?"

"Well, I was wondering if we could talk, I have some questions."

"I'd enjoy that, let me just set up here for tonight's service." He went back to the altar and continued setting up.

"That was one of my questions, communion."

"What about it?" he asked.

"I don't understand the differences between denominations. Why do they all think it is something different?"

"That's a very good question and I can't really speak to the history of each belief. For some, communion is at the center of worship, for others it is on the edge. The more important it is, the richer the theology behind it. For example, Catholics consider it the most important. They believe in transubstantiation, the belief that the bread and wine physically become Christ's body and blood in your body. By the way, we call it the Eucharist."

"That is what Jesus said isn't it?"

"Yes it is."

"So why don't you and others believe in that?"

"Episcopalians believe more in the symbolic language of scripture rather than in literal interpretation."

"And what is communion for you?"

"Well on the other end from the Catholics are most of the Protestants. They do it infrequently and believe it is just a memorial. The bread and wine are merely symbols, nothing more."

"That's interesting since most of them are literalists."

"I agree. All of us view the bible in one way or another and then justify our beliefs even when they are so obviously contrary to what we claim."

"And the Episcopal Church?"

"As with so many things, we are in between the Catholics and the rest. We believe in con-substantiation. That means that it's more than a memorial and less than physically changing, but we don't know what it is other than a mystery."

"A cop out."

He laughed. "I guess you can see it that way if you want. I prefer to accept mystery, do you not enjoy mystery?"

"Mysteries are wonderful, but I believe we are supposed to figure them out."

"And what if you can't?"

"We should never stop trying even though we accept it for the time being."

"Well that is probably where we are in the church. We accept the mystery while trying to ponder its depths and allowing the Spirit to be revealed to us.

"And how do you discover mystery?"

"You mean how do you discover God?"

"Yes."

"If you are seeking God, you will find him, he has already found you."

I wondered what he meant—I'd spent more time than he trying to find the secrets of the universe, I'd probably done some things he could only dream about. "Do you believe that God can be found outside of Jesus?"

"Hmmmmm, another interesting question-----I'm sorry, I've forgotten your name?

I tried to remember what name I'd used, it was a chance you took when revisiting a site. "I'm Bob."

"Yes, now I remember, Bob with the mother who is not well. I'm Steve. How is she?"

"She died two days ago."

"I'm sorry to hear that but I'm glad you could be with her at the end. Was she a woman of faith?"

"Very strong faith---in Buddhism."

"I see. I hope it served her well."

"It's one of the reasons I'm asking these questions. Is God in Buddhism?"

"This is only my opinion Bob but here is how I see it. The world has been full of people for a long time, even when Jews started there were millions of people around the globe. I don't believe God ignored them. God is revealed to those who want to see. His goal is always the same, to have people love one another, to have justice prevail and to be at one with his creation. Jesus is the Son of God. He personified exactly what God wanted in his life. There is no easier or clearer way to God than through Jesus. On earth I believe he is the only way to truly find the fullness of God. Sure, you can find aspects of God in and through other religious traditions, but not the totality."

"So do you believe that God reaches out to us in our dreams and through symbolism?"

"Certainly, constantly—dreams are perhaps a unique language of God that he can use within us when we won't listen," he replied with confidence.

“And things like astrology, numerology, alchemy, and mysticism?”

“I personally don’t think most of those are Christ centered, but in and of themselves they are not evil. Christian mystics had a very unique perspective and I suspect they were closer to God than most of us. It’s funny you should mention alchemy, we had a woman here that studied alchemy.”

“Really, who was that, I’ve always been fascinated by it?”

“Mary. Wait, I think you and she got into a bit of an argument at the bible study.”

I’d pushed too far, now I had to back out fast. “O yes, that was her, a wonderful woman.” I couldn’t help myself. “How is she, she didn’t seem well that day?”

“To be honest I don’t know. She was a regular at bible study but didn’t attend church very often, sometimes just coming in for communion. I haven’t seen her in a couple of weeks and we have never had her phone number or address. I too hope she is all right.”

“She probably just took a vacation or got caught up in something.”

“I hope so,” said the priest with concern in his voice.

“Do you believe in healing?”

“Of course, not only do I believe but I’ve seen it.”

“Really, what happened?”

“Well, probably the most amazing was when I served a church a long time ago. We had a man who had read the lessons for years. He was slowly going blind and hadn’t been able to read for a couple of years and could no longer get around without help. He couldn’t read, even with a book inches from his eyes. We had an outdoor service one Sunday and the priest said he felt God wanted this man to read the lesson. Everybody gasped. The priest called on us to lay hands on him, even with our doubts. We did. After the prayer the priest gave the man the bible and told him to read. He had 20/20 vision and kept it till he died."

"That's amazing, and you were there?"

"Yes. It was no act, he was blind and could see. So yes, I believe in healing, why do you ask?"

"What is it that heals?"

"That is the million dollar question. If I say God through Jesus, then you talk about medicine and other religions where healing takes place."

I had to laugh at him reading me like a book. "The thought had crossed my mind."

"To be honest, I am not really sure what happens, another mystery. I do believe Jesus helps us heal ourselves and others, but I have never doubted God's ability to work in and through anyone he wishes to work through. I also believe many of us are sick for emotional and spiritual reasons and when those are cleared up amazing things can happen. "

"Even blindness?"

Now he laughed. "Yes, potentially even blindness, but I don't think so in the case of that man, he was a saint."

"Even saints have problems."

"Very true Bob, very true."

I was wondering how far I should push things. Part of me knew I should pull away, yet another part, the stronger more aggressive wanted a witness. "What would you do if a series of healings took place?"

"What do you mean?"

"Well, let's say a bunch of people got healed and no one could explain how it happened?"

"I'd be very happy for them and praise God for the miracle."

"What if someone claimed credit but was---let's say just for fun—a Satanist?"

“It is against the very nature of Satan to heal, so it wouldn’t happen. Evil cannot heal, it can only destroy. The bible teaches us, as does history, that one of the best ways to separate those who claim to be from God from those who aren’t is to see what they do.”

“So Satan couldn’t heal someone?”

“Never. It’s not that he couldn’t, Satan has the power, it’s just against his nature and Satan is as true to his nature as God and Jesus are to theirs.”

“That’s good to know. So if you were to heal someone, you’d know you were on the right track.”

“I’d rather say you aren’t on the wrong track, there are a lot of tracks and they don’t all lead to the same place, even good ones don’t lead to the ultimate good.”

“What do you mean?”

“For me it all comes down to ego, and unfortunately ego usually wins. Christ calls us to battle our egos to let them go--- a very arduous process. Christians believe only in and through a relationship with Jesus can that be done. In essence, we are powerless over ourselves. Power corrupts as Marx said. I believe it. Look around, greed runs rampant in the world as people starve. We claim we are a generous people, but compared to what? Compared to what Jesus wants even monks who take a vow of poverty are greedy.”

“You sound angry about it.”

“Not angry, frustrated, most of all with myself, for I am no different.”

“So what’s the use?”

“It’s not an all or nothing game Bob. God does not say you either know all of me (which no one does) or you don’t know anything. The second we start a relationship with God, the potential is there for a full relationship. You and I are the ones who really control how things turn out, God is always waiting with open arms.”

"Very comforting I'm sure."

The priest let out a loud laugh. "Hardly comforting, I live in constant tension of knowing God and wanting to know God more. I'm sure you have been in relationships. There is always more to learn. Just when you think you know someone, they do something different. "

I was about to say something I'd regret. I looked at my watch. "Oh I'm sorry for taking your time pastor, I have to go, I'm late." I turned to leave.

"You are welcome here anytime, for prayer, worship, or to talk."

"I might take you up on that, thank you."

I walked out into the afternoon air, but things had changed in that church. I don't know if it was God, my ego, or something else, but I wasn't going home, I would stay and do the work here, which meant I had work to do.

The first step was finding a new lab. I needed a place away from everyone, preferably with a large room or barn, access to lots of electricity, and an environment where I could relax. Money was not an issue which made the search far easier. I went to a coffee house, pulled out my laptop and started fishing. For sale by owner was what I wanted. Whenever you bought a house from a broker, they bugged you forever. For sale by owner homes usually meant the owners were leaving after the sale.

Within a few clicks I'd found two possibilities. One was on the east side of town near Sandy, about 30 minutes out of Portland. The other was on the west side, not far from Vernonia. I called that one first. A delightful couple was leaving within the week, whether or not they sold it. They had 2. 5 acres, the house was off the road, a small barn and a pond stocked with trout just off a stream that flowed year round through the property.

I couldn't ask about the electricity, I'd see that when I got there. We made an appointment for the afternoon. Things were moving nicely.

By the end of the day I'd bought a house, most of the equipment I'd need and had it all set up to have a satellite on line for my computer. It wasn't cheap, but dial-up just didn't work for what I did, I needed speed and stealth.

I'd made the decision to fly home and drive a few critical items up from my house. There are some things that would attract attention to my new home I didn't want delivered. Things were on track for me to make my first move within two weeks.

Driving from my house in California gave me time to ponder some of the things the priest had said. I believed most of it, but still felt the true force of the universe was neutral, and he clearly thought it was good. For me, power was there for the taking, if it wasn't me, it would be someone else.

As with all things, I spent some time justifying my actions. I don't believe most of us do things wrong on purpose, we merely convince ourselves what we have done has a purpose or is right. Cult leaders and dictators are no different, the more power they have, the more they are convinced they are the truth. For me, the rationalization took the form of believing in the greater good. Mary and Philip were not using what they had learned for others. I on the other hand would. I would show the world within a couple of weeks what I was capable of.

By the time I arrived at the house, the people I bought it from had left the day after I bought it due to the 40% cash I'd given them. I was feeling great and ready to get back to work. I'd been away from the crux of my work for too long and need to get back into the flow. The property sat in a wooded valley, invisible from the road. A mix of grass, pasture, and woods covered the landscape. Light poured through all the windows, some of which would have to be blocked. The pond, about twenty yards from the house had a nice bench to sit on and was filled with large trout. I'd scoped out the electrical issue and was confidant it would work. There were several deciduous trees arrayed in their glorious red, yellow, and orange fall bouquets. Colors change faster in the country and at a higher elevation. The air was far more clear and fresh here than in the city and I couldn't wait to see the stars away from the city lights.

I spent about four full days and nights getting things hooked up. Once I got the furnace on line as well as the computers, I was back at. One of the best aspects of alchemical work has to do with space and time. I have yet to figure out how it works, but they seem to disappear. I can put in 5 days in a row, working 20-22 hours per day and not be winded. I am getting close to being in two places at one time, the marriage of sun and moon. For the present I spent most of my time working on Mary's formulas.

She'd done some phenomenal research on plants and minerals. I'd noticed in her lab that her plant library was extensive, there were specimens there I'd never heard of. Mary realized something past alchemists hadn't, as knowledge about the world grew, so did alchemy. Most of us rested on trying to figure out what had been done in the past. She assumed we'd learned it, incorporating much of modern science and moving past them, uniting science and religion, a remarkable woman.

Now my turn had come, my turn to show what alchemy could do, my turn to achieve immortality of body, mind, and spirit. I could taste the victory.

I rented a large P.O. box in Beaverton so deliveries wouldn't be made to my house. Using the computer I found all the plants and minerals I needed from around the world. Some were easy to find and some quite hard and expensive.

From Mary's notebook I saw she had been moved by the spirit to make and use things, but in the end used science to show how it worked. For her, just knowing something would work wasn't enough, she wanted to know why.

Another two weeks past as my potions and I fermented. Sounds odd doesn't it, a person fermenting. When you learn something new, like driving a car, all of the aspects don't instantly saturate your body, they take time. You start to relax as you learn to become aware of traffic, what the car can and can't do, and how quick your reflexes need to be.

The priest was no different. He had comfort levels within his faith. Part of that process was understanding himself. The more deeply we understand ourselves, the more fully we can help others in their own journeys.

And now I am the vessel of power. Potions in and of themselves are not enough. You've probably heard of the placebo effect. That's when you have a headache and you take an aspirin to get rid of it. The headache goes away, but surprise, they switched the medicine, you were actually taking a sugar pill. You healed yourself, not the medicine. Studies have been done showing doctors that patients believe in have more "cures" than those in whom patients have little faith.

Historically, alchemists were often medical people, using what they learned to heal people, but they never just handed out the "medicine," they delivered it, and that is what I was about to do.

I had two stops to make, my adrenalin flowing freely. I took to the freeway, heading on route 26. At first I was going to go to Hillsboro, a suburb of Portland, but I thought one of the busier institutions would be better. I'd done my research as I always do. The first place was a large nursing home with a special Alzheimer's wing. I put on my clergy collar and entered. I learned a long time ago that if you look like you know what you are doing no one bothers you. That reality proved true on this day, I walked straight to the wing. I walked down the hall till I found a room with an open door and a woman sitting in her chair.

These institutions were remarkable places of kindness and patience. Living with someone, especially in the advanced stages of Alzheimers can be more than difficult. Let them be where they can be safe and watched all the time.

"Hi Betty, how are you today?"

Betty looked at me a bit puzzled. "How are you Bill?"

Perfect I thought to myself. I gave her some of my elixir and held her hand as she drank it. I felt my energy moving into her, sensing the power of the elixir already working on her mind. I didn't stay long.

I did the same with 5 other rooms. I figured 6 people would be enough to shock people. By the end I was exhausted. Once Jesus felt energy drain from him and he looked at the woman who touched his garment, a woman of faith who was instantly healed. The process of healing takes energy and normally that comes from the one being a conduit for the spiritual energy.

I went out to lunch to rebuild my fortitude, relax, and focus on the next group.

St. Anthony's hospital is a large catholic institution with a cancer wing. Being a clergy person wouldn't work here, these people were rational and cautious. The only way I could get them to take a new medication was if I was a doctor. I went into the bathroom and put on my lab coat. Some doctor's wore suits, others wore coats. My hope was the patients wouldn't question a small new medication with no side effects. I knew I was taking my chances being caught, but it had to be done.

My luck was with me, something had happened at the far end of the hall and most of the staff was there. I walked into a room and found a gentleman, William, watching TV.

"Afternoon William."

"Bill."

"Sorry Bill. Dr. Schwartz asked me to bring this to you, a onetime medicine. Don't worry, it has no side effects."

"What is it?"

"Just something that seems to be having good results with your type of cancer."

He took the elixir without question. My hand had been on his leg, but I needed to hold his hand.

"Can I just listen to your heart and pulse for a second?"

"Sure."

I put my stethoscope on his heart as I took his hand pretending to feel his pulse. His cancer was taking more of my energy than I thought it would. I held it for about a minute.

"Everything ok?"

"I think you will find that tomorrow will be a new day for you. How are you feeling right now?"

"Like I have cancer, very tired."

"Are you a man of faith?"

"No."

"Well, don't worry, tomorrow will be better, get some rest."

I left being mad at myself for drawing more attention than I should. I wouldn't make that mistake again. I did the same with seven other patients, making sure they had an aggressive form of cancer that wasn't going to go away overnight.

Totally spent, I went home, now I just had to wait. I figured it would be two days before the news hit.

I watched the news and read the papers. On the third day it hit the fan. I saw it on the television first, the next day it hit the papers.

"This is Rick Johnson reporting live from the Cedar Crest Nursing Facility in Hillsboro. People here are still puzzled by what happened. Today, 6 people with advanced Alzheimer's walked out, apparently healed. No one has a clue as to what happened. We did have an opportunity to talk with Mrs. Soderberg. Can you tell us what happened?"

"I don't really remember. I've been here for 3 years, slowly deteriorating, I couldn't remember from one minute to the next. Two days ago a priest came in and chatted with me, although I don't remember what he said. The next day I woke up and was thinking clearly, I haven't felt this good in 20 years."

"Why did they keep you here yesterday?"

"They thought it might have been a fluke. Now they can't keep me, I'm going home."

"Susan, no explanation can be found. All 6 remember a priest, but no one else here remembers seeing one on the premises. These folks are happy for the miracle no matter how it happened. Back to you."

"Thanks Rick, now it's to St. Vincent's hospital where more remarkable activity is taking place."

"That's right Susan, I'm not sure what you call a group of miracles, but that is exactly what we have here. Eight people on the cancer ward are going home today---completely free of cancer. They were all considered terminal, but two days ago they woke up and told the doctors they felt great. The doctors told them they would have days like this, but one of the patients insisted on a blood check and a scan—which he volunteered to pay for. When the scan came back clean, they checked the others and released them, free of cancer. Susan, no one has an explanation. The only thing they seem to have in common is that they were visited by a Dr. Flood three days ago. He gave them something they said tasted sweet. The most interesting part of this is according to the hospital, there is no Dr. Flood here. Security has been tightened, but there are eight very happy people leaving the hospital. Perhaps an angel unaware?"

"John , is there any connection between these two miraculous happenings?"

"There is an ongoing investigation Susan, but nothing so far. One astrologist said the stars were aligned for miracles and one pastor has claimed it is a sign that Christ is about to return."

"Thanks John and keep us posted on any further developments."

The paper had it as a lead story the first day, an article on page six the second day and a tiny blurb on the third. After that it disappeared, just how I liked it. I knew the notebook was real, so I could finally move on and try the next series, more dangerous perhaps, but also more rewarding, I could hardly wait. The Fall had been a good start, the next few months would change history—I would change history!!!

5 MATT GOES INTO THE WORLD OF ALCHEMY

Time was moving more slowly than I'd hoped. From the police end of things, this was a dead end. No leads what so ever and not a high profile or priority case. Cases are usually puzzles to me. Why does God put me into the midst of one and not the other? We were now into our fourth week since the discovery of Mary. The bishop had put off his meeting with me yet again even though he claimed it was important. I spent a few hours making calls and keeping Julie happy, it doesn't pay to keep your assistant mad at you and doing all the work, especially when they don't make nearly what they should.

Julie loved the church and everything about it. Normally I prefer having assistants that aren't members of the parish I am running, but in Julie's case I made an exception. She was able to separate her church work from her life as a parishioner and she not only stayed out of the political battles, but let me know when they were coming. She wasn't a spy, but knew when trouble was brewing and thought it better to head off the problems before they got started---I couldn't agree more.

The latest upcoming battle royale of the moment had to do with our Christmas Bazaar, a yearly event entering its 90th year. The ladies of the church sponsored the event and took great pride in its success, although the $50,000 it brought in wasn't a great deal. There were three facets of the bazaar. The first was the sale itself, the parish hall filled to the brim with knick knacks for the holidays. Food and presents; parishioners had been making things for this celebration for 90 years and many had ancestors who started it. The central party at the fair was a reunion of sorts. People would fly in from around the country to participate. The date of it was fixed, like Christmas itself. You could set your calendar 100 years in advance if you wanted to. If Christmas was on a Wednesday or later, it would be on the previous weekend. If it was on a Monday or Tuesday, it would be two weekends before. About 15 years ago we'd added a sing-a-long Messiah to the festivities.

The women ran the fair and did so like clockwork. This was a well-oiled machine with a pecking order of duties that rivaled the Masons. Shelly had been the head for two years and this was her last shot, the torch would be passed to Helen next year, Mildred would become Vice-chair, Cindy the Treasurer, and thus the tradition was set for another 12 years. A third of the parish hall was reserved for parishioners and their wares and the rest was for high quality vendors, picked of course by a committee of the woman. The merchants were guaranteed 2000 people through the building over the weekend and many people saved some Christmas shopping for the fair. The past year we'd had over 4000.

The second aspect of the Bazaar was the "men's" lunch. Up until now, the men had provided a soup and sandwich lunch. The kitchen was filled with laughter and the "guys" loved getting together and doing it. When the list went up each year for volunteers, it was full before coffee hour was over. In fact that was one of the biggest Sundays of the year, made me proud. Last year however, some of the ladies were not happy with the presentation of the food, there had been rumblings about it after the bazaar was over. Because it has been going on forever we really don't do formal evaluations, word just spreads, that's how churches work. Some of the men thought it would die down, but it was percolating with reckless abandon. Tempers were starting to flair and I decided to put an end to it before friends turned into acquaintances.

"Shelly, Matt here. How are things going with the bazaar?" Pause. "I'm glad they are moving along smoothly, as I had no doubt they would with you at the helm. What a joy to be able to sleep at night knowing all the traditions are being kept, there is peace in the kingdom, and you are smoothing out what little ruffles might arise from time to time." Pause. "I've heard a few rumors floating about in regards to the men's lunch. I'm sure they are just in jest as no one would dare even think of taking it from the men, why if that happened, I don't know, I might have to cancel the whole thing, after 90 years." Pause. "That's what I thought Shelly, I'm glad you cleared it up for me and will stop the rumors you hear floating around. I know the men are excited about cooking and are always open to suggestions----which you might want to filter through me, you know how sensitive those men can be about their lunch—haha." Pause. "Well thanks for the call—anything I can be doing for you?" Pause. "Yes I know, that grandchild of yours will be getting baptized before you know, and then you will have to put on another party." Laughter. "You take care too Shelly and thanks again for your leadership."

And that was another brilliant save. Believe me, I put my foot in my mouth more often than I have a good save, and I suspected this particular battle wasn't over just yet, but I was ahead of the curve.

Now onto the next item on my list, the chat room.

I called Sue, she knew what I wanted. I'd spent a couple of weeks starting to learn about alchemy, I didn't want to enter the room completely ignorant.

"Sue, Matt."

"Hi Matt, I was wondering when you were going to get back to me.

"Got busy."

"That's what I figured, happens to the best of us."

"So what do you have for me?"

"Well, I've done some research and I think I found a good chat room for you, seems to be a national group that know each other and are mostly people who know what they are doing. I watched for a while and didn't get much of it, just sounded like some very strange people."

"My guess is computer geeks like you have a language most of us would find weird as well if we entered a hacker's room."

"Me, now Matt you know me better than that."

"That's the problem Sue, I know you far too well."

Sue and I go way back. I met her when she was in high school, about 20 years ago. Her mother was in my parish at the time and died of cancer. She was a senior in high school and didn't want to leave the area, even though her dad wanted her to come live with him in Miami. She moved in with me. We were the talk of the town, rumors were rampant and the bishop encouraged me to move her out. I didn't. She was an extraordinary person then and still is. I used to love having a glass of wine in the evening and listen to her practice piano. She was always on the cutting edge of the computer world. I put her through MIT (along with some scholarships she earned) and helped her get into grad school at Stanford. From then on she didn't need my help. In fact she made many generous contributions to my church and agencies where I was on the board of directors. I wasn't exactly sure what she did, but she lived in a waterfront house she owned in Portland---she'd done well. To date she still wasn't married, telling me she was far too busy. Encouraging her to get out, she would laugh and say sure, but rarely did.

"Don't go down that road Matt, let's get back to business."

"Ok, what is the address?"

She gave it to me and told me to know as much as I could before entering for they were a very cautious group. Apparently something had gone wrong with a few of the people in the group and they weren't sure who it was.

"Can you find where the members are?"

"That depends on the chatter. If they are innocent, yes, I just trace their IP address. If on the other hand they are like me and don't want to be found, I doubt it; they will bounce off other addresses or break into a network and use their IP address."

"Ok, well maybe they won't be needed----but I suspect they will."

"Anything else?"

"Not yet, but I'm working on a few things that have popped up."

"Like what?"

"We'll get back to you if and when they pan out."

"I knew you would, take care."

"Bye Sue."

I had an hour before a meeting so I logged on to the chat room Sue had given me and thought about a good screen name to use. I'd recently gone through a period in my own spiritual life of purifying my body and spirit. I'd fasted for two weeks on a retreat, reread the bible from cover to cover, meditated at least two hours a day and worked with a spiritual director intensely for three months. Purification is one of the critical steps on the alchemical journey. Chemically, it's when you get rid of the impurities in the compound you are creating. I thought that adding a bit of Latin would increase my value in the room—Purificatio. That's me----what a scam.

At first I just signed in and watched. There are some Christian chat rooms I join from time to time, watching at first to see who is there and what the general feel of the room is before I speak. If there aren't many people in the room it can get a bit uncomfortable. They expect you to talk.

In this room there were 13 people. I noticed they were from around the United States. Sue had installed a piece of software on my computer that told me where websites were housed and where chat room people were located, at least what state or country. My sense was that they came from many levels of knowledge. The beginners spoke in literal terms. The more advanced stuck to the symbolic language except to translate for novitiates. Think about Jesus and how he spoke. Most people didn't understand what he was saying when he spoke in parables. Even his disciples struggled. They couldn't translate the spiritual to the mundane. That took a connection to the Holy Spirit. Jesus acted and acts as both the translator and the guide to teach you how to become a translator. The key for Jesus was to look for the meaning behind the symbols. Too often then and now we fail to see the symbol and instead act on the literal. The Gospel of John speaks to this in a powerful way. Unless you know God, how can you understand God? The mysteries of God are only understood by becoming part of the mystery, to be in relationship with it. I often wonder why people put more faith in the written word than in the living presence of God.

I was intrigued by their user names. Some, like me, were alchemical processes—Calcination, Fermentation, Multiplication. Others were historical figures within alchemy---Hermes, Paracelsus and still others were elements found within the system----mercury, antimony, salt. And of course there were those who probably didn't have a clue----Merlin, The Master, Yours Truly, and The Stone. I figured out quickly that no one paid attention to these folks. I couldn't figure out if the names changed each time or if they were the same. Probably the later because some addressed the others as if they were friends. Codes within codes within a little electronic box. What ever happened to face to face conversations?

Trying to figure out who was female and who was male was another puzzle. I had a small idea of what the stakes were in this murder and my own bias pushed me into thinking it was a male. There was no doubt a woman was more than capable of committing murder for the sake of perpetual beauty, but I just had that intuition I would be spinning my wheels looking for a woman and long ago learned to trust my intuition. God gives us so many gifts to use for the benefit of helping others and getting our own spiritual life in order. Intuition is a long lost gift. Don't get me wrong, I'm not against science, but the world of rational thought has driven much from our souls. We are in an age where the two need to merge, science should help the human spirit, not hinder it. I think there is a sermon in that.

Intuition can be cultivated. We learn to internally sense good and bad intuitions. Most of us don't pay attention to our inner voices and the voice of God within. We listen to others and blindly accept what they say. Why did God give us brains? So we could turn them over to pastors, politicians, and public media? God wants us to use our brains actively, and part of that process is living with intuition, we all have it.\

At times the room was like a classroom, everyone would read while one or two people carried on a conversation, teacher to student.

M: So F, what have you done with your substance since last time?

F: I've been purifying it.

M: With what process?

F: I diluted it with some acid and then calcinated it in the furnace.

M: And?

F: I think I might have silver.

M: LOL

F: What?

M: P, what do you think?

P: Well, let's try something, take the "silver" and pour mercury on it

F: Ok, hold on.

M: Salt, what is new in your corner while we wait, this could take a while.

S: I've been struggling with fermentation.

M: What's the issue?

S: Patience.

H: Isn't that a critical issue for all of us?

C: Certainly is for me, both in the lab and in my head.

M: Well, not only is patience a virtue, the work can't proceed without it. Look, when you have a child do you expect that new entity to instantly get a job? Of course not, there is much to learn, not to mention physically developing. Our lives and work are no different. The question is, how many of us have the patience to allow fermentation to take place in order to seek the rewards?

There was a silence, I knew he'd hit home, with me as well. How impatient I was with myself, others, and God relative to my own development. I had high expectations, but often forgot to count the cost and to see how high the mountain I had to climb.

I decided to enter the conversation.

PU: Pardon me M, but in most traditions people work together to achieve enlightenment, why do alchemists work alone?

M: I'd be pleased to answer that PU, but first, tell us about you, I don't believe we've met. You will find alchemy has some significant differences to other paths.

PU: Can you do two paths at once?

M: Of course.

PU: I'm a Christian, is that ok?

M: That is an excellent path, many of us believe Jesus was an alchemist of sorts. Many alchemists throughout time were committed Christians. Some were killed because others felt they were heretics, far from the truth.

PU: So why work alone?

M: Patience PU.

PU: I should ferment a bit?

M: Ahh someone with a sense of humor, we haven't had that in a while.

P: A welcome relief after what some of us have been through lately.

M: P, now is not the time or the place?

PU: Did I miss something?

M: Let's just say this room has had a busy couple of months.

TM: Hey, does alchemy help with sex?

M: In your case probably not.

TS: I'll help with that one TM.

TM: Add me, we'll talk, this is getting a bit boring. TheMaster2341@hotmail.com

M: Two down a few to go. So, PU, what part of the world are you from?

PU: NW U.S.

M: You wouldn't happen to be near Portland would you?

PU: Yes, I'm in it.

M: I wonder if this is coincidence or the stars aligning.

PU: I don't believe in coincidences, I also don't know what you are talking about.

M: Later. Do you have a lab?

PU: Yes, not a large one, but I'm starting to do things. I have been working more on the spiritual side.

M: They are linked, learn that up front. One cannot be done without the other. Doesn't the bible say that your body is the temple of God?

PU: Yes

M: Then you must take care of the physical as well as the spiritual. One is a metaphor of the other. Paul talks about the community of faith being like the body—1 Corinthians 12—read it.

PU: I'm quite familiar with the passage.

M: And what part are you?

PU: Perhaps a part of the brain.

M: Ah a thinking man, we can use more that use their brain

PU: Thank you. Now are you going to answer my question?

M: Anyone want to help the lad---you are male aren't you?

PU: Yes, does it matter?

M: Of course.

PU: Why?

H: Because we woman are built differently, physically and spiritually.

PU: Prayer is prayer, centering is centering, gold is gold.

C: You have a lot to learn, I remember when I believed that.

PU: I know that, but can gold not be gold?

C: When it is transformed into something more.

PU: But then it is no longer gold

C: Its essence is still gold, but the manifestation is something else.

M: Isn't your Jesus the Son of God?

PU: Yes.

M: He was God before he became human.

PU: Yes.

M: Was he still God or did he give up his divinity for humanity.

PU: He was both, fully God and fully human.

M: But you didn't see God when you saw him, you saw a human, what he did was the God within him.

PU: Yes.

M: What we do is no different. I will always be me, but my psyche and body are already transforming.

PU: Into what

M: Perfection.

PU: I want to learn more

M: I sense that, I also sense you will have a hard time because you like everything to fit into a picture you have painted. Alchemy breaks all the known rules, rules science has yet to discover but will.

PU: I'm open minded.

M: LOL, not even close, but I appreciate the effort. What are you working with now?

PU: I'm working on two fronts. The first is distilling lead, seeing what salts are derived from it. While doing that I am surrounding myself with the correspondences of Lead. I play lots of C major music, watch Saturn in the sky at night, study the attribute of Capricorn, and drink herbs that help my gall bladder.

M: Remarkable for a neophyte. How did you find all of this?

PU: Let's just say I'm a good reader.

M: Excellent. Well PU, welcome to the club.

PU: Thank you. I still haven't heard an answer to my question.

M: And you now deserve an answer----anyone?

A: I'll take it. First off, who is responsible for your life?

PU: Me.

A: Who else?

PU: Well, I suppose my friends and my boss.

A: So if something goes wrong, you can blame them.

PU: Well I wouldn't put it that way, but perhaps.

A: In alchemy, you and you alone are responsible. Other people are but excuses we use to justify our inaction.

M: Interjection if I might A. Jesus said the same thing. He always accepted responsibility for his actions and he forced people to accept responsibility for theirs. Look at the woman at the well. He pointed out her flaws and helped her confess. She did and look what happened? The rich man who had followed all the commandments asked what he needed to do to enter eternal life. Jesus told him to sell all he had.

PU: He went away sad, but Jesus said all things are possible with God.

M: Precisely. But it begins with you.

A: People are distractions. Have you ever tried to write something with a group of people? It's much harder than doing it yourself.

PU: But is the end product better?

A: We seek advice on what we are doing, we are not complete islands. M has held me accountable many times and has given me advice, but I had to believe it and accept it on my own.

PU: And what of M, do you have a mentor?

M: Good question, presently no, I'm not sure where he is.

PU; so you have one.

M: We all do, well all except maybe two or three.

I decided that I'd made a decent first impression and didn't want to take up all their time, so I tried to get off.

PU: Well, sorry, but I have to go, thanks for the chat.

M: Will you be back?

PU: Probably, you seem like knowledgeable and friendly people.

A: Most of us.

PU: What does that mean?

M: Nothing.

It was clear M held the power of the room and no one challenged what he said.

M: By the way PU, do you have a messenger?

PU: Yes, why?

M: I have a favor to ask of you in Portland.

I gave it to him and signed out. Then I signed onto messenger and waited, I didn't think it would be long. As I sat staring at the screen, the phone rang.

"Hello, Matt here." I knew the voice. "Hello bishop, where are you calling from?"

"New York."

"And to what do I owe this great pleasure."

"Sarcasm doesn't befit you Matt."

"Just trying to be friendly bishop, my apologies."

"Accepted. We are still on for tomorrow?"

"Have you penned in."

"I'm sorry to do this, but I'd like to move it up, can you come over tonight?"

"To your house?"

"Yes."

I couldn't imagine what the bishop would need to see me about that was so urgent.

"Of course, what time?"

"My plane gets in at 5, come for dinner at 6."

Click.

I couldn't imagine what could be so urgent. I thought of calling some of the other clergy to see if they had heard anything, but decided against it. They were a talkative bunch and I didn't need rumors flying around when I didn't have a clue what was happening. I also knew the bishop tended to get stressed over things that to me were small potatoes. Even though I disagreed with the bishop on most things, he was still my bishop and was still one of God's children and it sounded like he needed help.

My computer beeped and I saw M was on.

"Hi M."

"Hello PU. I would prefer to be on a first name basis on here if we could."

"Not a problem with me, I never quite understood the secrecy thing in the chat room."

"Let's just say that if you stay in this long you will.

"I'm Matt."

"I'm Phil."

"Hi Phil, what can I do for you in Portland, OR.?"

"I hesitate doing this because I don't know you, but I sense that you are a good person."

"Since you are being honest with me, I'll be honest with you, I'm a priest."

"LOL, I knew you were an active Christian, I didn't think quite that active."

"LOL."

"Well, what are you doing in an alchemy room?"

"It's a long story, for now let's just stay I've read about it for years in Jung and the mystics."

"Good for you, I hope your journey is a fruitful one."

"Has already been."

"Good."

"So what can I do for you?"

"You are an impatient one."

"When I know that someone has something on their mind, I tend to go for the jugular, let's get to it, rather than dance around for a long time."

"Some people need to dance."

"Then they should go to a different dance hall."

"You don't have parishioners that need coddling?"

"Look Phil, we both know you aren't a parishioner that needs coddling, you don't need coddling at all, so let's cut through it and tell me what you want. If you don't trust me, then we'll meet in the room and when you are comfortable you can pop your question."

I was baiting him, knowing full well he was very self-confidant.

"All right. There was a member of our group from Portland. She hasn't been on for almost two weeks, I'm nervous something might have happened to her, but I don't know who or where she is."

"And you want me to track her down."

"Yes."

"How would I do that without a name, address, or phone number.'

"I don't know.

"You make it very difficult."

"I know. The only piece of information I have is that she goes to a bible study every Tuesday at 11 for an hour and they are studying Matthew. The last I heard she was on Matthew 6. "

"Lots of churches in Portland Phil."

I knew there was something I was missing, but I couldn't put my finger on it. Something about Phil and his connection to all this. Probably just alchemy.

"She did mention the word Eucharist a few times, does that help?"

"Well, probably Catholic or Episcopal."

"Are you familiar with them?

Again, a hesitation as to how much to divulge, I erred on caution.

"Yes, we know of each other. No idea what part of town she was in?"

"My sense is pretty close to downtown. She didn't drive, and she wouldn't be able to get to what she needed for the work far from town."

"What did you know her as on the chat room?"

"Sun and moon, was her latest."

"Is that good?"

"She was the best of the best, well beyond me."

"Oh. Why didn't you use messenger with her?"

"She didn't want to."

"I'll do what I can and I'll either see you on here, the chat room or I'll email you if I find something."

"Be careful."

"Why?" I asked perplexed.

"She isn't the first to have something happen to her—I think."

"How do you know she didn't go on a vacation or get sick?"

"LOL, you don't know Sun and Moon, she was never sick, never missed our weekly chats in 8 years."

"How old is she?"

"Well that is an interesting question. I would say she is probably in her late 60's or 70's, but she may not look it."

"What do you mean?"

"Just trust me, don't be surprised if she doesn't appear as you might think she would."

For me, death was death, not a pretty picture.

"Ok, I'll do what I can."

We left each other. I wondered if I should have told him then what was known, but I didn't know him, and would have to find out more before returning the message. After all, it would take me some time to do the detective work and I was curious to know which church she was going to, probably Christ Church, a few blocks from where she lived, I'd have to pay Steve a visit. Another connection made.

I called Sue back and told her to get me Phil's information. I suspected she already had it, but didn't push her, I wasn't in a hurry and realized this crime was not going to come to a quick end.

Now and then I come to my senses, discovering I've done something selfish and I grow up. Such was the case with the bishop. Here was a man in distress returning from a week-long trip, cooking dinner for me after a six hour flight. How did I let that happen?

I called him back.

"Hello?" the bishop said.

"Bishop, Matt here. I apologize for my lack of courtesy, forgive me. Please come to my house from the airport, dinner will be ready."

"I appreciate the offer, but I have to show you something and that something is at my house. I apologize for the mystery; I'm just uncomfortable talking about it."

"How about this. We meet at your house, see whatever it is and then move to my house for dinner and conversation?"

"Fair enough. I'll see you at my house then."

"Have a good flight."

I can usually get a better sense of what is going on in someone's life from a conversation than I was having with the bishop. I did notice when he said there was something to show me, a shiver surged up my spine and made me shake. You know how it is when someone wants to tell you something and won't? You imagination goes wild. I was wondering if he'd made some discovery about a clergy person---but if that were true he wouldn't come to me. Perhaps it was something in the budget, the treasurer had embezzled funds—plenty of that going around. He knew I was on the board of several organizations, maybe it had to do with that. Speculating never led too much so I tried to let it go. I had 3 hours to make dinner, get the house neat and do a few other chores. I headed for the door.

Shopping is always a treat for me. Most of the local merchants had become friends and knew my tastes. I always bought my vegetables from the Saturday market while it was in season and I had a few friends with farms in the country that would keep me stocked with potatoes, beets, and onions. The butcher called me when some wonderful piece of meat showed up on his doorstep. I'd received a message that pheasant was now in season and that brought back childhood memories of hunting. The bishop and I would feast on sublime game tonight. While wandering around Northwest Portland, my mind kept trying to piece the puzzle together. Obviously the murderer wanted something from Mary. Had he gotten it? What would be his next move? Then it hit me. I remembered the healings. Could that be him? Could a murderer actually heal? I needed to ask Phil some more questions and probably be more candid.

I arrived at the bishop's house a bit after 6. The pheasant would be ready when we returned, I'd opened a very nice Merlot from a vineyard a friend of mine owned, Cuneo's Cellar. Amazing stuff. He gotten into the wine business on a lark and now had a successful organization on his hand, along with several others. I rarely saw him, just drank his wine. I told him I'd make it rain at the wrong time of year if he didn't give me some. A case at Christmas each year and the weather had treated him well.

The bishop lived in a neighborhood home. He liked space even though he'd been widowed for 8 years. His children were grown but lived in the area and he loved having the grandkids over when he could. Weekends were the bishop's busiest time, traveling all around the diocese visiting churches. One of many jobs I didn't want.

You could tell he had a spectacular garden, all but dead now in late fall. In the summer, it was full of flowers. The bishop often talked about how he loved seeing God in his yard, the infinite variety of God's creative spirit. I couldn't have agreed more, but I didn't have the patience or the green thumb to be a gardener. The few flowers on my property were taken care of by the landscaper. One of the benefits of living on a cliff with a view is that you don't have much of a yard.

The bishop answered the door and handed me a glass of red wine.

"Peace to you bishop. How was the flight?"

He seemed amazingly tense, even for himself.

"Fine, just fine. Let's get to this shall we?"

"Of course."

"You know Steve at Christ Church?"

The hair stood on the back of my head.

"Of course."

"He called me a few weeks ago. He said someone had left him a gift with a note. It was a woman from one of his bible studies."

"And for this you need me?" I knew something was coming.

"Read the note."

He handed it to me:

"Dear Pastor: I have appreciated your bible study and all I have learned from it. You have helped deepen my faith. I will not be attending anymore as I have been called home unexpectedly. I hope you will accept this small token of my appreciation. Mary."

"I'm still not sure why I am here?"

He asked me to follow him to the garage where he pointed to a box that sat in the corner. "Look in there."

Once again my imagination was going wild. What could Mary possibly give to the church? Her files would not be understood, her paintings and pictures were useless and she was far too practical.

I walked over to the box, a large wooden crate covered with intricate carvings. It measured at least two and a half by two and a half feet. The wood was a combination of teak and cedar, the etched pictures ones I recognized from alchemy. I opened the lid.

The box was filled with gold.

"They had to use a forklift to put it here."

"Oh my God."

"That's not all," said the bishop. He took a brown paper bag from a desk drawer. On the table he poured out diamonds, or at least what appeared to be diamonds. The smallest was over a carat and they went up to several carats.

"Now do you understand why I called you?"

"The picture becomes clearer and cloudier all the time."

6 BOB'S CONNECTIONS

I was pleased with myself, having taken care of Mary, healed some people, found a house and had a conversation with the priest. I decided I deserved a break and took the weekend off, after all it had been over 5 weeks since Mary—we had both moved on with no heart feelings.

As I drove to the beach I started to think about my life, what wonderful turns it had taken over the past 20 years, the lessons I'd learned and the edge I was closing in on. However, I'd done my research and knew more often than not, being on the edge came with a price. Most people who had made phenomenal discoveries had done so at the end of a bottle of booze or pills. They were egotists, depressives, and brilliantly strange. I was at a point where I knew I might have to make a choice—normality and back away from the edge or brilliance and jump in. There was no doubt which way I would go should it come to that. I wanted it all. I wanted my sanity and the power. I had worked hard for the prize, probably harder than anyone. I'd made sacrifices. Even Mary was a sacrifice. I had a relationship with Mary, a very deep one for two people that had never met. She taught me much. I had to sacrifice that relationship for the greater good.

But on my way to the beach I was having second thoughts. The nature of energy is neutral. The atom can be split and used to heat a home or to disintegrate people and their belongings. The Bible has been used to save and to destroy. The sun itself can create life or annihilate all organisms. Nature is on a course of its own. The earth came into existence and scientists have a pretty good idea of when the planet will be lifeless—a long time from now provided we don't speed up the process. I was getting very close to understanding the essential nature of energy and how to determine which direction it would go.

Stem cells in an embryo somehow know when and how to differentiate into bones, organs, nerves, muscle tissue and the vast array of cell types in the human body. No one yet knows how they do it. That is one of the mysteries of life and someday we will probably solve that puzzle, only to be followed by another.

I know Mary did solve many puzzles and now that I had her book, I was close too. The choice will be what to do with the knowledge. Of course the process can't be shared with anyone, greed would take over and life itself would change on the planet. Perhaps I needed to use the knowledge to help maintain a balance on the earth. Look at history. There is a pendulum swinging between good and evil. From time to time, evil, at least in certain geographic and cultural locations seems to win. Hitler, Lenin, and the white man invading Native American territory are but a few examples. But the pendulum swings back and good balances the scale. Is my job to balance the scales one way or the other? Was Mary doing something to balance the scales?

I spent hours walking the beach, trying to listen to the earth to see what was expected of me. I knew to those who had much, a great deal was expected. But who determined what the expectations were? Who made the rules? Perhaps I do, or at least I make the rules suit what I want and I believe the world needs. I started to ask myself questions.

What if I could end hunger?

What if I could eliminate all malevolent dictators?

What if I could end poverty?

What if I could give good drinking water to every person on earth?

What if I could give the world limitless cheap energy?

Would humanity change? Humanity itself seems bent on maintaining the balance of good and evil. You have to ask yourself why evil exists. Ask 10,000 if they are evil, all will deny and will say they want a good planet. Yet evil persists. If there were limitless energy, Exxon and Shell would just find other ways of making money, of abusing the planet and ripping off foreign countries. They will convince you they are doing it all for the good. Humanity in and of itself has not changed in thousands of years and it never will. Solving all these problems would only create others. I was thankful I'd figured that out and didn't have to worry about curing all the ills of the world.

My next challenge would be on two levels, both physical and spiritual. On the physical, I needed to start changing and creating a metamorphosis in nature. Changing one chemical compound into another was difficult, but very possible. Having elements change into other elements was a bit more tenuous. The spiritual change needed to occur in order to turn me into the Philosopher, not a philosopher, but The Philosopher. One who could comprehend all things and create a unified theory for humanity. Perfection. What I find interesting is this notion of perfection. Christians have devised an idea of perfection that necessitates good. Jesus was perfect. Satan is the opposite of perfect. I claim that Satan is perfectly evil, just as Christ is perfectly good. Both are perfect. Is it possible to be both?

Most of us like to think of ourselves as much more good than evil. We seek forgiveness for the evil and lift up the good. When we find truly evil people, Son of Sam, Charles Manson, Hitler, some find excuses for them. They were that way because they were abused as children, their parents were alcoholics, and they had a traumatic event in their lives or a myriad of other rationalizations. The beauty of alchemy is there are no excuses, you are who you are because you chose to be. If you were abused, get over it. Yes it takes immense effort to break the cycle, but in the end, you make the choice to let the events destroy you or not.

Humanity often lacks the will be too good and defaults to evil. If you doubt that fact, look at the political world. They are all cowards, afraid to say what they truly know is right. They bargain away the lives of their people for political gain and future financial security.

I wanted to make the priest understand me. I knew I would be taking a chance, but he needed to understand, I needed someone to understand me from the inside, to feel my motives, to empathize with the sacrifices I made to achieve what I'd done. I would make an appointment when I got back.

I was always very cautious when chatting with my friends on the internet; I didn't want to be traced. I stopped in a bar that advertised internet wireless use on the sign out front. The old tavern was right on the beach, you could smell the salt air and hear the crashing waves inside. The evening was not a busy one, probably 15 people propped at the bar or sitting at table. Some football game was on and from the sound of things, most were locals. No one paid attention to me as I logged on, hacked their computer, changed a couple of settings and made it look like I was in North Carolina, should anyone trace me.

I logged on.

R: Hello everyone.

M: How are you, long time no see?

P: A moon's age.

R: And how long is the age of a moon, P?

P: Always asking the questions, some things don't change.

R: I've been quite preoccupied for a couple of weeks with the work, but I have made a break through and it was all worth it, although I will admit to missing you all.

M: A breakthrough?

R: Yes, I've made some profound discoveries of the soul and of the body, sun and moon are very close to converging and the salt has just about purified to gold.

M: Pardon my asking, but how did you accomplish this?

R: With great difficulty and sacrifice. All significant change comes with sacrifice.

M: Can you talk more about the sacrifice, we've been talking a great deal about counting the cost of the work.

R: Yes, all of us must make sacrifices and the larger the sacrifice the larger the reward. Early on in the work I made sacrifices of time and money. Then I made sacrifices of ideas, I needed to listen to others, mentors, rather than thinking I knew it all. In the end, we must be willing to completely sacrifice everything we are, our egos and all that went into creating them, in order to find the answers.

A: Can you tell us how you did that on a more practical level?

R: It wouldn't make sense to you, but when the time comes, you will know what you have to do in order to achieve a higher level. Let's just say I have done some things I didn't know I could do.

M: And the reward?

R: Amazing. I have healed people with cancer.

A: What?

R: You heard me, I have healed people with terminal cancer. Between elixirs I made and the state of consciousness I have achieved, I rid their bodies of cancer.

M: That's phenomenal, I haven't heard of anyone getting to that step other than….

R: Who?

M: Um no one I guess.

R: Well I know that Q was looking into that, have you seen her?

A: No, she hasn't been on for a couple of weeks, like you. Maybe you two were out at the beach together.

R: Always the humorous one. No, like I said, I've been holed up trying to get over this hurdle.

M: I'm glad you did, sounds amazing. So what is next?

R: I know I am closing in on the end, I'm just not sure what I need to do or who to turn to.

M: I think you are at the head of the pack.

R: I know, but there must be a way.

M: Won't the work in and of itself show you what to do?

R: If I am sensitive enough to it, certainly, but we are all so delusional.

M: I'm sure you will figure it out.

R: I suspect I will. How has everyone been? Any breakthroughs?

A: Everyone is making progress and M has been very helpful.

R: I knew he would be, he has certainly helped me in ways he will never know.

M: What do you mean by that?

R: You have been there for me on so many levels for many years and it's all paying off. How is your work coming?

M: Pretty good, minor setbacks, but nothing catastrophic.

R: Good, well let me know what I can do to help. I'm here for you.

Bob chuckled to himself knowing he'd had more than a minor setback.

M: I know. I have to go, but we'll see everyone soon.

R: Me too, take care all.

M: Before I go, I forgot to ask, has anyone seen Z?

R: I saw him the other day, our teacher is quite busy, but I know will have lots to share soon.

P: I'm glad, he is always so helpful.

R: Yes he is, more than you will know for a long time, just enjoy it.

M: Ok, take care.

M logged off.

R: Is M ok?

P: I think so, although he has been a bit tense lately.

A: Something happened to him, but he's not talking.

R: Happened to him?

A: Well, he mentioned having to go get stuff for his lab, things he should have had already. Don't know what it means.

R: Not to worry my friends, each of us goes through stresses; we just need to support him through them. Now I too must leave.

A: Will we see you soon?

R: I hope so.

The room felt a bit odd, almost like they knew, or at least Phil did. Probably my paranoia kicking in, I did burn his barn down. I was a bit surprised he didn't mention it to me. The more I search, the more I realize why alchemists and Christians had so much in common, their paths so similar. Here was Phil, keeping something very important inside rather than sharing it with the community. Mary had done that. She'd made amazing discoveries and strides in her own self-development and yet shared little with the bible study, or anyone else for that matter. The sin of pride is still alive and well in the world. One of the fundamental stages of alchemy (and with spiritual development) is letting go of pride, asking for help, and admitting your faults and weaknesses. The problem for me is there is no one to turn to. I am further along the path than anyone on the planet, at least that I know of. This is where alchemists and Christians part company. Christians believe that a new Christian can teach a mature Christian. God's power can overcome all things, even immaturity and there is no guarantee that a "mature" Christian will hear God. They are all in the same boat, moving together, each having a gift that others need, no one an island unto themselves---a beautiful model.

Of course there was Z. Z was a remarkable mix of human being. One day I would feel like he had already reached the end and then at other times he'd act like an idiot. He'd taught me much and said things that made me believe he was very, very, old. Perhaps he could help me. I suspected he and Mary were friends.

Alchemists live in a world of symbolic language. If you can't speak the language, you can't help, and the language changes as you grow. Let's say I speak Latin, or at least the language I am working with is Latin. Does it make sense to seek help from someone who knows not one word of Latin? I would hope not.

I kept coming back to Mary. Something drew her to Portland. It had to be more than just the energy of the area. There was someone here that helped her. There must be another advanced alchemist she was studying with or under. They were probably older so they weren't technologically savvy, thus I didn't see them in the chat room. I would have to find this person, get them to give me the final pieces of the puzzle I would need. But how do you find someone that doesn't want to be found? There are no want ads for alchemists wanted, there is no store for alchemists and they don't tend to hang out together. Then it hit me, like a clarion bell. How could I have been so stupid? I knew exactly where to start the search, in fact, I already had.

All the pieces coming together, this must be my destiny.

7 DIAMONDS, GOLD, AND OTHER GIFTS--MATT

The bishop and I talked about the situation over dinner at my house. The view of Portland from my balcony is mesmerizing. The glittering lights with the mountains in the background during the day always seem to drive away the pressures of life. During the winter I have the porch enclosed and heated so I can enjoy the view without freezing to death. I get a bit nervous with the winter rains. Having a home on the edge of a cliff presents its own challenges. Every year a few houses slide off their moorings, often into someone else's home. That would be a rude awakening.

I knew where the money came from, well I knew who gave it. I had no idea how the gold came into existence although the more I read about alchemy, the more ideas I had, crazy ideas, but ideas nonetheless. I knew I would have to chat with a physics professor at the University before long.

"So what do we do with it Matt?"

"Bishop, look, the gold and diamonds are perfectly legal. You and Steve need to cash them out and set up an endowment of some kind. I am certain Steve has many fine ideas of what to do with that kind of cash. Just estimating, I'd say about $20 million worth."

"Excuse me? How much?"

"You heard me, a lot of money. This is what you have dreamed of, it can take care of mission work in the diocese for decades and you don't have to have a capital campaign. I'll get in touch with my friend Dave at the Marshall Amato group and have him help you and Steve set up an account. He's done good work for me and the church and I think even the diocese has some money with him."

"Yes, we saw what they did with your funds so we put our funds with them too. No surprise, they are doing quite well. But I have no idea who gave it or what kind of money it is."

"If you think it is stolen or drug money, put your mind at ease. There is probably no purer funding on the planet."

"And how would you know that?" asked the bishop with some sarcasm in his voice.

"On this one you will just have to trust me."

"Matt, now is not the time to hold out on me. You didn't act surprised when you saw it. I just about had a heart attack."

"Bishop, I've seen a great deal in the last ten years, nothing surprises me. I am puzzled as to why it came to Steve's church, but other than that, this is not a surprise."

"I can see you aren't going to share anymore with me."

"Not at this time, there really isn't much to share." Had I chosen to, I could have spilled my guts with all my ideas about what was going on. I had yet another link with Mary and I needed to follow up with it.

We chatted over some port after dinner, some of the gossip floating around the diocese, our dreams about where we would like to see things move, and the bishop's sense that it was time to move on. He'd been the bishop for 13 years and had done what he could for the diocese. I thought he should have left about 6 years ago and he knew that. I was surprised he was being as open as he was this night, but he knew even though we had our battles, I could keep secrets.

After he left I sat out on the deck, admiring the lights and what they represented, God's creatures, struggling to have dominion over the earth and not doing a very good job of the process.

Dave usually went to bed around 8 so I didn't call him, but did get up early to give him a buzz at the office where he arrived between 5 and 6am to get ready for the opening of the market on the east coast.

"Morning Dave, how's life?"

"Good thanks, that time of year with lots of traveling."

"I've got a favor to ask."

"I'm all ears."

"A church has recently come into some assets of gold and diamonds which they need to cash out and invest and I was hoping you could help."

"Well, I'd be happy to do it, but you know I don't really work with smaller amounts of cash. On the other hand you know that, so this must be more than a little gold."

I laughed. "I knew you were a smart guy. My estimate is around $20 million." I waited.

"That's a nice gift. Do I get to know where it came from?"

"Not at this time."

"I had that feeling."

"I will tell you about it later."

"If I don't read about it in the papers first. I trust this has some connection to something you are working on."

"Good guess."

"Of course I'd be happy to work with them, have them give me a call."

"Thanks. Where are you off too next?"

"Quick trip to New York, Boston, and Dallas, then home for a few days, let's grab a beer."

"Sounds good, be good."

The next week flew by and I had little time to pursue the case and with no sensations coming to me from the

Spirit, I didn't worry. I trusted my senses and if God wanted me to act, he knew how to motivate me.

Churches are businesses and sometimes people forget the business part. Our church has a staff of 10, including 3 priests. We have weekly staff meetings, pastoral meetings, and meetings with the business manager and this week I had a vestry meeting and one with the outreach committee about the various projects with which we were engaged. I preferred cramming all the meetings into one week rather than having them spread out.

The only thing I did about Mary during the week was to visit with Steve, her pastor. I was intrigued to find out what he knew about her.

"So, what do you think about our new found fortune?" he asked.

"You are a very lucky man. That will look good on your resume—in one week created a $20 million dollar endowment." We both laughed. "I do hope you know with great wealth comes great responsibility, don't blow it."

"Yes, I know, I'm still reeling."

"What do you know about Mary?"

"Don't tell me you are involved with this?"

"Just a bit."

"God on the loose again."

"There is always hope."

"To be honest, I can't tell you much. She has been coming here to our bible study for many years. She rarely comes to church and she did not want to be considered a member. She did write a check each year for about $30,000. We tried to engage her, but she wasn't interested, quite a loner."

"Didn't even want the newsletter?"

"No one knew where she lived, her checks didn't have her address on them. I'd thought of following her home at one point, but felt that if she wanted to be anonymous, I should let her."

"She'd have known you were following her and stopped coming, you made the right move."

"How do you know that?" he asked a bit perplexed.

"I could tell by her house that she was extremely observant, intuitive and a bit paranoid."

"That explains a lot."

"Did she ever come in for a one on one?"

"Three times."

"Do you remember what she was after?"

"Hard to forget. The first time she came in wondering about God. She wasn't a believer but said that in her line of work, she was thinking she should be."

"What line of work did she say she was in?"

"That was the odd part, she didn't say and wouldn't, even when I pressed."

"We talked about faith for a while, she wanted to know what it did for people and what it meant on a theological level. I told her faith was a spiritual bond that connected her with God and all God represented."

"She asked if having God in your life added something to your physical life, like healing, or seeing things differently, didn't she?" I asked confidant of the answer.

"How did you know?"

"I'm learning more about Mary all the time."

"I told her being with God connected me with the Creator of the universe. She liked that and asked how to do it."

"She probably got on her knees right then and there."

"I told her she needed to accept Jesus as her savior and Lord, and yes, she got on her knees and asked me to pray with and for her."

"You don't see that every day in your church."

"To be honest Matt, it hadn't happened like that to me in about 10 years."

"How did it make you feel?"

"Well first of all I was a bit scared. Then while we prayed I was filled with a joy and peace I hadn't known in quite some time. But always in the past when I prayed with someone like that energy poured from me to them."

"And this time it came into you. You had a vision didn't you?"

"Oh my God, I haven't told anyone, how could you know?"

"I know Mary."

"Yes, I had a vision. I still don't understand it. Jesus and Mary were in some kind of laboratory. He was teaching her as she mixed chemicals. Then he laid hands on her and told her not to worry. Sitting in the top corners of the lab were a sun and a moon, and when Jesus prayer over her, they floated down, one on each of them and then in a flash the two became one and disappeared."

"Quite a vision," I laughed.

"I've never experienced anything like it."

"So that was the first time."

"Yes, the second was about 8 months ago. She came in and wanted to know about faith, the ego, service, monasticism and how they tied together. A very odd conversation. In essence, she was curious about how solitary monks became so spiritual since the bible seemed to be based on being in the world and in community. Could one find God just by being spiritual? She thought that faith necessitated service to others."

"And you told her?"

"I told her I did not claim to know the mind of God, but did believe being a solitary Christian was the exception to the rule and even then I was dubious. Yes, there are times to go away and work on yourself, but

God gave us gifts for the benefit of others, not of ourselves alone."

"Good work Steve."

"I appreciate your confidence. I sensed she was struggling with her own desire to be alone and not part of the world. She then asked if there was anyone in the parish that was quite ill. I was puzzled by the question and told her we had several sick people. She said she wasn't looking for sick people, but people on the edge of dying. I asked why and she just said she was feeling called to visiting them. I wasn't certain about it, but after making a couple of calls I found two she could visit. I figured she was feeling called to chat with the dying, a beautiful work we need."

"They were healed weren't they?"

"Why are we having this conversation if you already know the answers?"

"Because I don't know the questions."

"Yes, they were healed. I didn't know it was her, I didn't make the connection till just now. Who was she?"

"A very extraordinary woman who died long before her time."

"She shared with the group that she had paid these people a visit and how it filled her heart with joy to be with them and how much it taught her that being in the world is critical to finding God. She was crying when she said it."

"And the third time?"

"It was just a few weeks ago. She came in and….."

There was a knock at the door.

"Come in," I said.

His assistant walked in and handed Steve a letter.

"I thought you might want this now," she said.

"Why?"

"Look at the name in the address spot."

He looked on the envelope and in beautiful handwritten script was the name Mary. He looked at me.

"The letter is from Mary," I said.

"Yes."

"What is the post date?"

"Two days ago. What am I missing here Matt?"

"First, she's dead, has been dead for many weeks. She was murdered. She must have given the letter to someone and told them to mail it on a certain date."

"Why?"

"The problem, with murder and with spirituality is the same, the more questions you answer, the more there are to answer."

He opened the envelope and took out her folded letter.

"May I see the envelope?"

He handed it to me and I smelled it. Part of my gift is the memory of senses. I never forget smells, kind of like the salmon who remember the scent of their stream, even when there are only parts per billion in the ocean. I was like a separation machine in a lab. I could sift out the odors from her lab and see what was left. I closed my eyes, knowing Steve and his assistant were staring at me. Even within her lab, once I isolated the smell of death I put a smell profile on it, like a finger print. There were two other "prints" on the envelope. The first was the post office, that was an easy one to isolate. What was left was the home of the person who had delivered the letter.

"Well?" asked the impatient Steve.

"Another lab."

"What do you mean another lab?" his assistant inquired.

"Um, I think that will be all Alice, thank you for bringing this in."

She left in a bit of a huff, as would I.

"Mary worked in a laboratory."

"Like a cancer lab?"

"It's hard to explain, but I will when I know more."

"So you can smell another laboratory on the envelope?"

"Yes."

"Wow."

"The challenge will be to find the lab and the person whose lab it is."

"What if the person who killed Mary is seeking the same thing?

"Good point, I'd better find the lab soon than later. What happened the third time she came in?"

"I felt like I was being interviewed."

"For a job?"

"Not really. She wanted to know about my vision for the church, what ministries the parishioners were active in, and what could be done to bring Jesus into the world."

"I'm sure you gave her an earful."

"Well, I shared my ideas."

"And she was pleased."

"All she did was smile and said thank you."

"And left you $20 million. I'd say you gave her confidence the money would be well used. What did her letter say?"

"Thought you'd never ask." He opened the letter. "It says: Dear Steve: If you receive this letter it is because I am no longer alive. Please do not worry, all is well, Jesus and I are having afternoon tea. I hope the resources have reached you and that you will put them to good use. I am only sorry I learned about the importance of sharing my gifts so late in life. I waited 80 years to learn that lesson. I wish you the best of life. Mary. I wonder what she meant by the 80 years comment?"

"How old do you think she was?"

"About 40."

I laughed. She was at least 80.

"Not a chance."

"Trust me, she was, and you must not tell anyone, I tell you that in confidence."

"All right, but how?"

"More questions for which I do not have the answers. Is there something else in the envelope?"

"You are so quick Matt. Yes, inside my letter is a sealed envelope."

"Well, open it."

"That letter is not addressed to me."

"To whom is it addressed?" I asked.

"You." He handed me the note.

I smelled it and was a bit surprised to find my favorite smell, lavender. I wasn't sure whether to open it now or later, but decided fair play insisted I do so then. I read it first to myself.

Dear Matt: I hope I can call you that even though we will never meet, I feel I know you and will come to know you more in the months ahead. The lavender is for you. God has told me of your gift and of your love of lavender. You are reading this because you have taken on the case of finding the person who killed me. I do not know who will attack me at this writing, only that it is coming and cannot be stopped. I have had a wonderful life, full of surprises and grace beyond the imagination. As you know, there are others to carry on the work—and those that will use my efforts for both creative and destructive reasons. Don't ignore the creative, he will use the power for that as well. Such is the wheel of life and the nature of free will that God has blessed us with. I am at peace with my life and all is in order. I wish I could give you clues, but I know you will have already discovered the right path to take when you read this. I will tell you this, use your vision to find the common symbol, I know it is there. New England is beautiful this time of year, especially Connecticut. Don't let the police deter you, I have already forgiven whoever it is, but justice must be served. Mary.

"Wow, that is quite a letter," Steve remarked.

"No kidding." I was stunned. I knew Mary had talents beyond anything I'd seen, but this was well beyond that. In the few seconds I'd taken to read the letter I'd already come up with three things I knew. First, the chat room, second, translating her papers was the right thing to do and third, I needed to relook at the pictures along with finding other crimes to look into. The part about the creative was a puzzle, but I knew what to keep my eyes open for. She was right about free will. God can persuade us but not force us. Evil is a choice against the will of God and we are free to make it.

"How could she possibly know all that?"

"She had a special gift from God."

"I'd say so, wish I had that gift."

"Think again Steve, you might be dead."

I got up and left. I didn't tell Steve that there was a P.S. to the letter.

P.S. Matt, Behind the house you will find an old oak tree. In the tree is a hole and at the bottom of the hole is a box---enjoy , live long and prosper.

I had a feeling what was in the box and laughed at her use of Spock's favorite saying. Her home was only a few blocks away and I needed to debrief, so I walked. The crime tape was gone, the leaves were gone off the trees, but I could see the large broad oak tree even from the front yard. I strolled around back and was stunned on many levels. First, I realized the leaves on the oak were still green even though all other trees were bare. Then I noticed her garden was full of flowers. All other gardens I'd seen had been put to bed for the winter. More amazing tricks from the alchemist. I'd like to get my hands on some of that powder. I walked to the tree and found the box she's left for me. The carving on the wood seemed to be ancient. I opened the lid and took out the note.

"Matt, this will only work for you, drink one drop a day for three weeks, I think you will find the results very pleasant. If you want more, you will have to follow the path yourself—you already have half of it down. The box is from a group of asian monastics from the 9th century. I know you haven't heard of them and you never will, you can have the box tested for date if you want—I know there is a doubter in you." Mary.

I was honored to be considered by Mary. I sat at the base of the tree and cried.

I have always believed that breakfast is the most important meal of the day, gives you energy for the rest. I wake at about 5:30, get a cup of tea and get my mind set by spending time with God. Mostly I meditate, listening, quieting my mind so the Holy Spirit can work with my body, mind, and heart. I do throw in some prayers on behalf of others and myself, but that is more to tell me my own internal priorities, after all, God already knows what is needed in the world, he doesn't need me to remind him. I'm reminding myself about where my energies should be directed. I get frustrated by those who pray for peace or world hunger and do nothing about it, as if God will do all the work. I tell my parishioners not to pray for things they are not actively involved with. If you pray for the healing of someone, go and lay hands on them or at least talk with them.

I do a bit of yoga to help with my physical well-being and end my time with God reading the bible and other spiritual writings. Note that I said spiritual writings---I read Sufi, Buddhist, Jewish, and many other disciplines as well as Christian. All faiths have some understanding of God, I just believe Christians have the only path that will give you the fullness of God.

After my God time, I cook a leisurely breakfast and drink my Univera AgelessXtra to keep me young and take my Univera Prime. All good stuff. Then I watch the sunrise over Mt. Hood and take a shower.

Sometimes I will invite people over for breakfast. Why would I want to go to Denny's when we can sit on the deck? Besides, I enjoy cooking. Mary's bottle sat on the table and I stared at it through breakfast, wondering if I really wanted what she had.

I called Tom, wanting to see if he'd found anything over the past couple of weeks. I suspected the answer was going to be no, there had been a rash of murders in the city over the last two weeks and Mary's would be at the bottom of the pile.

"Tom?"

"Matt?"

"Yes."

"I was wondering when you were going to call."

"Well, I thought I'd give you a bit of time, but then I know you haven't been busy," I laughed. "If you need help, just call and deputize me."

"I thought priests were supposed to be forgiving types."

"Forgiveness and justice are part of the same thing in God's world."

"Don't hold your breath on becoming a cop, besides, you'd never pass the physical test?"

"I'm in better shape than you."

"But I don't have to pass the test, I did that when I was young and fit."

"Touche."

"Just stick to the God stuff pastor, let me take care of the bad guys."

"I'll let you wear the gun, but will keep working on some of the bad guys, especially the ones that are getting no attention."

"OUCH!"

"It's true isn't it? With all the crime lately, you've done little or nothing with Mary?"

"Yes, it's true, sorry."

"So have you found anything?"

"Nothing I'm sure you haven't found. The writing is mostly formulas and symbols, her bank account had 1.5 million dollars in it, she is squeaky clean. No credit cards, no phone, no tv and all her bills are paid early and she has never had an overdue book. "

"Could you loan me her computer?"

"What?"

"Could you loan me her computer, it wasn't a hard question."

"Why would I do that?"

"Because a year will go by before you look into the matter and I have some resources that could do the work tomorrow----and not damage a thing. I promise I will give you everything I learn."

"Hmmmmm, well ok, I will sign it out to the company you are taking it to, I can't send evidence with a person."

"CST."

"What is that?"

"Can't tell you, they are a source that don't want to be known. Trust me and just put me down as the delivery boy, you can track us both down if I don't return it."

"I shouldn't do this, but what the hell. When are you going to get here?"

"Soon."

"And what else do you have for me?"

"Right now, just guesses, hopefully I'll have more soon. I've been a little busy lately myself. And another thing, can you flag any odd crimes that happen in the next few months?"

"Like what and why?"

" I think the murderer is still around and I don't think he is done."

With that I hung up the phone. I love doing that, leaving him hanging. I headed straight to the station and picked up the computer which was waiting at the evidence room for me. A note was resting on top of the machine, unfortunately I can't print what he said on here, but I laughed.

The computer took a drive to Sue's home (CST). I have no idea what CST is, just another figment of my imagination. I asked her to look on there for a clue as to someone else Mary might have communicating with in the Portland area.

"By the way, I have some info you might be able to use."

"What is it," I asked, excitedly. Whenever Sue told me she had info for me, I knew she was playing down the value.

"Names and addresses of the chat room users. That is all but three. "

'Why all but three?"

"They don't want to be found."

"Even by your beautiful self?"

"Even by your friendly genius."

"I can't understand that. Do these people know you were tracking them?" I asked puzzled.

"No, I covered my tracks. They would have to be significantly better than me."

"Good, I think we are safe then."

"There were three more than those you told me about. One of them was Mary."

"But she died, how could you track her down?"

"All internet work leaves tracks, for at least months, if not years. Every email you write, every chat room you visit, every site you attend."

"Big brother."

"You're not kidding, now you know why I cover my tracks, who knows who will come after you."

"You'll have to teach me those tricks someday."

"Be glad to when you have a few hours-----in other words never."

"Sorry."

"Your loss."

"I'm sure that is true."

"By the way, there are two interesting things you should know. The first is that M is from Connecticut. He appears to be the current leader. The second is that R and Z haven't been on for a while. R just reappeared a few days ago. I don't know where, but he is somewhere in the northwest. Z stopped coming on 3 weeks ago, he is around here too. Make any sense?"

"Yes, too much, keep working." I had another thought. "Can you tell if either one had a history elsewhere before coming to the Northwest?"

"Hold on, I can figure that our fast. Want to take a guess as to which?"

"R."

When a computer hack was at work, nothing can distract them. I could wave a million dollar bill in front of Sue's face and the green wouldn't faze her. I wandered around, looking at her equipment, checking out some of her magazines. I even made her a snack. I heard her call me from the room.

"Matt, I've got it."

"What did you find out?"

"You were right, R has only been on twice since coming to the Northwest. He's from California, somewhere north of LA, around Santa Barbara."

"Thanks, that's a big help."

"By the way, you didn't mention Mary?"

"She's dead."

"But was she on?"

"I don't know for sure, but my guess is she was, her last conversation being about a month ago."

"What was her name?"

"S&M," she laughed. "An odd name for such a peaceful person."

"I think it stands for Sun and Moon, not the two you were thinking of. My oh my what a wicked mind you have."

"A product of the late 20th century."

"I keep forgetting how young you are, for such a mature girl."

I handed her a check for $2000 and knew she would pass on to charity. We'd gotten over me not paying ages ago. She didn't want my money and I didn't believe in doing things for free—unless you were a priest. Finally, she took my money and passed it on.

R was probably the murderer and Z was Mary's teacher. Now I knew what drew her to the Northwest. I wondered if R was aware of him. There was a chance I was guessing wrong and that by seeking out Z I would tip off the prime suspect.

I'm a bit of an odd duck when it comes to preparing sermons. Most clergy spend at least a full day working on them. They do research, pray, write and rewrite them. They try to find jokes and intellectual information to tie everything together. Most are more like short lectures. When I hear a sermon, I like to hear someone speaking from the heart. I want to know what makes them tick, how God is impacting their lives and what I can do to change mine. I'm a pragmatist. I also like metaphors and I understand when people see something or touch something the level of learning is deeper than when they just hear it. That being the case, I use lots of metaphors and am famous for my props. This alchemy thing had me on all levels. Entranced by what the alchemists had put together as a spiritual framework over thousands of years, I saw how it mirrored the spiritual journey of saints, yet on a more practical level if you knew how to interpret their symbols and I was getting better.

The lessons for Sunday were on the theme of transformation. The usual metaphor was the butterfly and a lovely one it made. But I needed something different and alchemy was what I chose. I spent no time preparing a sermon. That is I didn't take time out of any day to prepare. I figured I was going to talk for between 12 and 20 minutes. What I said was not going to change the world and the vast majority of people would forget what I said within an hour of hearing my words. Why spend a day for that kind of result. I love hearing clergy who believe people live by what they say. I say give the parishioners a test on the sermon 24 hours after they have heard it. Most will fail.

On Monday I read the lessons I would be preaching on. I also do that on Wednesday, Friday, and Saturday. My mind always has a part working on the sermon. You know how a computer can have a bunch of programs running at once? You can be writing a letter while the web, music, and a messenger are running in the background. My brain works like that, all of ours do. Rarely are we fully attentive to one thing. I gather ideas for my sermon throughout the week. I come up with a theme and then I gather practical ideas and metaphors. Slowly they become incorporated. By Sunday morning, I'm usually ready to go. The fact I am fairly adept at speaking off the cuff doesn't hurt, and of course let's not forget the Holy Spirit who is rarely at a loss for words.

The 9:30 service seemed more full than usual, probably 450 people. We had a devout choir led by a choirmaster who enjoyed a wide variety of music. If I asked for a jazz mass, I got one. This Sunday I had asked for medieval music. I had asked this two months before not having any idea why, but feeling the Spirit leading me in that direction. Now I knew why, alchemy was peaking during that time as a presence within the Christian realm. I doubt coincidence was at play when the lyrics to the tune they sang as an Offertory discussed a refiner's fire, gold, and the sun and moon.

I looked out at the congregation as I was about to preach. A sea of people with fears, doubts, and a struggle to find God more deeply in their lives. I loved my flock and felt blessed I could share with them. My name had reached the papers a few days ago in connection with the murder and word had spread like wildfire. That probably explained the increase in attendance. Numbers always went up when I became involved with a case.

I never opened my sermon with a prayer, although I probably should have more than most. I felt it odd people would start with a prayer beckoning God to be with them and the words they were about to utter when the words had been written days before. Shouldn't they have prayed then? The timing seemed off to me. Their prayer should have been something like: "Lord, I pray I didn't screw up this past week when writing this sermon down. I pray I might make eye contact at least three times, and my voice will show the intensity that burned within me as I wrote down the words." I am a bit impious, I'll admit.

"Today's topic is the world of alchemy. How many of you know anything about it?" I often enjoyed having a conversation with those listening. I called on a few people and found some knew more than others, some had wrong information, and most knew virtually nothing. That would change. One gentleman remembered the word from his crossword puzzle the week before.

"The world of alchemy is pervasive in our culture. Medicine was created by alchemists, Sir Isaac Newton was an alchemist. Herbal remedies were impacted by the work of alchemists over 2500 years ago. You will find alchemy in every civilization that has inhabited this planet. Alchemical symbols are found in the bible, in our songs, and throughout literature. The work of alchemy has always been very private, but the findings always make their way into the public arena. I have always been a fan of alchemy and have read off and on about the subject for years. Recently I have become more infatuated, I will go as far as to say that the Holy Spirit wants me to be an alchemist. Now, before you get excited and think I'm leaving, I am talking about spiritual alchemy, not about setting up a laboratory in our church." The congregation laughed. "There are processes the alchemist goes through on their journey, just as there are those we go through on our journey to Christ. Who can tell me some of the stages of our journey to Christ?"

Lots of hands went up.

"John."

"Well, first you have to believe in the journey, you have to accept Christ."

I knew what John would say being a very evangelical Christian. I knew what most of the people would say whose hands were up because of where they were in their own journey. Little did they know they were playing into my hand.

Others talked about going through trials, being tempted, confession, service, worship, being part of community, and having spiritual deserts.

"What you have all shared are right. They are all parts of the journey, all aspects that each of us must go through, in no certain order. Just because you have been in a spiritual desert and come out of it, does not mean you are better or closer to God than those who have not. These stages you mention are all part of the alchemical journey. Calcination is trial by fire, coagulation is being part of a community, and on and on. Alchemy is a metaphor for our lives and I believe the process to be a helpful one. Therefore we will be starting an alchemy group that will meet on Wednesday nights at the church. All are welcome and you can pick up your first reading and your assignment for this Wednesday in the parish hall after the service."

I rambled on a bit more about where I was in my own faith development, that I was working on aspects of pride that were getting in the way. I talked about how the woman at the well was transformed by Christ when she was confronted by his knowledge. I told them one of the best signs about how deep our relationship with Christ was, was in seeing how we were being transformed. If you weren't changing, you weren't in relationship with God. People who fear change have a difficult time with God, because God believes in constant unabated change. I pointed out that I struggled with some TV evangelists because I'd watched them over the course of ten or more years and they hadn't changed. How is that possible? God wants all people to be Christ like, to see justice and to be humble. I felt the Spirit telling me to shut up, so I said Amen and sat down.

I must have touched a nerve on many because they applauded, something that happened only a few times a year.

By the time coffee hour was over not only was I exhausted, but I had almost 200 people signed up for the class. Now the question was who was going to cook dinner. I was expecting 30 and knew I could make soup for that many, but 200 was different. I'd have to get busy and find some cooks.

I retreated to my office, took off my robes and was getting ready to go out and pay some shut-ins a visit with communion.

"Matt, we found something in the plate, we thought you might want to see, we have no idea what it is."

I looked at the head usher and knew he'd counted the money from the day's offering.

"Thanks, let me see."

He handed me a square token. The piece had been made from a mold and appeared to be brass. On one side was an image of a sun and moon. When I flipped the piece over and saw the peacock, I sat down.

"Matt, are you ok?" asked the usher.

"I'm fine, thanks for bringing this too me."

"What is it?"

"Just a piece of jewelry, I'll get it to the owner."

The truth was I'd been given a calling card and I'd see the piece before. I had to track down from where. The Holy Spirit and I had some work to do.

8 BOB ENCOUNTERS THE PRIESTS

The world is a giant unseen web, all things are interconnected, that is how God created the earth. Some people are able to sense changes in the web and still others are able to pinpoint specific parts. Pretend you are on the outside of the web and you have a thought. There are people on the opposite side that feel it, sense it, and respond to it, either indirectly or directly.

We are bombarded by gamma waves and microwaves all the time. Every television station and every radio station, not to mention thousands of cell phone waves are in the air all the time. We don't have internal radar to pick them up or we'd have a huge headache. The spiritual web is no different, only the frequency of waves is different and as of yet, science can not detect them—they will someday. Part of growing as an alchemist is being more sensitive to the web. We are most sensitive to the plight of other alchemists. I know when someone has made a major breakthrough. My sense of Mary's recent breakthrough is why I chose the time.

In order to see and feel the web at that level, one has to enter a very deep state of meditation, eliminating all other interferences to focus on the one. The practice of meditation and its physical and spiritual benefits takes great effort. Discipline and patience are the cornerstones. There is nothing inherently difficult about meditating, most people just don't have the discipline to sit still for an hour at a time and clear their mind or focus. Society almost demands we clutter our lives with unnecessary material and mental baggage. The only true way to learn how to meditate is to meditate. You can read books till you are blue in the face, but until you sit, meditation is a practice of the mind rather than the body, mind, and soul. The web is discovered at the heart of all three.

My lab had become my home quickly, I felt at peace in the space and had several projects percolating away in various lab paraphernalia. Things bubbling, distilling, melting, coagulating, and fermenting. The smells were sublime to my nostrils, the smell of change, power, and the creative forces that made the earth.

I entered a deep state of consciousness and started to observe the parts of the web I could see and feel. I do not pretend to understand how the web works. Why I am sensitive to the plight of some and not of others is a mystery. I know people I know well are always present; all the alchemists I have dealt with are there and I can tell how they are doing. I can even send energy their way to help. It's a form of prayer.

Today I was looking for something different, a very strong presence in the web. There was a tendency when you become aware of the web to focus on the weaker aspects because you are entering from a position of strength. But someone is aware of me as well. There are stronger people out there, not many, but there are a few and I was after just one.

I found him quickly, or perhaps he found me, I was experiencing his presence in a way I'd never felt before. My heart beat more quickly, sweat surfaced on my brow, and my mind raced---while thinking of nothing. While you couldn't exactly talk via the web, you can communicate basic feelings and understandings. Here was a true master, someone who had either reached or was near reaching the ultimate goal. Here was a man who had great power, I had to be careful. I knew he was a man because of the energy he had. All creatures exhibit specific energy depending on their species and their sex.

Z had been in the chatroom a few times but not often. I remember him telling Mary a few things which seemed odd. I'd taken notes in all of our sessions. I didn't understand what he was saying, but as I matured as an alchemist it made sense. He was well beyond Mary.

He was wondering when I would listen to his call, he'd been asking for me to listen for months. I laughed to myself while kicking myself for not paying attention. I'd written those feelings off as internal surges of ego, now I wished I'd gone to him early. I hoped it wasn't too late.

I pleaded with him to forgive me and to allow me to be his student, to teach me what he knew. Then the surge hit me, full in the brain. He sent the brunt of his anger through the web right at me and I knew the repercussions would be felt throughout the web. He knew about Mary and what I had done.

In chat rooms, if someone says something you don't like, you exit. I didn't like what the old man said, so I disconnected. I had to be careful about it because I was still part of the great web and he knew how to find me on it.

Now I knew he existed and lived in the area. My guess was he lived relatively close to Mary. She didn't have a car and I doubt he had a computer, which meant she needed to go to his house or visa versa.

Without a computer he had to buy his supplies and at his level of the process, they were unique and rare. In fact there were only two companies that supplied what he needed in Portland. Hacking their site wouldn't be difficult and hopefully they kept records of sales that were accessible.

I also needed to keep track of the police investigation and make sure nothing new had developed. I called the department and asked for Tom Frank, the head detective I'd read about in the paper. I called from a pay phone in a restaurant just in case he decided to trace the call, although I doubted he would.

"Hello?"

"Is this officer Frank?"

"Yes it is, who is this please?"

"I'm a friend of Mary Weathers and was just wondering if any progress had been made on the case?"

"I didn't catch your name."

"Jim Swartz."

"And how did you know Mary?"

"I was in her bible study at the church."

"Oh, right I remember that she was in that."

"So do you know who did it?"

"Not yet sir, we are working on it."

"Have you learned anything yet?"

"We learn things every day."

"I'm glad to hear that."

Then he laughed. "I'm sure Father Matt will have it figured out shortly."

"Father Matt?"

"Yea, you know, that priest who solves murders, he's on the case."

"O, right, that's great." I thought about pushing a bit more, but I didn't want the detective getting curious about me. "Well thanks and good luck."

"Take care."

I hung up and felt a shiver on my spine. Every neuron started to fire in my brain. Father Matt? I sensed fear even thinking about his name. I got onto the net and looked him up. Apparently he was a legend in Portland; a wealthy priest, a philanthropist, and a psychic detective who had solved some of the city's most difficult cases. He claimed God helped him solved crimes. While there were many pages about Father Matt and his prowess to solve crimes, he didn't have a web page of his own. I found his church, but all he added were his sermons, he appeared to like being low key about his life

My guess was Father Matt was a reasonable guy that understood the spiritual world. I was hoping with a few pointed warnings, he would back off. Today was Saturday, tomorrow I would go to church.

I hadn't been to church on a Sunday in years. I found the hypocrisy deafening. I lost all sense of who I was when in the church. From where I sat it was because of them. I needed to see and hear Father Matt, get close enough to sense whether or not I had a shot of convincing him to leave me alone.

I was glad he ran a large church. Lots of friendly people and I fit in as one of the minions. The music was fantastic-- what I would expect from a paid choir. The Episcopal Church came as close as any to having a liturgy worthy of raising the holy to levels it deserved. I was ready for another sermon that did little to feed me. I was pleasantly shocked.

Father Matt talked of alchemy and knew of what he was talking. He discussed the process and how it reflected Christian spiritual development. I was quite impressed. At the end he announced he was starting an alchemy group. I couldn't believe my ears, he was jumping into an arena he knew nothing about. At first I wanted to stand up and scream, "How dare you?" What did he know? He might have read a few books, but in truth, he knew nothing about how would he lead a group on alchemy? Were they going to set up a lab? I decided to not meet him, but to leave a calling card and see what happened. Years ago I had created a symbol to represent who I was, a token with the sun and moon on one side and a peacock on the other. When the offering plate passed, I put my money and the token in the plate. I took communion and left.

Hearing Father Matt and seeing him put me into such a state of agitation, I took two days off to get refocused. I focused on the substances I was creating in the lab and on some cooking. I was a man of the wilderness at heart and loved being outdoors. My property was situated in a way I could hunt and not be noticed----so I did. I could easily sit for hours in a tree, waiting for a deer with my bow and arrow. I'd shot one my first week in the house. Some of the meat was in the refrigerator and the rest in the freezer. I savored every bite. Good food helped settle my mind. After my meal I was ready to head back into the world.

Before I left I found the two companies the alchemist had to be using. I got into their back site and looked for anyone ordering what he needed. You may wonder why I'm not telling you here what he ordered, and where he ordered it from. The work still goes on. There are secrets you will have to find out for yourself. He made no attempt to disguise himself and within minutes, I had his address. I'd pay him a visit soon. My guess was that he was expecting me, just as Mary was. His fate would hopefully be better than hers, I just wanted information.

Some of my time was spent in the mountains, not far from Mt. Hood. I found a cabin and settled in with a couple of good books and some large sheets of paper. When I was near a breakthrough like I knew I was, I needed to get the images in my mind out on paper. Several large sheets were put on the wall and I started to draw. This might occur for 6-8 hours without stopping, then over a meal I'd analyze them, looking for patterns, for images of the unconscious. I'd brought all of the papers I'd taken from Mary's and found them to be quite useful; at least the one's in English and French.

My drawings were filled with images of water, the fundamental archetype of cleansing and the unconscious. I'd kept dream journals for years, knowing my unconscious revealed itself to me through them. Some had called dreams God's forgotten language and I couldn't disagree. Dreams are seen as a way God communicated in the Bible and throughout history. But these were waking dreams, my unconscious now surfacing while I was fully alert and aware.

What concerned me were the shadows. The shadows on the trees and even on the water. They were dark and seemed to change form in relation to what they were shadowing. I thought I'd reigned in the shadow, obviously I had work to do. On the other hand I couldn't forget the shadow had led me to Philip and to Mary, two key moves I'd made in this game. I was torn with what to do. The shadow represented the darker side of the neutral force. I felt significant pressure from the other side to maintain a force field against the shadow. Mary had taught me to befriend the shadow, but I'd never really accepted that way of seeing it and still don't.

I wanted to fully understand the shadow without giving in. Was that possible? Lucifer had done it and failed. But his ego was huge, mine was contained.

Before I left the mountains I took a hike up a hill, that gave me a vast panorama. There was snow on the summit and it was cold. I'd only worn a tee-shirt. I sat down to meditate. As my body slowed down, so did my mind. I saw the shadow encroaching on me and I let it take hold. My body was encased in light and then slowly grew darker and darker. I was being sucked in by a black hole and after a time, I couldn't stop. At some point I passed out.

I awoke several hours later, my body half freezing. I felt different, something had taken hold in me, giving me a confidence I'd never known. I started meditating using a form that increased energy flow dramatically. I felt my blood surge through my body, even as I shivered. My conscious mind separated from my physical body. I stood up and started to run down the mountain, my body burning with fire. I knew I'd entered hypothermia on the ground, if not more. But humans vastly underestimate what the body is capable of withstanding. When I reached the cabin my clothes were steaming, my body was warm and I had been reunited. I had a new appreciation for the cold.

The last drawing I did was interesting. The entire piece was in a shadow, even though I was standing on top of the highest mountain. Everything was dark.

Before I left the house, I sat down and drew up a plan. I was a plan kind of person. I always did better when under the pressure of a timeline. There was no one putting the pressure on me, but I felt it, not just from within but somewhere outside. Here is what I wrote down:

1. Call priest Steve and make an appointment—soon, need to understand his perspective
2. Figure out a way of contacting Father Matt without contacting him and let him know he needs to back off.
3. Visit Z, get his wisdom, one way or the other.
4. Pick up the resources needed for one of the final stages
5. Get to M and the others to see what they know

I needed to do all that within the week.

On my way back into Portland, I decided to visit Z. I drove to his house in the West Hills. His street was tree lined, a development from the 70's with modern houses and large lots. He fit in like all other neighbors, little did they know. His house didn't look different from any of the others. I noted again, like Mary's there was no phone line. There was a cable to the house, so I knew he used the computer at his home, he was just cautious. A very wise man.

The afternoon was getting on, darkness had set in and only one light was on in the home. I wondered if he was there. I'd parked a bit down the street, just in case. As I walked toward the door, I noticed a piece of paper attached to the knocker. My eyes stared at the image on the paper.

The sheet was folded in half. Two images were on the front, the two sides of my token. Z had never seen it, how could he know? I was furious. I opened the note.

"I do not know who you are, I just knew you were coming. I do not want to hurt you, but you know I can. I can't encourage you enough to stop your current path, you have done enough destruction to ensure your own. Pursuing your current course will only bring harm to you and to other innocent people."

I ripped it up and threw the note on the ground, wet with rain. Then I took a deep breath and sought clarity. I picked up the pieces of paper, knowing they were evidence. I put on my gloves, walked around the back of the house and was ready to break the window in the door when I saw another note.

"The door is open, no need to break the glass."

In my anger I shattered the door pane and then opened the door and entered. I was not about to follow his directions, how dare he not meet me, what a coward.

The house was essentially empty. Very few pieces of evidence that would indicate who was here and the power he had. In the basement was the space where the lab had been. A few things remained, but nothing that would help me. I needed him. He would have to set up shop somewhere and I would find him.

Before I returned to my house I bought a paper. I couldn't believe my eyes when I read the headline:

"Murdered woman leaves church $20 million in gold and diamonds."

Mary had done one of two things; either she had figured out how to change the form of matter or she'd used her powers of knowing the future to create a vast fortune. The difference between the two was significant. Picking stocks was one thing, changing matter was another. I think I knew which she'd done.

I stopped by a few places and picked up what I needed for the following week in the lab, getting ready for the next test, one of the last ones before the work was completed.

After I arrived back at my monastery I had two more tasks to complete. I went to Father Matt's website and sent him an email from one of my addresses that couldn't be traced.

"Dear Father Matt, you are a very clever man. Don't let your cleverness be your undoing, you have no idea what you are dealing with. Besides, if you back off, it will be more than worth your while. What that other pastor got is peanuts."

I figured his greed in and of itself would send him running. I smiled.

Next I had to visit the chat room.

We normally met on Tuesdays and Fridays at 9pm EST. That allowed for those who had to work on the east coast to be on at a reasonable hour. I'll admit to enjoying bringing others into the fold and sharing a bit of what I had discovered or learned with them. One of the moral obligations for those with spiritual information is to pass that on to others in one form or another.

At first I entered as one of my aliases, just to see who was there and what the tone was, but I left quickly when things started to feel funny. There were two new people in the room and they made me nervous, I didn't want to be caught as an alias, that would ruin my credibility. I logged back on as myself, R. I kept being surprised in this journey, seemingly one step behind a few others. My time this night in the chat room would be no different, but things were about to change.

9 MATT MEETS JOSEPH

The office was always busy after Sunday services so I needed to go to my house where I could focus. Lots of verbiage was being tossed about at coffee hour.

"So Matt, who are you voting for in the election?"

"Vote, me Miriam?"

"I know you haven't missed an election in 30 years, I just want to know if you are voting for or against the schools and the libraries. You are so fiscally conservative it makes me nervous."

"I would never vote against your advice, I've heard your passion about both institutions and you've convinced me. Besides I don't think the governor and legislature give them enough—you have my vote on both!." I wanted her beautiful 85 year old mind to think she'd converted me.

"Matt, you are such a charmer."

CeCelia came running over to me, a wonderful smile on her face and that mischievous look in her eyes. I knew I was about to get in trouble.

"Matt," she exclaimed. I insisted that we were all on a first name basis in the church. For some, the idea took some getting used to, but now they all enjoy it. The notion that we have to call someone Mr. or Mrs. or Father in order to show respect is a bit bizarre to me. CeCelia was a charmer, and the current head youth of the youth group.

"What is it CeCelia?"

"The youth group needs your help." She waited. She could read me like a book and always ended up getting what she wanted. "Ok, we will start with the easy ones. We are going to have a GPS party in two weeks, ya know, those machines that get you a position on the earth with the satellites?"

"Yes, I know of them."

“We are going to go around the city to different points, a race between different groups of kids in the church.”

“And how might I be involved?”

“We will have the final point be your house, where you will serve us lunch and give out the prizes.”

“I.......”

“You don’t have to cook.”

“But that is what I like to do.”

“Great, then we are on, at your house and you are cooking for about 30.”

I’d been had, she always did this to me and there was no way out.

“Date and time please?”

She winked as she handed me a pre-printed flyer with all the information on it, including a map to my house. Then she turned, whistled, got 400 people’s attention and announced it. Everyone laughed, knowing she’d gotten the better of me again. She is so sweet I don’t think I’ll ever learn, not sure I want to.

“Matt, what do you think about the gold?”

“You must be talking about Steve’s church.”

“Exactly, why didn’t that lady leave it here?”

“Well Max, I think she went to a bible study at that church for years, and besides, they need it more than we do.” Max was well meaning and didn’t have a greedy bone in his body. On the other hand he was a believer we should be good stewards of God’s gifts to us, especially money, and felt our church did a better job than most. I don’t believe it for a second, but I know he does. “Steve has some very good ideas of what to do with the money Max , you can relax.”

“I’ll sleep better tonight knowing that,” he said as he laughed and patted me on the back.

“Matt, we need to talk.”

Alice was a beautiful woman of 40. At one point I'd thought of asking her on a date, but decided against it. She was a wonderful person of deep faith and usually came to me asking prayers for someone in the parish. She had a way of finding out people's problems.

"What is it Alice?"

"Well, Jesus and I are having some issues and I'd like to talk them out with you."

I knew the issues were serious if she was coming to me at coffee hour.

"You name the time."

"Does tomorrow at 9 work for you?"

"Here or elsewhere?"

"Here is fine."

"See you tomorrow."

I kept talking with people for about a half hour. The other priests would take the next service today. I had to spend at least a half hour talking with people, but now I slowly moved out of the room and headed home.

There was something about this case that was disturbing me more than others. Usually, I am able to be completely objective, separate myself from the emotion of it all, but not this time. Night after night I lie awake trying to understand this alchemy thing. Feeling myself being drawn more and more into some kind of mystical fabric was unnerving me. I knew I could pull out, but found myself not wanting to. My meditation time had been significantly more active than usual and my dreams had increased in both number and intensity. There was no doubt God was trying to get my attention, just wish I knew for what.

I sat in front of the fire with all the pictures and writings I'd received from Mary's. I centered my mind so the Holy Spirit would have a chance of showing me something. I already knew the answer was here, I just had to find it. The feeling overwhelmed me to put the pictures on the table, so I did, spreading all of them out. My eyes gazed over each one. Then I fixated on one of them. There it was, an identical talisman that was put in the plate, sitting there on Mary's lab table. The murderer left a calling card and had been to church. Why didn't the Holy Spirit just tell me then?

However, God wasn't done, there was more. I reread Mary's note to me and got out a map---of Connecticut. I felt a pull to the Northwest corner of the state. The town of Lakeville jumped out. I knew of the village because a friend of mine had run a church there years ago and I stayed with him to enjoy the fall foliage. If I called the police and asked questions, they'd hang up on me. So the next best thing came to mind. I emailed Tom and asked him to do it for me---official business. I let him know there was a connection between Mary and something that had happened near Lakeville within the past 6 weeks—probably a fire. If they had anything sounding like a lab of any kind burning down, I needed the pictures of it, as many as they could send and a picture of anything that was left over from the conflagration.

I sat back, proud of what I had done---what God had done. God didn't take days off so it didn't bother me that I bugged Tom on his day off.

The doorbell rang. I wondered who would be calling on me. As I got up, I felt an amazing fullness of life within me. I can't explain the sensation, but I did know whoever was outside was the reason.

As I opened the door, I stared into the face of a man. Nothing special, probably 60ish, dark brown hair in a ponytail. His eyes glowed with life and he oozed a peacefulness.

"Hello Matt."

"Hello, and who might you be, since you already know me?"

He didn't say a word, just staring at me. Then I knew.

"You are Z, Mary's friend."

"How astute of you, I didn't realize you'd gotten that far already."

"I didn't. I just realized you existed recently and the power of your presence gave you away."

"Might I come in?"

"I'm so sorry, my apologies, do come in."

He walked into my home as if it were his, knew where everything was. He sat in front of the fire on the sofa.

"Can I get you something to drink?"

"A nice port will go well with what I have brought."

"Brought?"

"A small gift to time our conversation."

"Why do you need to time it, do you have to be somewhere?"

"No, but most conversations should end sooner than they do, this way I know when I have to start getting to the point."

"Alright, I'll be right back."

Eccentric was the wrong word for this person. I didn't recall ever having met someone so fully in touch with his surroundings and so in control of the situation—all while making me feel at peace.

I came back with my best Port. "Here you are………….. do you have a name other than Z?"

"I would hope so, my parents were more generous than that. My name is Joseph."

"Pleased to meet you Joseph."

He sipped the wine, then pulled out two cigars from his pocket.

"I believe you enjoy a cigar now and then?"

"Yes, I've been known to have one from time to time. Is this one special?"

"Try one, you tell me."

I took the cigar and knew I was handling a delicacy from the moment it touched my lips. The smoke was like incense, the taste miraculously mild. I'd never had anything like this.

"Where did you find these?"

"It's not really a matter of where, but more of when and what was done with the raw materials. I've been saving this for a special event and seeing your joy makes it worth the wait."

"Thank you. Can I ask why you are here?"

"Don't you think we need to talk? You were going to track me down weren't you?"

"Yes, but how did you know?"

"You are not the only one who communes with the Holy Spirit."

I was surprised to hear him use those words.

He laughed. "Did you think you had a monopoly on Christ and God?"

"Well no, but I thought alchemists were outside that tradition."

"Why do you think Mary was in that Bible study?"

"I hadn't thought about it."

"Alchemy is a physical and material path to wholeness. There is no being whole without God, and God has determined that the best, purest, and fastest way home is through Christ. There is no reaching the Philosopher's Stone without a deep and passionate relationship with Jesus. He is the Philosopher's Stone."

My mind was swimming. Joseph made everything seem so obvious and simple. Of course Jesus was the Philosopher's Stone, the perfection of humanity, why hadn't that come to me ages ago?

"Then why not just be a Christian, come to church and follow the normal path?"

"There is where you make your mistake----normal. What is normal about having a relationship with the

Creator? We are finite and yet can have a relationship with the infinite. That is normal?"

"You have a point."

"Normal doesn't work, never has. We are all unique beings and each of us must find, accept responsibility for, and act upon our path. Mine is alchemy. Look at your saints, each one did something unique with their lives, they didn't just follow the sheep."

"But why alchemy?"

"Another day, my cigar won't last that long."

"How long had you known Mary?"

"First let me ask you a question, how old was she?"

"80."

"You are a good detective."

"Yes I am---with the help of God."

"Mary and I have known each other for almost 70 years, I met her when I was nervous about getting old."

I must have looked a bit strange because he laughed.

"So how old do you think I am?"

"60ish."

"My, I wear it well. I'm 118. "

"You aren't Mary's friend, you are her teacher."

"Correct."

"I don't understand."

"What?"

"If you have the abilities you do, then why couldn't you stop the murderer?"

"Excellent question. Mary and I both knew something was coming, but the one who killed her is hardly a beginner. He is very advanced for his age, and greedy."

"He took things from her."

"Did you hear what I said earlier?"

"About God?"

"Yes, he will not get nearly as far as he would like. Unfortunately he will do more damage before he realizes it is too late so we must stop him."

"Call the police, tell them where he is and they will arrest him."

Joseph let out a long and loud laugh. "I know you have abilities that let you do such things. I however do not. He has guarded himself well. Even now he is at my home, seeking me out."

I stood to get the phone.

"Sit down Matt, he would be long gone before the police arrived and what would you tell them anyway? Here is the murderer!! What evidence do you have? None, I figured."

"How did he find you?"

"I have no idea, but he is very resourceful. I think he is a computer genius."

I started to pace, trying to fit the pieces together.

"Mary was a remarkable woman and student. She learned fast and had no fear. She felt the web like no one I had ever met. "

"The web?" I asked, wondering where all this was going, feeling a bit like Alice about to jump down the rabbit hole.

I'd heard of what I thought he was talking about, some mystical web that existed between all creation. The higher up the food chain, the stronger the web and the closer to you spiritually, the tighter the web. Hogwash. But I wasn't about to say anything.

His eyes were piercing and looking right into my soul.

"May I show you something?" he asked, as if I actually had the power to say no.

"Of course."

Expecting him to pull something out of his pocket or vest I tensed. Instead, he sat in front of me on the coffee table.

"You do pray don't you?" he asked with a smile.

"Of course."

"Good, then pray with me."

He took my hands, very firm for such an old man. I felt electricity running between us. Usually, I felt the Holy Spirit flowing through me to someone I was praying with, now I felt as if I was being prayed for, but for what?

"Lord Jesus, come, be present in our minds. Open Matt's eyes to see the wonders of your created order in ways he has been closed to. Help him to let go of his fears and all ideas he has held as true, so that he might see and feel your Spirit even more deeply than he already does. I know dear Jesus you use his senses, open them all to the power of your creation."

I was a pretty good meditator and I knew how to let my mind be receptive to the Holy Spirit. I wasn't exactly sure what he was up to, or what he thought would happen. I was thinking that here I was a priest, a believer, someone who had a deep relationship with Christ, and this alchemist comes in and wants to show me how to pray? Then it hit.

My entire body, mind, and spirit were slammed. I was experiencing something like I'd never felt before. A connection existed between me and the planet I'd buried. But I understood why, I was assaulted by the emotions of millions; their joys and sorrows, aches and pains, moments of ecstasy and of tragedy. I saw things about parishioners I never knew, yet in this moment I knew them to be true and not figments of my wild imagination. The web was real.

"Almighty God, help Matt to focus his spiritual energy, to help him bring justice for Mary. He has far greater skills than I in relation to his senses, but he lacks focus. Fill him with your presence and your eyes."

I had an image in my mind like Google Earth. Slowly I zoomed in on things. I saw the murderer in Z's house. Rummaging around, angry that Z knew he was coming. Then he was driving, but as he got deeper into the country, my vision blurred. I thought maybe the connections had to do with being around people, like in a city. The further away you got from people, the cloudier the vision became. I'd had visions before, but they were more dreamlike, this was real and a bit scary.

"Amen." He waited a few moments till I came back to this reality. "He knows we are after him."

"What do you mean?"

"He has progressed further than I thought. He is very aware of the web and is blocking you from connecting with him that is why it went blurry."

"You mean you don't need to be around lots of people energy to make it happen?"

"No my dear boy, in fact the opposite is true. Some of the most powerful people using the web are monks and nuns living in complete silence in the middle of nowhere. I think you may even use their energy before this is all over, they are very aware of you."

"I have monks and nuns working for me?"

"Have been for quite some time and they work for God, not you."

"God never ceases to amaze me."

"Nor I, so, now you believe in the web?"

"Did I ever have doubts?" We both laughed. "So what is next?"

"That is your job, I'm not the detective."

"How far are you in the process?"

"Which process?"

"Alchemical."

"I've just about arrived."

"What other process is there?"

"The most important my friend, the spiritual."

"And where are you in that one?"

"Close, I think, but then I have thought that before only to see another spiritual mountain range or desert looming in front of me."

I knew he was telling the truth. He was surrounded by a peace and energy I'd never known before and here he was telling me it was Jesus that gave it to him.

"Tell me why you use alchemy rather than more traditional paths."

"Traditional paths are stuck. They have put God in a cage, a cage God has no need for. We put limits on God, when God has no limits. Zen people will tell you in order to see what is really real, you have to let go of purely rational truth. That's what their koans are about. You know, the sound of one hand clapping? It doesn't make sense. You have to view it in a different light. What about Jesus and the camel going through the eye of a needle----the point of that story is all things are possible with God. Don't forget that, all things. We have barely scratched the surface and most people won't because they can't let go of their ideas, opinions, and notions of how the world works. If you want to find God in the deepest sense, everything must die---You must die to yourself to find yourself."

"And….."

"Alchemy is a very powerful tool to achieve that end."

"But can it be used for evil?"

"Much of the energy of the universe is neutral. Our friend has access to amazing amounts of power. I fear what he might be drawn to do."

"To do?"

"You don't know yet do you?"

"Know what?"

"How he has used the power."

"Well, he didn't need a lot of power to kill Mary."

"No he didn't. But what about healing those Alzheimer patients or the people he cured of cancer?"

I remembered reading about them in the paper. "He did that?"

"Yes."

"How do you know?"

"Trust me, he cured them----with God's help, even though I'm not sure he knew it."

"But why, if he is an evil guy, why would he do that?"

"First of all, within his own mind I am certain he believes he is good---Mary was probably wrong in not helping him, so he did what he needed to do----and he would do it to me as well. But I know he is getting close to having to make a decision about whether to follow God or himself. He may have already made the choice.

"Why would he choose against God?"

"Come now pastor, you and I do it every day, it's called sin."

"But he is so close."

"How close was Lucifer?"

"Touche." No other being the universe was as close to God as Lucifer and yet he made the decision to go it alone. "So what will be his next move?"

"I think he will have to do some more tests in order to convince himself he is on the right track. He wants to get there fast which is why he went after Mary and why he is coming after me and after you."

"After me?"

"He has made contact hasn't he?"

"Well, yes."

"He knows you are the only one that cares about him and can stop him. Trust me, he will stop at nothing to protect his interests."

"Wait a minute, back up."

"To what?"

"The part about him healing those people."

"What about it."

"What exactly do you think healing is?"

"Ah now we come to it, you want to play theology, they always do, trying to understand the infinite."

"I just want to know what you think healing is."

"All right , have it your way. You do understand the web."

"Yes, I get that part, not sure I believe it, but I get it."

"Good. Assume it is true. There are two critical things you need to understand in regards to healing. The first is the human mind and spirit are phenomenally powerful, that is how God created us. He wants us to use our brains. Secondly, God has created the universe with certain physical laws and he chose not to break those laws. Can God break them? Of course, he created them. But God knows once he starts breaking them for one person, why not for another, therefore he doesn't do it. What he does do is enable people to be open to their own and the energy of others. You've read about Jesus healing people and feeling power or energy leave him. He is completely oriented to others, not to himself. His energy is our energy, his passion our passion, his view of the world our view of the world—if we want it. There are certain substances you can take that will help that process along. I'm sure you are not surprised people other than Christians are healed? Now you are about to ask, why aren't some people healed? Even our energy and that of others can't change physical laws. Some people are in such a position on the web of life, they will not be healed. Their challenge, our challenge, is to discover how to live life fully, no matter the circumstances and when we are dealt a straight flush, find out how to use it to better life for others—internally and externally. Remember, Jesus was much more concerned about eternal life than temporal."

"So how did he heal?"

"Like I said, he was a conduit, he is not completely lost yet, but he is close."

"But how did they let him do it to them?"

"My guess is he posed as a doctor to the patients in the hospital and as a priest with the others. People they would recognize and trust."

"Is it lasting?"

"The healing? I can't tell you that."

"Are they stronger on the web?"

"All those who have a miracle take place in their lives are significantly stronger on the web for a while. But if they don't do something to engage the web and God, it drizzles away. You would be amazed at how many people have been healed and yet have forgotten what occurred within a year or two. Tragic, and I blame the church in part."

"Why?"

"You show no leadership in deepening faith. You expect people to grow on one bad sermon a week. You offer no reason to deepen your faith, no shared experiences, little pragmatic information and certainly no accountability. You care more about money and numbers than you do about their relationship to God."

"A bit harsh?"

"More importantly, is it true?"

"I would have a hard time building a strong case for the church in light of what we are called to do."

"Well put."

"Can you have strong healing power and not understand the web?"

"Yes, but most do, at least on a conceptual level. Their own theology probably keeps them from sensing the web or seeing it, but they feel the presence of others and of God on a deep level, they often sense when something is wrong elsewhere—a friend is sick or died, a major event in the world---like animals before an earthquake or major storm."

"I want to learn about this."

"I know you do and there is a chance I might be able to share some things.

"Might?"

"Matt, I don't know what will be asked of me or you in dealing with this murderer. I do know we are in a unique position and this alchemist will not hesitate in killing us if we interfere---which of course we must.'

"Hide."

"I can't run from reality, the forces at work are bringing us together on a collision course. The challenge is to have the meeting on my terms, not his."

"And he wants the exchange to be on his terms."

"Precisely, but he is greedy and overly confident, although I suspect right now he is a bit shaken."

"Then let's hit now."

"And how might I inquire, would we do that?"

I was puzzled. My assumptions had once again out grown the reality. Amazing how often we make false assumption about other people. I had to laugh at myself as I looked at this old man who had already disintegrated many beliefs I held---in one short evening.

I looked over at the cigars we had been smoking until the time of prayer when we'd put them down. Over a half hour had passed so I was looking forward to starting again, relighting the stoggie and knowing I'd extended the conversation. As I lifted the cigar to my mouth I quickly realized the flame was still going. My desert had been burning the entire time, yet had barely burned.

"Good trick isn't it?" he said, knowing what I'd discovered.

"I'll say, but it did extend the evening."

"Our work is not yet done or it would be ashes."

"So what's next?"

"I assume you have the internet?"

"Of course."

"Then let's go to it."

"Sit tight."

Now it was his turn to be a bit surprised. I retrieved my laptop (such a small screen, especially if you are sharing) and say next to Joseph. I had a flat panel TV on the wall, 6x8 feet—the real reason the kids wanted to come to my house. With the click of a few buttons, my screen appeared on the wall.

"That is quite impressive," remarked Joseph, sitting back and laughing.

"You see, technology isn't evil," I remarked thinking Joseph was probably anti-tech. He simply smiled.

I continued to be stunned at how long my cigar was lasting. I didn't need to smoke it a lot, each puff, like a fine wine, lasting.

"So where do I go?"

"I'll give you the address, it's a chat room for alchemists."

I typed it in and arrived at the home page. There were alchemical pictures and lots of other things to do; formulas, stories, biographies, galleries, tutorials, and of course, the chat room.

"My you are a quick learner, how did you find this, not many know about it."

"You have your resources, I have mine."

He didn't take the bait.

"Fair enough. Let me enter and chat, I think you should stay out for the time being."

I didn't argue.

Z: Hello everyone.

A: Hello Z, haven't seen you in a long time, how have you been?

Z: Preoccupied. A, how is your formulary coming along? Have you gotten through the fire that reigned upon you?

A: I think so, I'm discovering that sometimes even though the heat is on and I am in the fire, I have to turn up the heat.

Z: Very wisely said and a good discovery. And how might I ask did you do that?

A: The fire was in the midst of a relationship. I told the truth which not only surprised the other, but ultimately calmed everything down.

Z: Good intuition. Being blunt is not always the best, but certainly is more often than most of us do it. Remember what the Bible tells us, know the truth and the truth will set you free. Is that what you want---to be free?

A: Free of everything.

Z: I'm sure you have discovered that freedom comes with a price.

A: Well, I want to be free of my dark human side and find my divine side.

Z: You are on the right track, well done.

A: Thank you sir.

M: We haven't seen you in quite a while Z, have you been busy?

Z: Very busy, heading to the light and fleeing the dark.

R: The dark?

Z smiled at me. "I've got him."

Z: yes, the darkness surrounds us and we have to expend energy in order to keep it at bay. Certainly you know that R?"

R: Yes we do.

Z: And sometimes the darkness and the light get confused, the sun and the moon are both lights, mercury and silver both shiny metals and liquid at high temperatures, yet very different. Delusion is a problem for alchemists.

R: And how do you tell others how to tell the difference?

Z: That is the essence isn't it R? When we are clear about what is right and wrong, truth and falsity, life becomes easier. Have you ever done anything you knew was wrong, but convinced yourself it was right?

A: Yes I have.

P: Me too.

Z: R?

R: Of course.

Z: What tools do you use to choose?

R: The refiner's fire, my brain, silence.

Z: Three excellent choices, one big one missing.

Z smiled at me again, I knew he was baiting the murderer.

R: I'm not sure Z.

Z: How about the use of community, bouncing ideas off others? But then if one of us was tempted to steal something, we wouldn't ask anyone else would we, because we know that is wrong.

R: Of course, why waste the community's time?

Z: I see, so your refiner's fire would clue you in.

R: Yes, or I would know on an intellectual level it is wrong, or the Spirit would tell me in my silence.

Z: My brain and meditation can lead me down a wrong path, I have even convinced myself the Spirit of God was talking to me when it wasn't.

R: So what are you suggesting?

Z: That we were not put on this planet alone, we are social animals. Alchemists tend to be loners. Is anyone in this room an actively social person?

Nothing.

Z: Just as I thought. At some point, on the spiritual side of your work, you must seek out others, engage them and listen to them. This is difficult because you fear rejection and fear because of the alchemical work. I am telling you it must be done, otherwise there is far too much temptation to go the wrong direction.

R: But we share in here Z.

Z: You don't share it all, you hide things.

R: Me?

Z: Yes, you-----and all of us, including me.

Z looked at me. "Now for the real bait."

Z: R I know you are pushing yourself and gaining ground fast, I feel it. But you can't make the final steps alone, you will need help, I think it is time we meet.

R: Perhaps you are right R, what do you suggest?

Z: I will create a hotmail account, zalchemy tomorrow at 4, sign on and we will chat and find the right time and place to meet. To you others, no offense, your time will come. Do not write to that address I will only be using it one time.

R: I'll be there.

Z: I have no doubt.

R logged off.

Joseph had been at my house for a couple of hours and showed no signs of slowing down. The phone rang with Beethoven's 9th. General rings are so boring. For some reason I looked at Joseph. He smiled.

"Hello, Matt here."

"Matt, Tom."

"To what do I owe this pleasure."

"How did you know?"

"Know what?"

"About the fire in Salisbury?"

I loved teasing him. "Where?"

"I don't have time for this, how did you know?"

"A long story that is still unfolding."

"Talk to me."

"Not yet, but soon I think, so what did you find."

"A barn in Salisbury burned, might be arson, they aren't sure, although the gentlemen whose place it was--- a Mr. Phil Corbin--- said not to pursue it. I am faxing all the pictures to you. What are you thinking?"

"Tom, the murderer is on a rampage. He torched the guys barn, killed Mary and just tried to burgle another man's house. He isn't done and it will get worse, he is desperate."

"For what?"

"You wouldn't believe me if I told you."

"Try me."

"Next time, I have company, talk to you soon."

"How about now?"

"Bye."

I hung up the phone, such power. I knew he'd call back so I turned off the ringer. I was thinking he might even come over, but he probably figured I would assume that and leave. We were safe for a while. I told Joseph what I had just learned and about my messenger conversation with Phil.

Z: M?

M: Yes?

Z: Trust me, go on your messenger now.

M: Why?

Z: Trust me.

I opened another window on my laptop and waited for Phil. I didn't wait long.

Me: Phil, don't click us off. This is Matt, I'm with Joseph.

Phil: What is going on?

Me: I know your name is Phil Corbin, you live in Salisbury, Ct. and you recently had a barn burn down, your lab.

There was about 30 seconds of silence, I thought he'd left.

Z: Phil, this is Z, Joseph. Listen to him.
Phil: All right.
Me: Mary is dead.
Phil: Who?
Me: I think you know her as SM. You asked me about her last time we talked.
Phil: OMG (Oh my God)
Me: R murdered her.
Phil: Not possible.
Z: It's true Phil, he killed her, and is trying to come after me.
Phil: Why?
Z: Because none of us will share what we know with him because we know his heart is heading down the wrong path, you must have sensed this.
Phil: I had my suspicions, but to kill for it?
Z: Yes, and he's not done, we have to stop him.
Phil: What can I do?
Me: First of all, don't let him know you know. You will have to watch yourself, everything must appear as normal.
Phil: All right.
Me: Tell me what you are missing from the lab?
Phil: Everything, he burned it to the ground.
Me: I'm sorry. He came for something, think, what were you working on he would have wanted and is there any way to see if he got it?
Phil: I'm a techno freak, other than the actual experiments, everything is on the computer.
Me: Where is it?
Phil: Burned.
Me: Still there?
Phil: Yes.
Me: Get it.

"What are you thinking?" asked Joseph.

"Just a hunch, do you know what he was working on, what the murderer would have wanted?"

"He'd been doing work with Mary focusing on the transmutation of metals." Z said.

"Like changing things into gold or diamonds?"

"Yes, like that and I see she was successful."

"Very."

"Once again the student becoming the teacher, she hadn't told me that."

"I think the murderer knew, so he went after Phil first."

Phil: Got it.

Me: Looks like yours?

Phil: Yes, all the parts are there.

Me: Is it open?

Phil: No

Me: Open it.

Phil: That could be hard, it's charred.

Me: Rip it open, you won't ever be using this machine again.

Phil: I guess you are right.

Me: Tell me you had backup.

Phil: Yes, here and on a remote site, I backup every day.

Me: Good, I get tired of hearing about people that don't back up their computers and then get mad when the system crashes.

Phil: True.

Me: Is it open?

Phil: Yes. OMG.

Me: It's not yours is it.

Phil: No.

Me: How do you know?

Phil: The video card and sound card are different. I special order mine, very high end and very hard to get.

Me: He didn't have time to change everything out. So he has your computer, how will it help him?

Phil: Not sure. Most of what is on there he already knows, he's far ahead of me.

Me: What about the transmutation of metals?

Phil: Yes, he might be able to figure that out. I put things in code, but I know he is very facile with computers.

Me: How far had you gotten?

Phil: I've made some 3rd class diamonds and when the barn burned I was working on better ones. They were gone, but I thought they had been buried or burned.

Me: More likely stolen.

Phil: If that is true, they are like seeds, his work will be easier if he has them.

Me: We need to assume he does.

Phil: So what's next.

Me: We'll be in touch, take care of yourself, I don't think you need to worry as long as he thinks you are in the dark, he's after us.

Phil: Then you are the one's that need to be careful.

Me: We are, take care.

Phil: Bye.

Joseph had been talking with the room while I chatted with Phil. He worked with F and A, and others, giving them guidance on what to do next on their journeys. His memory was remarkable. Finally he signed off.

"Well I think that was a worthwhile evening."

I looked at my cigar and saw it had dwindled to nothing.

"Tomorrow I will talk with R, by then you will have a plan, won't you Matt?"

"Sure, if you say so," I said not having a clue.

"Pray and think about it, the Spirit will lead you, I have no doubt." Z rose from the sofa and gave me a hug.

"Thanks for coming."

"Thanks for letting me in."

"Thanks for the cigar."

"Thanks for the company."

We broke into laughter and hugged again. He walked out the door.

"Wait, where are you going, you can't go home."

"He won't come back, at least not till after tomorrow, and he won't meet me there, he's not stupid."

"How do I reach you?"

"I'll call you by 5."

"Ok."

I didn't know how he'd gotten my number, but I didn't ask. I was too tired, completely drained by what we'd just been through. Joseph on the other hand looked energized. I needed to get some of that juice.

I fixed some dinner and sat down by the fire for a quiet evening.

The doorbell rang. At first I was fearful, thinking perhaps the murderer had found me. He knew who I was and had been to the church. Looking up my address in the parish directory wouldn't be hard. I owned a gun and wouldn't hesitate to use it in self-defense, although I was a pacifist and believed Jesus would probably not agree with me. After all, he was completely innocent and let people murder him, without so much as lifting a finger. I always get a kick out of people who try to paint Jesus as a warrior, as anything but a pacifist---fortunately he accepts our humanity. Before grabbing the gun I decided to see who it was from the laundry room. As I peered out the window, I saw a woman, certainly not the murderer. I breathed a sigh of relief.

Upon opening the door I looked into the eyes of Alice. She was stunningly beautiful.

“Alice, what a pleasant surprise, I didn’t think we were meeting till tomorrow.”

“I’d rather not wait, but I’ll leave if you’d like.”

“Of course not, come in.”

I took her coat, the evening being brisk, a Portland drizzle in the air.

“Make yourself at home, can I get you something?”

“ A cup of tea would be nice Matt, thank you.”

She sat by the fire warming herself as I got her glass.

“So what do you need to talk about?”

Her finger moved along the rim of her cup her eyes going back and forth between the fire and me.

“It’s all right Alice, don’t worry, just spit it out.”

“I’m in love.”

“That’s wonderful, I couldn’t be happier for you.”

“With you.”

My heart stopped. I was speechless.

“I’m sorry, but I couldn’t figure out any other way of dealing with it. I’ve tried myself, but get nowhere, I needed to tell you. I don’t expect you to do anything.”

I still could think of nothing to say. Part of me wanted to hold her and yet that wasn’t what was needed. I just sat there like an idiot.

“Matt, I don’t think I have ever seen you speechless before.”

“I’ll admit, that condition is a rarity in my life, and at the moment I am.”

“Humbling?”

“Deeply, on many levels.”

“I don’t think it is going to go away, I’ve tried.”

My mind was racing. We’d been taught not to date people in the parish and other than Alice there weren’t any I was really interested in. I knew her well and considered her a deep and close friend. Now there was a decision to make. I could go with my heart or go with what tradition said was the best. I couldn't do it half-heartedly, I was either all in or all out.

"What is it you love about me?" the words coming out of my mouth even as I realized how stupid they sounded, how self-centered.

"Well, let me just tell you it isn't your money, I have more than enough."

That seemed to break the ice, we both laughed.

"You are a very bright, wise man who has a good sense of humor and is quite good looking. Certainly I am not the first woman to fall in love with you?"

"I don't have groupies waiting outside the door as you might have noticed."

"I told them all to go home for the night before I rang."

"Alice, I don't see myself as that attractive on any level. There are many men with much more to offer than me."

"That's your personal opinion, I happen to disagree, but I am sensing that I should work on letting go."

"I didn't say that."

There was tension in the air. The fire crackled, my cell phone rang, the grandfather clock chimed and the music played in the background, yet I heard none of it, all of my senses were in my eyes. I saw Alice in a new light, her beauty took on a new dimension, her inner spirit pouring into the room. I let the silence carry us for a while, she seemed comfortable with it.

"Alice, I probably shouldn't do this, but I have cared about you for a long time. I would enjoy having you come to my house again for dinner, to see what happens. This is not a door I want to close right now, I hope that doesn't come across as egocentric."

"Not in the least, I wouldn't have expected anything else. I couldn't have hoped for anything more."

She rose and headed for the door.

"Where are you going?"

"I don't want to wear out my welcome, I said what I came to say, now I'll go before I say or do something stupid."

I walked her to the door. After her coat was on, she kissed me on the cheek.

"Good bye Matt, thank you and I look forward to getting your call."

She was so gracious.

"Good bye Alice, thanks for coming over. I mean it."

When the door closed I felt like an idiot. I wasn't sure I'd handled that well at all, but I couldn't think of what else I could have done. I had not had a date in several years, well not one where I actually wanted or expected something to happen. Part of me felt like a teenager all over again.

I sat looking at the fire again, clearing my mind. I always tried to end my day in the palm of the Holy Spirit's loving hand, turning my sleep over to the Trinity. I kept hearing an inner voice, "Check email on messenger?" I knew I had direct connection with the Holy Spirit, so why would it send me message through email? The sense was persistent, so I opened my mail. I looked down the 55 messages awaiting my attention, most I could delete, even in the world of anti-spam and adware things got through. There was always someone out there one step ahead of the curve. Then I saw it.

To: Matt

From: R

"Dear Father Matt, you are a very clever man. Don't let your cleverness be your undoing, you have no idea what you are dealing with. Besides, if you back off, it will be more than worth your while. What that other pastor got is peanuts."

I felt so many emotions. Part of me was thrilled he was making contact. My heart raced. On the other hand I was angry at his writing. Not that I should have expected anything less. Clearly he was not coming around, this was one evil human being. I was always careful with notes like this not to read too much into them. I knew the police and the FBI analyzed them to death. This was clearly a bribe and a warning. The police wouldn't see the note. I hit reply

To: R
From: Matt
R:

Thanks for the note. I'll take a pass on your offer, I have more than enough financial resources already. I do have an idea what I am dealing with and I can only hope you change direction before it's too late. I'm not sure if you were making a threat, if so, I don't appreciate them. Just come in and let's talk.

Matt.

I told the email to let me know when he opened it and hit send. I did the dishes, watched the fire die down and was turning off the lights when the computer beeped, he'd received the mail. And replied.

To: Matt
From: R
Matt:
I'm coming, but it won't be for a chat. You've made your choice now I've made mine. There are a few others I have to deal with first. Hope you feel good about your decision.
R

That shiver went up my spine again. What was he talking about?

The coming days would bring so many challenges and surprises, I needed some rest, it had been quite a day.

10 BOB HAS A PLAN FOR SUE

Since my time with Mary's case I'd been mostly on the defensive. I was cautious, not wanting to sacrifice everything I had gained because my ego wanted something else. I went on the chat room, trying to see if anyone was acting suspicious. The only one I could find was M. He was always a cautious person anyway. Now I had his computer and before long, with the help of his crude diamonds and formulas I'd have a fortune. I chatted with many of the people I'd come to know.

Then Z arrived. It ruined my night. He was one clever person. I couldn't track his IP address, although I knew he was within 25 miles of my house. He was very pushy, trying to trap me. I didn't give in. Now the list of things to do just got longer, I would have to track him down before he got too clever. I'll have to give him credit, he didn't wait long. His ego was so large he thought he could handle me and set up a meeting. Well, he set up a messenger meeting which would lead to a face to face. That was his undoing. I don't care how far you are in the game, you can still die and you can't stop a bullet or knife, that is saved for the movies. I could hardly wait for tomorrow and what would transpire, but there were other things to occupy my attention.

I went into the lab and checked the pressure cooker. This was not an ordinary cooker. Were I to put a potato in here it would explode within a second. The pressure from this machine was about 25% of what was needed to make diamonds. There are other ways to create pressure and to transform matter. That was the secret I found on Phil's computer. I was glad he didn't link me with the fire, I would have hated to kill him. As I peered into the cooker I saw the diamonds glowing, I was close. Perhaps another few days. People find the transmutation of elements as something magical or absurd. Scientists will tell you energy is all that is needed, a lot of energy. Einstein showed how much potential energy there is in matter and the atomic bomb is evidence of his ideas. The challenge is creating and containing that energy. Nuclear reactors are probably the best example, but they are far too large. For millenia, the alchemist's furnace has proven to be a remarkable vessel for such work. What scientists fail to understand is the link between spirit and matter. The union of the two is what makes it all work. Physical energy contained by spiritual energy. Remember, the physical world was created by a spiritual being. My chief concern was my own spiritual journey. There were too many things getting in the way of that progress. I understand the eternity of life, how this physical phase is but a blip on the screen. Death is just an entrance into the next phase, so I don't really worry that much about killing, as long as it is in the name of future good.

Hurting Matt would only bring more attention to myself. Clearly his cop friend, Tom, was being kept abreast of what Matt was finding. I needed to find another way of getting his attention and knew exactly what I'd do. Matt cared about others, I'd get to him through them.

I created the bomb in my lab, a fire bomb. The house would incinerate so quickly there would be no putting it out. I always had to give them a sporting chance, a way out. I'd do it tonight and if she woke up, so much the better, I didn't really enjoy taking life. This one was very clever, it took me quite a while to find her, but she, like most of us, makes mistakes and leaves tracks.

I arrived at her beautiful home about 2 in the morning. All was quiet. She had a spectacular view and the city lights were laid out before me. This was a safe part of town and she left her kitchen window open. I threw in the bomb, the timer set for 25 minutes and left.

I wanted to be far away before it lit the night ablaze. Before I left I cut the phone line. The first of my several tasks was complete. The adrenalin was coursing through my veins, I felt more alive than I had ever been. This must be a sign that I am on the right track.

11

11 SPIRITUAL FLAMES IN MIND

I awoke with a start. My sleep had been peaceful until the nightmare, a giant fire, all consuming, night sky lit up, heat searing anything close. As I sat, covered in sweat, at first I thought it was symbolic of my life, perhaps of Alice. The harder I tried to convince myself of this the more I realized that conjecture was wrong. When in doubt, pray, so I did. Instantly and through no input of my own, I was attached to the web and focused in on someone that didn't know they were in danger. I could sense many bright spots on the web and could see many places where people were in trouble, but one stood out more than the rest. A brief glimpse into the intensity of omniscience convinced me I was glad I wasn't God. Something was very wrong and there was no time. I got dressed and headed for the car. Who and what could it be, I couldn't just start driving around the city. My eyes closed sitting in my driveway looking over the city. Then I saw the fire in my mind. Sue's house ablaze and she was inside, sleeping.

Lucky for me the streets were empty this time of day, unlike the rest of the time when gridlock seemed to be the norm. The city and state seemed to believe having construction on every major artery and freeway all the time was a good thing. Our tax dollars at work. Concentrating on the roads, my car flew around corners, going 60 on local streets wasn't that safe. I tried calling Sue to warn her but she didn't answer.

I ran two red lights not seeing anyone around and didn't really need to get stopped right now. Imagine me telling an officer I knew where a fire was about to be started and I was trying to save someone. I'd end up either in the nuthouse or in jail for arson. How did I get myself into these situations?

I was two blocks away when I heard and felt the blast. My foot pushed the pedal to the floor. The top of her house, her computer nest was gone. The blast had taken her house from being calm and peaceful to a conflagration in a matter of seconds. I'd been in her home enough to know where her rooms were. If she was home, she'd be in bed on the lower floor.

Looking in through the window I saw her in bed, probably knocked out from the concussion of the bomb. I threw rocks through the 8x8 foot double paned window. There was a hole in her ceiling, the stove sitting about two feet from her bed, she was lucky. The heat was already reaching her room, I grabbed a blanket and used it to keep the heat from my face. As I gazed up through what used to be her ceiling, I could see the sky where the roof once was.

I threw Sue over my shoulder and headed out, just in time, turning around to see the refrigerator falling onto her bed, crushing it into a flaming pile on the floor. I carried her to the car and putting the seat all the way back I laid her down. Then I thought of going back to get anything I could, but nothing would be saved, he'd seen to that. My eyes were transfixed by the absolute desolation before me. In a matter of minutes a home had been annihilated. People were already starting to come outside their homes to see what had happened. They would probably think a gas line was left on, somehow I didn't think that was the case.

The fire engines drove up and started to put out the blaze. The house was gone, there was nothing but a large burning pile of wood, metal and glass. I called the ambulance driver over and he took a look at Sue. Using smelling salts she started to come around.

"Matt, what is happening?" She didn't take long to discover her dream was gone. Tears welled in her eyes and I held her close.

"It's ok Sue, you're alive."

"What happened?" she said with a dazed look in her eyes.

I couldn't really tell her the murderer had just bombed her house with the EMT guy present.

"I don't know."

"You know her?" asked the EMT.

"Yes, she is a friend."

"And what might I ask were you doing driving around her house at 2am?"

Saying that I just happened to be in the neighborhood would sound stupid. "Do you have a phone?"

"Yes"

"Call this number, ask for Detective Tom Strom, ask him about Matt Peters."

"Wait a second, you are that priest guy that solves crimes."

"Yes."

"Are you working on one?"

I saw my way out.

"Yes, I was following a lead when I heard the blast."

"Wow, maybe God really does lead you to things."

"Of course he does." I remarked like a smart alec.

That seemed to suit the EMT and he left. I noticed people on the streets staring at the home, or what was left of it. I'd never seen a fire do this much destruction so quickly.

"Sue, this is my fault, I'm sorry."

"What do you mean?"

"The murderer sent me a threatening email, he is trying to get at me through people I care about. He bombed your house."

"How did you know to come and save me?"

"That will take some time to explain, another day, for now we need to get you out of here and to safety."

"How did he find me?"

" I think he is a better hacker than you gave him credit for."

I told the EMT to give the number I'd given him to the firemen, someone should call Tom and tell him to call me. I gave them my number and we left. The EMT driver wanted her to go to the hospital, but she signed a waiver. Driving home was much slower, Sue seemed to still be in shock.

"Do you think everything is gone?" I asked.

"All the hardware, I always keep a backup at a remote location."

"I'm thinking you should do that for me." I replied.

"You don't do it already?" Sue asked, obviously stunned by my lack of computer savy.

"No."

"Matt you are a slow learner. How do we stop this bastard? Pardon my language."

"You are forgiven. We are working on that, getting closer."

"Not soon enough from where I used to sit."

"I know.'

My day had been full enough. We sat watching the city lights for a bit and when I saw her starting to dose I took her to the spare bedroom and let her sleep. I too would try to catch a few winks before the new day started. Now I was angry. Instead of getting me to stop looking into the murder, I was about to redouble my efforts. I do realize that acting out of anger clouds the mind, so I meditated and prayed asking God to take the vengeance away and just help me see clearly.

Just as I was about to dose off the phone rang.

"Hello?"

"Matt?"

"Tom, I assume you heard."

"I'm here now, this guy is a bastard."

"Sue agrees with you, but she asked me to pardon her for her use of language. How did you put the pieces together so fast?"

"Fire, you, young woman, lots of technology—bomb, you figure it out," he said laughing.

"I thought all the technology was burned?"

"She has enough satellite dishes and other wires and stuff outside the house to make it obvious she is not your basic homemaker."

"I'll have to clue her into that. How did you know it was a bomb?"

"Gas explosions have a different burn pattern than a bomb, besides we smelled the plastique. You aren't the only one with a nose. Why did he do this and why to the woman?"

"He wants me to stop my search and she'd been doing some research for me, I can only guess he tracked her down—a known accomplice who could get in the way."

"My guess is his strategy didn't work. Wait a minute is the computer you took in that house?"

"You are such a smart detective, of course not, I'm more committed than ever and my guess is yes, the computer is gone."

"Did you look at those pictures I faxed?"

I'd totally forgotten with Joseph and Phil, Alice, and the fire. What a night. "Hold on."

I retrieved the faxes and started looking at them carefully. There were about 20 pictures, but eventually I found it, his talisman, right there on the lab table or what was left of it.

"Ok Tom, same guy. He left the same token at Mary's that he did at Phil's and my church. Here is another tip for you. Show the pic of the talisman to people at the hospital and the nursing home where those healings took place a while ago. He left one there as well. I'm sure there is one at Sue's too."

"This guy gets around. What makes you think this nut case did the healings? Doesn't really fit the MO."

"You'll just have to trust me on that one, it's all part of the escalation of what he is up to. He's already done enough crime to put him away a longtime. You can add bombing to the list, along with who knows what else. Any early idea what started the blaze?"

"Not completely, but we do know he used an incendiary device with magnesium and other high intensity metals along with the plastique. He wanted the fire to burn fast."

"On that front he was successful."

"You want to come down and share what we have both found?"

"Look Tom, I'd love to and will in the next day or two, but it's been a very long day and I have an early start tomorrow, I need to get to bed."

"Wimp."

"You've got that right. Night."

I took a quick shower and was asleep before my head hit the pillow.

12 BOB GOES TO A LECTURE

Having refined and purified the home of Matt's friend Sue, I decided it was time to pull in, to not do any more public things for a while, but to work on myself. I also decided to cease all communication with the outside world. It was to be a month of solitude, my own hermitage. I wanted the trail to go cold, they were getting far too close.

Before my self-imposed exile, I did decide to write Matt a final note.

To: Matt
From: R

Dear Matt:

I heard about the blaze. So sorry your friend was sleeping. I would hate for things to happen to other friends of yours and I trust you get the message. I'll be gone for a while, but I am watching----------closely.

R

While I needed Matt and Z out of the way, I could bide my time. They had taken control of the situation and I couldn't have that, so I took it back. Now they had to wait for me. I deleted my email account so even if they sent messages, I wouldn't get them. I would deal with them on my terms, when I wanted.

I still had hope for Z, Matt was a goner.

I spent the next several days reading old texts of alchemists, steeping myself in the vast tradition of the work. I plastered my laboratory with alchemical drawings and formulas and I had several chemical experiments going on at the same time. This is truly where I am most at peace, in the lab, doing the work. All alchemists find this to be true.

One of the pleasures of having land and an old farm with a barn is I could raise my own food again, just as I had in California. My feeling is if you eat meat, you should have the courage to kill it yourself. Buying packaged meat at the store so separates one from the reality of what you are eating. Not knowing how long I would be here, I ordered two cows, three pigs, 30 chickens, and 15 rabbits. They all got along well. My property was blessed with a large pond that I stocked with trout as had the previous owners. While I eat mostly vegetables, two or three times a week I would make something special. This week I stuffed one of the larger chickens I was raising. Having gone out and killed it and plucked it, I bathed its body with oil that had been infused with herbs. I've always thought I should have my own cooking show where I share my recipes and mix in a bit of alchemy on the side.

During my second week of isolation---I really shouldn't call it that because it connotes something negative, while in reality I relish the time and peacefulness---something in the paper caught my eye.

Priest to Start Series on Alchemy

The Rev. Matthew Peters will be starting a series at his church based on the understandings of alchemy. We all know Rev. Matt because of his work with the police department. He is a gifted teacher and shared with us why he was choosing this topic to teach on:

"I have studied alchemy for many years. Carl Jung, the great psychiatrist, used alchemy as a cornerstone of his theories. Alchemy is traced through virtually every culture on the planet and can be seen in writings from as far back as 3000 up to the present. While there is much mythology involved with alchemy, there is also a great deal of reality. My hope is to distinguish between the two and to give people some tools whereby they can deepen their self-understanding and their relationship with God."

We asked Rev. Matt if there was any connection to a case he was working on.

"At the moment, I'm more focused on this work than on any cases. There are some loose ends that will be coming together shortly. As the alchemist's would say, the peacock is about to get plucked and he doesn't even know it."

Much of what the pastor says is often cryptic and this was no exception. He is highly entertaining and even courts being wise. We encourage the community to join in this most interesting event. Wednesdays at 8:00pm.

I couldn't believe his audacity. A neophyte to the work and here he was teaching? Publicly? How dare he. I threw the paper down and started pacing, always a bad sign. I'd done well keeping him out of my mind, but now here he was forcing his way in again. On the other hand he didn't mention the case, so perhaps he'd gotten the message and was backing off. His reference to the peacock seemed like a direct challenge to me, although no one else would understand. He thought he could pluck me? I don't think so.

No one knew me or what I looked like. There was certain to be a mob there so what did I have to lose? For the next few days my home was filled with blissful music, the smell of gastronomic feasts, and the intense heat of the alchemical fire.

The lecture started late. Initially they were going to have people listen in the parish hall. That seated about 300. Twenty minutes before eight they announced everyone should move to the church. By the time we all moved and several hundred more joined us, it was 8:20. I couldn't believe this many people would come and listen to an amateur speak on alchemy. Perhaps he could be of use after all. There was certainly nothing wrong in bringing new people to the truth. I tried to meld in as best I could. I was quite social, introducing myself to many and finding a pair that I sat with. If Matt was watching, I knew he'd be looking for a loner, I'd come with friends. The key was to stay ahead of them, anticipate their actions, and then be on the offense rather than the defense.

Matt actually gave a better lecture than I had expected. He had clearly done his homework and as a speaker was quite captivating. For those who might be interested, because I am certain this won't be included in Matt's section, I'll include my notes. If you aren't interested, just skip ahead to the next set of lines. Most of this was found on the internet. I am told by Matt that resources can be found at the end of the book.

I put on a disguise, assuming in part at least that Matt was putting on this display to attract me. I didn't need to give them any more help than I already had. Mustache, glasses and earrings all helped distract the eyes from details and yet with this crowd I didn't stand out.

Alchemy History

"Hermes Trismegistus, " an Egyptian king and given this name by the Greeks, is thought to have been the founder of the art of alchemy. He lived about 1900 B.C. and was highly celebrated for his wisdom and skill in the operation of nature. The document attributed to him is the Emerald Tablet. The Emerald Tablet is one of the foundational alchemical documents from a historical perspective. From it all others flow. For those not versed in alchemy it will be meaningless.

The word Khem was used in reference to the fertility of the flood plains around the Nile.

By 332 BC, Alexander the Great had conquered Egypt. Greek views of how matter is made up of the four elements of nature - Fire, Earth, Air and Water, were merged with the Egyptian scientific ideas and ideals. The result was Khemia, the Greek word for Egypt.

When Egypt was occupied by the Arabs in the 7th Century, they added 'al-' to the word Khemia and al-Khemia meaning 'the Black Land' is now seen as a possible origin for the word alchemy.

Taoists in China wanted to combine external elixirs and internal processes. By using the chi, an internal source of life as well as minerals and plants, the believed they prolonged life.

Avicenna was a 3rsd century Arab scientist. He is thought by many to be the father of modern medicine. He also helped to bring Plato and Aristotle to the west.

EUROPE

A 12th century writer discloses the following: He helped situate alchemy in Spain.

"I, Artephius, having learnt all the art in the book of Hermes, was once as others, envious, but having now lived one thousand years or thereabouts (which thousand years have already passed over me since my nativity, by the grace of God alone and the use of this admirable Quintessence), as I have seen, through this long space of time, that men have been unable to perfect the same magistry on account of the obscurity of the words of the philosophers, moved by pity and good conscience, I have resolved, in these my last days, to publish in all sincerity and truly, so that men may have nothing more to desire concerning this work. I except one thing only, which is not lawful that I should write, because it can be revealed truly only by God or by a master. Nevertheless, this likewise may be learned from this book, provided one be not stiff-necked and have a little experience."

Albertus Magnus (1234-1314)was perhaps one of the best known and respected alchemists. He wrote a great deal about the work and passed his understanding onto Thomas Aquinas. Magnus is considered to be one of the 35 “doctors” of the catholic faith and Aquinas another.

Roger Bacon was a 13th century scientist who gave a stamp of authority to alchemy. A renowned scientist of his day, he helped propel alchemy to center stage.

Philippus Aureolus Theophrastus Bombastus von Hohenheim better known as Paracelsus was a 15th-16th century scientist and doctor. He is considered to be the father of toxicology and talked about the psychological underpinnings of disease.

Jean Baptista Van Helmont, was a disciple of Paracelsus taught about the chemistry of the human body. Van Helmont has been called the "Descartes of Medicine" for his probing philosophical discourses. But he was also an accomplished alchemist. In his treatise, De Natura Vitae Eternae, he wrote: "I have seen and I have touched the Philosopher's Stone more than once. The color of it was like saffron in powder but heavy and shining like pounded glass. I had once given me the fourth of a grain, and I made projection with this fourth part of a grain wrapped in paper upon eight ounces of quicksilver heated in a crucible. The result of the projection was eight ounces, lacking just eleven grains, of the most pure gold." He brought what he learned from alchemy into the day to day world around him.

Alchemy led to the development of many elixirs and amalgams as well as many apparatuses.

Two groups developed within the world of alchemy. The first group focused on the discovery of new compounds and their reactions - leading to what is now the science of chemistry.

The second continued to look at the more spiritual, metaphysical side of alchemy. This group split into two groups as well, one focusing solely on the spiritual and one seeking the spiritual through the material, continuing the search for the transmutation of base metals into gold. These led to the modern day idea of alchemy.

AMERICA

Rosicrucians fleeing religious wars and tyranny in Germany set up their lives in Pennsylvania. There, in Ephrata, hints of an alchemical laboratory were found in a wooden gothic structure they'd built.

Harvard was teaching the transmutation of metals into the late 18th century. The Governor of Connecticut and Massachusetts dabbled with quicksilver now and again as well.

Even with the death of New England's last known practicing alchemists in the third decade of the 19th century, alchemy did not completely die out. While there are many practicing alchemists carrying on the work in private and a few places more public, there are no real leaders of the movement at this time.

THE ALCHEMICAL PROCESS

There are four distinct stages characterized by the original colors mentioned in Heraclitus: melanosis (blackening), leukosis (whitening), xanthosis (yellowing), and iosis (reddening).

These colors were gradually replaced by the four elements: earth, water, fire, and air with their qualities of hot, cold, dry, and moist which corresponded to the three colors black, white, and red.

The blackness symbolizes the initial state of chaos or prima materia, prime matter. Out of this prime mater comes everything. Or it was thought to come back as a thing of many colors, sometimes described as a peacock's tail. From black to colors to silver to white, then the gold or sun state. This was done in a very intense fire. The red and white are the King and Queen who, at this stage, celebrate their "chemical wedding."

The alchemical process is exactly that a process, unique to each alchemist, no two are the same.
There are no fixed definitions or set order of stages in the alchemical process because each alchemist has his personal concept of his goal.

STAGES OF ALCHEMY

There are many stages in all chemical process. This is equally true of the spiritual process. Alchemy offers a wonderful metaphor for these stages.

CALCINTION

In the laboratory Calcination means heating a substance until it is reduced to ashes, usually over an open flame. In alchemy this process was symbolized by sulfuric acid at times because of its physical intensity and ability to corrode.

Psychologically spiritually, this process is where we "burn" away the ego and our attachments to more worldly things. The heat of temptation in the desert, the various trials and tribulations we all find in our lives are all part of the fire, the refiner's fire. Are we able to let go and find the depth of heart and soul to get through them as gold or do they etch their way into our being and pull us into regression?

Physiologically, this has to do with cleansing the body , finding a physical discipline, and intensely turning our bodies into the temples of God they were created to be.

DISSOLUTION

Now we take the ashes and dissolve them in water. Water in any state is eventually corrosive. In the alchemist's laboratory that nature is heightened. Iron oxide is often seen as the biproduct of this stage of alchemy in the laboratory.

Spiritually and psychologically we start to work on the unconscious and discover the soul within our natures. We look at those parts we either cling to that we need to let go of or we begin to discover those things we lost in our innocence. This is a stage of letting go, of letting God and the Collaborative Unconscious more deeply into our lives. Dream work is critical at this stage since dreams make the unconscious more conscious. We also start to see the world differently---as it is rather than as we want it to be. In modern times we aren't really sure what "pure" water is, in the spiritual sense it becomes obvious.

Dreamwork, meditation, contemplation, journal writing are all possibilities at this stage.

SEPARATION

"Now we isolate the components of Dissolution by filtration and then rid our laboratories of any unworthy material. Separation is represented by the compound sodium carbonate, which separates out of water and appears as white soda ash on dry lakebeds." In the laboratory it is imperative that things are purified, that we separate compounds and then reunite them in specific ways. There are a wide variety of ways of doing this. Filtration, straining, and boiling are but a few.

During Separation we face the reality of who we are, let go of that which holds us back and grab hold of that which moves of forward. We may find nightmares as our friends, our unconscious screaming at us because we are not listening or paying attention. We find our shadows and discover it is our friend, a part of us. It is finding the essence of what makes us whole and what gets in our way—separating the wheat from the chaff in biblical language. Ultimately, there is only one path that leads to gold. For many this is where they spend a lot of time, unable or willing to let go. Many chemical bonds take immense energy to break, we spend a life time attaching to the ways of the world, it is hard to take a different path.

CONJUNCTION

"Here we recombine the saved elements from Separation into a new substance. Conjunction is symbolized by a nitrate compound known as cubic-saltpeter or potassium nitrate, which the alchemists called Natron or Salt." This is a rebirth of compounds, taking elements to forge steel. In the laboratory we now have a series of pure substances, how to mix and merge them to bring us to the philosopher's stone is important. Too much of one and not enough of another changes everything. The Butterfly Effect plays an important role in this stage. Minute changes can have significant consequences.

Psychologically and spiritually, this is the merging of opposites at an elementary level. We bring together the animus and the anima, the masculine and the feminine. We unite our spiritual, physical, and psychological selves. Our emotional and rational natures reflect each other than being at battle. Intuition starts to become a stronger part of our day to day lives. The alchemists referred to it as the Lesser Stone, and after this level is reached, the student is able to clearly understand what needs to be done to find lasting enlightenment, which is union with the our deepest natures. We are more connected with the realms around us and synchronicities become more prevalent .

FERMENTATION

This is the stage of patience. Patience is a prime virtue during this phase of the journey. We allow chemicals to simmer, to meld the chemical bonds. By disturbing this too quickly we don't allow chemicals to mature into their new state. Many alchemists do not have the endurance to get through this process and wind up disturbing the new substance before its time. Good wines need perfect fermentation. Some fine wines continue to mature for decades or centuries.

Spiritually and psychologically we rest into "the new creation" which comes with a deeper union with ourselves and with God. We go through deserts as we allow this fermentation occurs. As we come out of our dark nights, ecstasy often takes place. Its arrival is announced by a brilliant display of colors and meaningful visions called the "Peacock's Tail" which we say a form of earlier in the process. Fermentation can be encouraged through various activities that include intense prayer, desire for mystical union, breakdown of the personality, therapy, dream work , and deep meditation. This fermentation comes ultimately from something external to ourselves. It is an internal process, not an external one. It is the work of the Spirit not of our minds. How do we let go?

During this phase the work things remarkable start to happen. We see things we didn't see, we have gifts and talents we didn't have before or the depth and passion of our talents deepen—especially when put into practice for the purpose for which we were given them. Many alchemists at this stage become narcissistic and the work breaks down and regresses. In the end, the Philosopher's Stone is not meant exclusively for the one who discovers it.

DISTILLATION

"We see the boiling and condensation of the fermented solution to increase its purity, such as takes place in the distilling of wine to make brandy. Distillation is represented by a compound known as Black Pulvis Solaris, which is made by mixing black antimony with purified sulfur. The two immediately clump together to make what the alchemists called a "bezoar," a kind of sublimated solid that forms in the intestines and brain."

All of us have the Philosopher's Stone within us. The bible says we must "die to ourselves to find ourselves."

True in all aspects of life. This is not dissimilar to dissolution, we purify that which has been discovered, getting rid of the last remnants of that which keeps us from being purely who we are created to be. Paul talked about praying three times for God to take away something he was struggling with---distilling. This comes near the end because the final threads in life we cling to are the deepest seated. At times we go from this stage back to the beginning. Alchemy is not a once through process, but one that takes place over and over again with different aspects of our lives. It is here we find that "peace that passes all understanding" in an ongoing and pervasive way.

COAGULATION

This final stage is where we are left with the purified substance of distillation. It is called Pulvis Solaris or Powder of the Sun. It is this substance which can turn anything into gold or perfect anything to which it is added.

Psychologically and spiritually, this is a mystical stage of permanent union. It is enlightenment, a sense of understanding reality as it is. There are only pure attachments This is where Paul claims that it is no longer we who lives, but Christ who lives within us. It is the unification that the mystics discuss, a merging of the sacred and the profane, anima and animus. This does not mean there is no unconscious, but we accept the mystery of it.

Physiologically, our bodies know how to care for themselves. We know there is no physical immortality, but were someone to achieve this state, they would live a long time. There is no guarantee someone will stay at this stage. You might think once you reach enlightenment you are good to go forever. Temptations are always around and free will necessitates we can choose to become unenlightened, to hand back the precious Philosopher's Stone.

It should be noted that many of these stages can take place at the same time with different parts of our laboratories, or spiritual selves. Each stage is not an all or nothing adventure. We distill and move on, only to return to distill at a deeper level.

The lecture ended with some questions, Matt explaining that many he couldn't answer because he didn't know enough—a vast understatement. He did say he hoped other alchemists would come out of hiding and help with things he didn't know. He'd be waiting a long, long time. I wanted to raise my long outstretched hand and give them the information they so desperately wanted, but I couldn't take the risk. How many knowledgeable alchemists were there in Portland? Three. I laughed to myself, now two.

Matt said a good night and came down from the podium. About 30 people surrounded him with questions.

"Pastor, you talked about the transmutation of matter, turning things into gold. Is that what happened at that other church that just received a large gift of gold?" a young man asked.

"Now that is an interesting theory. You might recall I didn't say anyone had ever achieved that goal, just that they tried. If someone had accomplished this feat, I would hope they would share the secret with me."

The crowd laughed.

"I am very interested in this work, where do I go to get help?"

"That is a hard question to answer because most alchemists are very quiet about it. There are some websites that give information and a few books out that have information, but as far as I know there are no groups actually doing the work in the Portland area. If I find them I'll let you know and will post them on my website. You can find the books and websites there or on flyers I left out front."

"Are you an alchemist?"

"As I said, I've been intrigued with the subject for decades. I find it hard to ignore a subject that has been around for millenia and has impacted virtually every major civilization on the planet. Saints and psychologists, artists, scientists, and writers, have all been affected by alchemy. There must be something there. On the other hand, I do not have a laboratory and no, I didn't make the gold and give it to my friend. I also don't believe alchemy is salvation, there is only one route to pure union with God.

"Is your public interest in the subject related in any way to a case you are currently involved with?"

Matt looked around, obviously struggling with his answer.

"As I've said before, my interest in the subject is long standing, the timing just seemed right. Thanks for your questions, but I must go." I didn't lie.

With that he turned and left. I was thrilled because clearly he'd ended his work on the case and I was home free. I would be on my guard, but felt as if I could do what I needed to do. The next test of power could now take place and ahead of schedule.

I returned to my lab and got busy. The smell of the woods, the fabric of the laboratory and the essences of what I was creating were all intoxicating. I had to sit down and catch my breath. The challenge at this stage was to keep things in balance, darkness and light. For all things I did that created, I needed to destroy, a balance must be kept. I thought I'd come up with two ideas that would do what I needed and keep the web in order. However, energy is like karma, only the universe really knows how things will shift. In the end, I didn't really care.

I put some Keith Jarrett piano music on to help rest my psyche as my brain worked feverishly. Making concoctions is both an art and a science. A non-alchemist could put the same ingredients into a pot and come up with a completely different solution. Shrodinger came up with the idea that experiments to some degree, depended on the one doing the experiment. Light acts as a wave if you want it to or as a particle if you want it to. Much of life is in the eye of the beholder. Alchemists seek to see life for what it is, without the baggage we attach. The process of eliminating all that stuff is tedious and difficult----but well worth the effort. The world of Noetic Sciences is bringing some of our work into the mainstream, but even they have underestimated the potential.

With alchemical formulas, the chemistry is 80% of the process and how things are actually created is the other 20, including the mental state of the creator. I'd meditated for four hours before I started and was quite meticulous with what I was creating. I had a good feeling.

13 MATT GIVES A TALK

I'd been preparing for these lectures for the past 30 years, the work had intensified since Mary's murder, but my intellectual knowledge about alchemy was fairly significant. I made a few notes to myself and an outline of the entire course. Tonight's introduction would be a bit of history, some psychology, a tad bit of chemistry and of course a good dose of spirituality. If I can't the audience how and why alchemy applies to their relationship with Christ and with God, then why do it? After all, I'm not running a university, I'm running God's church.

I had some coffee and did my morning prayers and bible reading. Luther had said that he couldn't imagine starting a day without a couple of hours of prayer, so he got up before dawn. My faith was not to that level yet, though I believed his insight to be true. I did center every day and do my best to ensure I was in the hands of the Holy Spirit before I walked out the door. I had good reason to believe that this day would find me more dependent on the Spirit.

When I got to the church a pile of messages were on my desk, I hadn't been in for a couple of days and everyone wanted a piece of my hide, certainly fair. Sometimes my office was a sanctuary, today it felt more like an office. I started going through the phone messages. Jill wanted to know about the wedding on Saturday, what color should the altar frontal be and did I have special requests from the altar guild for Advent? Advent is the four weeks before Christmas, it literally means "coming" and is the season where we celebrate both the coming of the baby Jesus as well as the second coming of Christ, at some point in the future. I'd been known to pull a few surprises on Sunday mornings and my doing so drove the guild members crazy. They were very committed to serving God's altar, to prepare the table and the surrounding environment in a holy and sacred way. They did their jobs well. But for me, God doesn't always work on a schedule. God doesn't always follow a pattern or the rules. I tried my best to think ahead and let them know, my intention was never to cause tension. I didn't always succeed. To Jill's credit, she never argued with my creative ideas. I told her about a couple I had in mind and she thanked me and said they would take care of them.

David wanted to talk about our work overseas. He was one of the wealthier parishioners and was very devoted to our international work. He thought it was time someone went abroad and checked on the work and he wanted to be that person. The conversation was short, I wished him well, told him I wanted the parish to pray for him by laying on of hands before he left. He was thrilled. A quick and easy conversation.

I saw the message from Alice and called her next.

"Hi Alice, Matt."

"Hi Matt, what's up?"

" I saw you called and just wanted to see how things were going?"

"Great."

"Glad to hear it."

"So can you go out on Friday?"

"That's in two days."

"You are very quick. Yes, it's in two days."

"Of course I'll go, where?"

"I'll pick you up at 7----it's a surprise." I had no idea where I was taking her.

"Good."

"There is something you should know."

There was nervousness in Alice's voice. "What?"

"A friend of mine's house burned down last night, she is staying at my house."

"Should I be worried?"

"No."

"I'm glad to hear that, so I'll see you on Friday, and don't worry about it."

"Thanks, Alice."

As soon as I hung up, the phone rang.

"Matt?"

"Hello bishop, how are you?"

"Better than you from what I hear?"

"And what does that mean?"

"For starters, you are dating a parishioner? A woman is staying at your house? You are giving seminars on alchemy? What are you thinking?"

"First of all where did you get all this rumored information?"

"I have my sources."

I knew who'd sent them to him. "Bishop, they came to you via email. Try replying to the email. "

"I did."

"It came back didn't it, the person doesn't exist."

"How did you know?"

"Because I know who sent them, someone trying to mess up my life."

"Who is he?"

"Well I don't know his name, but he is a murderer."

"Is this tied to the diamonds?"

"Yes."

"I don't want to know."

"That's why I didn't call you, plausible deniability."

"Are the rumors true?"

"To a certain extent, yes, but don't worry bishop, it's all ok."

"I hope so, we don't need another mess in this diocese."

"I'll try to avoid landing you in one."

For another two hours I chatted on the phone, took care of church business, signed some checks and then left for lunch. I went to my favorite restaurant, the head chef and owner knew me well and I always got great service. I sat looking at the river and finished my preparations for the lecture that night. I'd asked a friend to videotape the audience. I wanted a good look at every person, I had a feeling the murderer was coming. I also wanted it for a Podcast and YouTube.

The publicity I had set up for the lecture worked quite well. I was going to be thrilled if 100 showed up. By the time I started, we were over 500. The crowd was very diverse. There were young and old, well dressed and those who made casual look good. Most seemed to be seekers, people interested in finding a deeper sense of meaning in their lives and my interviews had clearly stated that this was a way to do find that meaning. My personality is one that gets fed by the energy of others. The more people around, the better my speaking. The reality is that I read and think a lot, but when the time comes to talk, either in a sermon or a lecture, I just let the Spirit lead me, and most of the time, when I get out of the way, the Spirit does.

I'd dressed casually, although I did wear my clergy shirt. Often I wouldn't wear my collar, my personal belief being that uniforms have a time and place, but living and sleeping in them are not called for. Tonight, the lecture being in my church and on a subject where most would not make a positive connection to the church, I wanted people to see that Christians could indeed either be alchemists are at least use some of their ideas to further their own journeys to God.

When the people settled down we opened with a quick prayer and I dove in. First I gave a brief history of alchemy, then I laid out the core stages and processes through which alchemist's work, both on a physical and spiritual level. I could tell as I looked at the audience that I had them hooked. I could have kept them there for 4 hours, but knew that if I wanted them to return I'd leave them wanting more. I'd had a clock put up in the back of the church so I could know what time it was without having to look at my watch, which in the middle of a church service sends the wrong message.

With 30 minutes to go I started taking about alchemy and Christianity. I'll admit that the whole idea of alchemy is still a bit foreign to me, I'll never become a Joseph or a Mary. I know how much of their lives they had to dedicate to get where they are and were. Their path was not my path, but their ideas still intrigue me. Partially because in the context of Christianity, it all fits.

I. The Awakening of the Self II. The Purification of the Self III. The Illumination of the Self IV. The Dark Night of the Soul V. The Unitive Life

I've included a few notes for those who might be interested in this final piece of the lecture.

The process in the Christian tradition of becoming one with God is perhaps best illustrated by looking at the process of mysticism and the best writer on this was Evelyn Underhill and her work entitled Mysticism. Within that book she outlines the stages of mystic union with God.

Self Awakening

The process of moving towards God starts with an internal understanding that we have a need for God. If we believe we can do all things on our own, that we have no need of the transcendent, we will not even start the journey. We may move forward with our humanity, we may be able to psychologically become quite mature, but humans are more than just our bodies and minds, we have souls, and the soul can't grow without becoming attached to the Creator. This awakening of our self is a deep sense of who and where we are in the universe. We learn perspective, that we are not the most important creature on the planet, that life does not revolve around me, that my ego, needs to disappear if I am serious about becoming one with God and hearing his will. This stage tends to be one of humility; as we focus on what is truly important, we find on the one hand how unimportant we are and yet how much God loves us. The lens of God helps us to focus internally, comments come our way (invited) that continue the process of becoming more humble. To be honest, many never really leave this level. They are unwilling to give up the ego, the live under the delusion of their self- importance and they can't let that delusion go. There have been many saints that were powerful people, but at the same time, they were humble, having a larger perspective in God's kingdom. Mother Teresa of our own time would be such a person.

If you are true to the process, you will ask yourself some questions: Who am I? Who am I in relation to God? What do I need? Do I need God? Why? Do I need humanity? Why? What beliefs, ideas, opinions and material things am I unwilling to give up?

These call for more than 30 seconds of reflection. Each answer comes with a cost. The bible tells us to count the cost. Please do.

Starbuck puts it this way: "Conversion," says Starbuck, in words which are really far more descriptive of mystical awakening than of the revivalistic phenomena encouraged by American Protestantism, "is primarily an unselfing. The first birth of the individual is into his own little world. He is controlled by the deep-seated instincts of self-preservation and self-enlargement—instincts which are, doubtless, a direct inheritance from his brute ancestry. The universe is organized around his own personality as a centre." Conversion, then, is "the larger world-consciousness now pressing in on the individual consciousness. Often it breaks in suddenly and becomes a great new revelation. This is the first aspect of conversion: the person emerges from a smaller limited world of existence into a larger world of being. His life becomes swallowed up in a larger whole."

You and I must have some kind of conversion experience.

In alchemy, the process of calcination is similar. On a mental state we give ourselves to the work, understanding that within ourselves we cannot accomplish what we want. We come to know that this is a process that takes heat. Changing the physical world came primarily through heat and pressure, but pressure causes heat. The center of the earth is thousands of degree hotter than the atmosphere, partially because of the heat of pressure. During this phase, we understand the fluid nature of reality, that all things are not quite what they seem. Hydrogen is hydrogen until it mixes with oxygen and becomes water. The rest of the alchemical process on a material side is discovering how to enable these changes to take place.

Purification of the Soul

Here, we are on the road. Ultimately, the more we rid ourselves of baggage and sin, the more we detach ourselves from the ways of the world and attach ourselves to the ways of God, the deeper the union.

A quote from Underhill:

"So, with Dante, the first terrace of the Mount of Purgatory is devoted to the cleansing of pride and the production of humility: the inevitable—one might almost say mechanical—result of a vision, however fleeting, of Reality, and an undistorted sight of the earthbound self. All its life that self has been measuring its candlelight by other candles. Now for the first time it is out in the open air and sees the sun. "This is the way," said the voice of God to St. Catherine of Siena in ecstasy. "If thou wilt arrive at a perfect knowledge and enjoyment of Me, the Eternal Truth, thou shouldst never go outside the knowledge of thyself; and by humbling thyself in the valley of humility thou wilt know Me and thyself, from which knowledge thou wilt draw all that is necessary. . . . In self- knowledge, then, thou wilt humble thyself; seeing that, in thyself, thou dost not even exist." You and I, in this sense do not really exist apart from God. In alchemy, matter does not truly exist outside the Philosopher's Stone. We seek it, because with the Stone we see things as they truly are. When we are at one with God, we see the world as God sees his creation.

How do we achieve this state? For Underhill there are two ways, one looking at getting rid of the negative and the other, to raise the positive. Again, Underhill?

" 1)The Negative aspect, the stripping or purging away of those superfluous, unreal, and harmful things which dissipate the precious energies of the self. This is the business of Poverty, or Detachment . (2) The Positive aspect: a raising to their highest term, their purest state, of all that remains—the permanent elements of character. This is brought about by Mortification, the gymnastic of the soul: a deliberate recourse to painful experiences and difficult tasks.

We are called to deliberately challenge ourselves, to enter deep self-reflection and overcome all obstacles that get in our way, that lead us to sin.

Alchemically, we start to break up the original compound. Dissolution is separating the different essences, eliminating the bad and keeping the pure. There are many ways to physically do this, just as there are many ways to purify ourselves. In the next stage, we physically separate each substance. We see them for what they are and make a choice as to which ones we want to continue working with and which ones are discarded.

Illumination of the Soul

When we have purged our bodies and souls of the baggage that keeps them from the mind of God, we have another conversion experience. We tend to have these during intense experiences like retreats, times of fasting, and dreaming. The world is illuminated by the light of God and we see all things clearly. The light always points away from the self. This is one way to tell true "prophets" from false ones. Cult leaders point to themselves. Television evangelists far too often lift themselves up—ignore them. Saints have always pointed to something greater than themselves.

This is the stage where things become much more experiential. This is where we read about wild dreams and visions, about God physically speaking to people, about the transcendency of our souls into a greater universe.

Underhill talks about this in three primary ways:

1. Practicing the presence of God. Here we feel God with us in and through all things. Whether it is while washing dishes as was true with Brother Lawerence, worshipping, working, driving kids to a soccer game, or having an argument, God is consciously present. Most

of the time our sense of God's presence comes and goes. Sometimes, like while in church, we might have a strong feeling of the Spirit. While deeply engaged at work, God may be very distant to our consciousness. To the person whose soul has been illuminated, God is constantly present. What happens in this context is that we feel the peace and love of God, as well as the power and wisdom. Our wills are more united with Gods. This is not however, unification. It is still transitory.

2. We view the world differently. Things are no longer as they seem, they are as God intended. Again, dreams and visions are common. The prophets had many visions, always as the world appeared to God, contrary to how we perceived it. Here we see the web of the spiritual world in its fullness. We know how we are interconnected and we are able to use those connections for the benefit of God.

3. Finally, internal energy increases dramatically. We have energy to share. Mother Teresa seemed to go and go, even though most of us would be exhausted working a day in her shoes. Because, as Paul says, "It is no longer I who live, but Christ who lives in me," we have direct access to the energy of God. Amazing things happen when we use this energy.

We also see during this stage the coming together of the Anima and the Animus, the male and female aspects of our personality. We understand that we are not whole without both, without not only acknowledging both, but using them. We have long known that men and women are different. We know what feminine characteristics are and what the masculine ones are. As we purify ourselves, we let go of those ego strands that keep them apart. Our minds begin to see and accept the part of our personality that we have denied. In our world, no one comes into balance naturally. Overall, our world tried to make boys be very masculine and ridicule the feminine. We tell girls that there are certain ways females don't act and things they don't do. Who makes the rules? God says there is no male or female, there are just his children. Illumination helps us to clearly see when to use our anima or animus, each has its place.

Alchemically, this is conjunction, the bringing together of substances that move
towards the Philosopher's Stone. The order and methods are metaphorically identical, amazing.

Dark Night of the Soul

All good things must end. Marx said that power corrupts and absolute power corrupts absolutely. We see this time and time again. Normal good people get too much power or too much money and become evil. Candidates for political office tell you they will be different than those in power, yet a year after they are in power, they are as bad as the last bunch. The cycle never seems to end, and the same cycle exists in our spiritual lives, sorry.

We all come to points in our lives when God seems absent. Perhaps he is busy with others, perhaps he is visiting another galaxy. I am good, he is gone. We'd become used to his presence and now we must cope with his absence. Our faith tells us that when we call out in anguish he should answer, yet all we hear is the dull echo of our own voice. Our souls enter a dark night, a desert in the spiritual wilderness. We feel impotent, powerless, and alone.

"Think not," says Tauler, "that God will be always caressing His children, or shine upon their head, or kindle their hearts as He does at the first. He does so only to lure us to Himself, as the falconer lures the falcon with its gay hood. . . . We must stir up and rouse ourselves and be content to leave off learning, and no more enjoy feeling and warmth, and must now serve the Lord with strenuous industry and at our own cost."

This is a very difficult stage, not only physically, but mentally and spiritually. We begin to doubt all we have struggled for. We start to question all we thought was true.

From where God sits, we are expected to move on faith, not needing to feel his full presence all the time while still knowing he is there. In reality, this is the last vestige of letting go of the ego. We are still clinging and God wants it all. He is willing to wait patiently for us to let go. We must look ourselves in the mirror and see who we are without any cloud cover. Within each human being lies a hero and a villain. Fortunately for the world, the hero wins out more often than the darker side. In order to die to ourselves, we must face, acknowledge, and defeat our shadow, our dark side. Part of this is accepting, yet controlling those parts. Another is to use that force to our advantage. There are far more heroes in the world than villains.

When Jesus was in the desert, this is what he did, he faced the potential darkest side of his being for he could have given in to Satan. He didn't. He chose the light, he chose to deny himself to find God.

But please understand, this is not just mere temptation. The dark night is not wanting a cigarette or having a bit of lust. That is child's play compared to this. The dark night tears at the very fabric of who we are, and don't forget, by the time you have one of these experiences you know yourself much better than 90% of the planet knows themselves.

In alchemy, there is a time when all substances become black. Alchemist's know it must come, but getting through it is difficult. Patience is a must, as well as endurance.

Fermentation and distillation are the key stages. Things are fermenting in the sense that they sit, they go through a foul stage before coming out fresh and different. The bible tells us to be renewed in our minds. The bible talks about not putting new wine in old skins. The soul is transforming itself into the image of God, squashing the ego in its path. When wine is fermenting, the vintner must have patience. Open the cask to soon and you have nothing, too late or too much air gets in, vinegar. The process of fermentation must be endured while creating the right environment. Wine casks are kept in very specific conditions depending on what is being created. Our spiritual souls must be kept in the right environment while they ferment. Our external lives need to be disciplined, just as they were to reach this spot.

Distillation acts within the fermented substance to finally cast out doubts, fears, and obstacles to God's grace. Distilled water is simply water with all the minerals taken out. If you leave a glass of water on the counter to evaporate, a very slight residue will be there when the water is gone. When you do the same with distilled water, nothing is left. A super filtration system takes everything out but the H2O. Our deepest selves and the Holy Spirit are slowly distilling our psyches so that all impurities are gone.

I hate to say it, but I doubt one person in this room, perhaps not one in the city will ever get to this state of being. So why mention it? You and I have to understand that all things are possible, that we have barely scratched the surface of what we are capable of doing and becoming. The responsibility for who we are rests with you and with me, not with God.

Unity of Self

Finally we arrive at union with God. An eternal union that is never broken. No more dark nights, struggles or doubts, must bliss, understanding, and enlightenment. For most of us, unity takes place after death, what a shame to not be able to see the world and humanity as God sees us. What a shame to not be able to use the gifts God gives us fully in this life.

Coagulation is the final stage when the distilled substances are brought together to form the Philosopher's Stone. It is the union of king and queen, the elixir of life, the birth of the eternal. All things are possible when knows all the rules of the game and what all the players are doing.

I am not going to say more about this stage because, I don't want to sound pessimistic, none of us will get there---and if you do, this lecture will seem like child's play.

I hope you have seen what some of the stages are in this spiritual process and how they relate to what the alchemists are doing. I have only given you a thumbnail sketch. There are volumes written on each if you are interested. Bibliographies are available in the narthex on your way out.

Wrapping up the talk answering some questions, finished with a prayer, and answered a few more before heading out.

I was exhausted, feeling like I had given every ounce of energy in that lecture, like people were pulling it out of me. Perhaps they were. I wondered if the murderer was there and thought about looking at the film they'd taken, but decided to wait till the morning. I left very grateful that so many people showed an interest and that my pastor friends came to support me. They were a group of local ministers who joined together each Thursday morning for sharing and prayer. Several were far more conservative than me, but we all believed in Jesus and the work of the Holy Spirit. They tolerated me well.

I opened the door to my house and my senses were attacked by the most amazing smell. Obviously Sue had been cooking. The aromas pulled me like a magnet to the kitchen. She looked right at home.

"Hi Matt, hope you are hungry."

She gave me a hug and went back to cooking.

"So what did you do with your day other than make a meal fit for the gods?"

"Well, to be honest, it was quite productive. I sold my lot to a developer for more than I bought the house for, bought a new house, and set up shop in a new temporary space."

"All in one day?"

"Why not?"

"I'm tired just hearing you talk about all of it. I couldn't have done one of those things in a day."

"You are too modest."

"Just honest."

I tried to sneak some pieces of what she was making, but she smacked my hand with the spatula. I backed off as I saw the glass of wine sitting for me on the counter.

"So I guess you won't be staying long?"

"The end of the week I move in to my new digs. You going to miss me?"

"Of course. Where is it?"

"I decided for a change of view. I bought a loft downtown. I see the city lights, the Sound, and the Olympic mountains."

"Wow, that's great. Enough room?"

"Of course!" She laughed.

"Cheers!"

Our worlds were so different that we didn't talk about work much. We tended towards politics and philosophical discussions. We always enjoyed each other's company but knew more than that would never happen. Relationships like that were treasures to me. There was no undercurrent about what else might happen, just pure platonic pleasure.

We ate and drank fine wine for two hours. I felt my mind drifting and told Sue I had to go to bed.

"I'll clean up in the morning, and thanks for such a divine meal."

"You're welcome. I'll invite you over to my new place."

"I expect an invitation within the month."

"By the way, Alice called to remind you to be at the restaurant tomorrow by 11. She seems like a very nice person."

I was very glad I'd told Alice about Sue.

"Yes, she is very nice."

"And thinks the world of you."

"Hmmm."

"In fact, if I didn't know any better I'd say she has a thing for you."

"She's a parishioner."

"Does that mean she can't have a thing for you?"

"No."

"Awwwww now I see, you might have a thing for her."

"Very perceptive, but that discussion will have to wait."

"Fair enough, but by then I suspect you will have more to tell."

"Undoubtedly."

I kissed Sue on the cheek and left.

My sleep was fitful, full of dark images. I was thinking that perhaps I'd entered the dark night of the soul. Then I saw myself laugh. I wasn't close to that experience yet. The dreams were still scary and when I finally got out of bed at 5 am, I knew something was going to happen, and it wasn't good.

In my prayers I asked the Spirit to heighten my senses during the coming days, to alert me to danger. I had a feeling the murderer was going to make a move, but had no idea what it might be. Recently, he'd taken charge and I didn't like the feeling.

15

14 MIRACLES FROM THE DARK SIDE OF LIGHT--BOB

Working in the lab changes the sense of time. I'd been working for over a week on the latest elixirs since the lecture and I was ready.

My first stop was the Harman Swim Center in Beaverton. I'd heard about this pool in the paper. Harman was the warmest water in the city because this is where they held sessions for handicapped people. I was impressed with the programs they had for a variety of ailments from obesity to arthritis, people in wheelchairs to the elderly. I was hoping to help their cause. I hadn't quite figured out how to get my five gallon container into the pool. The process would have been easier in the summer when the outside door was open. Now, in the winter, the temperature around freezing, the door was shut. I put on a little disguise and entered the building.

"Hi, how are you today?" I asked the lifeguard at the desk.

"Fine thank you, are you swimming?"

"No, I'm just here to collect a water sample." I'd put together an official looking document from the water authority that required me to take a large sample from the pool based on the idea that a chemical had been found in the neighborhood water supply and they wanted to see how many parts per billion were in the pool. I handed her the form.

"Wow, is the water dangerous?"

"Not at all, just a precaution."

"We treat our water."

"Probably not for benzene chloride." I tried to say it quietly, not wanting to upset the other customers or draw attention.

"True."

"So, can I get my sample?"

"Sure be my guest."

I went into the pool area with my container. While the liquid I was putting in was a bit less than clear, no one would notice, the pool being quite crowded. I was lucky the lifeguard at the desk didn't join me. I'd purchased a container with a large mouth. I watched the lifeguards on duty and then poured the formula in, filled up my container and resealed the top with an official looking seal. Another lifeguard came over and asked what I was doing. I gave him the same story and he went back to work.

I thanked the woman at the desk and left. With any luck, some results would be immediate. They would continue for a couple of weeks. Then it was onto part two.

I'd looked at the outreach schedule for Matt's church and saw they were part of a feeding program downtown on the 1st Sunday of the month. A little digging turned up the fact Matt was usually there and said the blessing but might not make it today. Perfect. He'd be ashamed he wasn't there to do something about it.

Sundays were very quiet downtown, not much traffic or many people. I'd made a large pot of soup, enough for about 50. The broth smelled divine. I was able to park right by the place where they fed people. I took my pot up and placed it on a table, along with paper soup bowls and spoons. Other churches and people from Matt's church were setting up and a good crowd was gathering. I chatted with a few of the people from the churches and a few of the homeless, not standing out, but at least letting my presence be known.

When Matt showed up I was a bit shocked and faded more into the background, watching and waiting. This time, the effects would be very quick, I could stay and watch and enjoy. Some would be happy for what I was about to do, others would be saddened. Everyone would be shocked, with nowhere to turn for answers. The media was about to have a very busy few days figuring out the yin and yang of all this. Had they been paying attention to Matt—attention seeking pastor.

16

15 DEATH AT THE SOUP KITCHEN

A message was on my machine. I had my phone turned off in my bedroom. My parishioners knew my cell phone number which sat on my night table in case of emergencies. They wouldn't dare call me in the middle of the night to chat. The regular answering machine was in the kitchen. There was lots of stirring about the lectures, all the crazies coming out of the woodwork to start a laboratory. I called my friend at Powell's books who asked that in the future I warn them about lectures so they could stalk up on books on the subject. I'd wondered if sales would increase. It was Sunday, gorgeously clear as Mt. Hood rose majestic in the distance. Some would be going skiing, some going to church, some having a leisurely day---and God said, "It is good."

"Matt, Joseph. Something is wrong, be careful today. By the way, what is the plan?"

I still hadn't come up with one. I was at a loss. All had been quiet for weeks. Joseph told me that alchemy—and spirituality—took patience. He believed the murderer was working on something special.

Throughout the morning, everyone was making comments about my seeming nervousness.

"Something wrong Matt?"

"Matt what's the matter?"

"Rough night Matt?"

"You don't seem your normal perky self Matt?"

"Father, should I be praying for you?"

"Matt, you need a vacation."

I could only take so much and left for a long walk n shortly after church. A plan was starting to take shape in my mind. The scheme had to be one that left no doubt who the murderer was while protecting Joseph, my parish, and myself. That's where the problems lay. This person didn't really seem to care who he hurt. The question was why was he lashing out, what did he need and was there a way of giving it to him without really giving it to him.

I loved walking in Portland at this time of year. There was a chill in the air, everything was lush green, and the air was always pure. Today was one of those magical days when the sky was blue and the mountains were covered with the early snows of winter. My mind seemed very settled here, surrounded by God's creations, the mastery of his creative power evident at every turn. I kept pondering until I figured out a direction to go. At the same time I realized how late I was to meet Alice and others at the soup kitchen downtown. I was in my collar, so I got to the busiest street and started hitch hiking. I didn't have to wait long as a gentleman pulled over.

"Hi, you need help Father?"

"Well, I could use a lift if you are heading downtown."

"Exactly where I'm going.'

I climbed into the Lexus.

"So what are you doing hitch hiking if I might ask?"

"I was out for a walk and then realized how far I'd gone and how soon I had to get to an appointment downtown. I was hoping my outfit wouldn't scare people off."

"Well I wasn't sure if you were a murderer in disguise or a priest, I decided to take my chances."

"Glad you did. I'm Matt."

"Oh right, the priest that works with the cops, I thought you looked a bit familiar."

"That's the one."

"On a hot case, are you?"

"Not so hot, but hopefully things will perk up. And what line of work are you in?"

"Retired."

"And what are you retired from?" I asked a bit puzzled because he looked quite young.

"I taught internationally for about 20 years. Every year I bought a new house and rented it out. Now I have 35 houses—they pay the bills."

"Wow, that is impressive."

"I see a bible on your back seat, do you go to church?"

"Yes, my wife and I attend Solid Rock in Beaverton."

"Fantastic ministry they do there, I'm glad you like it. Which of the ministries are you involved with?"

"My wife and I have recently taken on a foster child."

We had an outreach fund at the church that we used for special circumstances, I always carried a check with me to share our good fortune with others in ministry. I wrote the man a check for $5000.

"Here, put this towards helping the ministry," I said as I handed him the check at a stop light.

"Really? No wonder God had me pull over and pick you up," he said laughing.

"God does indeed work in mysterious ways. I know you will use it wisely. We're here. You can just drop me off on the corner, thanks for the ride."

I got out of the car and headed for the park where the meal was served. I was just in time. I noticed Alice starting to look for me.

"Hi," I said, giving her a hug.

"Hello," she replied kissing me on the cheek.

We'd gotten to the point in our relationship where everyone knew we were seeing each other, but we were not overly romantic in public.

"I like those greetings."

"Good. I think everything is about ready and we have a great crowd today because the sun is out."

"What are you serving?"

"For you pastor, nothing, I'll take you out after lunch," Alice remarked as she winked at me.

"Interesting, going out to lunch after lunch, why don't we eat here?"

"We can if you like, if there is food left."

"I wouldn't think of cutting in line."

We got everyone's attention, probably 150 people and I said the blessing. They were very tolerant as their stomachs growled, so I kept the prayer brief, after all, God doesn't need to listen to me for 5 minutes in order to bless the food while people are hungry.

There was a wonderful order to the meal, the homeless and poor being very gracious with one another, knowing there was plenty of food. They went through the line and found places to sit on benches, curbs, and the edge around the fountain.

I stopped.

Something was wrong and my senses kicked in. I looked around and noticed two people bending over. I ran to their side as they vomited. I screamed at the top of my lungs.

"Everyone STOP!!!"

They all looked up, wondering if I'd just lost my mind.

"Don't eat anything yet. Alice call an ambulance for those people."

"They're just a bit sick Matt."

"Trust me on this one, they are more than just a bit sick they've been poisoned."

I looked at the plates of those who were sick, tried to figure out what they had in common and then went to the tables. I tasted the stew first, letting it sit in my mouth, tasting all the flavors. One of the benefits of my gift was I could tell what was in something and how much. Colonel Sanders divulged his 11 herbs and spices to me a long time ago. I'd make it at my house and everyone wanted to know why I'd bought KFC. I loved going to the top restaurants and stealing their recipes.

There was nothing wrong with the stew. Next were some vegetables. The woman who cooked them was dishing them out, I didn't think it was her, besides she wasn't going anywhere. Then there was a giant pot of soup. I second I smelled the broth, I knew this was the home of the poison. I removed the pot, much to the chagrin of the crowd."

Not everyone had listened to me and there were a couple dozen people violently ill by the time the ambulance arrived---they called for several more.

"Sorry, a bad batch, " I said trying to calm people down.

I tasted it and while I couldn't determine what poison was laced in the soup this was where the death lay. I could feel his presence in the soup. The murderer had done this.

I called Tom and told him to send someone down to get the soup in order to determine what poison was used and if the cook left any clues on the pot.

Within 15 minutes the park was smothered with ambulances, the fire department and police, most of the homeless had moved out.

I asked the man who set up the tables if he remembered anyone putting it down.

"Yes, a nice gentleman from your church."

"How do you know he is from my church?"

"He made a point of telling me."

"What did he look like?"

"A good looking man, about 45, dark hair, mustache, glasses, and a good sized nose."

"A policeman will be coming soon, I'd appreciate it if you could work with him to see if you can help them come up with a picture."

"I'd be happy to help, what did he do?"

"I'm not sure, but whatever he did wasn't good."

I walked away just as Tom was walking in.

"Hey Matt."

"Hi Tom, glad you could come."

"My favorite spot for lunch."

"So what happened?""

"I noticed some people getting sick, so I tested the food and discovered that the soup was tainted. Trust me on this one, this is the work of our friend.. Hold on." I walked over to the person who seemed to be in charge of the medical teams.

"So will everyone be OK?" I asked.

"I'm sorry father, four are already dead, 6 are being taken to the hospital in serious condition, and another 7 seem to be doing all right."

I was deeply shaken by what was happening. I don't claim to understand God's ways, but I couldn't help but wonder why I didn't find the poison before people got sick. I didn't blame God or myself, I just didn't get it.

"It could have been far worse Matt, they were lucky you were here, do you think the murderer knew this would happen?"

"I don't think so, I wasn't planning on coming today until pretty late in the game."

"Can we help you maam?" Tom asked.

I turned and realized that Alice had been standing by me.

"Forgive me. Tom this is my friend Alice. Alice this is my cop friend Tom."

"Please to meet you Tom," Alice said with her winsome smile on her face.

"The pleasure is mine Alice, although I can't figure out why you hang out with this guy."

"Trouble does seem to follow him."

"I'll say." We all laughed.

The ambulances left and some other policemen came and took away the poison.

"Let me know what it is, will you?"

"Looked like beef noodle to me."

"Why don't you go have a bowl Tom?"

"Cute, very cute. Why did he do this?"

"He is exerting his power. Give me your phone."

"Why, where is yours?"

"I left it at the church when I went for a walk, I didn't want to be disturbed."

Tom handed me his phone and I dialed Joseph.

"Hello?"

"It's Matt."

"What did he do?"

"You knew?"

"I knew he was up to something, but I couldn't figure out when or where, did you get there in time?"

"Yes and no. Six died so far, maybe more, could have been dozens."

"The Spirit moves in strange and mysterious ways."

"No question about that. So what does this mean?"

"It means two things. First of all, at the stage he is at, he needs to have balance, for every evil act, there must be one of goodness. He hasn't made his decision yet, although he is very close."

"But his evil act wasn't successful."

"He doesn't know that yet, I'm sure you will be hearing about something amazing happening on the good side of life."

"And then what?"

"Number one, he will be very angry that someone stopped him. When he finds out that it was you, he'll go ballistic."

"Good, I want him agitated and on edge, not thinking completely clearly."

"He'll be on edge, but with fury comes power."

"I know, I plan on using that to my advantage."

"So you have a plan?"

"Yes I do, I'll call you later with the details."

"I can hardly wait. By the way, did you find the talisman?"

"I completely forgot, thanks for reminding me, bye."

I walked around the table where the soup had been and found the coin. What was I to do, announce to the world be on the lookout for this coin and if you see it, run?

"Tom, do you have your scanner with you?"

He unhooked his walkie talkie.

"Here, all yours, didn't really like it anyway."

"Call in and ask if there is anything strange going on in the city."

"You've got to be kidding, they will lock me up."

"Just do it."

"Headquarters, this is Tom, officer 2314, is there anything strange going on around the city at this time?"

There was a long pause.

"Hello, headquarters, do you read?"

"Yea, Tom, Rex here. How did you know?"

Tom looked at me knowing he'd lost another.

"Just tell me what's going on."

"Harmon Swim Center in Beaverton. Masses of people are showing up, traffic jams, almost a riot to get in, don't know why. They say they've never seen so many vehicles with handicap stickers in one place before."

"Let's go." I pulled Tom and Alice and headed to his car. "Put the siren on and get me there as quickly as you can."

We drove in silence. About a quarter mile from the pool, normally on a quiet street, we pulled over and parked, the street was a parking lot. People had abandoned their cars in the middle of the road.

As we walked past people in wheelchairs, people with canes and an assortment of others I chatted with a few.

"What's going on?"

"You haven't heard?"

"No."

"God has visited the pool?"

"What are you talking about?" Tom asked, a bit exasperated.

"People who swim in the pool are getting healed."

Tom stopped talking and walked faster. When we arrived at the pool, there was a long line, several hundred long winding along the sidewalk. We walked to the front of the line as Tom flashed his badge.

An officer stopped us at the door.

"What brings you into our district officer?"

"We think there may be a connection between what is happening here and a case we are working on. We'd like a sample of the water."

"Trying to sneak in are you?"

"No officer, I'm on duty. If you want to call my Captain, that would be fine. I will say that if you obstruct us from the pool and it turns out that you hindered an investigation, I'll have your badge."

The other officer had that look in his eyes that showed he couldn't make up his mind whether to challenge Tom and take his chances or let him through. Finally, wisdom won out. He took out his pen and notebook and wrote down Tom's name and badge number.

"Be my guest officer."

We entered the pool area. There had to be over a hundred people in the pool. The lifeguards were apparently keeping track of how long they were in. I asked and found out they were putting them into the pool in groups of 20 for 20 minutes.

I could tell from just the smell that this was not normal water. Then I tasted the warm pool and knew something had been added.

"Tom, we need a jar, I don't know how long the substance in the pool will last."

Tom left to find a jar. I went and started talking with people exiting the pool. After talking with about 10 of them I realized that whatever was in the pool seemed to help those with arthritis issues the fastest. They claimed they were walking better already.

I'd seen many false and real healings in my day. I knew that some people were so revved up by a healing service that they thought they were healed and their bodies acted like it. A week later, they were back to their old selves. I took names and addresses so I could follow up. Others said they didn't notice anything, but claimed they felt better. The blind did not see, and the lame did not walk, but clearly something in the water was having a powerful effect.

I called Joseph again.

"So, what was it?"

"He made something that he put in a pool and people are being healed."

"A big crowd is there no doubt."

"Word spread fast."

"That's what he wants. He wanted the good thing to balance the bad. Just out of curiosity Matt, if he'd been successful with the soup and 50 people had gotten very ill or died, which would have received more press?"

"The bad of course."

"Exactly, and he knew it. I believe he has made his decision about the direction his work will take him. We now have a very powerful, dangerous, and out of control enemy, we will need to act fast."

"Don't worry, within two hours his rage will be at a peak and he will be coming for me."

"What are you going to do?"

"No, it's what are we going to do, stay close to your phone, I'll be in touch."

"This has to end now," I said to Tom.

"And how might I ask are you going to bring that about?" asked Tom.

"Nothing dangerous I hope?" said Alice.

"Of course not." I lied.

"So what is the next step?"

"I have to call a friend and ask a favor."

"And what about us?" asked Alice.

"You are going home and I don't really care what Tom does."

"I'm not leaving you alone," she said.

"Alice, you have many gifts, but none of them are of use when dealing with this guy."

"And yours are?"

"Some are and for the others, I have friends."

"Just tell me when and where and I'll have the place surrounded."

"Can't do that Tom, he would know it before you even started. This is no ordinary person."

"So I gathered. But I can't let you do this alone."

"First of all, I won't be alone; secondly, I have a special role for you."

"Which is?"

"In due time, right now, get me back to the church as fast as you can, I have work to do."

16 BOB'S DISTRACTION

I was enjoying my wine, feeling good about my work. But the more I spent time thinking about life, the more I realized I had to make a decision and the reality was the decision was making itself for me.

Think about the situation this way. Yin and yang exist in the world. There is matter and anti-matter, good and evil. There is a balance of sorts. The world focuses on the evil in the world, primarily because that is what the media feeds us. You would think the world is rampant with evil the way things look. Evil dictators, drug dealers, perverts, crooked politicians everywhere----the evil never ends. Reality is far different.

Goodness has reigned on the earth for millennia. There is vastly more good than evil. Slowly the dark side of the world is being eliminated; the light is winning the war while losing some battles. Darkness is trying to win by being flashy and the strategy won't work. That's why they need some help. I'd be happy to side with the light, but they don't need me, I can't be a player on their team. I can be near the top of the pile on the dark side.

From my view, when things get too far out of balance, chaos begins. By helping keep a balance, I'm helping perpetuate the planet. Amazing, I can actually be good by being bad.

The beauty of energy is there is no good or bad, there just is. I love my house in the woods. I walk outside and instantly become aware of the necessity of balance. In order for there to be life on earth, there must be oxygen. To have oxygen, you must have oceans and forests to create that oxygen. I'd love to have the planet be warm year round and only rain twice a week, but if that happened we'd all die. We need heat and cold, wet and dry, darkness and light. With the power I am about to acquire I can start to tip the scales back into balance. I haven't decided how overt or covert I will be. No one will be able to touch me so which way I decide to go won't make a difference. I can be a dictator or I can work behind the scenes, I will be untouchable. At times the power overwhelms me, as if the force has a life of its own. But I know I am in control. I make the decisions, I have the vision. I will create rich from poor and take from the rich, a Robin Hood for some. I will give life and I will take it away as I already have. Power will flow to me, through me, and from me to those whom I chose.

The key now was three fold:

1. How to overcome the final hurdle and find the Philosopher's Stone
2. How to show the world my power
3. How to get rid of Z and Matt.

I'd thought about working on number one and having achieved that, 3 would be easy. But three was getting in the way of one. In fact, Z could keep me from getting what I need and want. That being the case, Matt and Z had to be eliminated. I'd tried to reason, but they are unreasonable people. I knew rushing into this was a mistake; I had to be methodical and patient. The key was to avoid being sensed by Matt or having Z track me down. The closer I came to the end game, the easier it was to find me.

Six hours had passed since my experiments. I went for a long walk, poured another glass of wonderful Oregon Merlot, and turned on the news. I was pleased with the first pictures—a line around the block at the pool. Police were all over the place and there were massive traffic jams. Word had spread faster than I thought. Then came the interviews.

"This is Jim Johnson with K2 news. I'm here at the Harman Swim Center where many have come, believing the water heals. This is Thomas Walker a man who comes to Harman three times a week because it is the warmest pool in the area and he has arthritis. Tell us what happened today Mr. Walker?"

"Well, like you said, I come here two or three times a week. I can't walk without my walker and the pool always gives me an hour of feeling better. When I got out of the pool today, I just felt different. I put my clothes on without sitting down, I don't need my walker and I don't have any pain. It's the water."

"So you believe you were healed in the pool?"

"There is no other explanation. You've talked with others, something is in that water."

"This is Mrs. Goldstein. What's your story?"

"I've had back pain for 30 years, I'm 82. Now I have none, it's gone." Mrs. Goldstein did a jig for the camera and the crowd roared with laughter and approval.

"Do you think the pain is gone for good?"

"I don't know, even one day is good, but I think it is here to stay---I'm going dancing."

Everybody around them laughs as she wanders away.

"It seems like something is happening here at the pool. One after another keeps coming out saying they feel better. Wait a minute, I think I see someone who might have an answer."

The reporter moved through the crowd heading for the front door. He grabbed the cameraman and dragged him along.

"Pastor Matt, Pastor Matt."

That got my attention. What the hell was he doing there? This was my show, how dare he. My anger was building.

"Pastor Matt, what brings you here? Do you know what is going on?"

"I'd say people are being healed."

"Did you have anything to do with this?"

Matt looked right at the camera, like he was talking to me.

"I've always had a special place in my heart for this pool and clearly God is up to something."

"So what did you do to the water Pastor?"

"Me? I am merely a tool for God's power and will."

"Then you did do something to the water?"

"You said that, not me."

"Well, did you?"

"I'm here, God is here, people are well."

"First he is a crime fighter, now a healer, what surprises does Pastor Matt have in store?"

"I can answer that."

"What?"

"I can answer that question, what do I have in store."

"And what would that be?"

"We are having a series of talks about alchemy. Come a week from Wednesday night and you will see things you've never seen before."

"More healings?"

"That is the least of it?"

"Can you give us a hint?"

"O geez, this is on TV isn't it. You can't put this part on, I don't have room for everyone."

"Right. Ok, fellas, let's go."

The camera went off. I threw my wine glass against the furnace, percolating in the middle of the room.

"Damn him. How dare he do that. He has gone too far, now he must pay and pay publicly," Bob said, his face turning red with anger.

They finished that story and turned to my other trial of the day.

"On a more somber note, 6 people died and many are hospitalized from apparent food poisoning at one of the outdoor soup kitchens today. Father Matt was there as well, here is what he had to say."

"This is a grave tragedy. We come to try and feed the hungry in God's name, I'm not sure what else to say."

"And you think it was food poisoning?" asked the reporter.

"It was definitely food poisoning, whether accidental or on purpose I can't say."

"You think someone may have done this on purpose?"

"If it was intentional they were not as successful as they wanted to be, but even one life lost is too many."

"Does that mean you are going to be on the case?"

"We have to wait and see what the police find and where God leads me, but I wouldn't rule it out."

"You heard it here; Father Matt is back in action, stay tuned for updates, back to you John."

I turned the TV off and started to plan. I had indirectly tried to hurt Matt, but I'd failed. Now I would have to take a more direct route. I still didn't want to injure him in anyway, that, in reality, would bother him. The key was to harm those whom he cared about, his flock, the ones he felt responsible for. I needed him to be off guard so when I did finally strike, his defenses were down.

I'd visited the church again on a Sunday and spent time at the coffee hour talking with some of the parishioners. Gossip is always rampant at churches, much of it true. Most of his flock adored him. They pined over him like some mythical figure. They loved how he used his gifts to get the "bad guys." Most of them didn't know much about what he was doing now, what case he was working on.

"What do you think of his alchemy lectures?" I asked.

"Superb presentation."

"Why do you think he is talking about this particular subject?"

"Haven't the faintest, but he is always into something interesting."

"Is he an alchemist?

They laughed as if I'd made a joke.

"I doubt it, he's far to grounded to be an alchemist," replied one elderly woman.

"What do you mean by that?

"Alchemists were mostly crazy people and there really aren't any around today—not real ones."

"You don't think so?"

"Are you one?" They laughed again as they said it.

"Um, well, no," I said trying to hide my interest.

"I will say Matt is pretty convincing, makes the whole topic sound fascinating. Just think what you could do with that kind of power."

"Yes, just think."

I turned away, listening, watching, and trying to figure out who would pay the price for Matt's interest.

Another woman had overheard our conversation.

"Dorothy, you are such a skeptic."

I couldn't resist. "Isn't skepticism a good thing?"

"Young man, there is a large difference between asking intelligent questions and doubting everything. My friend Dorothy tends towards the later."

"Just because I'm not a sheep led around my a leash doesn't make me a doubter, I just like proof."

"Then why are you in the church? God is not interested in having to prove anything, he wants you to believe because of faith."

"Blind faith?" I questioned.

"Well, ultimately, yes, but most of us have reasons we believe."

"And what might those reasons be?"

"Well, I feel God's presence within me, I see God's power around me, in others."

"How do you know it's God?" I'm fascinated by the beliefs of others. "Can human beings heal others?"

Dorothy jumped in. "My point exactly, God can't have credit for all the good things that happen in the world and take none of the blame for the bad things."

"I don't see why not," said the other woman.

I could already see this dialogue had taken place millions of times in the history of the church and the answer would not be found today. In back of me I heard someone talking about Matt, so I excused myself from the debate.

"I think she'd be a wonderful match for Matt," said an older woman.

"Well, they are birds of a feather," responded the older gentleman.

"Pardon me," I interjected, "is the pastor seeing someone?"

"Yes and we all think it's wonderful. Alice is a marvelous person and her personality suits Matt well. It's time he settles down," the woman remarked with a broad smile on her face, as if she'd made the match.

"Which lady is she, I'm fairly new here?"

"I didn't think I recognized you. I'm Ellen, and you are?"

"Bob."

"Bob what?"

"Bob Whitman."

They both extended hands to me as they introduced themselves.

The man, Sidney, nodded with his head. "Alice, to answer your question is serving coffee."

I glanced over and was struck by the stunning figure of Alice. After a few more minutes of chit chat with Ellen and Sidney, I went to get a cup of coffee. I looked at her name tag.

"Hello Alice, I'm Bob."

Alice carried herself well, a grace that few people had. "I'm pleased to meet you Bob, new to the church?"

"Well, I've been a few times, seems like a very friendly place and Pastor Matt is quite a good preacher."

"Yes he is, isn't he? I've been coming here for over 20 years and he is the best of the four Rectors I've heard here."

"And what else do you do here Alice?"

"A bit of everything. Altar Guild, Adult Education Committee, and believe it or not, right now I'm helping with the youth group."

"You are a busy lady, how do you find time to work."

"I squeeze it in."

Other people came for coffee, so I looked at her name tag again and then left the parish hall. I found my way to the office and looked her name up in the parish directory, writing down her name, number, and address.

At times I felt it was three steps forward and two back, but I had a few ideas that should slow Matt and Z down. Now I was about to turn up the pressure. I needed to be clear when I made my move and Matt needed to be distracted.

17 BOB GOES TO CHURCH

I'd been following Matt off and on for a while even before the recent events. He was a creature of habits and one of his favorite pastimes was attending Church on Sunday nights. Before you think he is a zealot, Church is the name of a weekly gig at a local Pub. I guess he finds it healthy to blow off some steam having a beer with friends and listening to good music.

The Pub was on the corner of an eastside neighborhood. Tattoo parlor next door, neighborhood slowly getting gentrified as much of the inner city was. Inside there were two sections; one where the music played and another with a pool table. While I wouldn't describe the venue as intimate, after all it's a Pub, the space is cozy. The clientele was amazingly mixed. I'd seen folks from their early twenties well into their seventies. Just about everyone liked to dance and the music made it hard to stay seated. Matt always came to the first set. I sat in back for a couple of Sundays watching him. He knew the band members and many of the regulars pretty well. I'm sure it was good for him to come to a place where he was not known and could blend in with some potentially non-religious types. Lots of tattoos and long hair filled the pub.

In the back of mind was what I was going to do with this place, how I would destroy it and who would not be joining in the after party. Poisoning would be difficult since the drinks came out of a tap other than the water and I didn't have a poison that was tasteless so I needed something to cover the slight flavor. Arson always worked best in empty buildings or where people were sleeping. Neither of those fit the bill. An explosion might be the best option. Plenty of chaos would let me plant the device, a timer would let me determine when it happened, and there was no security. There were bags and coats all over the place, a briefcase could sit there for days and not be found.

While Matt usually sat near the front, it wasn't always true. I had to figure out if he had to go in the blast or just scare him—or did it really matter?

Those who came to the pub were very friendly which made me a bit nervous. I decided after my first visit to go in disguise. In some ways it was like a church here. Same group of people at the core who knew each other, letting go of the woes in their lives for a couple of hours, singing along with the band when they knew the songs, dancing like a group of fundamentalists, and some quips from the band that could be mini sermons. I wanted to fit in so I watched and noticed a few people writing or reading—the ones who weren't dancing. I brought a book with me that slowed down the conversations and interruptions. You would think placing a bomb in a crowded pub would be easy, which indeed it would be. The challenge was in determining how much destruction and who to take out. I made the mistake of actually getting to know a couple of people and not really wanting to kill them. The bartenders were particularly nice and it was through no fault of their own they were in this place, but they would die. The irony is not lost on me that here in this "holy" church, a bomb would rip the sanctuary to shreds and dismember a significant number of people.

I'd done bombings before, but this was the first time I was going to take a life. In the past it was to practice, to create confusion so I could get supplies I needed without drawing attention to myself, or just because I liked to see things blow up. There were rarely investigations because no one was hurt. I usually tried to make it look like a gas leak and they were always done in different places so no one would connect the dots.

I noticed the band sold CD's and had a large tip jar that was passed around. I had no idea how much they were paid, but it was certainly less than they deserved. The weeks I was there I put in $200, they might as well enjoy their last weeks on earth.

The band was set up on a small stage, perhaps I should say crammed onto a small stage. A full drum set, several amps, five band members, three guitars, a bass, violin, and saxophone. Next to the stage was a covered piano that was pulled out now and then when one of their friend's would join them for the night. These were all very talented musicians who could pick things up very quickly. My first night there I'd purchased some CD's and had learned many of their songs. I enjoyed seeing the subtle differences between the studio and stage work.

When you listen, you can learn a lot about people. Turtle, one of the guitar players was a butcher at a local high end store. I chuckled thinking about who was about to be butchered. The cuts wouldn't be as nice as his work, but I didn't have time for that. Another irony of the work I did.

The backdrop for the stage was a cloth with large stars, alchemy. I felt called to this work, to this place.

I'd made a nice bomb. One of the places I'd done some "work" was at a demolition site in Pennsylvania, a mine. I'd walked away with about six pounds of C-4, a very nice plastic explosive. I set a timer in it, put it all in an old brief case and was ready to go. I'd set up the device so the timer was activated by a remote. When I saw Matt enter, I'd leave, push the button, and about an hour later, bye, bye. I was hoping they were in the middle of one of their great rock and roll songs. Might as well disintegrate while enjoying life. I knew of Matt's remarkable ability to find things, so I set a fail-safe mechanism. If they tried to open it, KABOOOM!!!!

I got there about 5:15, ordered a beer and a sandwich and sat down up front. I immediately put the bomb by the piano where it wouldn't be noticed. There were only about 15 people in the pub at the time. When it detonated there could be well over a hundred. I enjoyed my repast and moved to the front door at the opposite end of the building. As I got up, I put a special token of my appreciation on the amp and in the tip jar. I wanted to see Matt come in but not be forced to say hello. He had gifts that might let him know who I was. Inside, my heart was starting to beat fast, I was taking a chance that he might sense me just in his presence. Perhaps that was just paranoia.

This Church was not unlike other churches in that a lot of people poured in the few minutes before things started and into the start of the service. Roger, the drummer, usually showed up first with the drums. He loved to play tennis but was about to be given a serve he couldn't handle. But then he wouldn't be playing any more. Lex, the guitar, violin, and sax player was the second to arrive. He usually parked across from the front of the pub in his Toyota wagon. Took Lex awhile to set up and get everything tuned. I was thinking what would be left of his ears and fingers after the blast—fiddling days are over. Dave, who was the bass player (not the stock broker) had a car from the 50's---was a miracle it started to look at. He often came very early and played pool. Jimmy was the other guitar player, he'd just put out a new CD, too bad it would be his swan song. There were times the others showed up, plugged in and started playing with about a minute to spare. I was feeling sad that these fine men, many in their 50's were about to attend church in a different fashion—in their coffins. I was wondering how I could save them, but couldn't, so that was it.

Matt showed up with his cop friend, Tom. This was my lucky day. The stars were with me. They ordered some beer at the counter and sat up front. Matt introduced Tom to Roger and Lex and then sat down and started chatting. Once the band started, there was no talking; the music was far too loud for that.

My work done, I left and knew I'd see the results on the late news. They would be cautious as to what they showed. I'd probably see a shredded guitar (pun), pieces of a drum set, glass everywhere and perhaps a few body parts if the director was feeling like they needed some ratings.

18 MATT'S THIRD CHURCH OF THE DAY

I loved Sunday evenings. I tried my best to keep them free, not always possible but normally I was able to. Most people felt ministers must be exhausted after all that work in the morning. To be honest, worship filled me with energy. I usually needed something to calm me down after church. I often went out to lunch with some parishioners then went home and read a book or watched some sports on TV, not having a yard took care of that possibility. Shopping on Sunday's was crazy unless you loved waiting in lines, which I struggled with.

Believe it or not, I liked going to Church on Sunday evenings. This was no normal church. It was a band, the Freak Mountain Ramblers, who played at a local pub every Sunday night and called it church. Their brand of fusion of rock, country, bluegrass and who knows what else, was a bit of a religious experience for those that attended. I'd been coming for years as often as I could. I'd introduced many people to the boys and the pub, some of whom had become regulars as well. I probably knew about half the people there. I liked arriving early to say hi to the band members who came early and to talk with whomever I brought or to some others. Once the band started at 6:00 talking wasn't really an option. I have no idea why, but on this night I'd invited Tom and to my surprise he agreed, said he could use a break and had heard about the band.

We got there about 5:30 and ordered some dinner. I introduced him to Roger and Lex and we sat at a table right by the small stage. I tried to find ways of helping the band out. I'd commissioned a bluegrass mass for the church which they came and played for us during a service. It was a bit of a shock for the parish, but hey, they needed to be shaken up now and then. If you read the bible, worship is supposed to be meaningful, worshipful and fun. By the end of that service, people were dancing in the aisles. I'd also hired them for some fundraisers and auctions. I saw a few people I needed to say hi to, so I excused myself and moved around the pub. The engineer, the male lawyer with a ponytail, the woman who was both a drummer and a naturopathic doctor, a few guys my age who just loved to come and let loose, and a few students who loved the music. Dues paid, friend's made.

"So this is where you hide," Tom said.

"No one thinks of coming to find me here and I can't hear my phone. The floor shakes so much I can't tell the difference between the building vibrating or my phone."

"I could use a place like that now and then as well."

"Now you know, we'll see if you like the music."

"So what do you think this nut case is up to?" Tom asked getting serious.

"You want to know the truth?"

"Of course."

"He's up to no good. He is very dangerous because he is both a genius, focused on reaching the end of this process he is on, which by the way is very real, and he's a nut case. All those add up to a bad combination, I don't believe he is going to be making many mistakes, if any."

"Matt, all nut cases make mistakes, that's why they get caught."

"So you are telling me you solve all cases, there are no "cold" cases in your station?"

"Ok, ouch, you got me, but most of those are one incident cases. Very few serial type cases are unsolved. But before you ask, yes there are some."

"I think you will be able to add this guy to the list unless we find a way of bringing him out."

"And how do you propose to do that?"

"Not sure yet. I hate to say it, but we may need to see if he makes another move."

"You mean wait till he tries to kill more people."

"Unfortunately, yes. Doesn't mean I'm not working things, but I can only work with what I have and God hasn't shown me enough yet, don't know why."

"All in God's time I guess."

"Yes, all in God's time."

"Why do you think God does that, why doesn't he just take over the steering wheel and lead you to the house, save us and the world some trouble and grief?"

"That my friend is on my list of questions to ask when I get to heaven. Right now, I just count my blessings that we get the clues we do."

"Ok, I suppose I can be grateful for that. You have helped put some very bad people away."

"I take very little credit."

"I know, you give it all to Christ."

"You are catching on Tom, perhaps one day you will actually come to see."

"Don't hold your breath," he said with a laugh.

"I'm not, but I do have hope.

Tom had that cop look to him.

"Hi Matt, bring one of your cop friends tonight?" asked Roger.

"Yes, is he that obvious?"

"Just a bit and I know the circles you travel in. Sorry I wasn't more chatty earlier, had to get set up."

"Not a problem, glad to meet you," Tom replied.

"So what's the occasion?"

"Don't know, just had this feeling I should ask Tom tonight."

"Hmmmm, you don't think there is going to be a murder tonight do you," asked Roger with a smile.

Something stirred within me but I wrote it off as to my own paranoia. I was as good as anyone at shutting down the voice of the Holy Spirit.

"Not really a very good place to kill someone Roger, I think you are safe," I said laughing.

"Had me worried for a minute."

"Me too," Tom said.

"Any good cases going on right now?"

"Just a few nutcases out there taking lives and leaving destruction in their path," said Tom.

"You know what I call that?" I said.

"What?"

"Job security for Tom." We all chuckled.

"I'd be very happy to retire and have no crime, but it's a job and someone needs to do it."

"And I can't think of a better guy than you to be on the job."

"By the way Matt, are we set for that Youthfest in August?" asked Roger.

"Yes, we've got the permits and park all set. You are the heathen band and we have a couple of good Christian bands. Should be a lot of fun."

"We don't normally play for the younger set, should be a good time."

"Just watch the language."

"Hey, we can be good."

"I have my doubts, but I know you'll try."

Roger went and talked with the other band members as they drifted in and set up. Tom and I talked about family, the woes of the city, and the case at hand, not much new to add to what we already knew.

I could feel myself unwind as the band played. My feet tapping and hands keeping rhythm on the table. To my surprise, Tom got up and danced. I was not a big dancer. Now and then I'd join it, but that was a rarity. About forty minutes into the set I had one of those feelings. I tried to center myself in the midst of decibel levels that would challenge the Holy Spirit on a good day to get through. I started looking around, being attentive to details. It took me about 5 minutes but then I saw it, on top of the amp. I grabbed Tom with a frantic look in my eyes.

"What!!!?" he screamed in my ear. I pointed to the top of the amplifier. Sitting there was the token we'd seen before. He'd been here and wherever he left a token, he left destruction.

"Damn!!!!" was Tom's next line. "We need to clear this place out."

"Give me five minutes." I started to smell things. Pubs are a bit overwhelming when it comes to smells. I had to quickly let go of the 20 beers they had, the food, the human aromas of colognes, sweat and bodies. Even the amplifiers gave off smells. Finally I was hit by the smell of C-4.

"Tom, don't be nervous, but there is a bomb in here."

Lex was looking at us, knowing something was up. I waved and smiled. In this place I knew several things. First I must be close to the bomb or I wouldn't be able to smell it with all the other odors in the pub. Second, the murderer didn't have time to place the C-4 openly somewhere, it must be inside something he could bring, set down and leave. I looked around for a package of some kind. Within a minute I found the briefcase. I lifted it up and looked at the band pointing to it. Each of them nodded a no with a bit of fear in their eyes. I set it on the table and was about to open it.

"Are you nuts?" asked Tom pressing the top down.

"What, let's see if it's a bomb."

"Gee, let's just see if it happens to be triggered by some idiot opening the top," screamed Tom. "Why don't you just smell it?"

"Good thinking." I placed my nose against it and nodded my head.

He grabbed the briefcase and headed for the door. I followed.

When he got outside he looked around and seeing no one on the streets he threw bomb across the street. The bomb hit the pavement with a loud thud, the top opened as it slid under a car—Dave's car as I noticed immediately.

The explosion almost seemed to vaporize the car, and destroyed the one's in back and front. The fireball blew branches off the trees and knocked us on our rears. A few windows were broken by the concussion and debris and I could feel glass embedding in my face. Tom and I were lucky to be thrown down in back of a car as shrapnel blew over us. The car took the brunt of the force, had we been sitting down in the pub; let's just say a great deal of time would have been spent trying to figure out who had actually been inside at the time. While my ears were ringing I could tell the music had stopped.

One of the problems about being in an enclosed space when a bomb goes off outside is where do you run? You don't want to run to the bomb and yet staying inside feels unsafe. The music somewhat covered the sound of the explosion, but the windows shattering and people screaming quickly created mayhem. The pub emptied. Tom was quick to be on his phone to the station calling for the bomb squad. People were all over the place. Some just took off, others stood and stared. Those who had cigarettes lit them up. Some came out with beers in hand as if a parade was taking place and they didn't want to miss the show. No one knew they were meant to be the show and they'd been granted a reprieve to dance another day. Tom and I took a good minute to catch our breath and regain focus. Two of the patrons were doctors and were looking to see if anyone was hurt. I told them I didn't see anyone around. If someone had been in the car a doctor was not going to do them much good. I told them to see if anyone sitting near the windows had chards of glass in their faces. Because the thrust of the bomb at the window was behind us, Tom and I were pretty free of damage.

"Tom, thanks for not letting me open the case."

"I've lost track of whether you have saved my life more or I've saved yours."

"This one goes on your side of the ledger and I'll buy you a beer for doing it," I said.

"On the other hand, had you not found the bomb in the first place we'd be toast."

"Some truth in that, but still, I'll be generous and give you this one."

"Thank God for small favors and while I don't believe in things like this, that almost makes me cross that line."

"Not to get off topic, but how else do you explain what just happened other than God telling me?"

"You'd make a very good detective Matt, I have always told you that, you've got a good eye and nose for it."

"In your dreams Tom, in your dreams."

The band found us.

"What happened," asked Lex.

"Someone trying to make sure it was your last concert," I said.

"I knew some people didn't like us, but this is going a bit far, don't you think?" Roger put in.

"This wasn't about you, it was about me."

"Maybe you should think about not coming to church for a while," Turtle said. "Oh and by the way, our price just doubled for your concert," he said laughing a bit nervously.

Most people had no idea the bomb had been in the pub and that they were lucky to be alive. Police arrived and cordoned off an area to be checked for evidence. I was looking for the people whose cars had been destroyed.

"Hey," screamed Dave.

"What?"

"That was my car."

"I know, lucky you." Dave's care was older than dirt, most people wouldn't have given him $20 for it, but it ran and he liked it.

"Yes." He had that deer in the headlights look.

"What is this about Matt," asked Roger.

"To be honest Roger, I'm not completely sure and right now, the less you know the better. Unfortunately, you were collateral damage."

"How did you find the bomb or even know it was there?"

"Just be thankful I go to regular church."

"Pastor, we are always thankful for that," Turtle said as we looked at the destruction of the bomb, each having our own images of what could have been.

"You saved our lives, maybe we should do a free concert for you," said Lex.

"Yea, but on the other hand, if I wasn't here this wouldn't have happened."

"So you both saved us and caused it," said Dave the bass player. " I feel a new song coming out of this."

"Bit of a predicament and I look forward to hearing the new tune Dave," I said mustering a smile.

I gathered the band together. "Fellas, I think it is in everyone's best interest that we publicly say the bomb was not in the pub. As far as you know, it wasn't, I just happened to tell you it was. Agreed?" They didn't really have a choice and they all nodded. I knew they could be trusted. "And just in case someone decides to tell, which

I'm sure the word will eventually get out, I will be in complete denial and I don't think you have much evidence to prove there was a bomb in there---no video cameras as far as I know."

Tom and I were very aware the media would be here shortly, so we got our stories straight and agreed we had just come outside for a minute when the bomb went off. We kept our fingers crossed no one had seen us leave with the briefcase or had seen Tom chuck it under the car. It was dark so the odds were in our favor and as fate would have it, no one did. We would make the 11:00 news; a bomb had exploded under a car on the eastside, no one hurt and no explanation as to why. One of the stations interviewed Dave because it was his car and he was his normal calm self.

"I guess someone just doesn't like my music," he said smiling.

The dust settled, the air being as cold as it was, most people went back inside. The boys were going to play another set but the bomb squad put the kibosh on that, claiming we were invading a crime scene. All the patrons finished their food and drink and left. I'm sure things would have been different had parts of bodies been strewn all over the street and a building disappeared.

Tom and I were about to leave when I had a thought. Tom had taken the token but I just had this feeling we were missing something.

"Hold on Tom."

The band was putting their instruments away and sharing a beer. Roger was in charge of the tip jar. He counted the money and then laughed as he stood and was heading to the bar.

"Look fellas, glass blew all the way into the tip jar." He showed us. In the bottom of the jar were pieces of glass. He took them over to dump them into the trash.

"Wait!!!!" I screamed. Roger looked at me with crazy eyes, like there was another bomb.

"Let me see that." I took the jar from his hand. "Look around you, do you see any glass on the floor this far away?" Everyone looked around and shook their heads.

"What are the odds all the glass would have landed in the jar?"

"Zero," said Jimmie, one of the vocalists and guitar players. I was always amazed how three guitarists could work together so well, each had their own unique style yet blended in with any given song. .

I pulled out the glass, five pieces. I put one in each of the band member's hands.

"What do you these look like to you? Window glass?"

"If I didn't know better, I'd say they were diamonds," Jim remarked.

"Probably some cubic zirconium from a fan," replied Dave throwing them back on the table.

"I'll tell you what Dave and anyone else, I'll give $100 for anyone who wants to give me their piece. But I have to be honest, I think they are real, I think each of these is worth around $3000. My guess is that if you take these to a dealer they will tell you they have never seen anything like it. So it's your choice, you can keep it and take the chance it is worthless, give them to me for $100 or trust me and get your money---or make your wives, girlfriends, or yourself happy."

Each of them either put the rock in their pockets or wrapped their hands tightly around them.

"Matt, who put them there?" asked Roger.

"I have no idea, let's just say someone liked your music and you probably just had the best night, money wise, of your careers."

"Matt wait, that's evidence, you can't do that."

"Tom, there can be no link to the pub. We've already lied about where the bomb was, let this one go, we know what we need to know. Oh and band members, just so you know, you are now accomplices, so if you ever leak this happened, you'll go to jail." Those that were holding them quickly slipped them into their pockets.

"What are you talking about Matt? Just another quiet night at Church," said Lex.

Tom hated lying and knew his job was over if it ever got out. We'd done this before on other cases, fortunately things went our way most of the time. You might be reading this and saying, "By telling us this, they know he lied and will get him." I'll just say, it's part of the story, not everything in here is factually true, I add a few things to perk it up. There is no proof. Tom groaned every time we fabricated a story.

I was still feeling bad this had happened. The owner, a friend of mine was already boarding up the windows. His margins were very small and I appreciated the free music he offered to the community. I told him a friend would be out to fix the windows in the morning at my expense. As we left I called my carpenter friend and told him to send me the bill. I paid top dollar, but always moved to the front of the line. He actually offered to come out right then, but I knew the police would be working through the night.

"Was there a fight or something? Hope you are OK," said the window guy.

"No fight, just a bomb, turn on the news at 11 and thanks for doing this for me." Click.

It had been about an hour since the detonation. Tom walked over and talked with the bomb squad for a few minutes while I helped the lads load up their cars, the ones that were left.

"They say it was probably a briefcase---no surprise there. Early indications are C-4, with both a timing mechanism and a fail-safe if the case was opened," said Tom grinning ear to ear.

"Glad I brought you along tonight."

"Yea, quite the coincidence."

"And you know I don't believe in coincidences," I said.

"Yea, don't remind me."

"We will never know when he intended the bomb to go off will we?"

"Unfortunately no, that evidence is gone."

"My guess is we had 5-15 minutes. He either wanted to kill me or send a message, a very loud one."

"You actually believe he meant to kill all these people?"

"Yes. It also tells us he has been following me, knows my habits."

"Let me put someone on you."

"Thanks but no thanks, he'll be watching for that."

"So?"

"We need to draw this guy in, not scare him off."

"I may not be going out with you much until this guy is caught."

"You are going to be on the news to, smile."

The cameras came over to us, a reporter I knew.

"Hi Pastor Matt," he said.

"Hey Sam, how are you, got the night beat tonight?"

"Yes, mind giving us a comment?"

"Of course not."

"We are live outside the Laurelthirst Pub on the eastside where a bomb exploded about an hour ago, destroying three cars and breaking windows. Fortunately, no one was hurt. In the pub at the time was Pastor Matt, a well know priest in the community. So tell us what happened."

"My friend and I were inside, got a bit warm so we decided to come out and get some air. When we walked out the door, the car just blew up, knocked us down, which actually may have saved our lives."

"So there is no connection between the bomb and you or any case you are working on?"

"Not that I know of."

"You seem to be around these kind of things a lot Pastor," he said.

"Just lucky I guess."

"I'm not sure I'd see it as lucky."

"I get your point."

"And you are?" the reporter asked, shoving the mic into Tom's face.

"Tom, from the police department."

"Lucky you were here tonight as well."

"Well just having a beer with a friend. Wrong place, wrong time. I'm glad everyone is safe, that's all."

Tom was not very good on camera so the reporter came back to me.

"Any guesses to what this was about?"

"None. The car was one of the band members, I can't imagine they had enemies. Perhaps it was just a prank."

"A rather large prank don't you think?"

Tom giggled and under his breath said, "Just a bit."

"I suppose, but I know the police will investigate the matter and hopefully catch this whacko. I don't know why, but for some reason I don't think the car was his intended target."

"What makes you say that?"

"A hunch, a Spirit driven hunch."

"Well we know your track record on hunches, do you plan on following up with this?"

"Only if asked to do so by the police although at this point I don't know what help I would be."

"Officer, do you think Matt will be asked to look into this?"

"Well we don't often ask civilians to get involved, but Matt does have a good track record of helping the force. That isn't up to me, bombs aren't really my detail." Tom grabbed my arm, an indication it was time to go. I knew my sound bite would be on TV and the murderer would be watching and not pleased.

"Thanks Sam, hope you get it on the air." The band was standing there.

"Are you the band members Pastor Matt was talking about?" They all nodded, smiling for the camera.

"Whose car was the bomb under?" Dave raised his hand.

"Any ideas? Why you?"

"Ummm, no, maybe they didn't like one of my songs or wanted me to get a new car."

"That could be said for a lot of people," said Turtle. The band laughed.

"Turtle, they are your songs too, let's not forget."

"I'm not parking out front."

"Maybe it was some of your liberal bumper stickers pissed someone off," said Jimmy.

"They went a bit overboard for a bumper-sticker."

I was surprised how well they were all acting as if the bomb was intended to be under the car.

"Gentlemen, any last comments?"

"Come to Church, every Sunday at 6, right here, we'll be here, bomb or no bomb," said Roger, always marketing.

"Fellas, just so you know, they will take a total of about 15 seconds from everything they have taped. Nice try on the advertisement, but I don't think that will make the news.

I noticed the other stations and made sure I'd gotten my sound bite to all of them. As a matter of fact it did, and the following week they couldn't hold the masses that showed up.

The bombing was my fault and I was feeling bad. I knew the damage would have to be reported and I knew how insurance companies dealt with stuff like this. If they got any money it would take months and then the premiums would go up. I found the other two people whose cars were trashed. I asked for their addresses and they gave them to me without question. I'd make sure they were given an envelope with plenty of cash to buy a new one, cash that couldn't be traced back to me.

"Dave, I'm sorry about your car, I hope this helps," I said as I handed him a check for $5000.

"Um Pastor, the car isn't worth $2000," said Dave smiling.

The band laughed. "It wasn't worth $100," said Jimmy.

"Then it was worth having it blown up."

I went home shaken by this event. I was underestimating the depth of evil in this person. I'd have to be on guard more now and that in and of itself took energy. Strategies would have to change. If he was willing to kill friends where would he stop? This failure would enrage him even more. I couldn't protect everyone. I started to doubt why I got involved with these things at all. Perhaps I should just publicly announce I was not doing this work anymore. Then I realized it was a calling and turning one's back on a call from God is not a good thing to do, tends to fracture the relationship and I had no plan on doing that.

19 BOB GOES ON A RAGE HUNT

I was enjoying my wine, feeling good about my work. But the more I spent time thinking about life, the more I realized I had to make a decision and the reality was the decision was making itself for me.

Think about the situation this way. Yin and yang exist in the world. There is matter and anti-matter, good and evil. There is a balance of sorts. The world focuses on the evil in the world, primarily because that is what the media feeds us. You would think the world is rampant with evil the way things look. Evil dictators, drug dealers, perverts, crooked politicians everywhere----the evil never ends. Reality is far different.

Goodness has reigned on the earth for millennia. There is vastly more good than evil. Slowly the dark side of the world is being eliminated, the light is winning the war while losing some battles. Darkness is trying to win by being flashy and the strategy won't work. That's why they need some help. I'd be happy to side with the light, but they don't need me, I can't be a player on their team. I can be near the top of the pile on the dark side.

From my view, when things get too far out of balance, chaos begins. By helping keep a balance, I'm helping perpetuate the planet. Amazing, I can actually be good by being bad.

The beauty of energy is there is no good or bad, there just is. I love my house in the woods. I walk outside and instantly become aware of the necessity of balance. In order for there to be life on earth, there must be oxygen. To have oxygen, you must have oceans and forests to create that oxygen. I'd love to have the planet be warm year round and only rain twice a week, but if that happened we'd all die. We need heat and cold, wet and dry, darkness and light. With the power I am about to acquire I can start to tip the scales back into balance. I haven't decided how overt or covert I will be. No one will be able to touch me so which way I decide to go won't make a difference. I can be a dictator or I can work behind the scenes, I will be untouchable. At times the power overwhelms me, as if the force has a life of its own. But I know I am in control. I make the decisions, I have the vision. I will create rich from poor and take from the rich, a Robin Hood for some. I will give life and I will take it away as I already have. Power will flow to me, through me, and from me to those whom I chose.

I turned on the 11:00 news. At first I was excited, almost ecstatic as they talked.

"A bomb has exploded at a pub on the east side, details in a minute." I was puzzled because they showed the broken windows of the pub and a disintegrated car. There should have been more damage to the pub. I switched stations.

"Tonight's lead story is a bomb has exploded under a car on the east side, across the street from a local pub that was packed for Sunday night "church" as they call it—music and dancing. No one was hurt, but many were shaken by this event."

I screamed at the top of my lungs. Then I saw his face, once again on camera, talking calmly, claiming to know nothing about the bomb. Just happened to be in the area. He had raised the bar on the war. While I didn't believe he was indestructible I was coming to see he had vastly more resources than I had thought. It was time to change strategies and go after him more indirectly, make him suffer.

I did not feel like containing myself. I was glad I didn't have neighbors. My mind and body were filled with a rage I'd never known. Mary and Z had talked about controlling our emotions because they clouded our minds. I'd never felt more in control. I grabbed my bow and arrows and went outside. This time of year the elk always came down from the mountains. I fed them so they were constantly on my property. It didn't take long to find them. In my mind's eye I saw Matt as one of the elk. This wasn't sport, he just looked at me. I looked him in the eye and shot him. I didn't want to have to work, so I quickly shot him with the rifle. The others scattered as he fell. The first two shots took the edge off the rage, but I know I needed to do more. I grabbed the hatchet from the garage and proceeded to hack him up. By the time I was done my body was covered in blood. I lit a fire by the pond and threw my clothes in it, jumped in the pond to clean off. The slaughter of the elk and the intensity of the cold water calmed me down.

I stood by the fire, dreaming, refocusing, centering. Matt was now on guard, but couldn't protect all his friend's all the time. This time I couldn't leave things to chance.

Returning to the lab I gazed into the furnace. The seed diamonds Phil had given me were doing the job. I was thinking of telling him what the next step would be, but I had this sense he was already with Matt and Z, so no dice. The ones I had left as a parting gift at the pub were crude compared to what was happening now. I meditated for hours in front of the furnace. I had visions of those people in the book of Daniel thrown into the fire and not burning, soon that would be me. The heat made me sweat but nothing more. I felt attached to the furnace in ways that made intimacy with another human pale in comparison. I was being purified. Obstacles were literally being sweated out of my body. Now and then I would have doubts or visions of me going in the wrong direction—I let those drip out of my soul in sweat.

In one corner of the furnace I saw the small cauldron I was using to create gold. The colors had been changing over the past weeks from red to white to black, silver and slowly moving to gold. Another month at most and I'd be complete. I tried to not let the excitement lose my focus, but it was hard.

After an intense evening in the lab I often slept for 18-30 hours. I woke refreshed and clear headed.

20 MATT'S DISCOVERIES—INTERNAL AND EXTERNAL

I went home from the bar once again feeling like my body had been pushed beyond the brink. Every ounce of energy had been torn from my soul. I collapsed on my sofa, I don't even think my head hit the pillow before I was asleep. I woke up at 3 am after having a dream of Joseph talking to me----which he was.

"Awwww the sleeper awakes. I hope you don't mind that I helped myself to building a fire and some wine. Don't worry I didn't open your best, although you do have a nice cellar."

"How did you get in?"

"You didn't even bother to close the door, let alone lock it. I had a feeling this was not a good night for you to be alone."

I sat up, rubbed my tired eyes and just looked at him dumbfounded. "Joseph, you are a very strange man, but I appreciate it."

"I'll take it as a compliment, warranted or not. Quite a day you had from what the news had to say."

"So you saw me?"

"It was hard to miss you. You were on the ads for the news, every station and I saw you on two national news shows. I'm surprised the vans aren't parked outside your house."

"I know how they cut and paste, did they wipe out everything about the meeting in two weeks?"

"Fraid so, if that was your plan."

"Do you think he was watching and got a bit mad?"

"Of course he was watching, he lived to see his miracles and destruction. Having every ounce of glory taken from him and put on you----I can't begin to imagine his rage. God's very wrath may not be as large.

The pool and the lunch events were bad enough, which by the way they reminded people of."

"Well let's not go that far Joseph, remember, God did obliterate the planet once."

"I'm assuming this was part of your grand plan."

"Of course. I know far too well how people don't think clearly when they are in a rage; they react rather than plan and think. The teeter totter keeps going back and forth, for a while he has had the upper hand, now I've got it back, feels good."

"Do not let your guard down for a second, I feel you are already underestimating him. He has far more powers than you can imagine."

"That's where you come in."

"I know I'm intuitive, but I can't protect you."

"I just expect you to do your best. Oh and one other thing."

"Yes?"

"I need you to gather as many people who well on their way as you can. I need them at the meeting."

"You are hoping he'll be there?"

"Joseph, I'm counting on it and I hate to show my doubts, but I'm not sure I, even with God's help can beat this guy."

"On that count, I think you are right."

"Sometimes I wonder if giving humanity free will was such a great idea," Matt said with a heavy heart.

"Matt, I don't really think you mean that, but I do understand."

"You're right of course. Now if you will excuse me I need some more rest, I have several big days ahead. And I may be needing your help again, I'll let you know. Do you think he will strike again?"

"I don't know, I have my doubts, but he is way off track and staying off the spiritual web."

"I didn't know that was possible."

"You sacrifice certain things, but yes it can be done. If he is going to do something big, he'll have to reattach in order to get the energy he needs, but there might not be much time between when I sense him and when he acts."

"All right well, stay in touch." With that he left, as quietly and quickly as he had apparently entered. I locked the door, set the alarm and went to bed, in my clothes.

I'd planned on getting on some of the talk shows in town to plug the upcoming events and talk about all the activities that seemed to be buzzing around me; explosions, healings, poisonings. I liked starting my week off in the church, in silence, listening, absorbing, and feeling.

The light through the bright stained glass windows always gave me pause. They poured colored light onto the pews and in their abstract way outlined major events in the bible. All in all a very worshipful service for me.

My energies were now on the murderer and I had a hard time focusing on other things, even though I needed to. I talked with CeCe about the upcoming event that ended at my house, checked in with the ladies about the bazaar---the chit chat seemed to have ended and the men were gleefully back in charge of the meal. The next couple of days were taken up with business and church work. I didn't have time to be a full time detective. Most people know that I take Wednesday afternoons off.

I was in my office packing my bag when Alice walked in and closed the door behind her.

"So where are we going?"

"For?"

"For whatever. I'm not leaving until I hear that we are spending the afternoon together."

"I guess that takes care of a relaxing after noon watching a movie on my couch for me.

"I'm up for that."

"Really, you are up for that?" I was impressed.

"As long as it's action, I don't have the attention span for drama."

"Hmmmmm, almost sounds like a challenge, but for now, let me finish packing and we'll go. I got the new Bond movie."

"It's not in the theaters yet," Alice said surprised.

"I have some connections."

"Full of surprises aren't you pastor."

"I do have a few up my sleeve."

"You do know word is spreading about us.

"Does that bother you?"

"I'm more concerned about you Matt."

"Don't be, and word has been out for a while, the bishop called. One sighting is all it takes and we make the National Inquirer of church gossip. While I feel our relationship is evolving fairly quickly, I do think it is evolving. We are both grown-ups and can stop the train at any time."

Slowly she pushed me against the door. "I currently have no intentions of stopping the train." She planted a kiss on my lips. As usual, I didn't complain.

We spent a quiet afternoon at my house, primarily because we unplugged the house phone and turned off the cells.

Our conversations always flowed so well. There was no pressure to be anything other than who we were. We talked about art, music, God, and politics. We didn't agree on everything, but we'd known that for a long time. The one thing we seemed to avoid talking about was us. On my part it was intentional. We weren't going to be tying any knots soon so we just decided to fully enjoy one another rather than being pushy. I did enjoy having her in my arms and I could certainly envision her in my house. I was falling in love, or perhaps I had been for a while and was just getting around to admitting it.

We cooked dinner, enjoyed an evening by the fire and I took her home around nine. While we did fall asleep on the couch for a couple of hours, I was still tired and would need my energy. I always try to be a gentleman, even though I fail at times. I took her to her door, a lovely condo not that far from my home and kissed her goodnight.

My car is fairly tidy, a place for everything. I carried a few CD's with me, each in their respective boxes. A bit of jazz, folk, old rock, and classical, to fit any mood I might have. I noticed a CD in a cover I didn't recognize. Since no one had been in the car other than me, I couldn't figure out where it came from. Maybe someone gave it to me at church and I just forgot about it. Or perhaps they dropped it in through the sunroof as a gift. It said Matt on the CD, so I put it in. As soon as I heard the voice I pulled over.

"Well hello Matt, I'm sure it won't take you long to figure out who this is. No I haven't gone away, although in hindsight I probably should have left shortly after I got what I needed from Mary. You are turning into quite a nuisance. I try to do things and you undo them. I do this, you do that. You trust your God too much. I'm not happy about you taking credit for the healings--—saving those poor slobs downtown he wouldn't be missed if they died. I'm amazed and puzzled how you found the bomb, that was a sad turn of events, made me change my game plan since you are so clever. That is the point isn't it? I'm balancing things and you are keeping things off balance. Not good. I wouldn't want you to lose sleep, but you are never safe, do you understand, you are never safe. I know your every move and at a time of my choosing you will be hurt and then you will die. You think you are in control. That is an illusion and a delusion. I am in control. Soon I will be unstoppable. I am so close to getting the Stone----and I'm sure Mr. Alchemist knows that is true. I need to do a few more things, then I will be ready for the final act and then my friend, history will change. It's too bad you won't be around to see it. Your glory hog days are about to end. I hope you enjoy the one's you have left. By the way, I'll be sending Z along with you. He has worn out his welcome on this planet. Enjoy the wait."

My body cringed at this voice. I didn't really worry about the threat, I'd had those before. There were many people who didn't like me, well that is being kind, who hated every fiber of my being. Fortunately, the Spirit always seemed to warn me it was coming. I wasn't as confident this time and that made me more nervous than anything. I always wondered if my clock was ticking and someday the Spirit would say, "Sorry Matt, this is it" and bingo, I'd be gone. All of us somewhere in the recesses of our minds have a list of questions we will ask God when we die. God will have to block out a few days to get through my list. I suspect God is more than up to the challenge and will enjoy putting me in my place.

I arrived home, cleaned up and went to bed. I didn't think he'd try anything for a little while; he wanted to punish me first, set things up. It wasn't a matter of if, but when.

The flurry of media attention around the poisoning, healings, and bombing carried on into the middle of the week. Julie did a great job of diverting calls I didn't want. There really wasn't anything to add and my suspicion was the murderer was not going to be watching, he's had enough. Now the attention would merely increase my ego which was not the point, that was all for show. In reality I didn't really enjoy attention, I much preferred passing it on to others.

Magicians are great at misdirecting the observer for sleight of hand tricks. I was trying to divert attention as a distraction for the alchemist and as a crowd pleaser for the rest. I needed the attention and energy of a lot of people. Besides, I had one more media blitz in me for the session next week, but there was a lot to do before then.

My primary goal this week was to strengthen and deepen relationships: God, Alice, Joseph, other alchemists, Tom, and my parish---- in that order.

Building bridges with God is pretty easy when we are honest with ourselves. God sits waiting and when we take the bait he reels us in, a very natural process. Most of the time humanity fights nature, very sad indeed. I carved out four hours each day for the next 10 days to spend with God. Some of those times were at 1 in the morning, but I was there. My normative way of being with God is to meditate, Insight Meditation, a Buddhist method of clearing the mind. They would have me let go of the voice of God, but I tend to ignore that step. In the midst of my meditation three things kept coming back. God is patient but tends to get annoyed with me when I don't listen and obey.

The first was to return to Mary's house, there was more there of import. I got in my car and drove over. Winter had finally set in, the back yard was all but bear, no one taking care of the garden. I brought a flashlight knowing the electricity was off. I'd gotten the key from Tom who asked to join me.

"It's a spiritual thing Tom, sorry, I promised God." He understood and let me go alone.

I felt sadness upon entering. The police tape was still on the house and I'm sure it wouldn't be taken off till her estate went through probate. They found a will under her pillow. Everyone wanted a piece of the estate and people were coming out of the woodwork claiming to be her heirs. Her diary and pictures made it clear there were no heirs and I was standing in what was left of the estate. When I entered the lab I could feel her presence, physically feel her presence, it took my breath away. I don't personally believe it's possible to talk with the dead, but somehow she was there. Her warmth and wisdom, grace and power were all present. I stilled my mind and listened. I was called to the basement. I was unclear why I was back at the house, certainly the police had made a thorough investigation. The basement was dark and damp, a quick look showed nothing here other than a furnace, an old one. I was told to listen. Then I heard it, the sound of cooing. I followed the bird noise. I found a door in the wall and opened it. Inside was a pigeon in a cage. The side opposite what I was looking at had a door that was open---to the outside. The pigeon could come and go. I remembered being in the backyard earlier and seeing multiple bird feeders and a pigeon at one of them. I thought it a bit odd a pigeon would be in someone's backyard, but thought nothing of it. I wasn't sure what to think now. Attached to the cage was a piece of paper.

"Matt: If you are the one that found this, good job for listening, there is hope yet. If someone else discovers this, please take the bird and box to Matt and don't open the second note. If my murderer gets here first---- it isn't over till the fat lady sings."

I appreciate Mary's sense of humor. Inside the envelope was another one, and on top of the cage was a small box.

"Matt: I can only hope you are the one reading this. First of all, this is a very special bird, a special type of carrier homing pigeon. Trust me when I say this, the bird knows where the murderer lives. Before you get excited there are a few things you need to understand. First the bird must be released from here when the time comes.

Second, you need to have a general idea of where the murderer is because the bird is fast and the GPS unit you attach to the bird is only good for a couple of miles. There is no way you can keep up with the bird. I'll let you figure that one out. Finally, don't release the bird until you are confident the alchemist is either engaged in the final throws of his work or is in chaos. He knows I am after him, even from the grave and will sense it when you let the bird go. Finally, and I hope you are reading this fast, grab the bird, the cage, the box, and run. I think he has cameras on the building and has bugged it, my guess is he is about to blow you up."

I didn't need to think about this one. I grabbed the bird and box and flew out of the house. We ran down the street, taking the hand of a middle-aged woman and her child about to walk past the house. We were a hundred feet down the street when the concussion hit us. I turned to see a large cloud of smoke come from under the house, where I'd just been. Then the house simply melted into the hole. Slowly I walked back to the house, what was left of it which wasn't much. Probate would go more quickly now. No damage was done to the neighboring houses. Within minutes people poured onto the streets and the sirens were coming.

The bomber certainly knew what he was doing. He'd placed the explosives to cave the house in on itself, not obliterate it.

I placed the call. "Tom, you might want to come to the house."

"You aren't what the explosion was about I hope."

"Ok, so the house that used to be here and isn't anymore is a hallucination?"

"Damn."

"My sentiments exactly. Bring the bomb squad, they are going to get tired of seeing me."

I tried to comfort the woman and her son and after a few moments they left. There was no fire, just debris. About 20 minutes later Tom and the squad arrived.

"I need to know if it was set off remotely or by a motion sensor." I'd done a preliminary look around and didn't see any cameras or cables, but I was no expert.

"Do you mind me asking why you have a bird cage in your hand?" Tom asked.

"Another present from Mary, I think it might come in handy soon."

"Care to explain?"

I handed him the note.

"Wow, this is great, let's get cracking."

"The time has to be right. We have one shot. If we let the bird go at the wrong time we will either lose it, he'll kill it, or he'll move. The bird can't find him now because he's not going to be living here, since here doesn't exist. Poor bird probably needs grief counseling. You are just going to have to trust me on this one---and don't tell the chief."

"I rarely tell the chief anything you tell me and he doesn't ask. Separation of church and state he always says."

After about 20 minutes one of the members of the bomb squad came over to us.

"Motion detector in the front door. Bomb was in the basement under the lab. House foundation exploded out and then the house collapsed on itself. Kind of like those buildings you see. Whoever did this I think was hoping a bunch of people would be in the house. How long were you in before it went off and how did you know?"

"I was in about 10 minutes tops. As to how I knew, I didn't I just wasn't in very long." Once again I lied, but this time my fingers were crossed behind my back and I hope that counted.

"A very lucky man."

"Luck my ass," said Tom. The bomb squad looked at him quizzically but didn't ask any more questions.

I took the bird home and set it on the porch. Mary gave me good instructions on the care and feeding of the pigeon and told me not to worry, it wouldn't get lost even though it may disappear for a while.

Joseph was sitting in the café when I arrived. The Pearl district was the center of the art world in Portland. Lots of funky cafes and hangouts. I liked meeting down there, seeing what was new in the windows and chatting with the younger crowd that tended to spend more time there than in the west hills.

"I think you've had an exciting morning."

"I'm not surprised you knew, but why didn't you give me a warning, even Mary did---and she's dead." I laughed.

"Matt, while I was Mary's teacher, she had some things on me. Because she spent more time with people, she was far more intuitive and could see the future much better than I. I just get general ideas, she could see specifics. I'm glad she lent a hand."

"If she hadn't I'd be sitting in her basement with her home on top of me, literally."

"Well I'm very glad you got out in time. Now, more to the point, what are we doing?"

"I appreciate your cutting to the chase Joseph." We spent an hour going over what we knew and what I was contemplating doing to trap the murderer. In the end, Joseph wasn't truly a believer, but he had no alternatives and agreed to everything I'd ask for. We parted and I didn't think I'd see him again until my seminar in two weeks. My laptop was on and we went on the chat room and to a list of email addresses Sue had obtained for me of the major alchemists that Joseph and Phil knew about. They were clued in to what was going on and how we were planning on dealing with the issue. If any of these people decided to or had already gone over to the murderer's side, we were in trouble. Joseph didn't get any feeling that this was so and I breathed a sigh of relief.

The second thing I was called to do was spend time with Alice. That wasn't a problem. We both made time in our schedules each day to have lunch or go for a walk, sit by the fire or catch a movie. But each night I felt this wasn't what God wanted. By Thursday I'd figured it out, we were meant to pray and meditate together. She giggled at first finding it odd that we would do it and then both of us wondering why we hadn't done it before. In my experience there is little that compares with the intimacy of prayer and meditation between two people that are in love. We tend to bond on very human levels; our intimacy is often purely physical. The ultimate bond in a relationship is being joined together in and through the one that created you. In meditation you clear away all the human baggage and exist purely in the presence of God. We were both taken to a different place. No words were needed. We did this for about 40 minutes even though it seemed like hours. When we were done we opened our eyes, each beaming with a smile, our hands caressing each other's, tears streaming down our faces. After that we simply held one another. We didn't talk about the experience for weeks; we felt it was almost a violation of what occurred. We also knew it wouldn't always be that intense. I knew why God had called us to do it. While we were meditating I saw the spiritual web. I felt God, Joseph, and myself attaching Alice more fully to us. She was being pulled into network of grace and power in ways she didn't understand. I had a sixth sense it would be an important connection in the future.

Friday night I figured out the third item on God's agenda: Go to the beach. My nature is to question everything. There was so much to do and so little time, why go to the beach? I was having fun with Alice and feeling pretty calm, what was this about? Tonight I didn't question, I tried to be like Samuel: "Yes Lord, your servant hears and obeys." I called Alice and told her to be ready a 6 am for a beach trip. She laughed and said fine.

The trip to Seaside is a short and easy one. Things get busy on Saturdays, but hitting the road early meant we wouldn't fight traffic. We'd be coming back when most people were heading out. Route 26 takes you out of the city through the vineyard country of Yamhill County. Then you head into the coast range, a low range of "mountains" with wonderful smells so different from the city. Finally you find the river and follow it to the ocean. We went to the beach where Lewis and Clark are said to have camped. Always fun to be part of history. What would they think today? I still didn't have a clue what we were doing here other than going to the beach.

We walked up and down the beach for about an hour.

"Stop." I heard the voice as clear as day. I looked around and saw no one within a hundred yards of us and it wasn't Alice.

"Pay attention Matt, look, learn, and listen." Remarkable how quirky God's voice can sound.

"Ok Alice, we are here, let's just stand." I had Alice in front of me, my arms wrapped around her as I watched the surf, the tide coming in, now and then moving over our feet, our shoes on my back.

I'm as dense as the rest of humanity, perhaps a bit more. Some parishioners would say significantly more. I also love metaphor and God knows it. Slowly I let go of my thoughts. My Zen master I had worked with during seminary told me that part of the point of Zen was to get us to see reality differently. "You will never become enlightened through your mind, it only sees one small part of reality, one small piece of the truth. To see it all you must let go." I let go and the ocean exploded in front of me. A sea so vast, called many names by humans; the Pacific, Atlantic, Indian, Red and so many more, and yet, just one. Without the sea there was no life and the sea itself was filled with life, almost an infinite variety of creation. The surf had always been one of my favorite songs; I could listen to it for hours. At times a ballad and at others, a symphony. Never ceasing. I looked at the sand, each wave revealing and hiding things. Tide moves in showing a sand dollar, foam covers it and when the water goes out, the dollar is gone. Brief revelations we either grab or lose. Tiny pieces of gleaming shells or agates shining in the sun, being uncovered by the forces of God. I watched as birds landed right on the edge of the water line, hunting for food. They knew where God put the food. The water felt warm on my feet even though I knew it was 48 degrees. Perhaps I was numb. I watched the seagulls soaring overhead and remembered the story of Jonathan Livingston Seagull—being true to himself. I turned for a moment and saw the power of the ocean, the mammoth logs piled high where the winter storms had dumped them, now simply driftwood to play on and burn. On and on, the metaphor building, seeing alchemy at work right in front of me, holding that which I loved being caressed by the sands of time and the hand of God. Was I in heaven? Finally, Alice turned and kissed me. We turned to walk back to the car. Just as we turned away from the water I heard the voice one more time.

"One more look."

We turned just as a grey whale; no more than 200 feet from shore surfaced and blew its spout. It and two other whales circled for about five minutes and then went under and left.

"That was stunning God, thank you," I said out loud.

We walked back to the town in silence, breaking it over breakfast. My driving has been considered a bit fast by some. Normally it takes about an hour and a half to get to the beach. I made it in just under an hour going and just over an hour heading home. We made it back to my house for lunch. I've always said you know when you have been touched by the Holy Spirit because you are changed-----Alice and I were changed.

Three amazingly powerful experiences, all different, all unique, in less than a week. Don't ever underestimate God. The metaphor of the sea would last deep in my heart for a long, long, time.

I'd covered all the bases I needed to during the week, save one and that was the next meeting.

Big Red's is a nice restaurant not far from the Zoo. Not overly busy on weekends and yet busy enough, I found Tom sitting in a booth when I arrived. We hadn't talked since the bomb;

"I haven't heard from you so I'm assuming the rest of your week has been fairly quiet."

"Fortunately, yes. And just so we are clear, I'd be very happy if things like this didn't happen to me."

"I have my doubts, but I am glad you weren't hurt."

"I know I've been quiet for quite a while, but I'm ready to lay it out for you."

"Good, I was starting to have my doubts, thinking you were going to do one of your Indiana Jones' routines."

"No, I just didn't want us chasing wild gooses."

I told Tom everything I knew and everything I surmised. Then I laid out my plan on how to draw the murderer out and catch him.

"So let me get this straight. You and God will draw the murderer into a trap. There a group of alchemists will subdue this animal while a bird shows me or someone where he lives just in case he doesn't show or escapes."

"That's about it, but the way you put it makes it sound crazy."

"Matt, it is crazy."

"I guess, but that is what I have." I tried to sound like I knew what I was doing. In reality, I didn't have much of an idea.

"You know what is really wild?"

"What?"

"In a strange kind of way, it might actually work. I must be as insane as you are."

"Or perhaps you are starting to believe."

"In your dreams my friend, in your dreams."

"It's already happened there."

"What?"

I let it go and moved on, talking about some details that still had to be worked out. We spent some time talking about family and friends. He needed to know I believed in him. He'd given me information about some research he done around the country looking for things I knew the alchemist would eventually need. There were some leads he and others were following, a few in Portland. But I knew this guy only let tracks be seen he wanted seen as a distraction. His mistake would not come via a slip on a credit card, but on his self-confidence and ego.

Home was calling me, I needed to bake the big pot of soup for the youth group meeting at my house tomorrow afternoon after church. I was making chicken corn chowder and a chili. I put up my feet and read the paper, the aromas taking me to another time and place, catching my breath for what lay ahead.

21 BOB'S BAD KOOL-AID

I love Sunday mornings. Somehow the air feels crisper, textured in a unique way that I feel in my pores, not just another day on the wall calendar. I always cook myself a special breakfast on Sundays. The more deeply I have entered into the world of alchemy, the better cook I have become. I'm sure that is not a coincidence. My senses are heightened and I have an intuitive ability to know what will go well together.

Fresh coffee, nice chocolate croissant out of the oven all helped start the day off right. There were times when I wished I'd had someone to share them with, to cook for, one of the downsides of the life of an alchemist. That was about to change, at least temporarily. I bought my Sunday paper on Saturday so I wouldn't have to go out and spoil the day by being part of the grocery mobs. There was little news about anything that pertained to me, but there was a full spread on Matt. That too would change, he would fade and I would grow. Today was the beginning of the end for him and my breakfast tasted all the better for it.

I decided not to attend church, not wanting to push my luck. Instead I went for a long walk, communing with the forces of nature. I felt the trees lowering their branches for me. The firmament was my grounding as my spirit soared into the clouds. The mist that lay around me, coated my skin with the primordial soup I was close to controlling. These were the times when life was complete, the world and I becoming one. I felt the intricacies of its webs, through the ground making connections with all of life, every living organism feeding me and I them.

Matt's recent egocentrism still bothered me, I felt the anger in my heart, but my mind was clear and I knew what had to be done. I checked Matt's church's website and saw his sermon would be on line that afternoon as a video, I'd watch it when I returned.

Around 11 I loaded my car and left for the city. I sat in my car, just down the block from Matt's house so I could see the comings and goings. He arrived with a smile on his face. I waited 10 minutes and then made my call. Now I had to wait to see if he took the bait.

Alice, sweet Alice, and the kids arrived shortly thereafter. Within a minute, Matt left. As soon as he pulled out, I drove in and knocked on the door. Alice answered.

"Oh hi Bob, what brings you here?"

"Wow, Alice, you remembered my name."

"Well, I guess I have a gift for names."

"True. I thought I'd see if I could help with the youth group today?"

"Matt had to leave, sure come on in."

I said hi to a few of the kids and did what needed doing in the kitchen.

"Alice, do they know that Matt had to leave?"

"No."

"Ok. Hey kids, Matt won't be back for a bit, everyone get a drink, let's have a toast."

We all filled our cups with Kool-Aid.

"Here's to a wonderful group of people, a great leader (I looked at Alice), a wonderful priest, and hopefully some good times ahead. Cheers."

Everyone said cheers and guzzled their cup. I put mine down. The effect wouldn't take more than ten minutes. I was a bit surprised they drank so easily, not really knowing who I was although Alice had introduced me earlier.

The smaller ones were hit first. They went into the living room and sat down.

"I feel a bit funny Bob," said Alice.

"Hey kids, why don't you all go in and get comfortable in the living room?"

They filed into the living room, dragging.

"Listen carefully Alice. I have just poisoned you all. I am the only one with an antidote. If you go quietly with me the children will live."

She had the look of horror in her eyes, but I could see she'd resigned herself, besides, within minutes she'd be asleep, along with the rest of them. I helped her to the car and then went back into the house. The 20 students were all asleep. A price had to be paid.

I loved it when plans went smoothly.

The ride back to my house was quiet. I carried Alice in and set her on the sofa. She looked beautiful. Her grace filled the home. I was sorry her life had to end, but she would be living in and through me for a long, long time. Our marriage would be a unique one. Male and female had to become one in order for the Philosopher's Stone to be born.

While she was still asleep I called Matt's house.

"Hello?"

"Well Matt, how was the hospital."

"What have you done?"

"Don't fret, they are only asleep, they will be waking up soon."

"Why are you doing this?"

"I know you understand. Balance. Be glad I didn't kill them, things are still not right, you took the lives of those people downtown that were mine."

"I saved them, you tried to kill them."

"Semantics."

"Where is Alice?"

"Ah, lovely Alice. She will make a wonderful wife for me."

"A what?"

"I am the king and she the queen, I the male, she the female, I the Alpha, she the Omega. You've been replaced."

"You kidnapped her? Lay one finger upon her and I will kill you."

"Matt, you sound angry. I'm sorry to inform you I will be doing more than laying a finger on her, I think you have said your last goodbye to her. Then I will come for you."

"Come for me first you coward."

"I hit a nerve I see. Matt, you've lost control, it's my show, yours is about to end."

"Bring it on."

"I plan on it, but you won't know when or where or how."

"If you are so powerful, why are you so afraid?"

"I fear nothing," I said with confidence. The furnace was glowing more brightly.

"You run from your own shadow," Matt replied with clear tension.

"My shadow is stronger than your largest anger," I screamed into the phone.

"I repeat, you harm a hair on her head and you will die." I could sense Matt was already fading, losing control, letting go of that which was the only way he could get through this. I'd won.

"I don't think she will suffer, it's kind of up to her. But you do know from your vast studies that to bring it all together there must be fire."

"Tell me, why have you chosen the side of darkness and evil?" he asked.

"I have chosen balance, there is too much yin, the world needs some yang. I will be a strong dose of yang."

"The world needs lots more yin."

"I believe you are wrong. You tell people lies every week, I will speak the truth."

“What lies?”

“That God is with them. That he hears their prayers, that he walks with them, holds them. Garbage.”

“Just because you are so egocentric God can’t find a way in, don’t hold it against the rest of us. God walks with those who walk with God.” He walked with Mary until you murdered her.

“Said like a true priest.”

“I say it because I know it to be true. Your God is yourself. You are trying to become something you cannot become solely because of your intent.”

“What do you know?”

“More than you obviously. Joseph would agree with me and you know it.”

“He’s very old Matt, you shouldn’t listen to him, he is no match for me.”

“We are all a match for you, your cowardice is the proof.”

“Soon you will see how cowardly I am.”

“How soon?”

“Very.”

I was getting angry and distracted. He’d taken away my peace.

“Good bye Matt.”

Before he answered I hung up the phone. Alice was rubbing her eyes. I sat next to her.

“Where am I?

“At my house.”

“You kidnapped me.”

“Let’s just say that in the end you would have come on your own, I just jump started the process.”

“I would not go to see you thrown in hell!”

“I like a tough woman. Let me tell you what is going to happen. You will be here a few days, and then you will be free. During that time you may not leave the house. You might note you have a collar on. Kind of a dog collar, the kind people use with the invisible electric fence. With yours, if you leave the house without me, 1000 volts will surge through your neck, giving you instant cardiac arrest. I don't know if I will be able to save you. I'd invite you to try it, but doing so may be the last step you ever take. There is no phone, so don't bother looking. You are welcome to eat whatever you want, make yourself at home."

"What are you going to do with me? And what did you do to the children?"

I could sense her fear, but also the depth of her womanhood. To trick her made no sense, she would read me like a book.

"Alice, the children are fine, they were simply sleeping. Do you know who I am?"

"I assume you are the alchemist who burned down a house and murdered a woman."

"The house was a warning to Matt he ignored. The murder, as you call it, was a missed opportunity on behalf of another alchemist."

"You don't murder people on account of a missed opportunity."

"She refused to teach me what I needed to know. Teachers have a moral responsibility to teach; she broke her moral obligation and had to pay the price."

"Whose moral code did she break?"

"Mine."

"Since when do you make the rules?"

"Since I can."

Power has a way of stopping conversations, so does truth. There was a long silence.

"You haven't answered my question," she said stubbornly.

"Do you know much about alchemy, other than what your boyfriend has taught you?"

"First of all, he's not my boyfriend, secondly, no."

"I'll educate you. Alchemy in part is a merging of all the forces of the universe. Slowly but surely you bring together the masculine and the feminine, the shadow and the light, the trickster and the hero, all the archetypes of humanity plus the forces of nature. You learn to become gravity, electricity, magnetism. All of these lie within your grasp. I have only a few more pieces to add before I am complete. One of those pieces is….."

"Let me guess, the feminine."

"How wise of you, and a fast learner. Yes, I am the king and you are the queen, we will have a marriage of sorts."

"And if I refuse?"

"First, you don't really have a choice, you are a woman, like it or not. You can willingly give me your femininity or I can take it away."

"What, do you eat me?"

"Nothing so crass. I want the feminine spirit, not your flesh."

"What is left when my feminine side is gone?"

"I have no idea, I've only read stories. But know this, you will become a conscious part of me, you and I will live as one. That is what the bible said isn't it? "The two shall become one?"

"I think the writer was talking about being united sexually and spiritually."

"Ahhhhh, a biblical scholar as well. I think you are wrong. Do you believe in the soul?"

"Of course."

"And that soul exists outside the human body.:

"Yes."

"Then that spirit can exist anywhere, it could exist side by side another soul---in another body."

"I don't believe that."

"If I say I don't believe in God, does God disappear? Does my belief connote truth?"

"Of course not."

"Then your ignorance has led you astray. Souls can indeed transmigrate. Most do not, some do. When it is against the will of the other soul, that is what you call possession. Sometimes, schizophrenia. In the best of worlds it's a merging of spirits, a true and eternal marriage. In our case, we may live another hundred years or more, the complete person."

"I think I will pass."

"Unfortunately, that is not an option, the only option is whether you join me willingly or not. If you choose to go against me the suffering will be great. Tearing your soul from your body is not easy and you will feel it all. The process from what I have heard takes about 3 days, we will start tomorrow morning."

"You are mad."

"Actually, I'm the sane one, the world has gone mad."

"My spirit will fight you all the way."

"Your spirit is weak compared to me, my guess is you might last a day, then the intensity will become too great and you will beg to marry me."

"Never."

"We will see."

"Matt will find me."

"Matt is clueless. Had he any idea of where I was he'd be here. Besides, by the end of the week he will not be a problem."

"What are you going to do?"

"Not to worry, you won't be around in body to see it, but you will be part of me and will enjoy his end."

"I'd rather freeze in the Ice Queen's winter."

"There will be no ice where you are about to go. Just in case you were thinking of doing something to me, know I have set my laboratory furnace to explode if I do not punch in a code every three hours. So try to kill me or knock me out and you die. Your cell phone is gone by the way."

She turned and cried. I'd shattered her world, I didn't expect less, but I was hopeful she would come around and join me. The next two days would be spent preparing Alice and myself for the marriage. Wednesday would find me married, complete, and invincible.

22 MATT AND JOSEPH GO FOR A DRIVE

My adrenaline was pumping. I was trying to pay attention to the road, but my mind was on the nightmare that probably awaited me at my house. My wheels squealed around the corners as I drove.

"Tom, Matt."

"What's up?"

"I don't know, but it's not good. Get a bunch of ambulances to my house."

"What happened?"

"I don't know, but Alice and the youth group are there, so is the murderer."

"What? How do you know?"

"Just do it."

I clicked the phone off and kept trying to call Alice, always getting her answering service. The closer I got to the house, the more I was filled with fear. He swore he'd get back at me and he needed to do something bad.

Her car was in the driveway. I heard an ambulance coming up the hill and I ran in the house. The sight took the breath out of me. Twenty kids lying in various positions on the floor. I went to the closest and felt for a pulse. I spent the better part of 30 seconds finding the throb, but I felt it, barely. I checked a few more with the same results. All alive or so it seemed. The ambulances started flowing in and as the first paramedic walked in the door with the same shocked look I had when I first saw them. I said hi and the phone rang, my heart started beating faster and every sense in my body went on Defcon 1. I knew who it was. I called Tom as I turned off the answering machine so the phone would ring for a while. I knew he wouldn't hang up.

"Tom, don't ask questions, just tap the call coming into my house." I gave him the number.

"Ok."

We'd set up an instant tap on my phone believing the murderer would make contact at some point.

I answered the phone, wanting to reach through the phone and kill the guy. But I knew he had Alice and needed to keep him on the phone for a while to make sure they got the trace.

I went back and forth between being calm, blasting him, and taunting him. I made it clear if he hurt Alice he would die. I was confident from his voice he didn't really care what threats I made at this point.

We played back and forth for a few minutes, and then he hung up. I called Tom back.

"Did you get it?"

"He used a cell phone; the closest we can get is a cell tower."

"Where?"

"Out 26 not far from North Plains."

"You can't narrow it down more?"

"No, I'm sorry Matt, don't worry we'll get him."

"He has Alice."

"Oh God."

"We'll need all of God's help on this one," knowing I was well out of my league.

"I'm on my way."

"Did you take on a new role?"

"I'm glad you can see some humor in all of this?"

"Faith is capable of amazing things Tom."

"I guess."

He hung up and I went back to the living room. The medics told me the kids were all ok, a few were starting to wake up. I called a couple of the parents I knew had calm heads and told them some of what happened. It was only a matter of time before the news hit the media and I needed to figure out whether to let the news of the kidnapping out or not.

The murderer was playing the same game I was, trying to create chaos, to keep me from following the path I knew and trusted. If he could break my spirit or create doubt, he'd win. I was puzzled as to why he didn't kill all the kids. Perhaps knowing he can do something is enough, or perhaps…………

The phone rang.

"Hello?

"Matt, what is going on? I got a call from Channel 2, something about 50 kids dying at your house?" the bishop asked with concern in his voice.

"Wow, they got that one wrong."

"I'm glad, figured they must have been mistaken."

I loved playing with him. "It was only 20?"

"WHAT?!!! 20 kids died at your house?"

"They didn't die."

"Why don't you just tell me what happened Matt?"

"A murderer I have been tracking, the same one that killed the woman with the gold and diamonds, is trying to take me out of the picture. He's threatened me and now he is showing he can hurt those I care about—today it was the kids. He gave them a sleeping potion."

"How did he give it to them?"

"In their Kool-Aid."

"Weren't you there?"

"He also used a ploy to trick me into going to the hospital on a false call."

"I'm sorry."

"It's ok."

"What about the other adults that were there?"

I had less time to talk about Alice than I'd thought. I knew if I told the bishop, word would get out, so I lied. Well, a white lie.

"They are all OK."

"Something to be thankful for."

"Are you getting close to finding this crazy?"

"I hope so, by the way, what are you doing Wednesday night?"

"Right now it's free."

"Come to my lecture, I might need you."

"What is the lecture on?"

"Alchemy."

"I don't know anything about it Matt."

"I know, but you have spiritual authority and power, I've seen it."

"And why would you need that?"

"I'm not sure, just a hunch and a sense."

"I'll be there. Let me know if there is anything else I can do."

"Thanks bishop."

Over the next hour, the parents arrived, I did my best to tell them what happened and to plead with them to not spread the news, and it would only fan the fire. Most of them agreed with me and I trusted their word. A few had that look in their eyes.

The kids all seemed to be fine. Five or six got sick, all of them had a headache. I tasted the Kool-Aid and immediately knew something bad was in it. My mind raced back to Jim Jones, I'm sure the irony was not lost on the murderer.

I was cleaning the house, glad to have a few minutes to think. I'd dispatched the media quickly, telling them there was something wrong with the drinks, but not divulging it was an outsider, although I knew they'd be back, word would leak fast, they weren't stupid.

A giant pot of chili sat on the stove and wouldn't get eaten. I'd take it to the local soup kitchen for dinner. Sitting down, I prayed. The Holy Spirit filled my pores and opened my nose. Dogs and salmon smell amazing things, millions of things we don't, all the time, and yet they are able to pick small scents out and follow them, sense them in other places. God gave me the same type of gift. My kitchen was filled with smells, the overwhelming smell of chili, that of me, and that of the kids and Alice. I moved them all to the side. Kids smell different than adults and males than females. Biology has used this for ages. Imagine a giant bulletin board, with one hundred pieces of paper on it. You are trying to isolate one piece of paper. You ask questions that eliminate certain pieces and hopefully, in the end, leave the one. Smells stick in our deep seeded memory banks. I took the kids names, Alice, parents, and the medics off the board. All the normal smells of food, fire, and all my personal things were pulled off. I breathed in deeply when the final smell was on the board. I could tell a few things about this guy from his smell. He was probably in his late 30's, bathed regularly and didn't use anything on his skin---that was good news for me. While perfumes and deodorants may seem to caste a wide net of odor, they are confusing because so many use them. They cover the real smell, that is their purpose. I can't really bust into every house in a ten square mile area where I detect Irish Spring soap. But I had a clear scent, I would have to get very close to know for certain, but I had some ideas on how to narrow the field.

I made another call and picked up Joseph 30 minutes later.

"Where are we going Matt?"

"Just for a ride."

There was a tension in the car, both of us nervous about Alice, but not interested in talking about it. We both knew ultimately you had to act on what you wanted to be true. If I die and it turns out Jesus and God were delusions, I won't have any regrets. I choose to belief he is real and I act upon that reality to the best of my ability. We both want Alice to be ok, so we act upon that belief, talking about it would only increase our fears. I'm sure many therapists would disagree.

I asked questions about alchemy, about his life, wanting to know who this remarkable man was. I also asked more about Mary, feeling guilty. I hadn't before, I knew very little about her.

"Tell me about Mary."

"Mary was a saint, you have no idea what she'd done, with her own life and for others. I met her at a soup kitchen, she was living on the streets when she was 35. I won't go into the details, let's just say she'd made some mistakes along the alchemical journey and didn't reach out to others for help. I was serving. When she came through the line our eyes met, I was already in my 70's although I didn't look it. She sat down and didn't take her eyes off me for a second, staring with those piercing blue orbs of wisdom and tragedy. When I was done serving I sat down with a bowl of soup. She came and sat across from me and looked me in the eyes. "I know you can teach me, I know you are the one to raise me up," she said. I was stunned. I'd been looking for someone to guide, but this woman? She had many strikes against her already and I had my doubts to her integrity. She was stunningly beautiful and in talking with her I could tell had a solid brain. She told me she didn't know how much longer she could last on the streets of Portland. I told her I would return in the morning, that I had to think and pray about it. She asked if I was praying to God or to John Newton. I was stunned. John was an alchemist; I'd heard rumors that he'd sacrificed his life for the sake of a young alchemist. Now here she was. I'd been doing a little work with John but he was not my teacher. She could tell she'd hit a nerve, her intuitive powers were beyond imagination.

I went home and asked God to guide me. I didn't see how someone with so many problems could do what I needed them to do, not to mention to follow the path of

God. I asked God to show me where he'd used people with faults. The list ended up being lengthy.

Noah was a drunk
Abraham was too old
Isaac was a daydreamer and a liar
Jacob was a liar
Leah was ugly
Joseph was abused and lied, cheating his own brother
Moses had a stuttering problem and committed murder
Gideon was afraid
Samson had long hair and was a womanizer
Rahab was a prostitute
Jeremiah and Timothy were too young
David had an affair and was a murderer
Elijah was suicidal
Isaiah preached naked
Jonah ran from God
Job went bankrupt
Peter denied Christ
The Disciples fell asleep while praying
Martha worried about everything
The Samaritan woman was divorced, more than once
Zacchcus was too small
Paul was too religious and murdered Christians
Timothy had an ulcer..AND
Lazarus was dead!

"If God could use them, why couldn't he use Mary? I picked her up at the shelter in the morning and she lived with me for a year. She was a frustrated alchemist because she wanted to go from M to Z in two weeks. She'd already gotten to M with the help of John and her own devices in college. Patience was a virtue she worked on till her death. After a year she'd become very confident in herself, got a job, moved out, and built a lab. I'd rarely heard about anybody progressing that fast. She faced her demons head on and cast them off, she threw herself on the mercy of God and he surrounded her with his love. Mary was deeply spiritual. Her faith in Jesus and God were phenomenally powerful. Perhaps her greatest attribute was her humility. She never wanted or needed credit for anything. She healed, lifted spirits, counseled people from the brink of death, eased people into death, and yes, even helped people and organizations financially. She and I had many discussions about her ability to create wealth, something she'd gained in the past year. While I couldn't deny the substances were real, I did contend that flooding the world with that kind of wealth would create havoc. She told me only when God clearly directed her did she do it. I brought up numerous cult leaders and tyrants that had said the same thing. She laughed at me. She wanted to know if I believed she was one of them, knowing full well that I didn't. "You have to trust me Joseph, at some point you have to trust me." She knew my darkest fears about her. I cried that night more than I had in decades. From that point on our relationship changed. I was still technically her teacher, but I am sure I learned more from her than she did from me. I knew more on a purely alchemical level, but her soul had left me in the dust. She understood that no matter who you were you couldn't finish the spiritual part of the journey alone, that's why she got involved with the church. I have yet to do that."

"Hold that thought," I said. "We are here."

"Where?"

"That is the cell tower near Alice. I know you can sense presence in the web. I want you to see if you can find Alice or the murderer."

"I have never done that before."

"Just try."

I'd made a map of the area, a grid of sorts to drive trying to sense his smell and having Joseph sense the web.

We didn't talk for an hour. I had to get home and I wasn't at all sure this method was going to work, but I didn't have any other ideas and I didn't want to wait. As we were driving off Joseph stopped me.

"Wait, stop the car."

He jumped out, slowly turning around.

"He's started," Joseph said, I could see the fear on his face.

"Started?"

"Do you not know why he took Alice?"

"He said something about marriage, but Alice won't do that."

"You are thinking too literally, think alchemy. What is one of the final stages?"

"The merging of opposites and of the elements."

"Exactly, male and female."

"But that is a metaphor."

"You forget the murderer has lost any sense of metaphor, for him it is a literal necessity. He must find a way to unite a woman to himself, not just sexually and spiritually, but at a deep physical level."

"What does that mean?"

"Are you sure you want to know?"

"Yes."

"My guess is it has to do with fire. He has always used fire—with Phil, Sue, and others. He sees fire as a refining force that unites chaos into order, burns away the chaff to save the wheat. First he will prepare the vessels, one for himself and one for her. I'm certain he has been working on this for weeks if not months. He has all the things he needs now."

"He can do this even against her will?"

“He is not having a ceremony of marriage; he is going to literally take away her feminine spirit and unit it with his.”

“What will happen to Alice?”

“You don’t know want to know. In the end, she will die.’

I thought I was going to pass out.

“What did you sense?”

“His home is not far from here. There was a large surge in his energy, remember, when I feel your energy I only sense you personally. When I sense his, I also sense his home because his laboratory is a direct reflection on who and what he has become. My guess is he is turning up the heat, figuratively and literally.”

“How long do we have?”

“Three to four days at the most, if she can last that long.”

“Can I stall him?”

“I don’t know. He is very focused now and knows that when he is done, no one will stop him----he may be right.”

“You mean a bullet from my gun couldn’t kill him?”

“Oh it would kill him, but first you have to find him and keep your mind from being challenged by him. My fear is you underestimate the power of the human mind to change itself and act upon others.”

“Alice is very strong.”

“I hope so.”

“Can’t you trace it more than just here?”

“The web is a spiritual entity, not really tied to the physical world. It doesn’t really care where in the world you are, just that you are. He has set up an elaborate system around himself to protect his location and his essence. He is using the dark side of things now.”

“So use dark against him, or light,” I said in desperation.

"I have never ventured into the dark world, nor do I think has he. I fear for what he might discover and how he might use it, if he isn't destroyed first."

"That would be a good thing, let him die and then we find Alice."

"Matt, you don't understand. The murderer's house and he are one. If he were to die, the house would disintegrate."

"Damn, so I actually have to pray this mad man lives."

"Do you not think Jesus at some level would have loved to see some of his adversaries die? Didn't he die for the evil?"

"Touche."

We drove back to his house in silence. I arrived home and collapsed into bed not realizing how tired I was. My sleep was dark, no dreams. I couldn't remember a night like that in more than a decade.

While making breakfast in a home that seemed eerily empty I wondered if I should cancel all my appointments and just drive the roads looking or rather smelling for Alice. Were it a development of tract houses I wouldn't hesitate. All those homes are within 50 feet of the street. There were millions of smells, but I only need to sense one of them. Out in the country there were homes hundreds of feet from the road, homes you didn't even know were there. I could spend the whole week looking and never find a thing. I didn't know whether or not he was aware of my gifts, but I suspected there weren't going to be any welcoming balloons on his driveway. Maybe I'd go out later in the afternoon, but I made the decision to stick to the plan, confident he'd make contact. I could tell by the tone of his voice he was enjoying being in control. If we were to have a chance, I'd have to rattle his cage. I suppose God could just hand me a map, but God, in my experience, didn't work that way. The answers were in front of me I just hope I'd thought of them all.

I headed for the TV station for my interviews. They'd be on the morning programs and the news. I had numerous interviews, all of them very similar.

"Pastor, your life has been very busy as of late."

"I have been a bit pre-occupied as of late, I'll admit to that."

"What has been the focus of your preoccupation?"

"There is a murderer loose in Portland. He has killed at least one woman and tried to kill dozens of others. He is a coward who claims to have power, but does all his acts of evil in fear and hiding. What kind of human poisons the weak and innocent? But his time is coming."

"You know who he is?"

"I'm getting close."

"Can you tell us anything? What you know about him? How you are tracking him down?"

"God is a force to be reckoned with. I believe the murderer thinks he is stronger and smarter than God. He is mistaken. He has told me he wants to challenge me, I've told him to do it, and he cowers. He is weak. He is in his 30's, a loner because he can't get along with people, and lives in dreamland, avoiding reality."

"What do you think he is doing now?"

"Packing his bags and leaving town. He doesn't want to get caught and he knows we are close, he feels us breathing down his neck."

"If he leaves town, what does that do for you?"

"First, it lets me sleep a bit easier and secondly, I will see him for the true coward he is."

"Sounds like you are challenging him."

"I have no fear of him. He cannot touch me. He thinks he has, but he hasn't, not one bit. He knows his life is a fraud or he would come out. His parlor tricks have all failed. God does the healing, he does nothing but destroy."

"And what about the police, are they doing anything?"

"I won't speak for them, but they are working very hard. They have some great leads, have tracked down evidence that is tightening the noose. Don't think for a second I am out there on my own."

"And what is all this about alchemy?"

"Well, I have always been fascinated by the topic."

"We've heard from several sources the murderer is an alchemist."

"The murderer thinks he is an alchemist, he's not really a very good chemist."

"So he isn't an alchemist?"

"I don't know what he thinks he is, all I know is he is a murderer. I'm sure you've known people that claim to be great athletes or musicians but when you actually see them you wonder how they could live in such delusion. Look at the first few weeks of American Idol, America's Got Talent, or So You Think You Can Dance. Some of those people actually think they have talent when they have none."

"What about the situation at your house, we understand your youth group was there and were poisoned. There was also a poisoning at the soup kitchen you were part of, is that right?"

"I'm sure the audience could read into this that I had something to do with it. I was the one that discovered the poison at the soup kitchen and I certainly didn't poison anyone. We are not yet clear as to what happened at my house. I think we had a bad batch of juice."

"That isn't what the calls we are receiving tell us."

"Well we are all entitled to our beliefs, let's wait for the police to decide, let them do their job---shall we?"

"Let's talk for a second about the lectures you are giving---on alchemy."

"They are a series of talks, I don't really lecture well, and we are looking at how the history of alchemy can help all of us in our spiritual journeys. Alchemy is a metaphor for the spiritual process and we are working on the different aspects of that."

"What is the topic this week?"

"Glad you asked. On Wednesday night, 7:00pm at our church which I believe is on the bottom of your screen or will be given after the interview on the radio, we'll be discussing some very pragmatic ideas of alchemy. I hope to literally transform people's lives on Wednesday and hopefully some of that transformation will include significant healing of body, mind, and spirit. Others will be there to share their stories and show what they have accomplished. I think it will be quite a night."

"What do you mean what they have accomplished?"

"Let's just say people will see things they've never witnessed before."

"Those are strong words."

"I have a lot of faith in my boss."

"The bishop?"

"God."

"Oh, right. Well best of luck to you and thanks for joining us today. We'll be right back after these messages."

I hoped he was watching and would take the bait. He had to, Alice's life depended on that fact. I was a bit taken aback by the insinuation I had something to do with the poisonings and was sure the murderer would jump on that. I had to watch for ways he would find to tie me to the poisonings and motives he would give. I called Tom to tell him as much.

In the middle of our conversation I had an insight. I love life when I have an insight. Is this a great country, or what!!!!! I thought I'd found way to significantly narrow the field, maybe even isolate the house. I hoped I could do it in time and kicked myself for not thinking of it earlier.

You might be wondering why I didn't take the pigeon with us to the country, he hadn't returned to his cage.

20

23 BOB AND ALICE GET MORE ACQUAINTED

Alice and I spent the rest of the afternoon and evening getting acquainted. My journey would be far better, easier, and more enjoyable if she was part of the process. She was going to become part of me one way or the other. Why not join in the grand journey? She seemed to be calming down and was becoming more communicative, even volunteering to make some dinner. Before we sat down to eat I turned on the furnace in the laboratory, things were going to start heating up.

The furnace is the center of an alchemist's life. The further into the work one got, the hotter the flame needed to be. In order to have the flame reach the levels I needed, I added three circuits to my fuse box. I told the electrician I did some glassblowing and needed a very hot furnace. He'd asked why I didn't use gas and I mentioned I'd created a new form of glasswork that didn't work with a gas flame, which indeed I had. Alchemical furnaces need human intervention to reach a certain temperature, and then they took on a life of their own and created their own energy.

While most of the heat was contained within the furnace, the cabin usually rose to about 105 degree Fahrenheit. I needed the intense temperatures in order to transform the elements I was working with. In reality much higher temperatures are needed, but what science fails to understand is the connection between the spiritual world and the material one. Spiritual realities are capable of changing material ones. Within three days I would be changing mercury into gold and shortly thereafter I would be able to change just about anything into anything. Think about it, the ability to go back in time to the earliest stages of creation when elements were formed, to be able to transform matter. The potential was almost unlimited.

Alice was very quiet after dinner, watching the fire, commenting on how the temperature was rising. I told her not to worry about it and to get a good night's sleep, she would need it. I retired to the living room when she went to her room I'd created for her with all the comforts of home.

When one gets to the end of a journey, one tends to reflect on the beginning of the journey and some of the phases.

My journey started when I was a little boy. I was raised on a farm in the country; horses, cows, sheep, chickens, and lots of room to roam. My mother was a coward, leaving me with beliefs as to what all females were. My father was a tyrant. His ego was larger than the earth, his ability to listen to others zero, and his need to show he was better than we were, constant. Barely a day went by when he did not ridicule me or beat me. I've found a refuge in the woods in my books and in my mind.

I spent time each day from when I was seven on trying to figure out how to kill my father. Now and then I would actually try, and the times he caught me I was almost killed. Finally, when I was 13, I skewered him with a pitchfork over and over and over again, and then dumped him in our well that was about 100 feet deep. We hadn't used the well in years and I knew nobody would go down there looking for him. That was the first real crime I ever committed. I'd done a good thing, I'd killed an evil man and made the world a better place. In reality, I don't believe I have ever committed a crime, we have unjust laws, and many times it's just people acting against those unjust laws. And the moral government should have taken my father away when I was a child and hung him, but they were cowards. In an odd sort of way, my father gave me the courage to kill him. I'll admit to being filled with energy and joy when I killed him. What is wrong with ridding the world of evil? I know I have talked about balance before, but my father did not believe in balance, he believed only in himself and his rule was law. He had to die.

I think in her heart my mother knew I killed my father. We didn't really talk about it much, no one questioned where he went. The truth was that in our town everyone was glad he was gone. For a while rumors spread, some saying he had skipped town others saying someone had murdered him and thrown him in the lake. My favorite was the idea that aliens had come in and taken him. When I was about 10 I read a book that talked about alchemy. I became intrigued from the very beginning. I started doing experiments and learning about plants and minerals, and I read all the books I could, even though our library was quite small. I had to hide my reading from my father who didn't believe in it.

I left home at 17 and went to the city. My mother had a job and I too got one and sent her money. My mother never recovered from my father, she was a shell of what she could have been. I felt sorry for her, for she certainly had potential as do we all. She lacked the will to reach it. I learned from my mother and father.

I learned early on from reading about alchemy that calcination was a critical component of growing up. I trained my will and my tolerance of pain by holding my hand over a candle. I got to a point where I could watch the skin burn off my hand or arm without screaming, cutting pieces of flesh off my body and wanting more. Pain meant nothing, so when my father attacked me, the pain was mild. My ego was crushed and yet oddly reborn in his death. I learned in the bible that we must die to ourselves to find ourselves. I have died numerous times in the past 25 years. Now I am about to find life. Kenneth Patchen is one of my favorite poets. He said there were so many little dyings in life, it didn't matter which was death. I agree.

I have always had a difficult time with women, I just don't understand them. Their view of the world is fundamentally different than my own. Even most men I struggle with, but at least I find common ground with them, with women, nothing. I have long understood the need to find the feminine within me, if for no other reason than to tame the beast that lives within. But the anima was illusive. At one point in my 20's I even went to therapy with a woman specifically to bring it out. We spent months battering the shadow that kept me from finding the feminine. I made progress, but not nearly to the extent I needed to in order to achieve the ultimate goal. Now there would be only one way to unite myself to the feminine, through fire and transmutation.

I remember one of my biggest moments of the stage of separation. You have to understand the stages go in cycles, over and over and over again. Different heat, different dilutions, different coagulations. The idea of separation is to figure out what parts of your being you want to keep and which you want to let go of. I was living in two worlds. During the day I was a good employee at a university. I was moving up the ladder and it more than paid the bills. At night I was an alchemist. But eventually they conflicted with one another. The values of the one negated the values of the other. I could be like most people and choose to soften the lines, living comfortably ignorant in both worlds. But I wanted to be fully alive, fully aware, so I had to make a choice. I separated out the world—I quit.

My mother died and through the selling of the farm I was able to stay alive till I figured out how to make money the easy way, stocks. I only made enough to keep my lab equipped, myself alive, and do the traveling that was necessary.

The work consumed me, I barely slept for years. Then, about 8 years ago I found I was not alone. I discovered a few other alchemists and learned from them. We were all hermits by nature, but would gather to share and encourage one another, knowing the world wouldn't understand our labors. This led to the chat room. I'd met all of the people at the beginning of the chatting, but within a couple of years others joined and somehow it became anonymous. Mary and Z showed up and shocked us all, they were so far beyond where we were, but they were patient and I was serious. I progressed at a rapid pace that even impressed them. My metallurgy was moving fast and they offered hints whenever I asked. But they refused to meet me and my frustration level started to grow.

At the same time, I started to see how I could use my new power. I could do some healings and make some sick, I could read some people's minds and I could sense trends in certain markets that allowed me to make all the money I needed. I didn't want to make a fortune and attract attention to myself so I made just enough to give me what I wanted and stay under the radar.

Five months ago, I had a major breakthrough and needed information others had that they unethically refused to give me, so I started taking what I deserved. If they were not going to use the information they had to help someone else, they didn't deserve to have it. Now I had more information than all of them and others can't handle it, so I have to use it as I see fit.

My body had become accustomed over the years to extreme temperatures and walking into the lab that was now 130 degrees did not feel that hot. I knew by the time it hit 170 I'd be feeling the heat, I'd burn whatever residue was left within me, the hedge of impurity.

Marriage takes place at 185 degrees. That would occur sometime on Wednesday before the festivities at the church. Once the marriage was complete, I could challenge anyone and beating Matt at his own game would bring me great joy.

I slept more deeply than I had in years. My dreams filled with flights of the phoenix, marriages, and the complete conflagration of my internal and external enemies.

There are no skies on the planet like those of the Northwest on a clear crisp blue sky day. I woke early, filled the kitchen with the smell of coffee, poured myself a cup and went for a walk.

My land was half trees and half field. The forest had little undergrowth so I could wander aimlessly. Trees were adorned with a thick white frost that might have passed for snow. The world glistened in pristine purity and I sat in the middle. I was pleased that even nature was understanding what was to take place. They were preparing for the wedding, how thoughtful. I was beginning to comprehend the immensity of what I was about to accomplish. Countless numbers of people had been trying for thousands of years to reach the pinnacle I was standing upon. I and I alone would hold the Philosopher's Stone and all the power the fabled stone contained. People from every corner of the world had searched the planet and their souls for exactly this. Scientists, theists, mystics, philosophers, nut-cases and the like had given it their best shot and had led the way. I wouldn't be here today were it not for them.

I took off my clothes and sat on the ground, meditating for about 30 minutes, letting my mind clear, my senses taking in all nature gave to me, all that was being offered as gifts for the king. Inside I was impervious to the pain of heat and out here to the pain of cold. I felt nothing.

I thanked the trees and headed back inside. As I reached the house I heard a crack and turned around. A large tree was falling toward me. I stepped to the side as if in slow-motion. The top of the tree missed me by about 3 feet.

"Must have been a bad tree, unwilling to join the banquet, and paid for it. I'll use you for wood in the furnace."

Nature has a mind of its own, but needs to play by the rules of the ruler.

Alice was sleeping in and I would wake her soon. I suppose the sedative I gave her was a bit strong. I wanted to watch a few of the morning shows to see what was happening. Then I saw him.

Surfing to find a good recipe, I saw Matt's face. I stopped and froze. He was on TV taunting and mocking me. He made light of the poisonings. Now that I had Alice I was on the verge of making his death an easy one. This changed it all. He wanted a challenge, he'd get one, but in reality, he was no match.

Then I saw another opening, a moment of genius. One of the interviewers had insinuated Matt might be involved. After all, two poisonings had taken place with him around---to save the day---how convenient.

I could certainly plant some evidence letting them see Matt was not quite the morally upright priest he'd led them to believe. This strategy would take some doing because most people believed he was a truly good person, incapable of doing such a thing. I had time, I'd stew on it, so many options. This might change the timetable a bit, but all the more joyous to see Matt humiliated and rotting in jail rather than to actually have to kill him.

I went out to check on the generators and to get more wood for the fireplace. When I came back into the house, Alice was cooking.

"Good morning," she said with a smile on her face.

"Morning," I said, curious as to her perky positive attitude.

"I don't even know your name."

"Bob."

"Is it all right if I cook something Bob?"

"Be my guest Alice, anything you want."

"It's getting rather warm in here don't you think?"

I laughed. "Warm? Not yet, but it will, by tomorrow night the house will be downright hot."

"Why?"

"Do you really want to know?"

"Yes."

"In alchemy, many things are accomplished by the application of heat, calcination. The further you are on the journey, the higher the temperature must be to create a transformative environment. I am at the end of all journeys, therefore, the heat must be intense."

"But won't you get burned?"

"Nothing will happen to me." She let that stand.

I felt free to tell Alice whatever she wanted to know, she was never leaving the house, so it didn't really matter.

"What are you doing in the lab right now?"

"I am preparing the furnace for the final event and for the transformation of mercury into gold with the tincture of the gods."

"What will you do when you have achieved what you want?"

"The million dollar question. I don't know. I do know I have gotten to this point by years of disciplined work and by turning my life over to the forces of balance in the universe. I suspect they will lead me. Your crepes are very good by the way."

"Thank you. Matt is not as appreciative as you."

"Matt's ego is too large to be appreciative."

“He’s a man, what can I say. He knows his God and his God uses him, I don’t see that as having a big ego.”

“Let me show you something.” I went into the lab and brought back a small velvet bag. “Hold out your hand.”

Alice’s gentle hands unfolded as I poured diamonds into them.

“What are they?”

“Diamonds.”

“Where did you steal them from?”

“I made them?”

“What?”

“I created them from nothing, surely you’ve heard of the woman who left gold and diamonds to the church?”

“Yes, but I thought she was rich.”

“She was an alchemist. Matt forgot to tell you that part.”

“Yes.”

“Such a secretive person, Matt is.”

“He can be.”

“This is just the beginning of what I can do.”

“To what end? Why?”

“I am tired of having people abuse power, tired of witnessing hypocrisy run rampant in our culture, tired of being scorned. I will have my day and others will pay.”

“And Matt?”

“I’m sorry Alice but he is at the top of the list.”

“If I promise to go along with you, will you make his end painless and quick, he is no match for you.”

“I’ll think about that, he has done so much damage to me. He is weak though, doesn’t really seem like a fair fight.” Part of me didn’t trust her, but Alice was smart and probably knew there was no escape.

“I don’t understand what he has done to you? You’ve haven’t even met have you?”

"He is interfering with the process and dragging others in with him. He looks only at the small picture and by doing so loses sight of the larger one. I am focused on the big picture, little incidents are meaningless."

"So taking a life here and there doesn't matter?" she asked with concern in her voice.

"To be blunt, no. I have never taken a life for no reason, each life I take has either refused to give me something I have deserved or earned, or tried to block me or was not a life worth living and supporting. I consider it self-defense or survival of the fittest."

"You make a good point although I don't know of each case. You seem to have thought all this out."

"Trust me Alice, I have been at this for years and everything is thought out."

We talked most of the day. She had to keep taking off more clothes because of the heat. I was becoming sexually attracted to her, a feeling I had to fight. Alchemical weddings were of a spiritual nature. I'd read many stories about people getting to this point and blowing it by becoming sexually involved. I would remain pure.

I moved the TV into the lab and from time to time would turn it on. Matt seemed to be on every show there was, his ego flaunting itself more and more. He actually appeared to have more and more energy as the day wore on. Well I hoped he'd enjoy himself, these would be the last interviews he would ever give.

When I returned to the room, Alice was looking at a picture.

"Ah Durer's Melancholia," I pointed out.

"What is it?"

"Alchemy in a nutshell."

"I don't understand?" she asked sincerely.

"Many of the symbols of alchemy are in that picture. Pythagoras was an alchemist. The sphere, compass, hourglass, polyhedron, and magical square are all his."

"Magical square?"

"Look at that square with numbers. First, note no matter what direction you add the four numbers, you get the same sum. Next, note the two middle bottom numbers, what are they?"

"15 and 14."

"The year of the engraving, 1514, very clever I think. This was one of four such prints. The others were to have to do with the three other parts of alchemy, but he died before they were completed, or at least that is the tale. Do you see the rainbow?"

"Yes."

"Hearkens back to the contract with Noah and represents the order of colors discovered in the alchemical process. You will note that red is last, where I am."

"Why is the woman so unhappy?"

"Remember this is called melancholia. She has fought long and hard for the Philosopher's stone and has yet to find it. I suspect you have had moments of despair or depression, this is hers."

"Is there a way out?"

"Of course, she has all the tools she needs, she hasn't put them together in the right way and has yet to release her own spirit to that process, you can see it in her face, she wants control."

"But isn't that what you want?"

"No. I want to be controlled by the forces that rule the universe."

"That is what I want to, to be controlled by God."

"God is not in control, at least not of the human race."

"What?"

"That's because of free will. You have all failed to see the power of the human mind, especially in the hands of someone who understands how the mind and the natural laws of the universe work. Jesus had this, he got it and used it."

"But he never killed."

"Well not that they tell you in your bible, but let's remember those books were put together by believers and the collection of writings by people interested in spreading a particular image of Jesus. Wouldn't sit well if it came out he actually harmed people would it?"

"No, but I don't believe he did."

"Belief, exactly, I just happen to believe differently."

"But why is yours right? Where is your proof?"

"You've seen the healings, the gold, diamonds… do you need more?"

"They are pretty convincing. And you are close to something?"

"By Wednesday I will have near complete understanding. And control."

"What will you be able to control?"

"Matter and mind."

"That isn't possible," Alice commented in a bit of shock.

"All things are possible, isn't that what your God says?" Bob said with a smirk.

"Through Him all things are possible."

"Consider it a loop hole. Alchemy has found a way to a second tier of physical laws. God's weakness, or God's true purpose for those who seek."

"And what is your weakness?"

"Other than another alchemist as powerful as me, not many. I am still human, it's not like I can't die."

"But you will be around for a long time."

"We will be around a long time."

"I don't understand?"

"I told you, when the marriage is complete, your spirit will live in me, aware, united in body ,soul, and spirit---one, just like they talked about in Genesis."

"I don't think that is what they meant."

"But it is, you have failed to understand many of the writings in the Bible."

We spent many hours talking about alchemy, her life, her spirituality and mine, and food. I was becoming more at ease with her and felt she was starting to understand me better and relax. I'd been saving a bottle of wine for a special occasion and I couldn't think of a better one.

I prepared dinner and we supped on delicacies that sent our taste buds into orbit. I heard her moan with each bite. Mushrooms from the property, home grown chicken and veggies and a bottle of wine she claimed was one of the best she'd ever had.

I ensured she had plenty to drink and by the time we were done, I put her to bed. The hour was still early and there were a few things I needed to do before I slept. Tomorrow would find me back in the world, doing some chores, one last distraction for Matt and Joseph, and a visit to the police. I was looking forward to the adventure.

24 MATT'S BRAIN FUNCTIONS

I rarely was at a loss of words or without an opinion. I was going nuts not knowing what to do about Alice. I couldn't just sit and wait. On another case I'd asked a judge to give a warrant to search every house on a block for a missing child. Because of my track record she agreed. While we did find the child, he was miles away. The judge just about lost her job by trusting me and I knew it wouldn't happen again. I couldn't walk in and say, "Judge, I need a warrant to search every house in a four square mile area because I sensed something." I could personally drive around, but I'd noticed on the last trip that many houses had gates and some of those folks were not appreciative of people hoping over their fences to say hi. I trusted Joseph would call me when it was OK to let the bird go, who by the way had been missing for a couple of days.

My attempts to connect to the web were in vain, probably my worrying was keeping me from settling down. I called Joseph, maybe he'd know something.

"She's OK so far Matt, that's about all I know. I feel her presence and while it's strong, she has yet to know how to use the web so I can't get much information about her. Besides that she is in his house and there is like a protective dome over it. This is not an amateur."

"Will she make it?" There was a long silence.

"I can only hope."

"That isn't good enough."

"I'm not sure what you want me to say Matt," Joseph said with sorrow in his voice. "I'm sorry you got dragged into this mess, but it was your Spirit that did it, not me."

"I know and I apologize for venting on you, I feel helpless."

"Trust me Matt, I know the feeling, but tell me this, do you not think your Holy Spirit knew this was a possibility?"

"Probably."

"Do you trust God?"

"I like to think so, but obviously I'm having my doubts."

"What did Jesus say on the cross?"

"My God, my God, why hast thou forsaken me?"

"And what did he do?"

"What God asked him to do. He trusted and surrendered himself."

"You have a choice to make."

"Who is the priest here Joseph?" I laughed.

"Certainly you aren't stupid enough to think priests don't need help or a good kick in the ass from time to time?"

"From time to time---how about daily. I appreciate the kick."

"My pleasure. By the way, I forgot to mention one pretty important piece of the puzzle."

"What might that be?"

"If you take alchemical writings literally which our murderer appears to be doing, you need something very special at the end, for the final ceremony."

"And that would be?"

"The blood of a master."

"What?"

"Think about it. These alchemists, at least most of them in the last 1500 years were Christians. What was the last thing Jesus did or gave the disciples before he left?"

"Prayed and the Last Supper."

"Right, and what did he tell them they were eating and drinking at the Last Supper?"

"His body and blood."

"They had to partake of the body and blood of the Master in order to be transformed.. Now you and I know that is at least in part symbolic, but he doesn't see it that way."

"So he needs your blood."

"Yes, he made a mistake at Mary's. He must not have known about this."

"How could he not know, isn't it written down?"

"Remember Matt, very few people have come this far. Everything that is written about the final stage is conjecture and notes left by people who did something wrong. At some level, he is guessing. On top of that things are revealed in time. When you first became a Christian did you have complete wisdom? The more mature you get, the deeper we get. Certain things don't make sense until you get to a certain point on the journey. The parables were a mystery to the disciples early on; Jesus had to explain them in terms they would comprehend."

"So let's assume he gets it wrong, which I assume there is a good chance of."

"Yes, a very good chance and in that, he will die if he fails."

"Along with Alice."

"Yes."

"I can't let it get that far."

"So he could have used Mary's blood?"

"Yes, she was a Master."

"But she never would have given it."

"Blood is blood. I don't think it would have mattered."

"But you said it was like Christ at the Last Supper. In the end he voluntarily offered himself, it was not forced. He could have said no."

"True. I haven't been this step, so I can't tell you for sure. As far as I know, no one has ever found the Philosopher's Stone. Perhaps it is an illusion."

"Then why do you seek it?"

"Do you believe you will ever be perfect as God is perfect and as he calls you to be perfect in the gospels?"

"Of course not."

"Then why do you try? Why do you chase after something you know you will never have?"

"Because it's not an all or nothing experience. I feel God's presence even as I struggle."

"And I am filled with peace and power even in the midst of the struggle to find the Stone."

"Is the Stone the same as the Holy Grail legend?"

"First of all, alchemy is not a legend, I think you have seen that. Secondly, many do believe the Stone and the Grail are the same. Perhaps the Grail started as a metaphor and became something physical to be sought just as alchemy started as a spiritual discourse and become more materially oriented as they found they actually could change matter."

"So what does it mean?"

"He will figure out that he needs my blood and will be at the meeting. Alice is safe till then, although I believe he was planning on coming to the meeting after the wedding. In order to come before he has done that, he will need to have you in chaos. Trust me, for the next 48 hours he will attack you with everything he has. He can't kill you because he knows he will never find me, but you need to be prepared to be hit from every angle."

Coming from Joseph I knew these were heady words. I could sit here and try to out think him all day long and still not have a clue.

People at the church were asking if I'd seen Alice. I told them she had to go out of town for a few days, but would be back soon. People called to see if I was all right after what had happened at my house. I gave them assurances. The transcripts of Mary's writings were sitting translated on my desk. Even in English most of it meant nothing to me. I'd been taking her magic elixir regularly and I felt great. I took an extra helping this morning before I prayed.

I found it impossible to concentrate so I went into the basement of the church. I'd had a little workshop built for me, a place at the church to escape. I enjoyed stained glass and was working on a window for my home about 2x4 feet. Mostly abstract, but with distinct flames that would catch the morning light in my kitchen, it was nearly done. I could easily become absorbed in this work, letting go of whatever was on my nerves, but not today, Alice was too important and it was my fault he had her. I took a large pane of glass and smashed it on the floor as I screamed. Sitting on my stool, I sobbed. I cried till my tear ducts were empty and I'd turned it over to God. There was a knock at the door.

"Matt?"

"Come in Jennifer." She was the youth director and her office was at the other end of the hall.

"You Ok? Thought I heard something while I was praying and felt I should come and see if you were here. Anything I can do?"

"Sometimes it just gets to be a bit too much."

"I know the feeling. You have a lot on your plate. Anything in particular?"

I know I'm supposed to share my burdens with others, but the chance was too great I'd pull others in. "Not really Jennifer, but thanks for asking, I really do appreciate it and your concern."

"What happened?" she asked looking at the broken glass.

"When I lifted it, I cut myself and dropped the pane."

"Your hand all right?"

"Yes." I'd have to remember to put a Band-Aid on to carry forth the cover. I didn't want her thinking I would smash things at whim.

There was an awkward moment of silence, neither of us sure where to go.

"How are the kids?"

"They are doing well, everyone is going back to school tomorrow. Something strange happened though."

"What is that?"

"Every one of them had vivid dreams last night."

"Well that isn't so odd, teenagers tend to remember their dreams more than adults and the induced stress and sleep probably added to that. Some probably had nightmares."

"But that isn't what was strange."

"What is it?"

"They all had the same dream, I mean exactly the same and they hadn't talked to each other."

"Why did you ask them about their dreams?"

"Well it started with just a couple of the kids I'd been talking to who were interested. When we were talking on the phone they just told me their dreams up front and they were the same, so I started asking each person I talked to. It was a bit spooky after 8 of them all had the same one."

"What was the dream?" I could already feel my insides churning.

"Well it didn't really make sense to them. There were three people on a sailboat in the middle of the ocean."

The ocean. I chuckled. Coincidence?

"One they said kind of looked like you, one was a beautiful woman with diamonds in her hair and one was a man that seemed to glow. They were looking for something. They landed on a beach and another man and woman came out of the forest; he was some kind of wizard and she was tied up. At first it looked like a trade was to be made, the glowing man for the woman, but then the wizard said no, he wanted all of them. The priest jumped out and challenged him to a duel with swords, all or nothing, willingly to the winner. There was a massive bonfire on the beach, the heat of which was felt a hundred feet away. As the duel went on, they kept moving closer and closer to the fire. When they got within about 30 feet and their skin was seering, a giant explosion took place. All they heard was the laughter of the wizard and they all woke up, exactly at that instant. Pretty amazing isn't it, what do you think it means?"

"The dream was not meant for them Jennifer."

"Who was it meant for?"

"Me."

"How do you know?"

"Because I understand it very clearly."

"What does it mean?"

"You will just have to trust me on this, it's better that you don't know for now. But come back to me in a week and I'll tell you." I didn't add the part about if I was still alive in a week. "And I wouldn't even bring it up with the kids again."

"Ummm, ok if you say so."

"I think it's for the best. But I truly appreciate your telling me. Can we pray before you leave?"

"Of course."

We spent about ten minutes praying for each other, the church and the kids. We both felt the power of the Spirit filling our hearts, minds and souls. That peace that passes all human understanding came into me and I realized how much I'd been trying to control the situation and how fruitless that was. Always best to let God be in control. I told Jennifer how much I appreciated her and how the Spirit brought her too me. When we allow ourselves to be led by the Spirit "coincidences" happen on a regular basis.

So if I'd have not come down here, gotten angry and broken the glass, would I ever have heard about these dreams? What are the odds of 20 young people all having the exact same dream on the same night? I just wish they'd dreamed a bit longer, would have been nice to know if we'd won or not. My belief is that dreams are a window into the soul and the unconscious, that God uses them to help us, as does our unconscious.

I went back upstairs and got some work done, met with some people I was counseling and then headed home. I stopped at Alice's house, knowing where the hidden key was; to water her plants and feed the critters. Her cat missed her deeply, I couldn't tell about the parakeet or iguana.

There were days when I wished I didn't have this special gift that I didn't have to watch lives disappear or smell death. But in the end, good always came out of the evil that had been done. The evil wasn't undone, but justice was served and I believe the true justice would reign in the end. I was walking back to my car when I stopped. I could hear dozens of voices when I attuned my ears to hear, none of them visible. One stood out, a man panting and struggling. I called 911 and gave them the address where I was. I had a few minutes to find the man, probably having a heart attack. My body flew down the street, the voice getting louder and louder until I stood in front of a large white home. I assumed if anyone was home they would have helped him and I'd have heard that, but I didn't. The door was locked so I broke the window and went in. I called 911 and gave them the address as I ran up the stairs. I found him in the hallway. He was about my age and unconscious. I started CPR and didn't stop till the EMT's arrived. I let them take over as they gave him the shock treatment. I was relieved when he responded and they stabilized him.

They hadn't said a word to me until they had him where he didn't take all of their undivided attention.

"Were you here visiting?"

"No, I was just walking by."

"How did you know he'd had a heart attack?"

"God told me."

With that I turned and left. As much as I complain about my gift, I do feel blessed and at times like this, I am the happiest guy on the planet. I just wish it didn't always come at the expense of someone else's suffering. I asked which hospital he was going to so I could pay him a visit. Perhaps a new member of the church.

I was twiddling my thumbs and needed something to do. There had been a question I was curious about for a long time and I decided that today was the time to get the answer. I drove to the OSHU (Oregon Health and Sciences University). It sat on a hill overlooking the city and was in a constant state of growth, adding a new wing seemingly without end and an infamous tram. A premier hospital for teaching and research, I had many friends there. One of them was about to get a visit.

"Hi, I need to see Dr. Maloney please, tell him Matt is here."

I knew he'd see me unless he was in surgery, which was rare. He was a neuroscientist. Brain stuff. He was not only a member of our parish, but I'd made some significant donations to his research because he was helping us understand both the learning process and the power of prayer and its impact on the brain.

"Hey Matt, what brings you here?"

"I need a favor."

"Well, we are a bit busy today."

I looked at him in the eyes as deeply as I could.

"I need a favor Bill."

"Ummm Ok, what is it?"

“I need you to take two of those magic pictures of my brain with your fancy machine.”

“Whatever for? You experiencing some pain or something?”

“Not even close, you will just have to trust me on this one.”

He knew me well enough to not ask questions.

“Ok, come on back. What are we looking for?”

I followed him down a hallway to a room that was about 20x20. In the middle was a large white machine. It reminded me of an MRI full body machine except this one had more wires and was just for the head. I'd seen the pictures this machine could take, quite spectacular. I changed in another room, getting rid of my jewelry. I didn’t really have to. First of all it wasn’t run by magnets and secondly, I was old enough my mouth was full of metal, had it been run by magnets my teeth would have been ripped out of my mouth. I wasn’t really into that today.

“Ok, so I ask again Matt, what are we looking for?”

“I don’t know, but here is what I want you to do. You can see my fingers from your room there, right?”

“Yes.”

“Give me about 30 seconds then take a few pictures, whatever you want, but at least one of the whole brain. Then watch my fingers. When you see any movement, take some more, then wait until I move them again. There will be at least two times I do that, there might be three. If I haven’t moved my fingers within ten minutes after the second time, then we are done.”

“What are we looking for?”

“I have no idea, but I think you might see something unique.”

“What if something goes wrong?”

“Can you hook me up to a heart machine?”

“Yes.”

"Do it, but only come in and disrupt me if my heart goes nuts, do not come in if you see weird things happening in my brain."

"All right, but you have to sign papers." Papers that waived all my rights and gave them no liability if I was stupid enough to die on his table doing something he knew nothing about. I signed.

I lay down on the table as they got me all hooked up and then left. This was going to be a three stage journey. The first was to meditate and I knew he'd seen plenty of pictures of brains in meditation. About 15 minutes in I wiggled my finger. My guess was the picture would show my brain with virtually no activity. A few areas might show a blip here and there. Now came the fun. I came out of the deep meditation and opened my mind to the spiritual web. I visualized it in my mind. Joseph was there along with a few others. I allowed myself to get pulled more and more completely into that sphere of being. I lost complete track of my body and savored every minute. Time disappears in the spiritual dimension. A minute may seem like hours and a day may be but a second. I returned to my mind and contemplated doing something else, but changed my mind. After a few more minutes I came back to full consciousness and told Bill to come and get me. They came in, all staring at me and took off all the gadgets.

"What in tarnation was that all about?" he asked. I could see his interns pouring over the pictures in the other room.

"Pretty interesting wasn't it?"

"I can't say I've ever seen anything like it. What were you doing?"

"Show me."

We all went into a conference room. A large wood table was in the middle with ten chairs around it. At one end was a good sized screen and at the other end, built into the table was a console where Bill sat. Apparently they had this room directly connected to the machine and could show the pictures on the screen.

"Here is you at the beginning. Normal activity in all areas."

"Can you tell my IQ from this?"

"Zero." Everyone laughed.

"This is you meditating. Pretty good job, not the deepest I've seen, but as you can see most of your brain is quiet and inactive. All the red and orange areas of activity are gone, just a few blue and green ones. It's almost impossible to completely shut down the brain. After all your heart does need to continue to beat. Your senses are still engaged and you need to breathe, those all take information to and from the brain."

"Gotcha."

"Now here is where it gets interesting. You go from deep meditation to your brain going absolutely nuts. The left brain which is the more logical side is still relatively quiet, but look at that right brain, my God I've never seen such activity."

He was right, as I entered the web and deepened my connection, the right half of the brain picture turned yellow, orange and then almost solid red.

"I've only seen pictures that come close to that on severely psychotic individuals and they didn't return. Should I have you checked out?"

"Or do you mean have me checked in?" I smiled.

"What was happening?"

"We aren't done yet are we, there is more."

"Why did you come to have me do this is you already know the answer?"

"Because I needed evidence, not just a story."

"Yes, there is more. About six minutes into this part, here is what happened." He clicked for the next picture.

I laughed I was so stunned. The first picture showed my left brain now lighting up, then in different parts of the brain lights flashed. It wasn't so you couldn't see them come and go, but they were the energies of the others on the web and how the web showed up in my brain. The next picture was perhaps the most amazing. In all of these pictures, the edge of the head and the brain were clearly visible. In the last picture the energy released in my brain and by the others expanded past my skull. I wasn't a big believer in auras and people that can see them although from time to time I would swear I had, but here it was in living color. An aura surrounding my head. Every color under the rainbow, moving and morphing with each new image. I was partly looking at the pictures and partly watching the doctors, they didn't have a clue.

"Hmmm Bill, maybe you need to have that machine checked, doesn't seem normal to me."

"Right, nice try buddy, you aren't getting off that easily. We both know it's not the machine. What is it?"

"You wouldn't believe me if I told you."

"Try me, I'm looking at the evidence before I have a theory to find evidence for, it's a little backwards in the scientific community."

"That's the main problem, science will never quite get this one."

"So you are telling me that something spiritual just happened to my machine."

"In a nutshell yes, that is probably as close as you will ever get to seeing the soul operate on a purely spiritual level."

"The soul?" said one of the interns.

"He's a priest, my priest unfortunately," replied Bill.

"Can you hook two people up at once to this machine?"

"No need to, we only look at one brain at a time."

"What if I told you those flashes of light were other brains, wouldn't you like to see what's going on in each brain at the same time?"

I could see lights flashing in his brain, dollar signs for research, fame and fortune.

"I'll see what I can do. But what is it?"

"To be honest I am not sure I can explain it yet, but I'm working on it. I wanted to make sure it was real first and not just a hallucination."

"Well I suppose it could be a massive hallucination, but I've never seen anyone come back to normalcy after an event like that and having the energy of the brain outside the brain cavity—that is a first."

"Let's not publish or talk about this yet," I pleaded.

"Why not?"

"First of all, we don't have a clue what it is that is going on. Secondly, no one will believe you and I don't think you or your friends can duplicate this."

"I'll just bring you back."

"Hmmmm, I don't remember ever having been in that machine. And do you think I am like this all the time? It is an act of will and of spiritual connectivity."

"Awwww Matt, you are killing me."

"You'll get your day, be patient. By the way, can you print out a few 8x10's for me?"

A few minutes later they handed me an envelope with a set of pictures. I grabbed the release form I'd signed and took it with me. No evidence now I was there. Just in case. I thanked them all and headed out. The best part of the exercise was it distracted me and gave me a couple of hours of relief from my worrying about Alice. I knew she was strong, but we all have our limits.

25 BOB LAYS THE TRAP

The jigsaw puzzle was nearly complete, each disfigured piece fitting into another. The furnace was getting hotter, although I was nervous about the electric bill bringing the feds to my door thinking I was a marijuana grower. The generators did some of the work but at this point in the process I needed more. I'd be gone by the time they noticed, gone to a larger house with lots of servants waiting on my every word and command. I was looking forward to having Alice become a deeper part of me as well.

Today would be busy with final preparations. I put the collar and ankle bracelets on Alice. Should she run, the electrical shock would put her out for hours, if not for good, and she knew it.

The goal of today was to rid the planet of Matt and Joseph. They were more of a nuisance than a real threat, but I was having to spend too much time and energy on them and I knew they wouldn't stop, especially once Alice died. It was best to end this charade now. I wanted him to be distracted. By making him play my game or at least center his mind, I would find him on the spiritual web that connects us all.

I'd learned years ago how to make poisonous gas, it's not really that hard, at least varieties that only make people sick. The threat of extinction is a strong motivator and how would they know it wasn't real? I created a pressurized tank full of it and added some rose scent both to throw them off and as a bit of irony in the rose city.

Security in buildings is never quite what it seems. I merely created a work order, got a uniform and made a sign for my van. I was in the courthouse without a problem and with my tank, right to the ventilation room. I set the timer and was on my way in minutes. No one ever checks these things, besides, I, the ventilation expert, had just been there. Then I went back to the house, lots of driving on this day.

Alice was cooking as I walked in.

"Where have you been?"

"Out." I didn't want to disturb her by letting her know that I was keeping her boyfriend busy.

"Would you like something to eat?"

"Yes, I 'm actually quite hungry."

She brought me a plate of food. I smelled it.

"Nice try Alice, but none of the chemicals you put in would kill me, just make me sick. Besides that, there is something you need to understand, do you see that furnace?"

"Yes."

"Believe it or not, the furnace is part of my living being, as I exist so it exists. If something were to happen to me, the explosion would be great, the house and everything in it leveled, including you."

"I don't care."

"I think you do."

"You are wrong. Matt will find you."

"After tonight, Matt will not be an issue, trust me." That caught her off guard. "You know how powerful I am getting don't you?"

"Yes, but what I don't understand is why you are using it to harm people rather than to help?"

"We've been over that, I made a decision."

26 THE INTERROGATION OF MATT

Normally I do not allow interruptions during a counseling session, I find it rude. Julie knows the difference between a want, a crisis and a full blown disaster. She only broke in when the later came to our church. It was about 10:30. We had a knocking code that told me it was her.

The look on her face was dire.

"Something up?" I tried to stay calm knowing something had gone off the tracks.

"I need to see you for a minute."

I apologized, gave the gentleman something to work on while I was out and closed the door behind me.

"It's Tom." She handed me the phone.

"What's wrong?" I asked.

"I don't know how to tell you this, but you have a choice. You can either come down to the police station on your own now, or the policemen sitting outside your church will come in and arrest you---which I might add is what they wanted to do, but I talked them into letting you come in on your own," said Tom with a very strained voice.

"Tom, what is going on?"

"It's out of my hands, just come in."

My mind was reeling. I couldn't figure out what had happened that Tom was out of control and I was wanted at the station. The one thing I knew was it wasn't good. I had to think of the worst case scenario. I wrote down some numbers and told Julie to call the people and tell them where I was.

I greeted the police officers, got in my car and drove to the station downtown. The building was modern and pleasant, not what one normally thinks of in a police station. I was put into an interrogation room.

"Hello, my name is detective Roberts. Tom is not doing this because of conflict of interest. We have recently been given some very disturbing evidence about you."

"Let me guess, they didn't leave their name and number." The murderer had been busy.

"We can make this easy,"

"Or we can make this hard. I have no idea what you think you have. As far as hard goes, you have no clue as to what hard is," I was getting testy which was not always a good thing to do when under investigation.

"Let's start at the top. I need to get in the trunk of your car. You can give me the key or wait here for an hour or two till I get a warrant."

I didn't have an hour or two, so I gave him the keys. They brought me a soda. I asked about my one phone call. They laughed. And left. About 10 minutes later they came back in and threw a small bag on the table. I had yet another bad feeling.

"Want to tell us what is in the bag?"

"Marbles?"

"I'm glad you have such a sense of humor."

"Let me ask you one question officer. When I am shown to be innocent and dozens, if not hundreds of people are murdered, which block will you want to be assigned to in order to dispense parking tickets?"

I could see the nervousness on his face. He was about to go into territory he knew nothing about based purely on hype----always a dangerous affair.

He poured out the tokens the murderer used onto the table.

"How did these get in your trunk?"

"Obviously the murderer put them there."

"Right."

"Tell me this officer, since you know so much. I assume you know about the fire in Connecticut where a token was found. How are you going to explain how I was preaching here on the day of that fire?"

"Perhaps you have helpers."

"Wow, that is impressive."

Next he threw the pictures at me. Pictures of me at Sue's house running around, pictures of me at the soup kitchen before things started.

"Oh, and before you get to it, we know you got a phone call to go to the hospital before the kids were poisoned at your home. We checked your cell phone record. No call was placed."

The alchemist was remarkable at covering his tracks. I was wondering if he'd been planning this all along, creating evidence against me.

"I have no idea what you have against all of these people, but I think it's over."

"Officer Roberts, it's not even close to being over. Get Tom in here and he will explain."

"Tom won't be helping you on this one. He is being interrogated in another room for obstruction of justice."

I couldn't believe this was happening. The walls were crumbling, he'd once again taken back control, and I could feel myself slipping, just as he would want. I was pulling Tom down the rabbit hole with me.

"Just a couple of other things before we let you start to explain yourself. First, the phone conversation you had with the TV station recently where you threatened them."

"What in the hell are you talking about?"

"Father, such language."

"What are you talking about? I'm on very good terms with the stations, in fact I suspect you have seen me on most of them recently."

"Yes I have and to be honest I'm a bit, but not totally surprised. I think your ego has gotten the better of you." He raised his hand and I heard a voice coming through the speakers. It wasn't mine, any idiot could tell that, but it was a decent imitation.

"This is Pastor Matt, is your boss in?"

"No Pastor is there something I can help you with?"

"I need to get on the news, now."

"It doesn't really work that way, I can get a message to the producers."

"That is not acceptable. I've been giving you people lead stories for years, now I ask a small favor and this is the treatment I get?"

"I'm sorry sir, I can give them a message."

"Give them this, they had their chance, it's a bit late now, hold on, it won't be pretty." Click.

"You actually believe that was me? I said petulantly.

"You identified yourself."

"Hello, this is President Barack Obama. Get me your boss."

"Is that supposed to be funny?"

"I said I was the President, why didn't you believe me?"

"Good grief."

"Just have the voice checked against mine, it isn't really that high tech."

"We are, but it will be awhile. Oh and there is one more small problem."

"What else could there possibly be?"

"A woman named Alice from your church, whom we have been led to believe has disappeared. You, by the way, have told people she is away for a few days. We know this to not be true. Like to change your story?"

I could feel my blood boiling. How could God be allowing this to happen? I understand free will, but come on, help me out here. I was losing focus at the precise moment I needed it most. It was humbling times like this I realized how far short I was of having the depth of faith expected of us.

"You wouldn't believe me if I told you."

"Try me."

I had nothing to lose at this point.

"The murderer kidnapped her at my house while the kids were drugged. He sent me to the hospital to get me out of the way and in the end to make it look like I had something to do with it. Alice and I are seeing each other and are very happy. Think about it, why would I kidnap her? What is the motive?"

"We are looking into that, but right now things seem to fit better with you at the head than some unknown guy who has all these magical powers you talk about. Where would you like to start?"

"Let's start at the beginning, but I've been in here a couple of hours and I need to go to the bathroom. Unless of course you'd like a lawsuit for cruel and unusual punishment of a prisoner."

"We are very polite here Pastor, an officer will escort you to the rest room. Would you like to call a lawyer?"

"No need, I'm innocent, but trust me, when this is over you will be hearing from one. I guarantee that you or someone here has told the media which mean my name is being slandered on the TV, probably even as we speak. The department will have two choices; pony up tens of millions of dollars for defamation of character or put you on parking ticket duty and strip you of your pension. I hope you have thought through what you are doing."

The internal stress showing on his face was obvious. I had no idea if I could do what I just claimed, but I could tell he thought it a possibility. Beads of sweat appeared on his brow.

"I'm just trying to get at the truth."

"If you were truly after the truth, I wouldn't be here. No, you are after breaking a big case and making a name for yourself." I had him. Wasn't going to do me any good, he was in too far now.

"Oh My God," I shouted.

"What?" Roberts said, a bit shocked by my outbreak. I contained myself.

"Can I see the envelope the evidence came in?"

"I don't see why not." He slid the large manila envelope to me. I picked it up and smelled it. The murderer's scent was there. He certainly hadn't held it with his hands."

"I assume you tested it for prints as evidenced by the black powder."

"No prints."

"Gee, what a surprise. Sounds like your Joe average citizen turning in evidence to me." He'd rubbed it on his clothing, it sat in his house and car, and he was on it. Shouldn't have taken the envelope out of the bag and used it fresh, didn't have the chance to collect other odors other than his and.............. there was something else. Roses. And something else, what was it.

"Oh my God," I shouted again not thinking.

"What is it with you?"

"Nothing, can I go to the bathroom now?"

I got up and left the room. I had a good idea what was coming. The threatening phone call was a precursor to his doing something at the TV station. I turned back.

"By the way, which station was that I was supposed to have threatened?"

"KOIN 6. Why?"

"Just need to know who to apologize to."

I had to get out of here, but how to do you break out of police station? I went into the bathroom and sat down, thinking. An officer was posted at the door, I didn't think I could take him out. I was in there about five minutes when I heard the door open.

"Are you going to stay in that stall the whole day?"

I jumped out of my skin. This couldn't be possible. I threw open the door and Joseph was washing his face.

"Odd place to be staying," he said.

"What are you doing here? Wait, Julie must have gotten the word out."

"You are a bright young man. Seems you are in a bit of a pickle."

"That's putting it mildly, the murderer has stacked evidence making it look like I did it all."

"Well just get them to see the truth, sort it out."

"First of all, that takes time, time we don't have. Secondly, he made a threat against a TV station which I think will be happening shortly, the nail in my coffin, whether I can stop it or not, but I'd rather stop it."

"How do you plan on doing that locked up in here?"

"I can't, so you will have to."

"Sorry my friend, I don't have the gifts necessary to do that."

"Then why are you here?"

"To break you out, are you ready?"

"I'm going to be a fugitive?"

"Do you have an alternative?"

"I guess not, so what is the plan?"

"First of all, you need to know you have many friends who are willing to go all the way for you."

"Yes, I know. We can't just walk out and a friendly call won't have them cut me free right now." I was running out of time and options.

"Calm down Matt." He checked his watch. "Ok, in one minute you walk out the door and out of the station, do not talk to anyone, stay focused, do not question what you see or hear, just walk. A green sedan will be waiting out front, running. I know you want to ask questions, don't. Take your one minute and center yourself as best you can."

He left the room. I stood by the door and got my breathing into a rhythm. Joseph's mere presence helped calm me down. After a minute I opened the door. Joseph was talking to the officer guarding me. He was in some kind of trance, oblivious to me as I walked by. I walked down the stairs past dozens of officers. They all nodded. Word had yet to get out that they had a celebrity in lock up. When I got to the front entry, two of the detectives who had been talking to me were talking to someone. As I rounded the corner she turned, making the detectives turn their backs to me and the entry. Then I saw who it was, Sue. She was showing them something, but I knew she was a distraction, more misdirection. It was hard not to take my eyes off Sue. She'd put on an unbelievably sexy outfit that highlighted her numerous beautiful features. The police were clearly enjoying themselves. I walked out the door and into the car that was waiting, just as Joseph had said. It wouldn't take them long to figure out I'd flown the coop. I just hoped those inside weren't held for aiding and abetting.

The TV building was only five blocks from the station. Twenty five floors of offices. What was he thinking of doing? I centered again. Roses. There it was again. He'd been here and left something, where was it coming from? I walked around until I had it. He'd gotten to the ventilation system. I saw a maintenance man in the lobby and told him I was from the ventilation company doing an audit check on some recent work and needed to the central machinery. He laughed.

"No you aren't, you are that priest guy."

"All right, you are right, I'm sorry. What do you know about me?"

"Well you and God healed some people and saved some lives and you have put some bad guys behind bars."

"Exactly. God told me a man has put some gas in your ventilation system, we need to get there before it's too late."

"Why didn't you say so?"

He got on his walkie-talkie and told others what we were up to just in case we needed help. He said it was right under the lobby. I was already noticing some people starting to act differently as we got on the elevator. People swaying, slurring their words, and the smell of roses becoming more and more intense.

We ran down a hallway into a room. A large tank was sitting next to the main blower with a hose stuck into the pipe. A timer was attached to the tank. The gas had been pouring into the system for about ten minutes. I turned the valve.

"Wow, looks like you and God have done it again."

"Couldn't have done it without your help.

"Glad to be a part of it sir."

"Just call me Matt. While I think of it, I have another favor to ask."

"Anything."

"Well before you say that you might want to hear what I need."

"Doesn't matter, you just saved everyone's life in this building."

"Well some police men are on their way here and they are going to claim that I am the one that put that canister here."

"They can't possibly be that stupid."

"Just a few of them, most are very, very smart.

"So what do you want?"

"A way out, they will be surrounding the building."

There were three of them in the room with me. They all agreed to help.

"Front desk, are you there?" said one of the guards into his walkie-talkie.

"Yea, I'm here."

We took that guy up to the tenth floor air conditioning room, just in case someone is looking for us.

"If they want you, they'll just use the walkie-talkies."

"I'm just saying."

"Roger."

"Ok, that will get us a little time. Roy, you stay with the canister, when the cops come, just tell them pastor said he was an air-conditioning man and needed to see the room so we took him to the tenth floor. John you go to the tenth floor and wait by the room. Don't wait too long, then leave. If the police ask you what happened, tell them you took the guy up, he went in for a couple of minutes, said thanks and good bye and left. Pastor, follow me."

We went down some underground hallways that seemed to go forever. He took out a key and opened a door and locked it behind us.

"Where are we?"

"Across the street. There are tunnels all over the place. Some of the maintenance people share keys, never know when you might need to get in or out of your building from a different access." I laughed.

"I think that is a fabulous idea. Are you happy with your job?"

"Very."

"Good, I'm glad. When this is over, I'll be sure to put in a good word to your boss for you and your friends. I see a raise in your future."

"I appreciate it pastor."

"Matt."

"Matt, sir."

We walked up the stairs and out a door that was on the other side of the building, clear of police whose many cars we saw out front. I took a cab to a café we'd all agreed to use at any time as a meeting point if there was ever any trouble. We knew if something happened our homes would be watched. I pulled in. I recognized Sue and Joseph, was surprised to see Tom, and wasn't sure who the other three people were.

"Well hello Matt, glad to see you, did you get there in time?"

"Yes, he'd put gas into the ventilation system, but thanks to some very helpful people we got it shut off before much was leaked and they got me here. So Tom, how did you get free?"

"I'm not sure. They convinced me in short order that with you gone the depth of my pain was about to increase, I was either all in or I was toast. Here I am."

"Yes, but how did they get you out?"

"Meet Officer Johnson---Phil Johnson," said Joseph looking at one of the men I didn't know.

"Awww so you are Phil from the east coast. "

"At your service."

"Impersonating an officer your first day in town, aren't you glad you came?"

"I enjoy a bit of fun, but I've had my fill."

"I'm Matt and you would be?" I asked looking at the woman I didn't know.

"Jennifer, you know me as A."

"Ah yes, A. And you are?" looking at the third person.

"I'm Thomas."

"He's not in the room you went to, he's a special student of mine," Joseph remarked.

"Well I'm glad to meet all of you and I'm sorry it's in this situation."

"It's not that bad Matt. The police are looking for you, you are back on TV although not in the best of lights, and they are talking about canceling the talk tomorrow night because you have disappeared from a police station. Oh and I almost forgot, they are looking for a few people that helped you escape, although they have no idea what they looked like," Sue said cheerfully.

"I think it's time to call in some chits, don't you?"

"This may be a very good time Matt," she said.

While the others chatted and enjoyed their coffee and croissants, I made four phone calls in this order and all were friends, two were parishioners; the Mayor, District Judge, Chief of Police, and director of KOIN 6 news.

"Hi Sam."

"Where are you Matt?"

"Enjoying some coffee."

"As a fugitive I understand."

"That's what I'm calling about. I'll make this short. I'm being framed—a good job I assure you, but framed nonetheless. The murderer wants me out of commission or distracted for 48 hours. If he gets his 48 hours you will be kicking yourself for the rest of your life, trust me on this one."

"Matt, you've dug a pretty big hole. You left the police station."

"Your honor, I came to the police station of my own accord, I was never placed under arrest, and therefore I was under no obligation to stay. I suppose you could make a case that I didn't give them the opportunity to arrest me, but legally, I didn't need to."

"I feel so comforted."

"I need 48 hours. I promise in 48 hours I will show up at the police station and will stay there until they decide to arrest me or let me go. I need the police off my back until then."

"You are putting me in a very precarious position."

"Then stay out of it, but when the chief calls you in 10 minutes, tell him to give me the 48 hours."

"Ok Matt, but just know that if you had anything to do with any of this, my pledge is going to shrink next year."

"Always glad for your sense of humor and thank you."

That went well.

"Hello, Sid please, tell him it's Matt." I didn't have to wait long.

"Matt, where the hell are you?"

"Seems to be the question of the hour. I'm safe."

"Thank God for small favors. What is this game you are playing? Why did you resist arrest and bolt, it's not like you?"

"Did officer Roberts tell you I was arrested?"

"He said you were brought in for questioning."

"The truth is I came of my own free will to the station. I was never arrested or even told what I might be arrested for, although innuendos were mentioned. My understanding is that if you walk into a police station of your own free will and are not arrested, you can leave of your own free will. Am I wrong?"

"Technically, no."

"Then we are good."

"Not remotely. You were seen at the KOIN building where poison gas was released."

"Yes, like the soup, I probably saved hundreds of lives, I'm so sorry for that."

"Matt, we both know it's not what it looks like."

"Sid, we are good friends, but you are starting to irritate me, so I will just lay it out. I'm being framed by a murderer who will do significantly more damage if I don't stop him. No, the police will never catch this guy, they've had months and have done nothing, not their fault, and he's just very good. I am making one request and one demand; it's your choice as to how you treat each. First, I need 48 hours to catch this guy. If I don't,

I'll turn myself in. When I do catch the murderer I want officer Roberts off the police force and put on parking patrol duty. This is not about vengeance, but about his abuse of power. He leaked the story about me and it's already on the news that I am a suspect in murders, arsons, and thefts. My reputation is severely damaged. So he goes on parking patrol or I sue the city for $12 million dollars and I think you know I'll win. This is not a threat, it's a promise. Along with giving me lots of rope with which to hang myself, you will pull the dogs off my detective friend, Tom."

"God you are pushy."

"I'm running out of time and don't have time for chit chat or to bargain or to play games with politicians and policemen, do it on your own time."

"Settle down Matt. I don't know why but I'll do the first and last now. I'll call the D.A. As to parking duty, we'll talk."

"No Sid, there will be no conversation, when the police have the murderer in their hands with clear evidence, you will have one week to get rid of Roberts or the lawsuit will start. By the way, his reputation is already gone, I'm going on the news in an hour and will specifically name him and what he has done for the cause of justice."

"Don't do that Matt."

"Sorry, I just don't trust the establishment. He's done."

"I don't think I have ever seen you like this."

"You have no idea what we are dealing with and the damage Roberts has done. I don't know if I can undo it in the limited time I have."

"He was following evidence from what I hear."

"No, he jumped to conclusions and acted as jury and judge in the public arena before even talking to me."

"How do you know it wasn't someone else who leaked the info?"

"I'll have my day in court and trust me, I'll have the evidence. I believe a simple phone log check from his phone will be enough. But I have more. You guys aren't the only ones that tape phone calls, oh and by the way, I'd check, my guess is that during at least part of my conversation with Roberts, your tape machine got the flu, kind of like Nixon's. Unfortunately, I have my own complete recording."

"All right, you've made your point, you have free reign for 48 hours, as does Tom."

"I appreciate this . And just so we are clear Sid, I mean complete free reign. No tails, no undercover people sitting outside my house or office. It's all or nothing, I don't need the murderer spooked by idiots, and might I suggest you let officer Roberts know this, his level of stupidity is rather high."

"Ok, Ok. Go."

"Thanks. By the way, if you want to see how to spin this, just watch channel 6 in two hours, I'll spell out the deal we made."

"Why don't you tell me now?"

"I haven't figured it out yet."

"I should have known."

"Can you get this done in the next 45 minutes?"

"Get what done?"

"My freedom."

"I doubt it, but I'll try."

That went far more smoothly than I had expected. I knew the lawsuit rattled him, probably pushed him over the edge of putting up a fight. He was a very good chief and his heart was in the right place. I wished him well with D.A. who I called next. That went more smoothly since the Mayor had just finished talking with him. Next up, the TV station.

"Martha please, tell her it's Pastor Matt calling." I had a feeling my name was buzzing around the station.

"Hello? This is Martha."

"Hey Martha, Matt here."

"What on earth is going on? I get calls from the police station, I hear a tape of you calling and going ballistic on the phone. I hear that there is evidence you are a murderer."

"All false and I'd like to come in now and talk about it, live."

"What? So tell me what this is about?"

"Off the record, for now?"

"Sure."

"There is a murder loose as you well know. I'm very close to getting him and he knows it. He gave information to the police implicating me in numerous things, including the gassing of your building, which by the way, I stopped, just ask your maintenance crew, they will tell you the truth. A police officer called you to let you know all of this. The murderer is playing into his hands and has taken control. I need to get control back and in order to do that I need to get on the air."

"Makes some sense, what about tomorrow morning?"

"Too late and I can't explain the details, you'll just have to trust me. If you don't agree, I'll just go to the other station." I was confident that one line would get me the air time.

"You do know how we work. OK come in, I'll get things lined up."

I returned to the crowd at the table.

"Ok, everything is a go. Yes Tom, you are clear, for 48 hours. Then we either turn ourselves in or we turn in the murderer. We've got some work to do."

For another hour we strategized and gave everyone something to do. Then I headed out for the station. I was not very secure Sid would be able to spread the word about not touching me in the 45 minutes I gave him which made me all the more pleased I'd taken down Terri, the maintenance man's cell. I called.

"Terri, Matt here, how are you?"

"Good."

"Have things calmed down at all?"

"Not a lot, still lots of cops here, asking questions and looking around."

"I was afraid of that. Can you do me a favor?"

"Of course, name it."

I met him at the same door he let me out of. We retraced our steps underground and avoided all people until we arrived at the service elevator. He took me to the 7th floor where the station was.

"You go to need help getting out?"

"No, I'm going to walk through the main door and hope everything is in place. If it isn't, come visit me at the police station."

We shook hands, laughed, and he disappeared. When you are a man accused of some pretty horrible things, especially being a priest, heads tend to turn when you walk through doors. There was dead silence when I entered KOIN 6's lobby.

"Don't worry, I won't hurt anybody."

One person laughed, several left the lobby in a hurry. Martha casually walked in.

"Let's go Matt, you are on in five minutes."

Most TV studios are not nearly as glamorous as they make them look on the screen. They are crowded, warm and very bright. Cables all over the place and three cameras peering at you. Any sense of intimacy you get on a show is created by those on the camera and their relaxed nature.

"This is Tanya Johnson with a special report. A few hours ago, we gave you a report that Pastor Matt, a well-known figure in Portland, had been accused by the police department of committing murder, arson, theft, and fraud. They gave us evidence to back these statements up, evidence given to them by an unknown person. One of the pieces that concerned this TV station in particular was a phone call Pastor Matt allegedly made to this station making threats. Two hours ago an attempt was made to gas everyone in the building. Pastor Matt was seen in the building at the time. He has asked to come on the air and explain himself. Welcome."

"Thank you for having me Tanya. First, let me be clear, I categorically deny every accusation made against me. I am trying my best to catch this criminal animal and he is doing his best to keep me off balance and frame me."

"So you are claiming all the evidence was fabricated and is false?"

"Every bit of it."

"We were told you ran from the police station, avoiding arrest."

"First of all, I was never put under arrest. Several officers have exceeded their boundaries of police process and will be held accountable for that when this is all over. I can prove it was an officer that leaked the information to you----highly illegal by the way. I went to the station to help them with their investigation and gave them information that would make it clear I was not the culprit if they were interested in checking it out---which they weren't."

I took out of piece of paper from my pocket.

"This is a piece of paper you will find the police officer's fingerprints on that was interrogating me. It has the evidence I was talking about that would clear my name. You'll note it is very crumpled. That is because he threw it in the waste basket. That will be seen on the video tape of the interrogation which has already been collected by someone other than the officer in charge."

"What about the threat to our building and the gas?"

"There was no threat, it was the murderer placing the call. Have you ever seen me threaten anyone? Have I ever done anything other than try to help people? Have I not been a friend of this station for a decade?"

"Well people do change."

"It wasn't me, any idiot can take the recording and do a voice comparison and find that to be true in about 40 seconds. Again, the police refused to do this. I left the station because when I heard the tape I knew the murderer was going to follow through with the threat and make it look like me. I came and found the gas. "

"How did you even know it was gas?"

"I smelled roses on the envelope that was left with the evidence. Roses don't bloom this time of year. I also smelled a faint hint of gas. I took a guess and turned out to be right. Besides, God helped."

"God helped?"

"God helps in all things, I just happened to listen this time.

"So what now?"

"Well, the police are still not convinced I am innocent. I arranged to be out on bail, $5 million dollars' worth. I have a church to run and a very important talk tomorrow night. I didn't want to give it from jail. I told them I wouldn't leave town and I would turn myself in on Saturday. After much discussion, they agreed."

"They are very trusting."

"Look, a lot of people know me in this city. I'm not going anywhere very fast and $5 million is a lot of money."

"So just to recap, you are claiming complete innocence and you say you once again saved the lives of many, perhaps hundreds."

"In a nutshell yes, but not without God's guidance. There is a maniac on the loose we will catch, he is not nearly as strong as he thinks, and he's a coward. And while I'm here let me give a plug. I look very forward to tomorrow night's lecture on alchemy, promises to be lots of fun. Some good laughs, some magic tricks and some things people have never seen before. The murderer is pretending to be powerful and is hiding. Tomorrow night people will see true power out in the open.

"Sounds fascinating, we'll be there."

"Well, I'm not allowing cameras inside, but we can talk afterwards if you want."

"Do you mind me asking why we can't be there?"

"This is a spiritual event and I don't want any distractions and to be honest, seeing things over the TV isn't the same. I've never believed in those shows where the preacher tells you to put your hands on the television and get healed. Hogwash. God is an up close and personal God and that is who we will be meeting tomorrow night---in a very big way."

"We appreciate your coming in pastor and good luck tomorrow night."

"Oh, one more thing."

"What is it?"

"If I were you, I'd be expecting something amazing to be happening, more on the positive side of life, something that will gather a crowd and make everyone happy."

She had the look of shock in her eyes. "How did you know?"

With a laugh as if I knew the answer I responded. "Whatever do you mean Tanya, know what?"

"Know about what is happening at Powell's Books?"

"I'm sure I have no idea what you are talking about, but tell us."

"We were going to cut to it right after this story. Someone has planted diamonds larger than a carat all over Powell's Bookstore. The place is a madhouse. So far 50 have been found."

"I wouldn't stop till you hit 100!" I exclaimed with great joy. "Enjoy the hunt!!"

"Did you have something to do with this?"

I thanked Tanya and the crew and left. As I went down the elevator, I felt my nerves tingling, more than a bit nervous about what would await me when the doors opened. The lobby of the building seemed to be almost back to normal, save the 10 officers milling around. Officer Roberts was at the door.

"Pastor Matt, I see you have friends in high places, good for you."

"Officer, a kind word of advice. Stay out of my way for 48 hours if you want to have a remote chance of seeing daylight."

"Is that a threat?"

"You will learn that I don't make threats, but I have no tolerance for the abuse of the law which you have clearly done. Oh and by the way, you will be making the news. That evidence I gave you that you crumpled up and threw away with your fingerprints on it and doing it on camera----should make the news—don't bother going back to the station to get the tape, the D.A. already has it."

He turned white.

"Stay out of my way and I will bring you the murderer. If I don't, I'm all yours for as long as you want, honest."

With a smile, if not a smirk, on my face, I left. Other TV stations were waiting outside for their own chunk of meat, but I'd had enough. I'd give them a story next time around. I climbed into the car that was waiting for me and left. This had been a major blip on the radar but once again I felt God had regained control. I felt good, centered, and was breathing easy once again. I had that deep sense of peace that passes all human understanding. Tomorrow would be a different tale.

25

BOB

27 BOB TALKS OF MARRIAGE

I went into the laboratory for a bit, checking on the potions for the evening performance. Then I returned to the living room and turned on the television. Matt's favorite channel. Sure enough, he'd made it in time and was live on camera. Alice watched as I went back to the lab and tried to find him in my mind. It didn't take long but he was so preoccupied with the TV I couldn't break through, but the strain I was putting on his psyche would pay off later, I wasn't done with him yet.

"He foiled you again," Alice said as I returned to the living room.

I laughed. "My dear, he didn't foil me, I gave him a choice, save people and be vulnerable, or let people die and stay safe. I knew he'd choose the people, he is weak."

"In his weakness he is stronger than you at your worst."

"I know you have strong feelings for him, but at least be realistic, he is no match."

"He saved all those people."

"He saved no one. The gas was very weak, would make people sick at best and only hit three floors, the lowest of the building. You see I am not that evil, I did not intend to kill anyone, just get his attention. I was successful. He didn't find it on his own by the way, I led him to it, like a mouse in the maze that can't resist the cheese."

"You underestimate God."

"I don't underestimate anyone or anything, but I do know my capabilities. God hasn't seen fit to stop me yet. Besides that, Matt has a friend, a master alchemist he found, someone as strong if not stronger than me. But he has been hidden all these years, he shares his powers with no one for no reason, what a waste. At least I am using what I have. And I look forward to having you share them with me."

"Never."

"As I have already told you, the choice is not yours, it can be pleasant or painful, but the transformation will happen."

She went and sulked in the corner looking out the window. I returned to the lab waiting patiently for the right moment.

An hour later I was jolted. Matt had used a great deal of energy doing something and was quite weak mentally, I crept in close and then attacked his mind, sending visions of the horrors he would soon be witness to. I'm sure his body was in agony. I would wear him down till his mind snapped. I could see that Joseph had yet to teach him how to avoid this pitfall. He felt like putty in my hands.

I was feeling his mind peel away, giving in more and more when suddenly I felt like he was holding a mirror to me, the full power of my mind reflected back on me. I was literally sent falling back and tripped on a table, sprawling across the floor. I was dazed for an hour. When I came to I couldn't figure out what had happened. He didn't have that strength. I doubted that he was surrounded by alchemists that were protecting him, he didn't know any and I knew that Joseph was not with him. I only knew of one force that could do that, electromagnetism. But it had to be of significant force and there weren't any magnets floating around like that and he didn't even know of this trait they carried. I went back to the laboratory and tried again, but he was gone, surrounded by chaos, I couldn't find him.

Magnets, like a lot of forces in nature are quirky. They have influence on both the material and spiritual realms. Alchemists have learned that seemingly material forces have a hand and an impact on the spiritual world as well.

I'd video-taped his interview in the morning and turned it on without Alice around to annoy me. He was on there, mocking me again. My anger raged. I dreamed of what I would do to him, how painful I would make his demise, how he would watch others suffer before he joined them. I walked in to Alice and slapped her hard on the face.

"That's for your boyfriend, may he rot in hell which is where he will be in four hours."

"I thought marriage to be real and valid had to be based on love, not just a piece of paper. The type of marriage you are looking for doesn't even include a piece of paper and yet you think you will merge with someone that despises every pore of your body?" Alice replied feeling confident.

I slammed her door and locked her in; I didn't want any more distractions. I hated the thought of my spiritual compliment having to enter the relationship unwillingly. I'd read ancient manuscripts of this happening. Women being kidnapped, traded, or bought because of their beauty, wealth, or intelligence. The alchemists felt they would "inherit" whatever they had through the melding. Sometimes the naiveté of some of these scientists was comical. We'd advanced not only in a technological sense, but in a psychological one as well. I understood it was the essence of Alice I would be adding to my own persona, her "femaleness."

For years I had studied feminine psychology. I'd isolated their peculiarities and had disciplined myself to focus on them in what I did and in the potions I created. In the end, nothing worked. I watched men that acted like women, but even they lacked the depth. The fact was they weren't women. The only real way to have the feminine at the core of your being was to morph with one, to somehow absorb their essence and alchemy was the only way to do it, the very process is at the heart of alchemy.

The furnace must be at its hottest in order to forge the two essences completely and each would have to drink a potion of metals that would fuse as well, living in the bottom of the furnace until completely burned, a process that usually took about 36 hours. The final jump in temperature came just before we entered as the gods filled the lab. I get goose bumps just thinking about it. My guess was that Alice would not do this willingly, she would have to be hypnotized or drugged in order to drink the metal. I've drunk a lot of metal in my life, but this combination was fatal except in this one process.

Part of the beauty of meeting Matt and Joseph is that I will be able to get the final substance I need for the potion---their blood. The metal composition must mix with the blood of a master alchemist and of a rival. There were other masters in the world and I could track them down, perhaps even get me to give me some of their blood, but this would work out perfectly. I didn't expect them to just hand their life force over to me, I'd have to take it from them. Doing so in front of a large group of people would only make the conquest that much better. .

The day was spent in peace and quiet. Not even I could enter the lab now, the heat so intense. I opened all the windows and doors which turned the home into a pleasant 85 degrees. Alice sulked most of the day. We chatted a bit now and then, but clearly she was losing faith in her boyfriend, the fight was just about gone. I decided one more show of strength might be helpful.

"Alice I want to show you something." I took her hand and she didn't fight. "I do this for two reasons. First, I'll be leaving shortly and when I return, we will be married. As I have said, if you go into it of your own free will, the pain will not be that great, if you fight, well I want to you give you a very small taste of what it will be like. I also want to give you a warning not to try to leave."

I had turned the voltage down a bit around the house. When I dragged her through the electric field the shock would be enough to make her pass out, but not to cause a heart attack or death. I could feel her tense as I walked through the door. She screamed as her body tensed in electric convulsions. Then she collapsed. I turned off the juice and put her on her bed. Then I turned it back up. If she tried to escape, I'd find her on the porch upon my return.

I took Alice her dinner. She was just coming around. "I'm sorry I had to do that Alice, but you are a slow learner." She remained silent. "You can enjoy the evening. By the way, you know doubt have considered cutting the collar off. I'm amazed you haven't already."

"I assumed it was boobie trapped."

"Indeed it is, a very powerful gas will leak out and kill you if you cut it off."

I got dressed and loaded my car. The final chapter was in play. I'd been waiting for this moment for a very long time. My blood was pumping through my veins, the adrenaline already building. There was one briefer stop on my way.

28 MATT'S SLEEP ATTACKS

The group gathered at my house for a lovely evening. We didn't even bring up what was about to take place, we just laughed and enjoyed one another's company. I'm sure the murderer was in the front or back of everyone's mind, but we'd all agreed to be distracted for tonight, without even mentioning it. Most of our attention was on Joseph. He kept giving these cryptic clues that he may not be long for this world and we all wanted to get as much out of him as we could. He seemed very patient and pleased to share his knowledge, much of which I didn't understand. Sue was completely out of touch. Phil and the others took notes. They all left around midnight. I was tired and went to bed. I said my prayers but drifted off quickly.

My dreams were active on this night. I had a couple of fairly sensuous ones, not uncommon in my life and some about alchemy. Then the web appeared. I saw a few lights on it. Then a light appeared that didn't seem to be on the web, but behind it. As the light grew, the web started melting from the outside. I noticed I was at the center of this melting process. One light after the next would disappear as the light burned the web away. It never caught fire, just melted into nothingness. In the dream I had no clue what to do. There was no were to run and somehow the light had kept me from waking up or fleeing the web itself. I was trapped. The heat and light were intensifying. Every ounce of spiritual and physical energy were being spent trying to hold on.

I sat up suddenly. I was in the room but not in the room. I was fully awake, my eyes open and the dream being played out before my very eyes. Nothing like this had ever happened to me. I wondered if this was like St. John of the Cross's visions. I was paralyzed on my bed. I knew my mattress was soaked with my sweat as I lay motionless. I heard the mockery of his laughter, his sucking everything out of my being. I tried everything; prayer, meditation, casting out demons, singing, and laughing. All to no avail. I was beginning to wonder if I would make the lecture, I must have been here for hours and hours. Finally I realized that perhaps I was going about this all wrong. Instead of fighting, surrender, open up and listen.

The second I opened up two things happened. First, the light crashed into me and I screamed, I was now firmly in its grasp. Secondly I heard a clear and distinct voice.

"Press the button, turn on your blanket." I hesitated, what was that all about?

I heard it again. "Press the button now!!!"

It took everything I could do, but my hand reached and turned on the electric blanket. I heard a loud humming noise. Within seconds the light exploded and was gone. I was surrounded by darkness and thought I'd gone blind. I still couldn't move. No longer paralyzed, my body just couldn't move due to exhaustion. I tried talking and couldn't. I quickly went back to sleep.

I awoke at 7. The previous night was a blur. My bed was still soaked so I knew that at some level whatever had happened was very real. I heard the hum and turned my body to the side. On each side of my bed were two giant pieces of metal. I figured they were what caused the nightmares. Somehow that evil man had gotten into my house and set these up. But how and when? And why didn't I see them when I went to bed? Well, yes, the room was dark and I was exhausted. Still.

The phone rang.

"I hope they worked."

"What are you talking about Joseph?"

"The magnets."

"The what?"

"Aren't you lying on your bed or do you have enough energy to get up?"

"Yes, I'm in bed, yes I had a bad night, yes I'm tired, but I still have no clue as to what you are talking about."

"Aren't there some large metal objects next to your bed?"

"Why yes there are, how observant. I thought they had to do with the nightmares I had last night."

"They did. You were so tired yesterday and so drained, I became concerned our friend would try an attack while you were sleeping, which I think he did."

"The burning light."

"That would be the one. Anyway, he came at it in a way I was helpless to do much. I was trying to get your attention, but you were so focused on keeping him at bay you didn't listen, until you let go, surrendered, then I got through and told you to push the button."

"Oh yes, the button, but why would I want to turn on the electric blanket?"

"I replaced the blanket with a very strong electromagnet which acts as a force field against what he was trying."

"It worked."

"Obviously."

"Why didn't you tell me before I went to bed?"

"Had I told you, he would have known it, you'd have unknowingly alerted him and then he would have done something different. Not only did you succeed, but I suspect he is now the tired one. The electro-magnet acts as a mirror, so all the intensity he focused on you was now on him. Wish I could have been there."

"You people do some weird stuff."

"Well to be honest, I didn't know the strategy would work. I'd done some reading, but never really tried it."

"So in the end, I'm a guinea pig?"

"Yes, sorry."

We both laughed.

"Well I'm going to shower, then maybe eat and take a quick nap before I get on with my day, there is a lot to do. See you tonight."

"Yes, and I wouldn't worry, he will be busy himself, I think the attacks are done, although I can't begin to know the depth of his rage at this point. I fear for all of us, especially the innocent ones who come tonight. I hope we are making the right decision, he will be bringing every ounce of evil energy he can find in the universe with him and there are a lot of principalities out there."

"I couldn't agree more, I'm going to light some candles on their behalf at prayers today. Fortunately, I happen to know that God is more powerful than all the principalities, that is where my trust will be."

"I may join you in that effort and I don't even believe in the candle thing."

I dragged myself out of bed, fixed some breakfast, took a shower and fell back onto my bed for a wonderful two-hour nap. I woke up around 10 feeling refreshed. Now it was time for the final preparations.

29 SHOWDOWN AT THE CHURCH--MATT

I arrived at the church at just about 6pm. The people would start arriving shortly. I made sure the crew was there setting up the other viewing areas, getting chairs up, coffee ready, and someone on the phones to give directions. It never failed that someone at the last minute wouldn't know where or how to get here, especially in the age of Mapquest, but it was always better to be over prepared than under. Seeing that all was in order I went to the chapel and locked the door. The chapel seated about 50, had 30 foot ceilings and was almost completely stained glass—at night illuminated from the inside, unless you flip a switch and then from the outside—I flipped the switched and was bathed in soothing colors and images, both real and abstract.

My prayers in the midst of silence were for protection for everyone there save myself, and for guidance. I didn't want to underestimate the murderer's power or depth of evil, nor did I want to hold back the power of God, which I knew to be infinite. I surrendered myself to God and to Christ and then sat in stillness. Usually at this point I felt that inner peace that passes all understanding; I physically felt the presence of God surrounding me. Tonight it was there, but not nearly as potent. I couldn't figure out if the reason was because of my fears and trepidations or because God didn't want to fill me with peace. I'd learned long ago to accept whatever happened in my meditations, not to question, just accept—and so I did. I sat in silence, clearing my mind and breathing deeply for about 20 minutes. When I was done, I knew there would be people wondering where I was, so I headed back to the church.

The sanctuary was packed. Many greeted me as I walked through the sanctuary and the rest of the facility only to find every space jammed with another several hundred sitting outside. The crew had set up speakers on the grounds but couldn't put video outside. When I returned I saw Joseph near the altar sitting in a choir stall.

"Evening Joseph, ready?"

"With great reluctance, yes." I hadn't seen Joseph this tense, the very sight of it made me nervous. I recognized a few of the people we'd met with the other evening, but there were strangers with him.

"Am I missing something Joseph?"

He laughed, looking at them. "These are our friends, I decided it was time for us all to meet, face to face and we can use their help." I'd already met Phil and a couple of others, now I introduced myself to each of them, made the connection and met a couple of new ones.

"I'm glad you are all here, although I'm not sure it is in your best interest."

"They have only one job Matt, to shield your mind. Our friend will be working on you the entire time."

"First of all, he isn't our friend, but an enemy. Secondly, I have a very high source that is going to shield me------------------and thirdly, thanks, to all of you, we will all need every ounce of assistance we can get. You are angels unaware."

Joseph knew better than to respond.

"I have a few more things to do before we get started, excuse me." I left and went to the sacristy—the room where the vessels for communion and our vestments are kept. I decided to use our oldest silver from the 13th century, pieces that were surrounded by legend. They were locked in a safe and we rarely used them, their value at over $2 million. To me they were just pieces of silver in the form of a chalice and a plate. But with the mythology that surrounded them I figured I could use all the help I could get. The church had received them about 80 years ago in a very auspicious way, but that is a completely different story for another time.

I set the altar ensuring that what I'd asked the sexton to do had been done. He was very efficient and all was ready. I gazed at the audience seeing many faces I had never laid eyes on before. Three TV camera crews were in the back and a number of photographers, I would have to remind them not to take flash pictures during certain parts of the presentation. I had bouncers in case there was trouble—outside what I expected. I'd given them clues as to what I was expecting and what words or hand signals meant to just relax and not worry. Four minutes to opening. No one had a clue what was about to happen, as if I did. I felt my pockets; one cell phone in my left pocket and another in my right, walkie-talkie in my coat. I had no sense that the murderer was here, I certainly hoped he wasn't pulling the plug. I looked over at Joseph who shrugged his shoulders.

When people arrived they received a rather thick bulletin. It outlined what they'd missed in the earlier lectures, gave some on line resources for alchemy and spirituality, some information about our church—encouraging them to join us for worship---and a questionnaire. I have always believed that our mental/emotional, spiritual and physical parts are intertwined. By learning about one we learn about the others. I offered a questionnaire on the Enneagram, a remarkable tool of self-discovery. A friend, Don Riso had written the definitive work on the subject and has a survey on his website to help people find out where they were in the system. I'd made copies for the crowd. It's brilliant in that it not only tells you about your core nature, but tells you what you need to become like in order to grow and on the other end of the spectrum, what personality traits you will take on as you disintegrate. I asked everyone to take the survey and I could see most of them doing so as they waited.

I have always been a nut about starting on time; services, meetings, weddings, dinners. People who knew me were aware of this and usually showed up early. Too many churches start everything late waiting for people to show up. They show up late because they know you will wait. My feeling is if I wanted the lecture to start at 7 I would have said 7. I said 6:30, be there. Harsh perhaps but it seems to work. I remembered one dinner party I gave for a few friends who didn't know this about me. They were to arrive at 6. I served myself a cocktail and o'dourves at that time. When they showed up at 6:40 I was eating dinner. I had them eat, although their food was a bit on the cold side. They were too embarrassed to apologize. At the end of the night which was actually quite pleasant, I told them I believed on being on time and that I only tolerated severe lateness twice, then the invitations stopped. They were never late again and are very good friends. Up front, honest, and to the point. On the other hand that strategy has gotten me into trouble on a few occasions.

At 6:32 I stepped to the lectern. I noticed that those who knew me well pointed at their watches with a smile on their faces wondering why I'd waited two minutes.

"Good evening everyone. Welcome to our church for this evening's talk. I am sorry that many of you are watching on television and especially those who are outside and can't see. Over the past four weeks we have been looking at the world of alchemy; its history, symbology, its impact on history and on our lives today. We have talked about its connection to Christianity and how we can use the symbols within the alchemical process to help our own relationship with Jesus. We have seen that alchemy has touched many areas of life. I hope you have seen how alchemy can help you in your own psycho-social-spiritual lives. In the bulletins you have been handed, much of what we have covered is included along with a few websites that will help you on the journey if you choose to take it. I can tell you from my experience that the process is more than worth it."

"Tonight we are doing something different and special. My hope is that after tonight you will no longer have doubts about the power of alchemy but will start to understand what a powerful force it is and in my opinion, how God can use this art form to change lives—with God at the helm of course. When God is not at the center, things do not turn out as expected because there are dark forces at work in the universe as well. It turns out that alchemy doesn't work very well without a connection to the one who created all things. Let me be very clear. Tonight is not an illusion; everything you see here will be real. There are no actors, no tricks. I know some will not believe it and that is fine; personally, I don't care it's a matter of choice." (I let that line sink in.)

"Alchemists have lived among us for centuries. Most have never let it be known who and what they are, their work is done in private. You may have heard of a woman who recently left a church a significant amount of gold. She was an alchemist. Sir Isaac Newton was an alchemist. He well understood that the boundaries of science and reality are shady at best. Tonight you will see things that science cannot explain. This doesn't mean they are not real, just that science is not mature enough in its language to comprehend deeper rules of the universe that alchemists do understand or perhaps I should say use."

"Before I begin I hope that of you found a survey to fill out in your bulletin if you could take that out and find what number it says you are. Just out of curiosity please raise your hand if you are a number one. How about number two? (I went through the 9 numbers).

I'm not surprised there are a lot of 4's, 5's and 6's here. More on that at the Enneagram workshop."

"While I am not an alchemist I have come to know some including a master alchemist. I'm sure many of you will think I'm lying when I tell you his age. Joseph has been working at the art of alchemy for over 80 years he is 110 years old. Tonight he will be the one doing most of the work I will try to keep up. Joseph if you could come and please join me." (As Joseph moved forward there was a loud gasp from the crowd for he didn't look a day over 60). "I gasped as well when I first saw Joseph obviously nobody in this room thinks he's 110. I've seen his birth certificate I've seen pictures throughout his life in an era to tell you that he is indeed 110 years old."

"As you all know the goal of alchemy is to find the Philosopher's Stone. Some mystics in Christianity believed that Jesus discovered the Philosopher's Stone and that enabled him to do all that he did. Obviously Christians do not believe that, we believe he is God's Son, his only begotten son and through finding power in and through God he could do all things. But is there a law that says God cannot work in and through other things? Could not alchemy be a vehicle for finding Christ, to finding the powers of the universe? Those natural powers? I believe it is exactly that and I think Joseph will tell you that as well as the evening wears on."

"So, Joseph, what would you like to do first? O and before I forget, please make sure you fill out the forms in your bulletin. We are not going to use these to send you junk mail, but to keep track of those who are changed by what happens tonight. I am familiar with healing services where people leave feeling healed only to become unhealed in a day or two. We want to know that you are changed forever, and give glory to God for those healings, so please fill them out. My estimate is that there are close to 2000 people here tonight, a very good sample for us to watch. If you would like to watch as well, there is information about the website that will track people, give new information about what we are seeing, a chat room and some more classes that will be taking place soon."

"By a show of hands, how many people in here have a headache or stomach ache right now, or get them on a regular basis?" (In the sanctuary about 60 out of 1200 went up). Joseph stepped to a large table set in front of the audience.

"I am not a public speaker so forgive me. I have never done publicly what I am about to do. I do not know if it will work, but I see no reason why it won't. Most headaches and stomach aches come from stress in our lives, or chemical imbalances in our brains. Getting rid of one is fairly easy, take an aspirin. But when they become more frequent or more intense, like migraines, drugs rarely work. There are really two critical parts of alchemy. The first is the tools you use, including the laboratory equipment and the various chemicals, minerals and plants we use. The second is the alchemist him or herself. You may remember something called Shrodinger's Cat where a scientist showed that the experimenter has an impact on the experiment simply by what he thinks. We know that if you look for light to act as a wave it will and if you look for it to act like a particle it will. To a certain degree our wills and minds create the reality we see." Joseph was settling in, I could feel his nerves dissipating.

"Now, you might be sitting there saying, "so all of our aches and pains are psycho-somatic, I create them all." No, some of our illnesses are internally created, but not all. Some religious traditions want us to think that illness is an illusion and if we can just overcome the illusion, all will be well. I do not believe this. The headaches we get are very real. For centuries, millennia actually, alchemists have been experimenting, meditating, and sharing information about what we find. Think of it, 4000 years of knowledge passed down from generation to generation, each succeeding group adding to the base of knowledge, deepening our understanding of how the world works and how we can deepen our own lives. For a variety of reasons, some good and some bad, much of this knowledge has been kept secret" Joseph said looking into the rapt eyes of the audience.

"Here is the fascinating thing about alchemy. I am now mixing a potion for anyone who raised their hand that wishes to try it out. It is a mixture of chemicals, minerals, and plants, none of which were made in a factory. If you take this, your pain will go away within twenty minutes and it will stay away, perhaps forever, depending on your attitude towards it and me. I could write the recipe out, but because you are not where I am in the process it will fail. There is a relationship between creation and the creator, between the substances being used and the one using them."

Joseph worked for a few minutes mixing a bowl of something. I couldn't tell what language he was speaking, but it wasn't English, probably Latin or German. The room was silent.

"Ok, anyone who wants to try it, inside the sanctuary or outside, please come forward. I apologize for making you wait while I do this, but I must be the one that gives it to them. If you do not have consistent and persistent headaches or stomach aches please do not come forward at this time. I could use the spiritual prayers of the rest of you, so just sit in silence and keep the people receiving in your hearts and souls. Try to send your spiritual energy that comes from God to them."

Most of the 60 made their way forward and others trickled in from outside. As they walked by him they took a sip from a cup, he grabbed their hand, looked in their eyes and winked. Then as they headed back to their seats, we would ask them for their name so we could follow up with them. Most of them did. I'd asked some musicians to come and they were playing light jazz in the background which the crowd seemed to enjoy. It took about 20 minutes to get to everyone.

"Some of the first people should already be noticing a difference, are you?"

Five people stood up and said their pain was gone or going fast. I could tell from the sounds and the faces that some believed and some didn't.

"Let me try another experiment, this will involve everyone here, all I ask is that you be honest when I ask questions. Some of you want to show me as a liar. But if what I say is true, face reality, don't run from it just to prove me wrong for you will only harm yourselves. You are all probably wondering why I have had people pass this massive ball of yarn around the room and outside. Everybody should have a hand on the yarn, if you don't please touch it now. Make sure the string is taut. This is one giant string, I believe over a half mile long. Spiritually we are all connected although most of us are too busy in our minds to sense the giant web that connects us. Webs are interesting things. A spider sits in the middle and no matter where a fly lands on the web, no matter how large the web, the vibrations reach the center and the spider knows exactly where that fly is. The spiritual web is no different. We are all giving off spiritual vibrations. Jesus was sensitive to those, he knew when people were trying to trap him, he knew when a woman touched him and was healed. I want to show you how the web works. First I want you to watch me write on this piece of paper. Now, just so you don't think I am a magician we are going to raise this over you. “

Joseph put the writing in an envelope and clipped it to a rope that was raised 60 feet over the audience.

“Now, please close your eyes. Breathe as I tell you to breathe. In and out, in …………… and out. Everyone needs to be in the same rhythm. Relax, enjoy the quiet and peace that fills the room. Keep hold of the yarn. Now, without letting go of the yarn, if one of your hands is tingling, raise a hand. Open your eyes and look around.”

About 80% of the hands went up.

“Close your eyes again. Understand that we are all connected on every level. We expend energy to stay apart from one another. Feel the yarn in your hand, everyone focus on the feel of the yarn in your hand. Imagine that I am at the center of the web that is the yarn. I am going to send a message to you through the yarn. You should receive something in your mind, don’t say it, just see and remember it. When the image and number are clear raise your hand.”

He waited about 30 seconds.

“All right, now open your eyes. You should all have some paper and pencil, write down what you saw. The reason I do this is so at the end people can’t say others just said so to be part of the group. Now someone tell me what they wrote on their sheet. Yes ma’am, you.”

“I saw a penguin and the number 264.”

I heard a murmur go throughout the crowd.

“First, how many had that image and number? Raise your hands.”

Over 90% did. Note, I did not say there would be an image and a number.

“Now, lower the envelope. Sir, if you would open it and show it to the audience.”

The envelope was lowered, the man opened it and turned it to the audience. It said Penguin and 264. This was followed by a loud applause.

"Before I go on let me say that those who did not see these images are not bad people, you just have very strong minds with great doubt. Doubt is a choice you make, a lifestyle. It's neither bad nor good, it just means you will not see things others do, will not be as sensitive to the spiritual web. You can change that if you choose. Let's be clear, this is not a magic trick or magic, this has to do with a relationship with the spiritual world that surrounds you and being open to it. Most of us are not most of the time, including myself."

Just as I felt the phone vibrate in my right pocket, Joseph grabbed his stomach and sat down. He looked at me and I nodded, the murderer had entered the building. We both looked up and saw a man in his 40's dressed in red sit down in the middle of the room. Show time.

I stood up. "As you might imagine, this is draining for Joseph, not only has he never done this publicly, but everything he does takes energy so we will give him a break. Most of us are aware of the notion of good and evil, yin and yang, lightness and darkness. The Greeks called this notion dualism on a philosophic basis. There are those who believe that good and evil must balance each other, they see so much goodness in the world, they seek to do evil to balance the scales. Others see evil and attempt to do good. "

I paused for effect.

"Tonight you will see a battle, a battle between good and evil, two sides of an eternal battle that has been waged forever. Now let me be clear; those that I perceive as evil count themselves as good and me as evil. But I ask you, do you consider poisoning people's food or gassing a courthouse a good thing? The biggest difference between those of us on this side, is that we make our views known and practice what we do in the open. I am standing in front of you saying and doing what I believe. I have been on TV doing what I do. Joseph is here now showing you, showing the world who he is and what he does. Let me see a show of hands of those that came forward. Are your stomach and headaches gone?

Virtually everyone raised their hand.

"You see, we are not hiding, yet there is a master among you that lives in fear."

I waited. Then he stood up.

"I do not live in fear of you Matt."

The crowd collectively took a deep breath. I wanted to let Tom do his work right now, to end this. But I was very aware that if I did that now, this would not end and I had told Tom that. There was only one way to move forward that would bring finality to this.

"I know you are very powerful whatever your name is, why don't you come up here so all can see and hear you. I do not fear you and I will give you a microphone so all can hear."

He started moving forward. The camera caught him. His eyes were on fire. His hands and arms slowly raised and he spoke in Latin and the lights dimmed. Joseph spoke and the lights regained their brightness.

"You are no match for me old man."

"Do you really think you are a match for me?" Joseph said in a thundering voice I'd never heard that echoed off the walls. "Your parlor tricks are a waste of your time and energy, I would save it."

"You have no idea what I have become and am becoming, but tonight you will see."

"It's not too late, change and join us."

"And be a pawn in your silly game when I can be a master of many?"

"You will be a master to none and a slave to your own selfish desires."

"You call me a slave? Look around you. All of these people here are slaves to what science and culture tell them to believe and what's most humorous is that they actually believe they have free will and are making choices."

"You've worked for years to free yourself from some of those ideas, why don't you share with others the wisdom of how to break free?" Joseph said mockingly.

"Because they will waste the wisdom as has been done for centuries. The world needs to know what true power is and I plan to show them."

"By what?"

"By finishing the process tonight and demonstrating to the world what can be done."

"You aren't ready?"

"More ready than you will ever be. Those people who drank Joseph's potion, raise your hands."

About 30 people raised theirs.

"What he does, I can undo."

Again he said something in Latin. Within seconds there was groaning, three people running for the doors in pain. The audience was growing restless and anxious. I couldn't let this go on much longer. Out of fear about a third of the audience stood to leave.

"Sit down," the man shouted at the top of his lungs. He said something and I heard the doors to the church which had been open all shut. "You will not leave until I say you can leave, I need witnesses. If you try to leave, you will die." Everyone sat back down and I swallowed hard. I wasn't sure if he could follow through with his threat, but I wasn't going to take the chance yet. I stepped forward.

"I wasn't sure if you were going to show, you've been rather cowardly for the past two years."

"I'm not cowardly, just in preparation."

"For this day. Was Jesus cowardly?"

"Jesus was close but hadn't completed the final step or he wouldn't have died. This is what thousands of years of alchemy have been leading to, the final triumph."

"Jesus was sensitive to what God called him to, even death. You have no sensitivity to God and that will be your undoing. But you aren't really in your 40's are you?" Matt stated bluntly.

"Matthew, you are such a clever man. No I am not. I'm proud of my 95 years."

Even Joseph gasped. Then his eyes lit up.

"You were Jonathan, weren't you?"

"Yes, you taught me almost 60 years ago for almost 10 years, but you were slow and I needed to surpass the master."

"You were an impetuous, egocentric young man who had no patience. I thought you'd died."

"That was what I wanted the world to think. For years I worked and now I am the master of masters. I need only three things," he said with arrogance.

"A bride and the blood of a master and an adversary." Joseph's face went ashen.

"How perceptive of you. As you know, I have my bride and soon, I will have the other two."

I chimed in. "Do you actually think we will go without a fight?"

"I expect a fight, but your fight will only end in massive bloodshed, do you want that written on your tombstone?"

"I hate to dissuade you, but I've been studying too and I'm a quick student."

He let loose a laugh that sent shivers up everyone's spines.

"You aren't even close."

"I know that you must mix my blood and that of Joseph in a potion that contains mercury. You believe that you are so advanced that the mercury won't have an impact."

"Well, well, you have done your studying."

"Then you return, take your bride into the furnace and just as the Phoenix, you walk out as the Philosopher's Stone."

"You catch on quick."

"By the way, might I have a name to call you by?"

"Bob."

"I would like to make a deal with you, Bob, call it egocentric. I believe my God will protect me from your concoction more than your alchemy."

"God is in the alchemy, don't you understand that?"

"Then you will not mind sharing the cup with me. If you are right, I will die and you will get what you want."

"Why should I, I can have everything I want."

"I don't think so."

"How do you think you will stop me?"

"Not just me, but all of us. You came in late and missed Joseph's show, everyone listening is attached to the web. On top of that, there are some friends here you probably don't know." I pointed to the choir stalls and 10 alchemists of the chat room rose. They each said their chat room name. "I know you have great power, but surely you do not feel you can overcome all of our collective energy? Even if you did, you would be so weak from the strain you would never make it past the police that will be outside. You have my word that if I lose the challenge, you can walk out free."

"What is the trick?"

"There are no tricks. You will be in charge except for one step, when I bless the wine that I will add to your tasty beverage. Even alchemists believe in the grail, you can't really refuse me adding wine that has been blessed.

If anything it will connect more strongly the yin and the yang."

"You make it difficult to say no, and besides what fun it will be to show these fine folks the possibilities."

I turned to go to the sacristy to talk with Tom.

"Where do you think you are going?"

"I have to get the wine; you are welcome to join me if you want. Look if I wanted you shot I could have done that as soon as you came in. You don't think I am so stupid as to think you wouldn't come tonight do you? You are not the only one with plans."

I could see the surprise on his face, he actually did think we were that stupid.

"All right, go ahead. Don't put anything in the wine."

"We will be drinking from the same mercury you put in the chalices and the same bottle I pour from, if I poison you, I poison myself."

I got into the small room and pulled out my walkie-talkie speaking with Tom. No word from Sue and he wasn't sure how they would get into the church since Bob had somehow locked the doors. I told him how to open the windows beside the doors, I doubt Bob thought of that. But timing was everything, I could feel Bob's power and if he was successful we'd all be in a lot of trouble. I returned to the altar with my wine.

Bob joined me. Two priests of sorts about to do spiritual combat, just like Elijah and the prophets of Baal. I didn't fool myself that I was an Elijah, but there was a lot riding on the next 15 minutes.

"Bob, you go first, do whatever you need to do."

I stepped back, praying. Looking out into the sea of nervous faces I couldn't help but feel a bit guilty for dragging all these people into this mess. Bob took a bottle out, filled with a silvery substance that was certainly mostly mercury.

Mercury poisoning is not a pleasant event. Some of us remember playing with liquid mercury when we were kids, rubbing it on dimes making them all silvery. The actual amount that got into our blood stream was very low, but in some cases did damage. However, drinking half of cup of mercury would bring rapid damage to vital organs such as the liver and central nervous system. Severe pain within hours, death within days. Hallucinations, the shakes, lack of coordination and speech are all impaired. Not a pleasant way to go. I should also point out there is no cure or antidote.

Bob raised each chalice as he said some things in several languages. I picked up some of the Latin and German, but the others were lost on me. Under each chalice I had put a little towel to protect the altar from any wine and mercury spillage. Now and then Bob would look at Joseph and say something. Joseph would respond in whatever language they were using and bow. Then he turned to the other alchemists and did the same. He raised his arms as if saying a prayer to the audience. His persona was very charismatic, captivating to watch.

"Matt, the altar is yours."

I stepped forward knowing I had to stall for time. I started in on the Eucharistic prayer, throwing in some Latin just for fun now and then. I filled the cups to about half full, seeing the mercury in the bottom of each chalice. I set the cup on the altar, removing the towel it was sitting on. I said some quiet prayers, not really wanting to invite God into this mess I'd created, but certainly wanting his help if he was around at the time—which I had no doubts he was. I knew I couldn't stall forever. I asked the audience to join hands and say the Lord's Prayer with me.

"Our Father……. Virtually everyone knew at least parts of this prayer. In the middle of the prayer I felt my phone ring. I looked over at Joseph and winked. Things were in place.

One of the people in the audience stood. "Don't do it."

"Please don't worry, trust in God, and trust in the ability of the human mind when surrounded by love to overcome all things. Besides, if I happen to die, I will be in God's arms, so be at peace, I win either way."

"Such thoughtful words on your deathbed pastor, shall we?"

He took the chalice closest to himself. I reached out for mine, my hand dipping in to make the sign of the cross on the wine. I stayed there a second praying, then lifted the chalice with my hand under the bottom.
I looked into his eyes.

"Cheers." We clinked cups and drank.

"O, by the way," I said with a smirk on my face, "I don't think your bride will be joining you, you'll have to find a new one."

"She is safe and sound and waiting for me."

"She is safe and sound all right, look." I pointed to the back of the sanctuary. It was one of the most beautiful sights I'd ever seen. Alice and Sue walking down the aisle.

"What? How is this possible? He screamed.

"Everyone grab hold of the yarn, close your eyes and think of someone you love."

Bob's focus was shattered, the energy he needed to make the transformation was dissipating fast. I knew he would regroup. Alice came up and gave me a big hug and a long slow kiss. The idea infuriated him. He touched her as he said something and she collapsed.

Joseph ran to Bob and grabbed his shoulders. At once light seemed to be flowing all around them, Bob's was blue and Joseph's was red. All of the alchemists in the choir stall ran over and joined Joseph. They were using their collective energy to stop Bob. I don't know why but I started to sing a contemporary Christian song that I knew most people were familiar with and they all joined in. The sound got louder and louder. They all stood and raised their hands, the yarn looking like a giant web connecting everyone in the sanctuary and I was certain all those outside as well. I could see that Bob was fighting it. He screamed something at the top of his lungs. Joseph and the others collapsed, a large heap of humanity on the floor in front of the altar, like a sacrifice or an exorcism gone wrong. I thought we'd failed.

"We are not finished Matthew," Bob said as he looked into my eyes with his piercing orbs. Then he too collapsed.

Tom came running up with Pete and several others I presumed to be doctors behind him.

"Take Bob first, get him into a secure jail. He will still have mental powers when he wakes up, if he wakes up. Do not let anyone near him before you talk with me. The mercury will kill him within a few days, there is nothing you can do for him."

"Matt, what about you?"

"I'll be fine."

"What are you talking about, we all saw you drink the mercury."

"Take a look at the chalice and the altar, trust me I'll be fine."

Tom went to the altar and saw the plug in the bottom of the chalice and the hole in the altar. When I was making the cross in the cup, I was pulling the plug, it drained into the altar. Bob couldn't see the hole because of the towel I put over it. The wine washed down what little mercury didn't, I got none. Bob on the other hand had just put half a cup of pure mercury along with other poisonous chemicals into his body and didn't have the energy to perform the transformation. The collective love of the audience and the alchemists saw to that. I went to Joseph who was just becoming conscious. The crowd was still in shock; spiritual, mental, and emotional.

"Joseph are you all right?"

"I don't know, I had to go places I hadn't been before in order to stop him, he may be taking me down as he descends, I can still feel his grip."

"Tom, get Joseph to the hospital now, 20 minutes in the MRI. Right Pete?"

Pete laughed. "Whatever you say Doctor!"

The other alchemists all got up and were OK as they watched Joseph being led out.

I stopped them and had everyone lay hands on Joseph asking for God's healing and blessing.

Alice slowly started coming out of her daze as well.

"What happened? She asked.

"In his fury, Bob attacked you, but I don't think he had it in him to kill his bride. I believe that up till the end he believed he would win."

"I've never loved being in a church so much."

I'd totally forgotten about the audience. You could hear a pin drop as I turned to face them, all eyes open and staring. Obviously a few were shaken, a few looked like Bob's energy had gone through the yarn to them. I told the alchemists to go and help those that needed it.

Then I turned and spoke to the audience. "You have witnessed something tonight you will never, I hope, see again. There are powers at work in the universe that most of us have little concept of and many of those powers are neutral and can be used for creativity or to destroy. I hope you have all been touched tonight, I hope you have learned something and I hope that you understand that the power of love, of God's unconditional love is the greatest force in the universe. Perfect love casts out fear as Jesus tells us. It often comes with a price, but in the end it is victorious."

"Most of us want to live a long time. Joseph did, and has. He worked very hard to discover what it is that will keep us alive as long as possible and obviously he discovered some things. But what I have learned most is that longevity is not the point, but rather how we live the life we lead. I feel sorry for atheists or for those who think that this life is it. You couldn't be further from the truth; this is only the beginning of an unbelievable life to come. Go on your way in peace knowing that God loves you. Good night everyone."

No one moved. There was no clapping, no questions, just 2000 people sitting in rapt wonderment and awe. I took Sue and Alice to the side room off the sanctuary, Tom and the other alchemists joining us.

"Matt, I still don't get how you found Alice?" Tom asked.

"I told Sue the general area where I knew she was, she put her computer to work and looked for houses that were soaking up electricity. I knew that to get his furnace to the heat he needed, he'd need an enormous amount of energy. He didn't worry, knowing he'd be gone within a few days. Obviously it worked."

"It was a great strategy, although cutting it a bit close for my tastes. The utility companies don't make it easy to break into the grid on computers. I figured you could use a little extra help, so as we were walking up the aisle I had my computer shut off all the juice to the house."

"Matt, the furnace has its own source of energy as well, when Bob dies, the furnace dies and he says it will be a large explosion, if there are people there get them out," Sue added.

Tom got on his phone and relayed the information. I could hear him arguing with someone that said there was no electricity at the house so no explosion could happen. He ordered them to be out of the house and to cordon off a square block around it.

"Matt what about you, shouldn't we be getting you to the hospital, didn't you drink the mercury? If Bob is going to die,……." Alice asked.

"Don't worry, I didn't have any, I rigged the chalice and the altar so that the liquid would drain before I lifted the cup."

"You are a devious one aren't you?"

"I just don't plan on checking out yet, too much left to do. I am a faithful person, but I am not stupid. I don't put God to that kind of test."

We all talked for a while getting to know the other alchemists. I didn't even know they were coming. Apparently Joseph had told them all about the situation and said it was time to come out of hiding and join the world. All of them came and I was thankful they did. I poked my nose out of the door and saw that finally people were starting to file out.

Eventually I thanked everyone for their labors, made sure they had places to stay and offered to pay for their trips if they wanted help. None accepted the offer, but we did decide to meet for lunch the following day at the hospital to say hi to Joseph.

I took Alice back to my house, said hello and goodbye to the bishop who was pleased it was over, put had a splendid glass of wine and held her as she fell asleep in my arms in front of the fire on the sofa. I felt I deserved it.

The following morning we all met in the lobby of the hospital. Normally that many people can't visit a patient, but this was not a normal situation. Tom made sure there wasn't a problem. We didn't know if Bob had accomplices so a guard was posted at his door and at Josephs, a floor down. We opened Joseph's room only to find it empty.

"Where is he?" I asked the officer thinking that perhaps they had taken him for a test.

"In his bed, I saw him 30 minutes ago and haven't left my spot."

"Look for yourself, he is gone."

"That's not possible."

"Do you know how tired I am getting of hearing people say what is and isn't possible?"

The alchemists joined hands and closed their eyes for about a minute, I had no idea what they were doing, but I didn't interrupt. After they were finished one of them turned to me.

"Don't' worry, he is fine. Thank you for all you have done for us and perhaps for the world. If you ever need us, don't be afraid to ask."

"But how do I get in touch with you, I don't know your numbers or where you live?"

"I think you know how," replied Phil with a winsome smile.

And I did. It saddened me that I would not see Joseph, not be able to thank him for saving my life and ridding the world of an evil man. The alchemists turned and left, already talking with one another about their next steps. I had no doubt I would run into them again.

I walked down the hall and down the stairs till I entered Bob's room. He lay on the bed on his back, staring at the ceiling, almost as if in a trance. I could see that they were already giving him intravenous drugs for the pain, his body whincing now and then.

"Hello Bob."

"Hello Matt. No one will come in and talk to me, how long do I have?"

"A day or two at most. I told them not to come in, I don't know how much power you still have and I will not allow you to create havoc in the hospital."

"Then why are you here."

"You have no power over me, I think I have made that clear. You will die like the rest of us, your house will self-destruct, and no one will remember you. Your entire life has been spent so you could die of mercury poisoning. Yin and yang I guess."

"Yes, yin and yang."

"I brought you a tape recorder. If you are willing I would like to hear your memories of the past few months, since you went to Mary's home and killed her. I would like to understand things from where you are. Will you do that?"

"I suppose it is the only thing I will leave behind."

"I know that you did help some of those alchemists, so your life was not a total waste, but it could have been so much more."

"The ego is a very powerful thing Matt, I will never claim to understand how saints can do what they do. I am sorry for what I did to Joseph, is he all right?"

"I don't know, he literally disappeared." I saw a tear slide down Bob's face.

"Perhaps I will see him in the next level of existence. Do you think God will forgive me?"

"I'm not the judge Bob. I'm not convinced you truly believe in your heart that you did wrong, but I do know that God's love is infinite, certainly larger than your evil."

"I always knew you to be a perceptive one."

I still didn't trust him, so there was no prayer, no shaking of hands. I put the tape recorder down. I know I am supposed to forgive my enemies and pray for them, in time I would, today my faith was not there.

"I do hope your last days are fairly pain free."

"Matt, pain has never bothered me and I will go down fighting."

"Good bye Bob."

I turned and left never seeing him again. The recordings were brought to me after he died.

I'd barely slept the previous night, so much energy in my veins. Alice was asleep when I'd left in the morning and gone when I'd returned home, although she'd left a note telling me she'd be back with dinner. I slumped onto the deck sofa and fell asleep. My dreams were filled with alchemical images, of journeys to be taken, lessons learned and the uniting of the King and Queen, sun and moon. I woke up refreshed even though I'd only been out less than two hours. I slept so soundly I didn't hear the phone ring, there were 13 messages. Several from broadcasters that wanted interviews, a few from church people, one from the bishop and then the final one.

"Matt, this is Joseph, I hope you enjoyed your dreams, you can look forward to more like that, I have much to teach you. I don't like hospitals and believe I can heal myself faster than they could heal me, besides don't people often get sick in hospitals? I appreciated the guard at my door, but it really wasn't necessary. Do not be hard on him, he just had an easy mind to manipulate, he truly did not see me leave and no I didn't walk through walls. I do not know when I will resurface, but you will be one of the first to know. It has been an honor knowing you, you have taught me things I needed to know and they have changed my life forever. Be at peace, take care of Sue and Alice and use the gifts that God has given you, along with a few I have left in your office. Don't forget the web."

I sat down and cried.

30 BOB'S GOODBYE

Most alchemists are loners; we work by ourselves for ourselves. We know the world will see us as nut cakes if we go public, so we don't. Most of us have a teacher or comrades who are on the journey that we share with. I tell you this because I was not ready for the crowd at the church. I knew there would be a lot of people, but as soon as I entered the building I had to expend extra energy to combat that which I felt assaulting me. Eyes staring at me and a feeling I hadn't encountered for a long time. I sat down searching my memory for the sensation I was feeling. Then it hit me. Joseph. He had taken me to a place on the spiritual plane that introduced me not only to new powers, but to new feelings. Now they were back, Joseph was here. I found him quickly once I knew what I was looking for. An ordinary looking man for one of the supposedly supreme alchemists of the world. Tonight the student would surpass the teacher. I chuckled to myself.

After that, things become hazy. I remember Matt talking about me in general terms and then me going up to the front, the final battle finally underway. We argued. I heard about his potion to heal people and I undid the healing. The masses were going to see firsthand who had the power. He had them connected to the web, I at least temporarily pulled the plug.

I apologize for being brief but my energy is drifting away, I know that I do not have much time left, but am confident that in one form or another I will be back.

Instantly the well became ill. I mocked them and their childish faith. Some started to leave so I locked the doors. Those who do not believe in mind over matter are fools.

There was more talking and the introduction of our chat room of alchemists. I had hoped some would join me in power, but it was clear they were all in mutiny. So be it, they would pay the price, and soon.

Then Matt put forth the challenge. He was playing right into my hands. I approached the altar and prepared my mixture, full of mercury, sulphur and other critical compounds of the alchemical process. I felt my heart leap when Joseph and Matt put their blood into the cups. I was so close I could taste it, feeling the depth of my power surging in my veins.

Matt seemed to take forever doing his part. I wondered why God took so long to accomplish such a modest task. He ended with the Lord's Prayer. I wondered if there was a trick and joined hands, feeling the power of Joseph through the yarn trying to garner that of everyone else. I pushed back and sent a surge of my own energy back through the yarn. As I looked out over the people I saw that it had shaken them, they would be of little use.

This was it, the moment I'd been waiting for, for decades. Every ounce of my being was focused on this moment. My concentration was pure as we clinked glasses and drank. As I waited for him to bend over in pain I looked down the aisle and saw Alice, my bride to be. How could it be true, how could they have found me. I felt the defilement of my sacred laboratory. She came and kissed Matt. I flipped out, lost focus and poured my venom into Alice. Then the hand and power of Joseph made me cringe. My concentration broken, the mercury poured into my system as an ordinary man. In an instant I knew it was over. As I collapsed I saw Matt holding Alice and smiling at me.

My 95 years on the planet were extraordinary. My sole regret was that I left no one on earth with my knowledge. I taped this in the hopes that perhaps someone will learn something, see things through my lens, understand that I am not an evil man; I just see the world through a different lens.

I am fighting as hard as I can, so that I can return to the work. I forgive Matt for what he did to me, but upon my return he will……………………..

At this point, Bob died as he was talking.

31 EPILOGUE--MATT

A week after the eventful evening at the church, life had returned to almost normal. Bob died within a few days, but lasted longer than science had predicted. Because he had no history he did not exist and had no family. Joseph told me that in the best interest of the universe I should attempt to let him be buried where and how he'd want. It took me a few days to figure out what he meant and then a few more to pull some major strings.

Two weeks to the day after he poisoned himself, I laid him back in his furnace. The electricity had been off for a week because of what Alice had heard would happen when he died. I was one of the first in the house the following morning after the lecture. Overall it was in order. I spent quite a bit of time in the lab, not really knowing what it was I was looking for. Just before I left I saw it. Someone had come before we'd arrived. Joseph. I have no idea how he knew where to come or what he wanted, but his insignia was on the counter. He knew I would understand it and no one else would. I suspect he took diaries and lab books that gave away secrets the world was not yet ready for. The police found nothing of interest. Alice did not want to return to the scene of her kidnapping. Evil was palpable.

When we were finished and Bob was in his furnace, I called Sue and told her to switch on the juice. We gave ourselves about 200 yards of protection. Most of the police and firemen laughed when I told them what was going to happen. I knew their bosses and they were ordered to listen to me, if only to humor the priest. Twenty minutes after the electricity went on, the house blew, and I mean blew. A massive explosion which put most of us on our behinds destroyed the entire house, right down to the foundation. We were pummeled by pieces of wood and plaster. Everyone looked at me. There was no fire to put out because there was nothing to burn, it was gone, completely and absolutely. There wasn't enough leftovers to even have a clean-up crew do their job. Bob was history. I preferred it that way.

Sue was also thrilled to have him out of her life. She did admit that through this she'd taken on a new client. It appears the electric utility wasn't very pleased with her ability to break into the grid and wanted her help---at a very nice retainer—to make it more secure, if she could crack it, so could terrorists.

Tom got back to his murders and reluctantly thanked me for helping get the bad guy.

Alice and I got our lives back on track, our love growing deeper because of what we now held in common. The more I learned about how she dealt with Bob, the more impressed I became.

This had been a very public case and while the end result was fine, the bishop was on his best chastising behavior when we met for lunch. He tried to have me promise I'd tone my life down, even though he knew it would do no good. I told him the church congregation had grown by 40% in one week. He pointed out that it was like people who came to see the wrecks, the crowds would slowly dissipate when they realized the fun and games were over. I asked him if he was sure they were over. He just groaned. Naturally I made him pick up the tab, after all he'd invited me to lunch.

Within a day of Bob's death the media frenzy ended, one of the local politicians was accused of doing some naughty things and that was a higher priority. Seems to happen a lot in Portland.

I was in touch with all the alchemists who told me they were in touch with Joseph and all was well. They were all going to start running courses around the country dealing with alchemy. They wanted to know if they could have a yearly conference at my church. I couldn't think of a reason why not.

It took me a couple of weeks to get my life back onto a more routine schedule. That was when I pulled out the bag Joseph left me. It came with the following note:

"Matt, as promised a few gifts. I can't begin to compete, nor would I want to, with what God has blessed you with. However, two of these potions may come in handy from time to time and if you would like to add a few other interesting traits to your already lengthy list of gifts, do what I've outlined in the little book. Most people take years to get to this point, but I have a feeling you can skip those steps. I'll be watching." Joseph.

I couldn't help but feel that in the end, Joseph had always been in control, he knew what was going to happen and how it would happen. Once again alchemy and the alchemist became metaphors for what was most important in my life, finding God and Christ. Joseph knew the same thing and I knew he was on the edge of discovering the stone. I had no doubts I'd be seeing him soon for what he needed to do was to take his gifts and bring them to the world.

Already I was hearing things. I knew the next task was awaiting me on the streets of Portland and beyond.

THE AUTHOR

The Rev. Stephen Rodgers is an Episcopal priest and a psychotherapist. He has been a spiritual student and admirer of alchemy for decades. He currently works at the Cedar Hills Hospital in Portland, OR., has owned a wholistic health center and has published a book on the soul. While very open minded, Stephen is a deeply committed Christian.

www.ingramcontent.com/pod-product-compliance
Lightning Source LLC
LaVergne TN
LVHW020526100826
845148LV00010B/1352

9780615854953